A COMPANY OF ROGUES

THE CUPIDS TRILOGY
BOOK THREE

A Company
of Rogues

TRUDY J. MORGAN-COLE

Breakwater Books
P.O. Box 2188, St. John's, NL, Canada, A1C 6E6
www.breakwaterbooks.com

**A CIP catalogue record for this book is available
from Library and Archives Canada.**

ISBN 978-1-55081-990-8 (softcover)

Cover painting: detail of *Young Woman with a Lighted Candle at a
Window*, oil on panel, 26.7 x 19.5 cm, ca. 1658–1665, by Gerrit
Dou. Museo Nacional Thyssen-Bornemisza, Madrid.

We acknowledge the support of the Canada Council for the Arts.
We acknowledge the financial support of the Government of Canada through the
Department of Heritage and the Government of Newfoundland and Labrador through
the Department of Tourism, Culture, Arts and Recreation for our publishing activities.

Printed and bound in Canada.

Breakwater Books is committed to choosing papers and materials for our books
that help to protect our environment. To this end, this book is printed on a recycled
paper and other sources that are certified by the Forest Stewardship Council®.

Canada Council   Conseil des Arts
for the Arts   du Canada

Newfoundland
Labrador

Canadä

Cast of Characters

Names marked with an asterisk are people whose names appear in historical documents, though they are portrayed as fictional characters in this novel. Children born after the novel begins are not included in this list of characters; for adult characters, the description indicates where they are and what they are doing as the novel opens.

In the New Found Land

Isaac Bell: A servant of the Guy family at Musketto Cove.

Stephen Butler: A settler who comes out to Newfoundland in 1617 and stays at Musketto Cove.

John and Sallie Crowder: Settlers at Cupids.

*****Thomas Dermer**: An English sea captain who comes to Newfoundland in 1618.

Alice Guy: Second child of Kathryn Guy.

Kathryn (Gale) Guy: Colonist who came out from Bristol in 1612 to join her husband Nicholas; now living at Musketto Cove.

James (Jemmy) Guy: Youngest child of Kathryn and Nicholas Guy.

Jonathan Guy: Eldest child of Kathryn and Nicholas Guy; first English child born at Cupids Cove in 1613.

*****Nicholas Guy**: One of John Guy's earliest Cupids colonists, now a planter at Musketto Cove. Husband of Kathryn Guy.

*Robert Hayman: An English scholar and poet who comes to Newfoundland in 1618.

Hal Henshaw: A settler who comes out to Newfoundland in 1617 and stays at Musketto Cove.

Higgs and Barry: Servants of Thomas Willoughby.

James Hill: A settler at Cupids Cove.

Jem and Elsie Holworthy: Settlers at Cupids Cove.

George and Jennet Lane: Settlers at Cupids Cove.

*Anne Mason: Wife of Cupids governor John Mason.

*John Mason: Governor of Cupids from 1615–1620.

Nancy (Ellis) Perry: Former maidservant of Kathryn Guy who came out to Cupids Cove with her in 1612. Kidnapped by the *Happy Adventure* in 1613; later a servant in the home of Pocahontas and John Rolfe in Virginia. Wife of Ned Perry.

Ned Perry: One of John Guy's original 1610 Cupids colonists; later a sailor and ship's carpenter aboard the *Treasurer* and the *White Lion*. Husband of Nancy Ellis.

Gilbert and Sheila Pike: An English pirate and his Irish wife, planters at Carbonear.

Hannah Porter: Sallie Crowder's sister, living with the Crowders at Cupids Cove.

Dickon Sadler: A settler at Cupids Cove.

William Spencer: A settler at Harbour Grace.

Daisy (More) Taylor: Servant to the Guys at Musketto Cove. Widow of both Matt Grigg and Tom Taylor. Sister of Bess.

Bess (More) Tipton: Servant to the Guy family and planter at Musketto Cove. Sister of Daisy and wife of Frank.

*Frank Tipton: One of the original 1610 colonists, now a planter at Musketto Cove. Husband of Bess.

Matthew (Matty) Tipton: Bess and Frank's second child.

*Tisquantum: Wampanoag man from Patuxet who was kidnapped, sold into slavery in Spain, and eventually made his way to England and from there to Newfoundland.

Will Tipton: Bess and Frank's eldest child.

Rafe Whitlock: Servant to the Guy family at Musketto Cove.

*George Whittington: One of the original 1610 colonists, still living
at Cupids Cove.

Nell Whittington: George's wife.

*Thomas Willoughby: Son of Sir Percival Willoughby, who spent
time at Cupids in 1612–1613 and later returned to the colony.

Beyond the New Found Land

Captain Bellamy: Captain of the *Fair Isle*.

John Gale: A Bristol stonemason; Kathryn Guy's father.

Lily Gale: John Gale's daughter; Kathryn's younger sister. Married
to Walter Tucker.

John Harvey: A sailor on the *Bountiful*.

Samuel Hollett: Navigator and mapmaker on the *Bountiful*.

MacLeish: Ship's carpenter aboard the *Fair Isle*.

Omar: A formerly enslaved man who befriended Nancy in Bermuda.

Dickon and Mary Perry, Mother Perry: Ned's family in Bristol.

Tibby: Longtime servant of the Gale family; believed to be Nancy's
aunt, but actually her mother.

Francis Withycombe and Red Peter: Sailors on the *Treasurer*; old
friends of Ned Perry.

Map detail from *The Coast of New-Found-Land from Cape Raze to Cape St. Francis* by Henry Southwood, London, 1675. Courtesy of the Digital Archives Initiative of Memorial University of Newfoundland.

This map, published about fifty years after the events of this novel, shows the section of Conception Bay where most of the story takes place, including Harbour Grace, Musketto Cove, and Carbonear. The original English settlement at Cupids (Cupids Cove) is not marked on the map, but is located immediately north of Brigus.

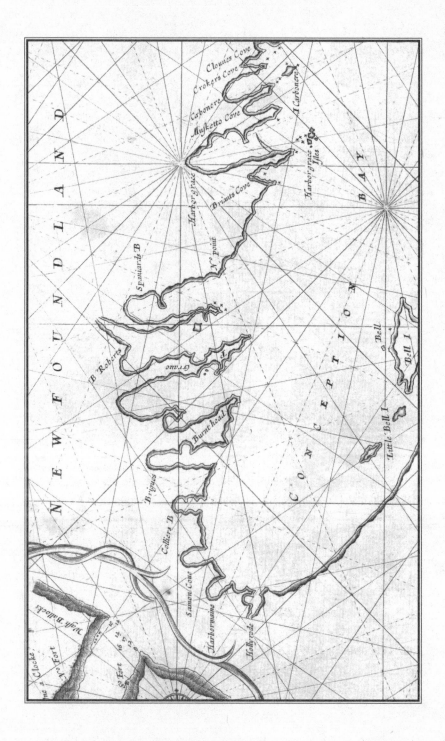

Author's Note

THE EPIGRAPHS AT EACH CHAPTER HEADING ARE TAKEN from George Chapman's translation of the *Odyssey*, originally published as part of his book *The Whole Works of Homer* in 1616. The edition I used was *Homer's Odysseys*, London: Reeves & Turner, 1897. The epigraph at the beginning of the novel is from *Quodlibets* by Robert Hayman, published in London in 1682.

To a worthy Friend, who often objects the coldnesse
of the Winter in Newfound-Land...

> *You say that you would live in* Newfound-land,
> *Did not this one thing your conceit withstand;*
> *You feare the* Winters *cold, sharp, piercing ayre.*
> *They love it best, that have once winterd there.*
> *Winter is there, short, wholesome, constant, cleare,*
> *Not thicke, unwholesome, shuffling, as 'tis here.*

—Robert Hayman, 1575–1629
Quodlibets, Book 2, 81

ONE

An Adventure Goes Awry

MUSKETTO COVE, JULY 1617

*A grove grew
In endless spring about her cavern round,
With odorous cypress, pines, and poplars, crown'd.*
              —*Homer's Odysseys*, Book 5, 86–88

I F ONLY I WERE A MAN, THAT I MIGHT GO HALF-NAKED IN *the sun!*

Summer days in the New Found Land were rarely hot enough that a woman would want to strip to the waist as a man might do. But today was such a day. Kathryn Guy thought for a wistful moment of how it would be to stride along shirtless, in breeches, letting the sun warm her bare skin. She imagined her shift and kirtle hung on a peg in some unused room, herself transformed, no longer needing them. She was entirely alone in the forest, a rare thing for a busy mother of three. For half a moment she entertained the idea of taking off her clothes altogether, of being naked as a wood-nymph.

An impractical idea as well as a naughty one: dryads, presumably, were not troubled by the prickling of branches or the scrape of pine needles. Being tree-spirits themselves, not bound by mortal flesh, they could slip through the forest unscathed. But Kathryn's arms were already scratched, and while her clothing felt heavy in the hot sun, it also protected her from a great many more scrapes and scratches.

A wood nymph would also not feel the warm, heavy tenderness in her breasts as she thought of nursing her son. Jemmy had begun to wean and Kathryn could go longer without feeding him than she had a few months ago, but her body still felt that tug towards her hungry child. Wood nymphs also did not need to crouch awkwardly in a bush to make water, trying not to wet their own skirts. No, she was far too much a creature of flesh and bone to flit through the trees like a nymph.

She had been in the forest an hour or two already; she had left the house after breakfast. Her servant Daisy was watching the children while Kathryn's husband and the other men were out fishing. Kathryn had been thinking for weeks that her store of plants, roots, and bark from the forest—things she used to make medicines for her household—needed to be replenished. She had seized on the opportunity of the glorious day to go to the woods and gather what she needed.

As a girl in Bristol, learning the secrets of the still-room from her mother had been Kathryn's favourite household chore. She could perform all the tasks expected of a young woman—bake and brew, clean and sew, dress a capon and stew it for supper—but the herbs and plants that her mother handled in the still-room, the unwritten recipes she passed down for how to prepare each remedy, had fascinated Kathryn. She had cherished the thought that someday she would use that knowledge as mistress of her own household, growing and gathering and brewing the remedies that would keep her husband, children, and servants healthy.

What she had never imagined was that she would be a wife and mother on the other side of the ocean, collecting plants from the wild forest that bounded three sides of her husband's plantation. She had, of course, an herb garden; the Cupids colonists had brought over many seeds from England. Kathryn had carefully tended the hyssop, thyme, mallow, and wormwood she had brought with her from England to Cupids Cove, and from Cupids Cove to the new plantation. These plants now formed the core of her own still-room stock. But she was ever seeking out wild plants as well, trying and testing them, asking the other women settlers, when she had chance to meet with them, what new cures they had discovered.

She had been in the New Found Land five years now, and was always adding to her store of knowledge. In some parts of the New World, she knew, the native people of the land traded with the settlers and taught them what local plants were good for healing. But there were no friendly native women anywhere near the Guys' plantation that Kathryn could learn from. In five years, Kathryn had yet to see one of them. So, it was only by trial that she had learned that spruce bark could be made into a brew that soothed many ailments, including the dreaded scurvy, and that the sap of the fir trees was ideal for healing the cuts and small wounds that everyone suffered while going about the work of a busy plantation. She was seeking these things today, as well as the ever-useful juniper berries, which could be brewed into a remedy for sick stomachs.

Between looking for plants and imagining herself as a wood nymph, Kathryn's mind was well-occupied as her feet found animal trails through the forest and her eyes spotted berries and bark to add to her basket. Only when she came out into a little clearing and looked up did she notice that the sun had climbed to its zenith and beyond. Back at the house, Daisy would be fretting that she had not returned for the midday meal. With the rare pleasure of time to herself, Kathryn had entirely lost track, not only of the time of day, but of the paths she had followed into the forest.

She did not worry. For her first two years in the New Found Land she had lived in the little settlement at Cupids Cove, but for these past three years her family had occupied their own land further up the shore of Conception Bay. Their plantation was the only one in a tiny cove that the fishermen called Musketto, tucked between the larger bays of Carbonear to the north and Harbour Grace to the south. They lived with the ocean to their east and the forest surrounding them on north, west and south. Since moving there, Kathryn had done a good deal of wandering about the woods, sometimes with her husband and sometimes with Daisy or Bess, often with the children in tow. Trails led from their cove to the fishing stations at Carbonear and Harbour Grace, and the Guy family had cut several other trails through the woods that they used regularly.

She still felt, as she imagined all the settlers did, that the "wilderness" was something strange and menacing, harbouring unknown threats. But she no longer thought of the forest around Musketto Cove as wilderness. It was where her husband and his men cut wood and hunted game and wild birds, where Kathryn and her maids picked berries. It was becoming tamed and known, part of their home. She left the clearing in the same direction from which she had entered it, confident that she would soon retrace her steps and find her path.

An hour later she was no longer as certain. *I am lost in the forest*, Kathryn thought, a strange thrill accompanying the fear that those words ought to bring. Anything might happen to someone lost in the forest. There were the everyday fears of hunger, exposure, wild animals and wild men, but also the possibility of being fairy-led or meeting some other fabulous creature. Just as the flowers and trees of this land were different from those in the tamed and gentle lands around Bristol, so the fae-folk might be different from those she had learned about back in England. Giants, ogres, unicorns: who knew what might dwell this deep in the forest?

Still, she could not shake the sense that this land was hers and would not harm her. Trouble had come to her and her family in the New Found Land, but none of it had come from the forest. Neither natives nor wild beasts nor fairies had come from the forest to attack her family. The harm had come from men of their own kind—fellow settlers who had betrayed them, and English pirates who had burned, killed, and captured. The land itself had never betrayed her.

The sun grew hotter still: even through the canopy of green above, she could feel it beating down. One path ended in a tangle of trees; she turned around and tried another. The sun was a little lower in the sky now. It was sinking towards the west and so she kept it at her back, knowing that walking east would bring her to the sea.

She did sight water, but it was not the ocean. Several brooks and one large river ran through the woods around their plantation, flowing into the pond that lay on the other side of the rocky beach near their house.

There was another good-sized lake further inland where the men fished for trout in the autumn. If she had come to that lake, Kathryn knew she could find her way home.

But this was not that familiar lake. Breaking through the trees, Kathryn saw a very small, sheltered pond in a grove of birch. She was quite sure that in three years of wandering these woods, she had never seen this pool before. She was further from home than she had imagined.

She sat on a stone underneath one of the trees and looked at the glimmering, inviting waters of the pool. Perhaps this was where the fae-folk dwelt; perhaps a naiad, a water nymph, would rise from the pool and greet her. Would the nymph curse Kathryn for stumbling upon her secret place, or bless her with a granted wish? The wish would have to be a straight path home, of course; it was well into the afternoon now, and her most pressing need was to return to her family.

But she was tired, and the pool looked cool and inviting. A few more minutes' delay could not matter that much. She hoped her little fable of a naiad in the pool was only a fancy, for Kathryn, already busy unlacing the front of her kirtle, was about to invade the water spirit's domain.

Kirtle and petticoat off, she stepped to the edge of the water, enjoying the freedom of standing only in her skin, the dappled sun pouring down on her body. The water eased the soreness of her full breasts, washed the sweat from her skin. It was as refreshing as she had imagined, the bottom of the pool a little muddy but the water clear. The pool was only the length of two bodies across, but it looked deep enough to bathe, and she stepped further in, letting the delicious coolness envelope her.

In the middle of the pool Kathryn dipped down, holding her breath and closing her eyes till the waters closed over her head. When she stood up again, she reached for the pins that bound her hair. She had gone bareheaded in the woods, but kept her hair pinned neatly up; now she let it down and dipped below the surface again, letting the whole thick dark length soak in the chilly water.

She stood up, water streaming down her face, and laughed aloud at the glorious freedom of the moment. No-one around to see or to judge her, only her own body and the woods and the water. It was, she thought, the most truly free moment of her twenty-six years.

"Ho-ho, what have we here? A water nymph in my pool?"

A man's voice, light and mocking, cut into Kathryn's perfect solitude. She spun around to see who was there. Her mind full of fairy folk as it was, she almost thought it was a river god into whose territory she had blundered, even as her mind told her it must be a human man, and that she was naked. She bent her knees so that her breasts were below the water.

Then she saw him—fully human, indeed, dressed in breeches but shirtless, as she had imagined herself earlier in the day. Not a creature of myth or magic but a creature from her own past: Thomas Willoughby, her one-time lover, leaning against a birch tree watching her bathe.

An Unexpected Reunion Occurs

The men
That here inhabit do not entertain
With ready kindness strangers...
                    —*Homer's Odysseys*, Book 7, 40–42

H E HAD THE DECENCY TO TURN HIS BACK WHILE
Kathryn got out of the pool—feeling not at all sylph-like as
she clambered over the muddy, moss-slippery rocks. Quickly,
she pulled petticoat and kirtle over her damp skin. What was Thomas
Willoughby doing wandering about the woods?

She had last seen him a month ago, when she visited Cupids Cove
with her husband. Until then, she had believed Willoughby safely back
in England, where he had returned four years ago. But his father, Sir
Percival Willoughby, still owned large tracts of the New Found Land.
Now that he was back in his father's good graces, Thomas was once
again in the New World pursuing the family interests. He had told her
when they met in Cupids Cove that he had brought men over to clear
land for a plantation, and had made the outrageous suggestion that she
might leave her husband and come live as his mistress. The words were
spoken in jest, of course—Kathryn was almost certain of that.

She fumbled with the hairpins scattered on the ground, finally laying them among the berries and leaves in her basket and leaving her wet hair loose. Thomas glanced over his shoulder. "May I look upon you now, Mistress Guy?"

"You may. How do you come to be here?"

"I should ask the same—you are on my land." He had put his own shirt back on; likely he, too, had come to the pond intending to bathe.

"I lost my way," Kathryn said. "Can you set me back on the right path to get home?"

"From here? 'Twill be a long walk. My house is but a quarter-hour's walk from here, but 'tis a good hour or more through the woods back to your husband's land. I can take you back by boat from my house."

Kathryn did not like to be at the mercy of this man. He was as fair to look on as when she had first known him in Cupids Cove years ago: light hair falling in soft curls, ice-blue eyes, a tall and slender frame that still looked boyish. He was as cocksure in his manner, too, as he had been then. But there was something else in him now: he had a rich man's assurance as well as a boy's bravado. He had been sent to the New Found Land five years earlier in disgrace, in hopes that hardship would hone him into manhood. And perhaps, after all, it had.

The path was not wide enough for two to walk abreast, so she followed as he told her how he and his father's agent, Master Crout, had brought a dozen labourers from England to help build a house and plantation in Harbour Grace. All but two of his labourers had given up within a fortnight, daunted by the challenges of life in the wilderness. "I tried to warn them," Thomas said, "told them to expect hard work—and they are used to hard work back in England, you know. But once we left Cupids Cove and sailed up the shore, and they found their first task was to clear the forest, they balked. What did they think the colonies were like? I told them no lies."

"What did they do?"

"Laid down tools and refused to work. Insisted on sailing back to Cupids Cove and taking the next ship to England. I told them they would owe my father for their passage, but what good is a crew of lazy louts? Master Crout is gone off exploring—he has taken some men to cut a trail through the woods, from Carbonear over to Trinity Bay. I am left with only two men, though I mean to bring over more. I have asked my father to send out an experienced carpenter to build me a proper house, though I am not yet certain if it should be built here in Harbour Grace, or at Carbonear."

"Nicholas cleared our land and built our house with only himself and three other men," Kathryn said. "It took a deal of work, but most of it was done by the summer's end." That had been their second summer on the land; she did not speak about the first summer, which had ended in tragedy. "Even now, we have a small household—one maid and two menservants. And we have Bess and Frank—Frank fishes with my husband, but he and Bess have their own little house near ours."

"Quite the lady of the manor, are you not?"

"I do not give myself airs. I know I am no lady."

"But every man can be lord of his own manor in this land. A cobbler like your husband might rule an estate as large as my father's in Nottinghamshire."

They topped a small rise of land and stood looking down the slope of a hill that stretched towards a pebbled beach. Along this slope, trees had been cleared, and a simple wooden building stood in the centre of the cleared area. On the shore was a small wharf with a shallop tied to it.

"Next year, I will hire fishing servants and some men to work the soil, so the place can sustain itself," Thomas said, leading her towards the house. "Some of the Cupids Cove settlers mean to join me here—John Crowder and Jem Holworthy both are eager to become planters, rather than dancing to the tune of the London merchants. We must fish to survive, but my father is convinced the true wealth in this country lies beneath the earth, not out in the water."

"You mean in growing crops?" Kathryn said, amazed at his foolishness. "I have heard men talk of the crops that make great profit on plantations to the south—sugar and tobacco. This is not the climate for such things. Sure, we can hardly grow enough food to live on! A man can feed his family on carrots, turnips, cabbage and the like—if he buys grain from English ships—but there's no wealth to be found in this soil."

As she spoke, she looked at the sweep of land around them: the rocky ground, the trees, the dark grey water beyond the beach. Harbour Grace was much larger than her little Musketto Cove; further out in the bay she saw scores of masts, for this was a busy place in summer, where ships of many nations came to carry out the summer fishery. Thomas had chosen for himself a stretch of land on the north shore of the harbour, well away from the fishing vessels.

"Not in the soil," he answered her. "Under it."

"Gold?"

"Gold, silver, copper, iron. That is what will make us rich. We will have a plantation, but our greater purpose will be to search for ore so that mines can be dug."

"That will not be the work of a year or two," she said, following him down the path. "You mean to stay some time."

"Aye, I will have men here for several years, and come back and forth from England as I please. I do not intend to bring my wife out, nor to raise our children here."

My wife. Kathryn was about to say, "You are married now?" but she kept her lips sealed. If she responded with surprise, he would take it as proof that she still cared for him. Of course, back in England, he had made some appropriate match with a young lady of his own class.

"I am sure she is accustomed to a gentler life," was all that Kathryn said. Then she added, "'Tis clouding over—and after such a fine day."

"I'll not delay long, then, in taking you home. Only—are you hungry? I have no fine table to invite you to, but I can offer you a simple meal before we depart."

She was, in fact, very hungry. "I will take something to eat, but we must not linger long," she said as he led her into the small house. The ringing sound of axes told her that Thomas's servants were at work somewhere on the property.

The house was crude indeed—little better than a tilt or a labourer's cottage, with a door and one window to let in some light, a table, a bench and a small bed in the corner. *The men must sleep outside*, Kathryn thought, *and cook there too*, as Kathryn and Nicholas and their servants had done before their house was finished.

"'Tis but poor fare," Thomas said, "though if you can wait awhile longer, my man Higgs will roast a bird or make a stew that is almost fit to eat. He is the only one of us who can cook, so the duty falls to him. We make what shift we can." As he spoke, he handed her some tough, dry bread—not as hard as ship's biscuit, but not far off it—and a little cheese he had wrapped in a cloth.

"You would get a better meal at my table. Perhaps we had best sail for Musketto Cove now, and I can invite you to supper." She took a bite of the cheese; it was very old and sharp to the tongue.

"You call your place Musketto Cove?"

"We did not name it. When we settled there first, we thought the place had no name, and that we might call it Guy's Cove, or some such thing. But then some fishermen who had been coming here for years told my husband that they had always called it Muskets Cove or Musketto Cove—something to do with shooting off guns there, I think."

"I will save the joys of dining at Musketto for another day," he said. "I've some dried beef about somewhere—and here's ale."

Kathryn took the ale gratefully—she was quite thirsty—but waved away the offer of meat. She did not trust the condition it was likely to be in, and she wanted to delay her departure no longer. The wind was rising, and the light through the small window had changed: the earlier sunshine had turned to a dull grey. She thought there were yet a few hours till sunset, but the sky was darkening for a storm.

"You must bide awhile. The breeze is coming up, and 'tis blowing the wrong way—I cannot sail north in this wind."

For the first time, Kathryn felt a touch of fear. Until now there had been the sense that she was having an adventure that was a little bit daring, a trifle foolish. Now it seemed possible that she might not, after all, get back safely to her husband and children today. "You must find a way to take me home!"

Thomas Willoughby spread his hands wide. "I am not the Lord himself, to command the winds and the waves."

"Then I will go back alone through the forest." She stood up and moved towards the door, but he put a hand on her arm.

"Do not be a fool, Kathryn. You were lost before I found you—what hope have you now of finding home before dark, in the rain?"

"This is your fault! You ought to have led me straight home, not here to this—this miserable hovel you live in. I thought you were in jest when you asked me to come away with you. Do you mean to hold me prisoner?"

He laughed. "Still the little spitfire underneath that proper matron, eh? Come now, Kat, would it be such a bad fate to live here with me? You can see the place needs a woman's touch."

"Live here, and be your cook and maid as well as your doxy? Thank you for the kind offer, but no. I want to return to my husband and children."

"I am sure you do. Just as sure as I am that some small part of you wants to remain with me—though perhaps in a better house and softer bed than this one."

A booming crash of thunder cut across his words, followed seconds later by a flash of lightning. Kathryn stared out at the storm clouds as rain began to pelt the trees. She was as angry as if Thomas really did have the power to conjure up a storm.

He moved closer, picked up a strand of her hair and twined it around his fingers. "Perhaps you will confess that you like being here with me?"

He was so close, his breath against her face. She pulled away as she heard, mingled with the sounds of the storm, men's voices approaching. Thomas's servants were coming to take shelter in the tilt.

The first man through the door, a burly young fellow with a yellow beard, stumbled on the doorstep in his shock at seeing Kathryn.

"Mistress Guy, these are my men, Higgs and Barry," Thomas said, as smoothly as if he had never touched her hair. To the men he said, "Mistress Guy's husband owns land in the cove north of here. I found her lost in the woods, and she is taking shelter here until I can bring her home."

With the men inside, the mood changed. The four of them crowded into the small room, ale was passed around, and Kathryn drew the men into conversation, asking about their lives before leaving England.

Higgs, especially, was glad to talk about his wife and three little ones on the Willoughby family estate, and how he hoped he could earn a better life for them, perhaps bring them out to the New Found Land to join him someday. "She's a fine brawny lass, my Liza, and I daresay she'd do well out here."

"Aye, I'm sure she would if she's not afraid of hard work," Kathryn said, and told them of the summer five years ago when she and her maid Nancy and all the other young women had come out on a ship from Bristol. While Kathryn had been going to join her husband, most of the others had been single women. "But all were matched and mated soon. A good many of them are still in Cupids Cove, and two of them are with me on my husband's plantation. I'll not say it has been easy, but you and your good wife could do far worse than to make your home here."

Thomas was quiet throughout this conversation, sitting back and sipping his ale as Kathryn talked with the labourers. He had drawn the shutters and lit a candle, so it was almost cozy in the small, close-smelling room. Every few minutes their talk was interrupted by another clap of thunder, and rain beat in through the cracks in the rough wooden walls and the gaps between the shutters. Higgs shared around the bread and cheese and dried meat; this time, Kathryn took some of everything. Outside, the sky was growing dark not just from the clouds, but from the lateness of the hour.

When Thomas said aloud, "I am afraid you will have to stop here with us tonight, Mistress Guy," she said, "No! I must go home." But her voice broke on the word *home*—a simple glance outside would tell anyone it was hopeless.

"Nonsense. You may sleep in my bed," said Thomas, giving her a sly, sideways grin before continuing. "I will join Higgs and Barry on the floor—we've little comfort to offer the fairer sex, but you shall have the one mattress in the place."

"I cannot—there *must* be a way that I can get home. What will my husband think?" She hated the shrill, frantic tone of her voice.

When the serving-men went outside to the privy, Thomas put a hand on her arm. "You must not be so distrait, sweet Kat. Even a man of such limited imagination as your husband will surely see you had no other choice but to stay here until the storm passed."

"You know what a fragile thing a woman's good name is. How can I spend the night in a tilt with three men?"

"You were bolder, once upon a time. Once you spent seven nights with another man in your husband's bed."

"That was hardly the same."

"How was it different? This is far the lesser sin—I will not lay a hand on you." He took his hand off her arm, as if to prove his words.

The heavy stamping feet outside saved her from having to answer. She retreated to the bed, which had some rough sacking hung around it in a poor imitation of proper bed-hangings. Though Higgs and Barry commonly slept outside, on stormy nights like this all would shelter indoors. Behind her makeshift curtains Kathryn heard the three men settling down to sleep.

She lay on the straw-stuffed mattress, thinking of her own down-filled bed and the simple hangings that seemed luxurious by comparison to these. Nicholas always made sure she had the best of everything, as far as was possible in the colony. Nicholas—who trusted her, who had never guessed at her unfaithfulness. True, his touch did not awaken her passion as Thomas's had once done. But now she lay in a room only a few feet away from Thomas and trembled with fear.

Surely he would not dare come to her, approach her, with his two servants asleep in the same room? Even Thomas Willoughby would not be so reckless, so foolhardy.

This is far the lesser sin, he had said, to take shelter under his roof. That she had once shared a bed and given up her virtue to him was a great sin in the eyes of God, but only God knew of it. Thomas was not thinking how he would view the thing if it were his own wife, that pretty and pampered young lady in England. The greater sin was always the sin that was known.

If she were to come home in the morning, in a boat rowed by Thomas Willoughby, and have her husband and all the servants know how she had passed the night—that could never be kept secret. *And what will Nicholas do then?* she wondered.

The rain beat down upon, and in some places through, the boards of the roof. The night had no answer for her.

THREE

A Marriage is Celebrated

BRISTOL, JULY 1617

The bride and bridegroom having ceas'd to keep
Observéd love-joys, from their fit delight
They turn'd to talk.
                                    —*Homer's Odysseys*, Book 23, 448–50

THE BELLS OF ST. STEPHEN'S RANG OUT AS NED AND
Nancy left the church hand in hand. Ned's family gathered
in the churchyard: brothers and sisters, nieces and nephews,
his mother, beaming. "I never dreamed I would see my Ned's wedding day," she said, her soft voice little more than a whisper as Nancy
bent down for the older woman's embrace. "I know you will make him
happy—indeed, you already have."

"Thank you," Nancy said. She said it over and over, to the gathered
family and neighbours. Words of thanks seemed so small against the
great tide of joy she felt, but she had not the gift of a honeyed tongue.
So she said *thank you, thank you*—to Ned's family, to the minister, to
the woman who lived next door to Ned's brother, and to the people she
thought of as her own family—Aunt Tibby, Master Gale, Lily.

They stood apart, a smaller and more sober group than Ned's family. Lily was hand in hand with Walter, her betrothed, no doubt thinking of her own wedding which would take place at the end of summer. Already Lily was beginning to move out from the grief surrounding the death of her mother and brothers, to think about the future. But her father was still bowed down by loss. When Nancy came to him, he took her hand in both of his, but did not smile. "I wish you every blessing. Ned is a good lad," was all he said.

Nancy met John Gale's eyes for a moment; he was the first to look away. *He knows*, she thought, and then, *He has always known. But does he know that I know now?*

She had grown up under this man's gentle authority; he was master of the household where she was a servant; he was the father of Kathryn, her mistress and dearest friend. He was master of the apprentices, of which Ned had once been one. What Nancy had not known until a few weeks ago was that John Gale was her father. If he was ever to own that, to acknowledge her as his daughter, surely her wedding day would be the time to do that?

But of course he would not. To do so would be to admit that he had been unfaithful to his wife. That he had taken his servant Tibby to bed, and brought their bastard child into his household. Nancy had grown up believing Tibby was her aunt and that her own parents had died of plague. As she grew, she had begun to wonder whether the woman she called "Aunt Tib" might, in fact, be her mother—but she had never guessed who her father might be, until Tibby told her the truth.

And what does it matter, after all? It was not as if the Gales were a wealthy family, where being a base-born daughter might promise some inheritance. John Gale was a stonemason, and the only thing he had to leave was his house and his business. That would have gone to his eldest son, if young John had lived; now it would go to Walter, as Lily's dowry. Nancy neither expected nor needed anything from John Gale.

She pulled Tibby into an embrace. "I hope you'll be happy, my dear girl," Tibby said.

"I am so glad we came home and got married here," Nancy said. She had thought that today, perhaps for the only time in her life, she would call Tibby *Mother*, but the word would not form on her tongue. It was a name she had never called anyone; how could this alien word convey any more love than simply "Aunt Tib"?

"You might stay home, you know," Tibby said.

"You might come with me." They had talked of it for weeks, but Nancy knew she would never coax Tibby out to the colony. She was as much a part of Bristol as the old city wall, as sturdy and unchanging.

"Come now, I'm famished, and there's a feast waiting for us," said Ned, tugging at Nancy's hand.

"Feast" was, perhaps, too fine a word for their wedding breakfast, but it was fortunate that Ned's brother owned a bakeshop. As the two families—and a few neighbour children hoping they might sneak in unobserved—squeezed into the main room of the shop and the savoury pies and pastries were passed around, Nancy felt wrapped in the warmth of the celebration.

There was more to this day than just her marriage to Ned. That bond had been sealed long ago when she first promised to wed him, and sealed anew when they found each other again after their long separation. But with the vows exchanged and the wedding feast eaten, she felt she belonged to a family, as well as to her husband.

And now they were going to turn their backs on all that, and cross the seas again.

Much later that night, behind the curtains of the bed that Ned's brother Dickon and his wife had vacated so they could have it for their wedding night, Ned turned to Nancy. "Have we made the right choice?"

"What, to marry? A bit late to be doubting that, is it not?"

He laughed softly. "Indeed, no turning back from that. But to go from here—to leave Bristol again. Are we doing the right thing?"

They had booked passage almost as soon as they returned to Bristol, intending to marry quickly and be gone. But when Nancy had returned to the Gale house, learned of the sorrow and suffering there, and heard from Tibby the true tale of her own birth, she wanted to linger for a time. Now midsummer was past, the fishing fleet long since gone to the New Found Land. Their plan was to seek the next ship they could find that would make port anywhere near the Cupids Cove colony.

Nancy sighed. "I had the thought today—'tis a pity to leave here, where we have family and friends. But the wedding feast is over, and your brothers and sisters will return to their work. Tibby will keep house for Master Gale, and Lily will plan her wedding while Walter runs Master Gale's business. When everyone goes back to their lives, what is there for us here? Would you go back to stonemasonry? Work for Master Gale and Walter as their journeyman?"

"I could," Ned said. "It was my first trade, and I am sure Walter could use another pair of hands. But what would you do?"

"Aye, there's a question." As a married woman, Nancy was unlikely to find a place in service. "We would have to rent a room or two, and I would keep house for you—not that there would be much house to keep."

Ned smiled, one hand tangling in her hair as it lay loose across her bare breasts. "Two rooms in a Bristol house would be little space compared to a home in the colony."

"It would be easier."

For a woman, work in the colony included much more labour than a town-bred serving girl had been raised to expect. Nancy had been taught to cook and clean, to brew and bake, to mend and sew. She had not been prepared to care for livestock, to plant and harvest vegetables, to help build shelters and walls—never mind learning how to split, gut, and salt codfish.

"Do you want that? An easier life?"

Nancy tried to answer honestly. "Since we have come back to Bristol, so many folk—your mother, your sisters, Lily and Tibby, the fishmonger's wife—have asked how I can think of going back to the New Found Land, to such hardship and danger. Even without such disasters as I have suffered, the weather there is harsher, and the winters colder."

"Not to mention the fear of wild beasts and wild men," Ned added.

"Though neither of those ever troubled us. And since I came to know Pocahontas and Matachanna and the other Powhatan, I have not so much fear of the native folk. But 'tis true—the New World is a harsh place to live." She paused, momentarily distracted by the play of his fingers across her body, then caught his hand and kissed it before going on. "It might seem like a safer life, here in Bristol. Yet think of the Gales.

Only Kathryn went to the colony, while all the rest stayed here—and half the family died of sickness in their own house."

"True enough—there is less of the plague over there than here in England."

"And I thought, also"—she searched for the right words—"after all I have seen in these last few years, two rented rooms on a Bristol street would seem small to me, now."

"I feel the same," said Ned. "In the New Found Land we may well have our own house and our own land—could you imagine? Two common folks such as yourself and myself, Master and Mistress Perry."

"Don't be giving us too many airs, now! You cannot be certain of a house and land. We were both in service to Nicholas Guy before; why should we not be again?"

"Ah, love, you cannot imagine how glad Kathryn will be that you are safely back. She will insist that Master Nicholas give us whatever we ask for, even to a piece of their own land to build our house upon."

"Your reward for rescuing me." Nancy laughed.

It was a jest between them—Nancy, the maiden in distress, and Ned, her rescuer. Of course, that was not the truth of the tale. He had left the New Found Land with that intention, and travelled far in his quest to do so—but by the time he found Nancy she had a good position in the household of Virginia planter John Rolfe and his wife, the Powhatan princess Pocahontas. Nancy felt she had done a credible job of rescuing herself.

"Then that is what we will do, if you are content—we will return home together, triumphant," Ned said, and kissed her.

The morning after their wedding, while Ned went down to the docks to talk to sailors about finding a ship bound for the New Found Land, Nancy cleaned up from the wedding feast alongside Ned's mother and sister-in-law. The older woman paused frequently in her work, seeming to need more rest than the tasks required. When she left the room, Nancy turned to her new sister-in-law.

"Is Mother Perry well? She tires so easily."

Mary lowered her voice. "She did not want to tell you or Ned, for she hated to bring any sorrow on your wedding day—but she's not been well at all. She has little strength, and she coughs up blood—just as Father Perry did before he passed away. She was glad to see Ned once more, and to see the two of you wedded. She said I wasn't to tell Ned, but..."

Nancy did not tell Ned herself, but urged him to go and talk to his mother. And when that sober conversation was done, Nancy suggested they stay in Bristol awhile longer.

"You will not be sorry to delay our journey?" Ned asked her.

"No—I think not. In England or in the New Found Land—I am at home as long as I am with you."

FOUR

A Wanderer is Brought Home

Nought beneath the sky
More sweet, more worthy is, than firm consent
Of man and wife in household government.
                    —*Homer's Odysseys*, Book 6, 278–80

KATHRYN WOKE, STIFF AND UNCOMFORTABLE IN A strange bed. She heard men's voices. Memory returned: the pool in the forest. Thomas Willoughby. His house; his servants; the storm.

Slowly she unfolded herself and got out of bed—she had slept in her petticoat and kirtle. Neither Willoughby nor either of his men was in the house; the door stood ajar, revealing a clear, sunny morning.

Outside, Willoughby tended a fire with pottage cooking over it. He scooped out a bowlful and handed it to her. "The storm is over; you must bring me home now," she said, taking it without thanks. "And bring one of the men with you, so my husband will see we were not alone."

"Ah—he will be happier to think you spent the night with three men than with just one," Willoughby said, smiling.

"I've no time to bandy words with you, Master Willoughby. As soon as I have eaten, you must take me back to Musketto Cove."

"I cannot spare a man to go with us," he said.

She had not heard Higgs approach until he spoke. "Begging your pardon, Master Willoughby, but it may be best if two of us go with Mistress Guy—you and I may need to row on the way back." He looked at his master as he spoke, but glanced quickly at Kathryn afterwards.

As Willoughby's shallop sailed out of Harbour Grace and around the point of land, Kathryn remembered the frantic search through the woods after the fire and pirate attack four years ago, when Nancy had gone missing. Would Nicholas and the servants have carried out the same kind of search for Kathryn last night?

At least they would soon know that she was alive and well. She did not dare guess how her husband might react to the news of where she had spent the night. If he had sense, he would be glad she had taken shelter with a neighbour on a stormy night. But men did not always show good sense where their honour was concerned.

Musketto Cove was a small, welcoming circle of water surrounded by a tree-lined shore that enclosed the little bay like a pair of embracing arms. The Guy family's house, outbuildings, and wharf were on the north side of the bay-head at the end of the pebbled beach that separated the ocean from a small freshwater pond. Kathryn had come to think of this place as home, and she was always glad, when travelling back from Cupids Cove by boat, to make that turn into the cove and see their plantation unfold before her. Now, for the first time in a long time, she felt a flutter of trepidation as her home grew near.

Thomas's only chance for a word alone with her came when they tied up to her husband's wharf. She had not seen any of Nicholas's boats out on the water, though normally at this time in the morning he and the men would be out fishing. His shallops were tied up at the wharf. *They are still searching the woods for me*, she thought.

"Stay here, Higgs," Thomas said as he helped Kathryn out of the boat. "I will see Mistress Guy to her door."

Kathryn was about to invite Higgs to come to the house as well, to say that she'd gladly give him a drink as thanks for bringing her home—but that would mean that Thomas would linger longer. So she said only, "Thank you" to the servant, and walked up the path with Thomas.

He bent close to her ear to speak. "I did not jest, when I asked you to come live with me. Now that you have been in my house, I mean it all the more earnestly—I would have you."

"You'd not take another man's wife, Thomas. What folly!"

"I would, if she left her husband willingly. Your husband has not the power he once had in this country, now that there is a new governor whose name is not Guy. Nicholas is only another planter. Will he fight to win you back if he knows...?"

Knows what? She knew Thomas could ruin her with a handful of words—could tell Nicholas that she had slept with him four years ago in Cupids Cove. He could even lie and say that she had gone to his bed last night. She would deny it, but whose tale would Nicholas believe?

At that moment the door to the house burst open and Daisy More came running down the path. "Mistress! 'Tis you! Alive!"

"Of course I am alive, Daisy!" Kathryn set down her basket and caught her servant in her arms and embraced her. "And 'tis glad I am to be safe home! Where is my husband, and the children?"

"Bess has your youngsters down at her house with her own two, trying to settle them. The men started searching again at first light, but—ah, here he comes now." They looked up to see Nicholas Guy emerging from the trees beyond the house, breaking into a run as he caught sight of his wife.

"God be praised, Kathryn, you are home, and safe! Where have you—?" He broke off to look at the man accompanying her. "Master Willoughby?"

Thomas quickly told his story of finding Kathryn in the woods, sheltering her in his tilt overnight during the storm. Kathryn added, "I tarried too long gathering berries and plants in the forest—I quite lost my way, and 'twas great good fortune that Master Willoughby was nearby." She held up her full basket, as if she needed proof of her tale.

Nicholas nodded, glancing down at Willoughby's boat. "Do you and your man wish to come in, take some ale before you start back?"

"'Tis kind of you, but no, we had best be back at our day's work. We will visit sometime, for I welcome any guidance you can give me in the business of starting a plantation in this country." His voice was so smooth and civil that it was impossible for Kathryn to believe that just a few moments earlier he had been urging her to leave Nicholas and come live as his mistress.

"You have my thanks," Nicholas said.

Kathryn had already moved away from the men, towards the smaller house where Bess and Frank lived. The children were tumbling out the door now, and the men's voices retreated to a murmur as Kathryn set down her basket and ran to meet her children.

"Oh, mistress! I was telling Jonathan and Alice all morning that you'd be back today, safe and sound," said Bess, who was carrying a crying Jemmy in her arms. "But this young fellow won't settle at all, wants his mama. We was all near out of our minds with worry."

"All is well," Kathryn said, telling Bess the briefest possible version of her tale as she took her crying son in her arms and sat on the doorstep of the house. She unlaced her kirtle and settled him at her breast, his suckling giving them both ease.

The older children, tugging at her skirts, interrupted Kathryn's attempt to tell Bess how she had gotten lost in the woods. Four-year-old Jonathan climbed up into her lap, while three-year-old Alice ran her fingers over her mother's arms, hands, hair and clothes as if to reassure herself that Kathryn was real.

"Mama, did you see the fairies?" Alice wanted to know. The older children had all been given stern warnings about the danger of being taken by fairies if they went into the woods alone.

"No, I was not fairy-led—I am your own mama come back again, I promise," Kathryn said, and thought, *Though that is just what I would say to reassure her if I had been taken by the fairies.* But fairies only troubled to capture sweet-faced little girls with golden ringlets and blue eyes, not sensible matrons.

Looking down at Alice's face, with its echoes of Thomas Willoughby, Kathryn remembered that when they had met in Cupids Cove last month, Willoughby had told her that if she had a son born after their affair, he would claim the boy, but a girl was not worth the trouble. *Let us hope that if he ever sees you, he will continue to think you worthless,* Kathryn thought, cuddling her daughter close.

Later, when the children were playing and everyone else was at work, Kathryn took advantage of a few moments' peace to go to her sleeping chamber and pull a clean shift and kirtle from the chest that held her clothes. She had only a few changes of clothing, and except for special occasions, most were worn for many days of work about the house and garden before being laundered. But yesterday's adventures had left her kirtle stained with mud and grass, and her petticoat soaked with sweat. Perhaps that was why she was eager to change out of them—or perhaps it was the knowledge that she had worn them in Thomas Willoughby's bed.

Nicholas surprised her; she stood there clad only in her shift, her hair loosed from its pins so she might comb it tidy again. She felt oddly exposed, though Nicholas was the only man in the world who had the right to see her in this state.

"So, you spent the night at Willoughby's plantation."

"I begged him to take me home straight away, but the storm blew up quickly."

"How did you come to be all the way over to Harbour Grace?"

"I told you—I lost my way. 'Twas a pleasant day, and I walked a long time before realizing I could not find the path home. I stumbled upon Master Willoughby in the woods by accident."

"The storm had not started then? Why did you go with him to his house, instead of returning home at once?"

"I did not know the way, and he said 'twas faster for him to take me home by boat."

He took a few steps towards her.

She had never been afraid of Nicholas. Seven years ago, when she was a girl in Bristol and they were first married, he had been a solemn stranger, but never a cruel one. He had never raised a hand to her. Over the years she had grown fond of him, been glad for his protection and company. Now he was that stern stranger again, his face closed and suspicious.

"I do not think well of Master Willoughby," Nicholas said. "Sir Percival is a good man, but his son is a fool, and not to be trusted with another man's wife."

"Surely, sir, the question is not whether Willoughby can be trusted with a man's wife, but whether a man can trust his own wife?" Kathryn's voice trembled a little, but she forced herself to look into his eyes. "You know I would never play you false."

Lies, lies—and yet, the truth. She had not been unfaithful—this time.

"You are a good woman," he said, moving closer still. "But women's virtue is frail, and Willoughby is a handsome devil. He would be quick to take advantage of any weakness."

"I only thanked him for his hospitality and told him I wanted to go home to my husband. I knew you were worried about me."

Nicholas's face softened. He stroked her loose dark hair. "Aye, that I was," he admitted. "I was frantic at the thought of you lost or injured, alone in the forest."

"God preserved me, and sent me help," she said. "And I promise I will never wander so far into the woods again." If he thought her only reckless and a trifle foolish, that was so much better than thinking her faithless.

He sighed heavily and drew her into his arms. "'Tis glad I am that you are safe. I will not lecture you about how it looks for you to have been alone at Willoughby's place, for I know you received a great fright, and you are sorry, and will not wander off again."

"I will not—I swear it."

"Ah, Kathryn, my little wife." She relaxed; anytime he called her his little wife, he was in a kindly mood, and sometimes an amorous one. But his voice was sober when he said, "I love this land, and I believe you love it too. But yesterday when I searched the woods for you, I thought of how it was here after the pirates attacked, how all was burned and ruined, how Tom was killed and Nancy taken. I could not help but think that perhaps this land is cursed, after all, and we should not be here."

An Ocean is Crossed

AT SEA, SEPTEMBER 1617

Nought is more wretched in a human race,
Than country's want, and shift from place to place.
                    —Homer's *Odysseys*, Book 15, 444–45

O N THE DOCK, MEN LOOSED THE SHIP'S LINES FROM
their moorings. Ned stood at the ship's rail beside Nancy,
waving at the little party of friends and family gathered below
to bid them farewell.

"When I first left Bristol, I never thought to make this voyage again,"
Nancy said as they pulled away from the dock, the faces of the people
onshore fading into distance.

"Nor I," said Ned.

His mother had died in August. Ned was glad they had stayed
through the summer, glad he had been able to sit by her side and see
her laid to rest, as he had not been able to do for his father. When they
heard of a ship sailing to Cupids Cove with a small group of colonists,
making port at Bristol before crossing to the New World, Ned had
arranged their passage. He and Nancy both had a little store of coins
from their last employment and could afford to travel as passengers.

They had agreed it was time to go, and yet he was not entirely surprised to see Nancy quickly wipe a tear with the back of her hand. He passed her his handkerchief and said, "Have you any regrets? I can ask the captain to give us a little boat to row ashore."

She smiled. "Nay. I am sad to say goodbye to Tibby, but I am content to leave."

"I am glad to leave also. England is a hard place," said the man standing beside them at the rail. He was sturdily built, taller than Ned and broader across the shoulders, with black hair and light-brown skin. He was dressed like an English workingman, in tunic and breeches, and spoke good English, but with an accent that was hard to place.

"It is that, indeed," Ned said. "You would be Tisquantum, then? I am Ned Perry, and this is my wife Nancy."

He knew of their fellow traveller—a native of the New World who had been living in John Slany's household for the past year. Slany was the treasurer of the Newfoundland Company, and one of his men who was also going out to the colony had told Ned that the native man would be travelling with them.

Now Tisquantum greeted them both, and asked, "Are you going out to settle in this New Found Land?"

"We are going back there," Ned said. "We went out with Governor John Guy when he first settled Cupids Cove a few years since, but we have been away for some time."

"Ah, yes. I too have been a long time from my home."

Nancy, who likely knew more about the natives of the New World than any Englishman aboard the ship, asked, "And where is your home? In Virginia?"

"No," Tisquantum said. "The land the English call Virginia is called Tsenacommacah in the tongue of those who live there. My people are the Wampanoag. My home is called Patuxet, well to the north of Tsenacommacah, but south of your Newly Found Land. The English think my homeland is new-found, also." He gave a wry smile, then said, "You were in Virginia?"

"I was," Nancy said, "for two years. I served the lady Pocahontas there."

"Ah," said Tisquantum. "I saw her in London—from a distance; I did not chance to meet her. We could have spoken, though their tongue is a little different from mine. Perhaps we would have spoken in English— I have had some time, now, to learn your speech."

"You speak it well indeed," Ned said. "But you are coming to the New Found Land with us, and hoping to make your way from there to your own country? You know the New Found Land is an island, surely."

"I do," said Tisquantum. Ned wondered if he had insulted the man by hinting that he might not have learned everything needful to know about the place he was going. "Master Slany said that the English governor in your colony wants one of our people as a translator, in hope he might treat with the people of the land. And that from there I might find a ship taking me back to my own country, in time."

As the long weeks of the voyage passed, Ned found Tisquantum an easy fellow to talk to. In a strange way he felt that both he and Nancy had more in common with Tisquantum than with the other Englishmen, all London or Bristol fellows who had never been out of England before. With Tisquantum, Ned and Nancy could trade tales of the far places they had been to and the strange things they had seen.

Tisquantum told them of the papist friars who had taken him in and cared for him in Spain, and how he made his way from there to England. He did not, however, talk of how he came to leave his own country, and Ned did not press him for that tale.

They had smooth sailing; good weather and good company made the trip almost merry. The ship did not stop at St. John's, the busiest fishing station on the island, but sailed around Cape St. Francis and into Conception Bay. Ned stood at the rail with Tisquantum and a couple of men who were coming out to settle, Stephen Butler and Hal Henshaw. Ned pointed out the fishing stations along the way.

"That's Carbonear that we just passed—you can see there's a good few ships fishing out of there for the summer. Just south of it is the cove where my old master was building his plantation when we were attacked, and his house burned."

"By Indians, or Frenchmen?" Butler asked.

"Neither. 'Twas a bunch of English pirates."

"What does this English word mean, *pirate*?" Tisquantum asked, though surely he had heard the word before. "Why do you call a man by that name?"

"Pirate ships and captains break the King's laws," Stephen Butler said. "Pirates steal what is not theirs by right, and take folks captive, and make an unjust profit."

"Ah," said Tisquantum. "It is true then—there are many English pirates."

All four men fell silent. Ned strained to see what was happening on the shore of the small cove, but he could see no more than the fishing boats out on the water. The Gale family had received letters saying that Nicholas and Kathryn Guy had gone back to this same cove and rebuilt their house, and that things were going well. How long ago, Ned wondered, had that last letter been written? A year or more, surely.

"'Tis strange to think," he told Nancy later as they bundled up the few clothes and belongings they had unpacked during the voyage, "how little we know of what has passed here since we have been away."

"I know. Four years—'tis a long time. I want to see Kathryn again, but for all I know, she may be—"

"Hush, now. We'll not tempt fate by saying ill things aloud. Things will be as we find them, and we'll make the best of it."

He smiled at her, and wanted her to smile back. But now, on the very edge of coming to the home she had tried for four years to return to, he saw fear mingled with hope in Nancy's eyes.

What struck Ned first when they landed at Cupids Cove was that he did not recognize anyone. New men had come and settled since he had gone away, and old ones had left. And of course many of the men here would not be year-round settlers of Cupids Cove, but summer fishermen.

Then he heard a voice call out, "Is that you, Ned Perry?" and turned to see Jem Holworthy, with George Lane nearby—men he had known for years, since they'd first come out together.

Lane's wife Jennet darted towards Nancy, crying out and putting her hands to her mouth. "Nancy Ellis! 'Tis yourself—alive!"

They all came then, those who were left from those early days, amazed to see Ned and Nancy again. Even George Whittington greeted

Ned with careful formality, though Nancy would not speak to him. The bad blood between them went back many years, to a time when Whittington's malicious accusation had almost cost Nancy her life.

Jem and Elsie Holworthy offered Ned and Nancy a bed by their hearth. Holworthy said that on Sunday he would take a shallop and bring them to Musketto Cove.

Ned did not know the place by that name, but he recognized it by description as the same spot the Guys had attempted to settle in the summer of 1613. "So they are all still there, then—Master Nicholas and Mistress Kathryn, their children and the rest of the household?" he heard Nancy ask Jennet Lane.

"Aye, 'twas but a few weeks ago Master Guy was here on some business with Governor Mason. They are all well—did you know she has two boys and a girl now?" The chatty Jennet Lane and the quiet Elsie Holworthy led Nancy away between them as Ned followed with the menfolk.

In honour of the new arrivals, all the colonists and many of the fishermen gathered on the beach after the evening meal. Fires were lit and some brandy passed around, as well as ale from the Cupids Cove brewhouse. The colonists were eager to hear all the news from England.

"Did ye hear Sir Walter Raleigh came back to England in disgrace? They say he will be sentenced to death—again," the ship's captain was saying to Governor Mason.

"I had not heard! What is the charge against him?" the governor asked. Ned did not catch the answer, for a voice near him said, "Very bad fortune—sentenced to death twice! How many times can an Englishman die?"

Ned turned to see Tisquantum standing beside him, half a smile on his face. For all the hardships he had suffered, Tisquantum sometimes seemed more amused by the English than anything.

"I thought you were still surrounded," Ned said. "When I saw you before there was a crowd of young ones around you—the women and children as well as the men."

Tisquantum shrugged. "The same in London. They are all..." he paused, searching for the word, "...all curious, to see the native man from far over the seas. They want to touch my hair and my skin, to ask questions. The governor's wife asked me if the monks in Spain baptized me as a Catholic, and told me it would be better to be baptized again in the Church of England. But I told her I had just come from the sea, and needed no more water put over my head."

Ned laughed, and Tisquantum went on, "The governor wants me to go with his men to look for the people of the land, to see if I can speak with them."

"Do you know anything of them?"

"No Wampanoag has traded this far north, but we have dealings with the Mi'kmaq, who go back and forth across the waters from this island that they call K'Taqmkuk, to the greater land. The Mi'kmaq have no camps near this part of K'Taqmkuk, but they have traded with another people who live here—I have heard that the Mi'kmaq call them Osa'yan'a, but I do not know what they call themselves. This is as much as I know; it is far from my land of Patuxet. Still, I will go, to see if I may be of use."

"You must come to Musketto Cove too, to meet Master and Mistress Guy, and see myself and Nancy again. I know you will be welcome."

"Perhaps. It may be so."

Three small children hovered nearby, whispering at each other and darting glances at Tisquantum. "They are daring each other to talk to you," Ned said.

"I know. Our children in Patuxet did the same when Englishmen and Dutchmen came to our shores. I should make the growl like a bear and scare them away?" But instead Tisquantum squatted down on his heels, to bring himself to the children's level, and spoke softly. Ned did not hear what he said, though, for someone else was making a growl like a bear—John Crowder, another of the first colonists, who was arguing with Governor Mason.

"All I say, sir, is that Slany sends out more of his own men, London men, and you are a London man yourself, sir! It seems to me the rights due to us Bristol men is being forgotten in all this!"

"Quiet yourself, man!" George Whittington said. "You cannot speak so to the governor!"

"You're a Bristol man yourself, Whittington, but you've never had an eye to anything but your own advancement," Crowder shot back. "If this colony goes all to the rule of London men, you'll be tripping along behind them, begging to empty their chamber pots!"

Ned had seen little of this Governor Mason so far, but he seemed a calm and commanding fellow—he had been a ship's captain before coming to Cupids Cove—and he was not much troubled by Crowder's outburst. "You know 'tis naught to do with me, Crowder. I enforce the King's law here, but the dispute is between your Bristol merchants and the London merchants."

"'Tis folly that the Bristol merchants go on tolerating this!" That was the usually quiet Jem Holworthy. "Begging your pardon, Governor, I know you try to be even-handed to all, but there is no profit in this company for Bristol men anymore."

"And that is why you are cutting ties, and going to Harbour Grace, then, is it?" a man Ned did not know called out—a recent arrival from London, guessing by his accent.

"Aye, for all the good 'twill do me," said Holworthy. "All this shore is ruled by the Newfoundland Company, and the company is ruled by London merchants."

"'Tis true!" Crowder put in. "When we came out here with Governor Guy, we were told we could build a thriving colony here. I'll not say we were promised we would all be wealthy men; that is folly and false promises. But we were promised more than we've ever got!"

"One colony, one company for all, is no good to anyone!" Jem Holworthy declared. "We need a second colony—a colony at Harbour Grace, settled by Bristol men and funded by Bristol merchants. And begging your pardon, Master Mason, but we need our own governor as well!"

As night dropped down, Ned slipped away from the group of arguing men to find Nancy sitting by a fire with several women quizzing her about her travels. She looked up gratefully and rose to join him, bidding the women good night.

"Are you weary?" he asked as they climbed the path to the big dwelling house that the Holworthys shared with several other colonists. It was the same house where they had both lived during Nancy's first year in Cupids Cove; this place was soaked in memory like a Christmas cake soaked in brandy.

"Aye, so tired." She paused by the door and looked out at the broad expanse of the ocean under the twilight sky. "Do you remember asking me to marry you, just here?"

"The time you said no? I'm not like to forget it."

"Ah, well. You weren't one to give up easily, I'll grant you that."

"And aren't you glad of it?" Ned said, and they went inside.

SIX

Bad News and Good Arrive Together

MUSKETTO COVE, SEPTEMBER 1617

This news dissolv'd to her both knees and heart,
Long silence held her ere one word would part...
—*Homer's Odysseys*, Book 4, 937–38

"WILLOUGHBY HAS A CREW OF TWELVE MEN WORKING on his site now, and his house is closed in," Nicholas told Kathryn as she cleared away the morning meal.

"He'll want something better than a tilt before winter comes," Kathryn said, trying to keep her tone light. Six weeks had passed since her unexpected stay at Thomas Willoughby's property, and she tried to speak of it quite naturally, without any shame. "He had only the two men before—the first ones he brought over turned around and went back to England when they saw what the land was like, and the work they were expected to do."

"Not everyone is cut out for this country," Nicholas said. "Holworthy has gone back to Cupids Cove after clearing his stretch of land alongside Willoughby's. He means to return in the spring to build his house. But Willoughby is wintering in Harbour Grace. I intend to take Frank with me today and go visit Willoughby. I've no great liking for the man, as you know, but with his father owning such a stretch of the country, 'tis best to stay on his good side."

"Are you going in the boat? Take me with you, Papa!" Jonathan, who had been playing outside, ran into the house and jumped into his father's outstretched arms.

"Nay, my lad, this is no journey for little boys. Mayhap on Sunday I will take you and Will out for a little sailing trip. And if your mother and Auntie Bess will come, then the little ones may come along as well."

"No little ones, only me and Will!" Jonathan insisted, and Nicholas laughed. Though the lad was only four years old, he and Bess's son Will strutted about the place like lords of the manor, enjoying their superiority over the younger children.

Kathryn's fervent desire was to never see Thomas Willoughby again, but she knew that was unlikely. They had few neighbours along the coast; most of the settlers who remained in the New Found Land year-round were at Cupids Cove. The only other English people in this part of Conception Bay were the Pike family further north at Carbonear, but they could not be counted as friends. Kathryn believed that Sheila and Gilbert Pike had known of the pirates' attack on the Guy plantation, and Mistress Pike had told Kathryn plainly that they did not want other settlers nearby, and that the Guys should go back to Cupids Cove, if not back to England.

Now that Thomas Willoughby was building at Harbour Grace, Kathryn had resigned herself to the fact that Nicholas would meet with and talk to her former lover. If only she could trust that Thomas would keep her secret! But he was an unpredictable man. If he took it into his head to say a few ill-placed words to Nicholas, Kathryn's whole life could crumble.

She had little time to fret about what might happen; a working day was too busy to allow for much worry. Nicholas and Frank going over to Harbour Grace meant that there were fewer hands to make the fish; when Bess and Daisy went to work on the flakes, Kathryn was in charge of all the household chores and all five children.

Summer was ending; the planation's success for the year would be determined by the price their stores of salt fish could command when the merchants' ships were ready to make the journey to markets in Europe. It would soon be time, too, to harvest the garden, providing them with vegetables for the winter. Tomorrow, perhaps, Kathryn thought she might leave the children with Bess so that she and Daisy could go berry-picking; wild berries were the only fruits the settlers had so far found growing in the New Found Land, and they could be made into preserves. As the air grew cooler and the days shorter, her thoughts turned to what had to be done to prepare for the cold, lean months to come.

The shallop returned as she was ready to put the evening meal on the table. Frank and Bess and their children joined them in the big house. With children and servants all crowded around the great board, Kathryn searched her husband's eyes to see if there was anything there that ought to concern her. But he smiled as he and Frank told the servants, Rafe and Isaac, about how much ground Willoughby had cleared and how his house was coming along.

Only later, when the meal was finished and the children in bed, did Nicholas come sit on a bench beside Kathryn. He was still then, and she thought he might have something troubling to say, but all he did was pull some papers out of a satchel. "Willoughby was down to Cupids Cove a fortnight ago," he said. "There was a ship there—out of Plymouth, but a Bristol merchant was aboard, carrying letters. There were some for you and me."

"Letters!" Kathryn had been surprised not to receive a letter from home in spring; her father usually sent a long missive bringing her up to date on all the family's news. Now she saw his familiar hand, and reached for the letter. "Have you read your own letters?"

"Yes; mine concerned mainly business," Nicholas said. He still owned a house in Bristol, in which his unmarried sister lived; his shoemaking business had been bought out by his former journeyman. "But I think yours may contain some heavier news."

"Did you read it?"

"No, but…Joanna's letter said there was plague in Bristol back in the spring, and that many families were hard hit. She said she thought the sickness had come to your house, but that you had better wait to hear news from your own people."

"How kind of her to spare my feelings," Kathryn said drily; Joanna had never liked her.

She held her father's letter in her hand. If he had written it, then he was still alive. Could her mother be dead? Or one of the children? Kathryn's three younger siblings, Lily, John and Edward, were all growing up, and she knew she would likely never see them again. But it was a comfort to hear news from home, to think of them all well and going about their lives.

She unfolded the letter, looked for a moment at the heading—*My deere daughter Katheryne*—and then handed in back to her husband. "Read it to me, please," she said.

Kathryn had learned her alphabet as a child, and could read a bit, but making her way through a letter was always a slow business. Nicholas usually read her letters aloud. Now his quick eyes scanned the lines before he began to read. "My darling girl," he said, "it is heavy news indeed."

"Read it to me, please."

"My dear daughter Kathryn," Nicholas began, "It has been long since I have written you and we have known hard times since the plague came to Bristol."

"Is there a date on it? When did he write it?"

"The thirtieth of June, this year."

More than two months, the letter had been making its slow way to her, across the ocean, then waiting at Cupids Cove until someone—Thomas Willoughby, as it chanced—would take his own letters back up the shore. Whatever had happened to her family had happened long ago.

"Some months gone now we all fell sick of the plague. Your mother had the worst of it and I am grieved to tell you she is dead," Nicholas read. He put his free arm around Kathryn's shoulders as he read on. "She loved you and I know that she would have wished you to be with her. Then fell sick all the children, John, Edward and Lily, and I myself ailing many weeks. When recovered I learned that only Lily was left to me. Both your brothers are gone to God."

"Oh, dear Lord!" The cry burst from Kathryn's lips, and she buried her face in her husband's shoulder. In her mind's eye she saw the little boys she had bid goodbye to five years go—the round faces and sturdy limbs she remembered. But those were not, of course, the boys who had died. They would have been young men now, apprenticing with their father, learning his trade. She had never seen John with the stonemason's hammer in his hand, never seen Edward tall enough to look down at her. She had missed their boyhood, and now they were both dead.

And her mother! It was hard for any woman to raise children without her own mother nearby to offer help and advice. Her mother could not write, so messages between them were appended to John Gale's letters. Last year his letter had contained a package of rosemary seeds with the note that "*yore mother saies you will knowe well what ailments it is goode for*," words Kathryn had sounded out for herself as if she could hear her mother saying them. Now her mother's voice was silent, her busy hands stilled at last.

"Poor papa—how lonely he must be! Just himself and Lily and Tibby in the house!"

"There is more to the letter," Nicholas said. "Shall I read on?"

"If it is more bad news, I do not think I can bear it. Read it over first, and warn me if there are more hard tidings to bear."

He was silent a moment, and then he said, "There is some news that will make you glad."

"Read on, then."

"It has been hard to bear, but we carry on," Nicholas read out. "Walter, who was my journeyman, has come back to work for me, and he and Lily will marry later in the summer. They will live here with me and I will be glad not to lose the one child still remaining to me."

"Walter and Lily?" Kathryn could barely remember Walter's face, but the match made sense, she supposed. Though if her brothers had been alive to inherit the business, her father would have looked for a better match for Lily. "If he is kind to her, then I am happy for them." A wedding should be glad news, but any joy that could be wrung from it was overshadowed by tragedy.

"There is more." Nicholas looked back down at the paper. "We have had another wedding of one we had not thought to see again. Nancy is returned with my old apprentice Ned. I am glad to tell you they were wedded at St. Stephen's a fortnight ago and will soon return to the New Found Land."

Kathryn sat up straight, tears still blurring her eyes. "Nancy? Nancy has come back—to Bristol?"

"It seems she has. Alive, and well, and married to Ned Perry," Nicholas said, a trace of wonder in his voice.

"And coming back here! When, I wonder?"

She did not know if Nicholas answered her, or if there was anything more in her father's letter. She got up from the bench by the hearth. In the chamber above, the children slept. The menservants were outside, having a drink of ale and talking at the end of a long day; Daisy was at her sister Bess's house. In that rare still moment, Kathryn walked outside.

Once there had been only a step leading up to the door there, but in the spring Nicholas had built a porch with a rail, like the deck of a ship, out in front of the house. She stood there now looking out to sea, out to the rolling waves that separated her from her dead loved ones, from her grieving father and sister. The waves that had taken Nancy away from her, and now, it seemed, would bring her back.

She tried, in the days that followed, to cling to that joyful news. Nancy alive! And Ned too, and the two of them married—and coming back to the New Found Land. She wanted to believe she would see Nancy again, but holding on to even that much hope seemed impossible.

The round of duties that accompanied summer's end continued, but Kathryn no longer felt busy and purposeful. Each day felt as if she were pushing forward against a headwind, making little progress. Even the tasks that normally brought her pleasure—playing with the children, compounding medicines in her little still-room—felt joyless.

"I know I would not have seen my mother again in this life," she confessed to Daisy one day as they harvested carrots and parsnips from the garden. "Why does it seem so hard, then, to know that she is gone?"

"Ah, while there's life, there's hope," Daisy said. "'Tis hard when life and hope are both gone." And then Kathryn felt ashamed for telling her sorrows to Daisy, who had lost two husbands in the span of a year.

I will school my tongue, she thought, *and not speak of this to anyone. And in time, it will grow easier.*

But it did not. Even her husband, not generally the most insightful of men when it came to the moods of women, knew she was not herself. Three weeks after the news had come from England, he ventured to say, "Jonathan asked me today, 'Why is mama so sad?' He thought he had been naughty, that you were not singing and laughing with him as you usually do."

"I am sorry," Kathryn said. "I will try..."

"I know you have had a great loss," he said. To her ears it almost sounded like an accusation. "But I have never seen you so weighed down, not in all the years we have been married, though you have had so many hardships."

It was true—even when their plantation had been attacked, and Nancy taken captive, Kathryn had not felt this blanket of bleak despair. Her anger and sorrow then had spurred her to action. Now she felt no emotion at all, only this deadly dullness.

In truth, she had felt this way once before, but Nicholas had not been there to see it. In the first year of their marriage, he had left her in Bristol and gone off to the New Found Land. She had been carrying his child then, and when the baby was stillborn, she had plummeted into despair as if she had fallen into a pit. It had lasted weeks, perhaps months; only the prospect of coming out to the colony to join her husband had dispelled that gloom.

Now there was no great adventure ahead, only the hard work of preparing for winter. She felt like a puppet in a puppet show, such as they used to put on in the town square in Bristol. Saying the words, miming the actions, but without any true thought or feeling behind it.

So it was that she barely stirred on that crisp morning in early October when she sat by the fire spinning wool, the children playing nearby. Daisy, who had gone to feed the animals, came in to announce that a shallop was sailing into Musketto Cove. "I wonder is it that fellow Willoughby, come over from Harbour Grace? Or perhaps the pirate Pike and his Irish wife? One of the people aboard looked like a woman."

Kathryn rose, the children following her like a flock of ducklings. She had not, of course, forgotten the good news that came along with the bad. But she had not been able to hold on to it. It did not seem that it could be real.

The shallop's passengers were not yet close enough to see, but Kathryn strained her eyes as if she could make out the face of the figure in the grey gown and white coif. Her heart beat faster. Perhaps, after all, one good thing might happen.

The sail was down; the oars dipped; the boat drew nearer. Then Kathryn saw one of the men in the boat point, and the woman looked up at Kathryn.

Four years now since Nancy had been taken, and everyone had tried to tell Kathryn that she must be dead. Kathryn had stubbornly refused to believe it. She and Nancy were bound by a tie of friendship stronger than any blood-tie; she was convinced that if Nancy had died, she would have felt or heard or seen something, some token of her passing. She had kept hope alive far longer than was sensible, until Sheila Pike had told her that the ship that captured Nancy had sunk off the Bermudas, and the captive maid had gone down with the wreck.

Now the boat was tying up, and Jem Holworthy climbed out, followed by Ned Perry. Young Ned, whom Kathryn had sent off with a tiny purse of coins in hopes that he would somehow find and save the woman he loved. He looked older, broader of shoulder and chest, his beard fully grown in and his skin sun-darkened, as though he had spent a long time at sea. Now he was helping Nancy out of the shallop, and she too looked different, though Kathryn could not have said exactly how. *And I must look different to her as well*, Kathryn thought.

She stretched out her arms to her friend. Nancy, who never cried, was crying, and Kathryn thought, *All will be well. It must be well, now that they are home.*

SEVEN

A Newcomer Arrives

MUSKETTO COVE, NOVEMBER 1617

Then took they feast, and did in parts divide
The sev'ral dishes, fill'd out wine...
                    —*Homer's Odysseys*, Book 8, 631–32

"IF YOU MEAN TO MAKE BREAD, YOU OUGHT TO DOUBLE THAT. Are you accounting for the new men?"

Nancy paused to count up on her fingers. "Master and mistress, the children, myself and Ned, you, Isaac and Rafe, Stephen and Hal. There's enough bread here for a dozen of us."

"But you'll have to bake again tomorrow," Daisy said. "I've been in the habit of making bread every second day in the cooler weather—it keeps."

Then perhaps you ought to still be making the bread, Nancy thought, but kept silent.

For more than three years, the Guy family had lived in this house and Daisy More had been the maid of all work, helping Kathryn with inside and outside duties as well as caring for the children. Nancy still thought of her as Daisy More, the name she had borne when she came out from England. Other people, on the rare occasion when anyone needed to use a surname, did the same; Daisy's two marriages had both been of such short duration that they did not seem to have left even the permanence of a sur-name. She had briefly been Daisy Griggs and Daisy Taylor, but she was forever Daisy More: small, worried, hard-working, and born to ill-luck.

When Nancy and Ned returned to Musketto Cove, they brought two of the new settlers who had come over on the ship with them. Musketto Cove now had four more mouths to feed. Having Nancy's help eased the burden on Kathryn and Daisy, but it led to a dozen tiny skirmishes like this one every day.

Nancy had no wish to quarrel with Daisy; they gotten on well back in Cupids Cove, years ago. But tackling the task at hand was Nancy's way of dealing with any new circumstances, and after nearly a month in Musketto Cove, she was still working out exactly what her task here was.

Ned and Master Nicholas had agreed that in spring, a newly cleared section of the land on the south side of the cove would be set aside for Ned and Nancy to build themselves a small house just as Bess and Frank had done. In the meantime, Nancy was a servant in Kathryn's household, as Daisy was, and she thought keeping the peace was surely the best policy.

"True enough; bread will keep for two days in this weather," Nancy conceded. "But now that I am here to help, I can bake every day and leave you more time for your other duties. There's scarce room in the hearth to bake a double batch, and I know having more of us here puts a greater burden on you."

"That it does," Daisy admitted, moving to the fire to stir the pottage. "Very well then, you go on with the bread." The women spoke in low voices; the room was lit only by the fire and a few tallow candles, as the sun would not rise for an hour or more. Upstairs, the master and mistress slept with their children. There was a bed up there, too, for Nancy and Ned, and one for Daisy. The four unmarried menservants—Isaac and Rafe, Stephen and Hal—had rigged themselves up a space in the store-room attached to the main hall. They would sleep closer to the hearth when the winter grew colder.

"Why could Stephen and Hal not have stayed down in Cupids Cove?" Daisy said, her voice low. "We need men in the summer for the fish-ing—in winter they're more trouble than help."

Nancy shrugged. She turned the loaves of bread into iron pots and then moved those into the niches in the hearth where they would finish rising. "'Tis something to do with this quarrel between the London men and the Bristol men. Master Slany sent out two men, and the company in Bristol sent four more. To make peace, Governor Mason divided them—Master Slany's two London men down in Cupids Cove, and the four Bristol men divided between here and Harbour Grace. 'Tis all to do with this dividing up the colony into two, with the Bristol merchants taking Harbour Grace for their own new settlement."

"I'm sure I don't know what difference it makes, except more work for us women."

"No more do I, but Ned says 'tis a bad thing for the masters to be quarreling, and all must pull together and do our part."

"Always glad to hear my good wife quoting my wise words," Ned said, appearing at the bottom of the narrow stairs. He was the vanguard: now the rest of the upstairs sleepers were waking. Along with Kathryn and Master Nicholas and the three small children came the men who had been sleeping in the storeroom, stretching and yawning as they headed out of doors towards the privy.

Kathryn was last downstairs, with her youngest, Jemmy, in her arms. "Forgive me—I should have been down in time to help," she said to Nancy and Daisy. "'Tis so hard to get up, these dark, cold mornings." She gave a heavy sigh and put Jemmy down onto the floor by the hearth with Jonathan and Alice, and looked about as if she had been gone a long time and needed to reacquaint herself with the familiar things about her. "What should I...?"

"We've not fetched ale yet," Nancy said, and noted the relief on Kathryn's face when her servant gave her a simple task to do.

"Has she been like this a long time?" Nancy asked Daisy later, when the two of them went to feed the pigs and goats. "I knew she would be sad at the news of her mother and brothers, but I had not thought to find her so—so broken in spirit."

Daisy sighed. "I' faith, she has been weighed down with grief since the word came from Bristol about her family. But if you want to know my thinking, there was a trouble that started even before she heard that news. Did she tell you of the time she got lost in the woods, back in the summer?"

"No, she has said naught of it." Kathryn had wept with joy at Nancy's return, but the flood of words Nancy had expected—all Kathryn's pent-up tales of the last four years—had not been spoken. Kathryn had been oddly quiet and subdued, and Nancy had wondered if this was simply the way she was now, an older and sadder version of the friend she had known from childhood. But Daisy assured her the change was more recent.

"Well, she went off in the woods one day to gather spruce bark and juniper berries and the like—for making cures, you know," said Daisy, throwing a handful of vegetable peelings into the sty as the pigs rooted eagerly. "A storm blew up, and we was all frantic with worry. Then she shows up the next morning in a boat with Master Willoughby and one of his men—they had found her and taken her in for the night. After that she was—well, I don't know quite how to say it. Quieter. Like she was lost in herself, you might say. My thought was—though I hate to say it…"

Nancy waited. She had her own thoughts about this story. In the old days in Cupids Cove, Thomas Willoughby had been a good deal too forward in flirting with Kathryn. Had the young nobleman, newly returned to this country, made improper advances to Kathryn?

But Daisy's thoughts ran in another direction. "I fear she might have been fairy-led. Alone so long in the forest—'tis what they say of changelings, is it not? That they are taken to the fairy kingdom, and they come back different."

"I only ever heard tell of children being fairy-led, not grown men or women."

"Oh no, the fairies will take anyone—you got to be mindful when you go in the woods. My granny told me tales of them, and I am sure they're here, as well as back in England. Mistress Kathryn was ever so quiet after she got lost in the woods, and 'twas but a few weeks after that she got the letter from home that told of her poor mother and the boys. That was the final blow. I thought perhaps, now that you're back—that might bring her back to her old self. That is, s'posin' 'tis not the fairies."

Kathryn's dark mood had clouded the joy of Nancy and Ned's homecoming. Indeed, Kathryn had suffered a great blow, learning that half her family was dead and knowing nothing of it until months after the fact. But she had suffered greatly before now, and the only time Nancy had seen her give in to despair was after she lost her first baby, back in Bristol. Then Kathryn had taken to her bed for weeks, shrouded in a gloom that seemed impossible to penetrate.

There was no possibility of Kathryn taking to her bed now—the mistress of a busy plantation had no such luxury. But she went about her work mostly in silence, her laughter and chatter stilled. Nancy felt the weight of all the unspoken words, the untold stories, lying on her tongue, but she had no idea how to break that silence.

But there was little time to give much thought to Kathryn's feelings, or her own. Nancy was learning the rhythm of life on a fishing plantation in the New Found Land: with the fish sold and the garden harvested, there was a brief window of time for other tasks before cold weather closed in. Today the men were working on the fences and outbuildings. "First winter we were here, we had to bring the animals inside in the coldest part of winter," Daisy told her. "Two goats and two pigs, we had then. I grew up in the country and I've shared quarters with livestock before, but I don't mind saying I'm glad we've a byre now."

Meanwhile, the women made preserves from whatever of the summer's bounty could be saved for winter: today it was the tart red berries that grew in the marshes, combined with sugar they had obtained when the merchant ships came to take their fish to market. A little sweetness, and a hope of staving off scurvy, for the long winter ahead. Bess came to join them, bringing her two little boys to play on the floor alongside Jonathan, Alice, and Jemmy as the four women worked.

"Did they have to go through all this same work down in Virginia?" Bess asked Nancy.

"We made preserves there also," Nancy said, "and when the tobacco crop was sold, 'twas much like when the fish is in here—time for the men to turn their hands to other tasks. But they've not got the same long winter to prepare for."

"I'm sure you'll not be looking forward to another New Found Land winter," Daisy said. "Last January we had snowdrifts as high as the roof."

"I am sure Nancy would find a little cold and snow a small price to pay for being home, and safe," said Kathryn, wiping her hands clean as she bent to pick up Jemmy.

"Of course, I never meant—"

"No matter," Nancy said. "Look to the pot, that's near boiling over. 'Tis good to be back here, even if the winters are kinder in Virginia. The summers there are too hot."

"The strangest thing to me is that you served an Indian woman," Daisy said as Bess moved to the hearth to see to the bubbling pot. "I cannot fathom it—a native woman married to an Englishman!"

"There's a good many strange things in this world," Nancy said. "I'm going out to the privy."

She did need to relieve herself, but more than that she needed to be out of the warm, busy room, away from Bess's and Daisy's questions and, worse, Kathryn's lack of questions. Outside, the sky was a brilliant blue. The birch trees, whose leaves had flamed golden a few weeks ago when she had arrived, were all bare. The sound of hammers rang out: Nicholas Guy was on the roof of the byre with Hal Henshaw. Not far from there, Rafe and Stephen were hacking at the hard ground with spades, enlarging the root cellar. Closer to the house she saw Ned working alongside Isaac Bell, the other manservant, laying stones in a circle atop each other.

"You've not built anything of stone for a long time," Nancy said to her husband.

"Not since I helped build the wall at Cupids, years ago now," Ned said. "But Master Guy thinks we ought to have a baking oven, with the place growing as it is."

"That's good sense." Nancy thought of her mild tiff with Daisy about how much bread to bake; it would certainly be easier if, as back in Bristol, there were a communal oven to which Kathryn's household, Bess's, and eventually her own, could bring their bread. Ned looked happy to be working with stone again; it was the trade he had trained for. While rocks were more plentiful than almost anything else in the colony, most building here was done with wood.

"D'ye think 'tis close enough to the big house?" Isaac asked.

"'Twill be fine," Ned said. "Next year, Nancy and I will build our house on the other end of the beach, but 'tis not too far to come to bake bread. And," he added, "close enough to your own place, should you take a wife and settle down here."

"Oh, no, no hope of that for me," Isaac muttered into his beard. He was a quiet and nervous-seeming young man; Nancy had observed him trotting after Daisy like a well-trained spaniel, while Daisy paid him no mind at all. "This has been going on for two years," Bess had told Nancy, "but our Daisy swears she'll not marry again."

Nancy had already heard this declaration from Daisy's own lips. "I lost one good man to the scurvy and another to pirates; I'll not risk a third, no matter how much Isaac fancies his chances. You may laugh, but 'tis a curse I have upon me. Two husbands be enough for any woman."

Nancy wondered, looking now at Isaac, how truly Daisy believed in the curse. Isaac was a scraggly fellow, wiry but thin, with a sallow, pitted skin and eyes of a watery blue. Did Daisy honestly believe she would curse him by marrying him, or was that belief merely convenient?

"Who's that, now?" Ned said, looking out into the cove.

A shallop under sail was coming towards their wharf; as it drew closer they could see three men aboard. By the time it had lowered the sail, most of the inhabitants of Musketto Cove had left their work and gathered on the beach, for the arrival of any boat was noteworthy. When the three men aboard were close enough to see, Master Nicholas said, "I believe that is John Crowder, is't not? And Master Willoughby? But who is the swarthy fellow?"

Nancy glanced at Kathryn as Thomas Willoughby's name was mentioned, and thought she saw Kathryn flinch. But she looked back at the men in the boat when she heard Ned say, "Why, that is Tisquantum! I told you, sir, I had asked him to come visit us here—you will be interested to meet him, for he has many tales to tell."

The men moved to the wharf to help tie up the shallop; the four women held back with the children. "Is that fellow really one of the native folks?" Daisy wanted to know as Tisquantum came ashore.

"Aye, Ned and I crossed over from England with him, along with Hal and Stephen," Nancy said. "He was brought over to Spain from his own country years ago and ended up in England somehow. He hopes to get back to his people."

"Is he from here?" Bess wondered.

"No—someplace to the south."

"He's surely a fine, well-made fellow—for a heathen, I mean," said Daisy.

As the two sisters sized up Tisquantum, Nancy looked over at Kathryn. She alone showed no curiosity about the newcomer: rather, her attention was focused on the equally handsome figure of Thomas Willoughby.

EIGHT

A Resemblance is Remarked Upon

MUSKETTO COVE, NOVEMBER 1617

A person fair is giv'n,
But nothing else is in thee sent from heav'n;
For in thee lurks a base and earthy soul...
                              —*Homer's Odysseys*, Book 8, 240–42

S HE WATCHED THE THREE MEN APPROACH: THE FAMILIAR form of John Crowder, the unfamiliar and striking native man, and, walking a little ahead of them both, the too-familiar figure of Thomas Willoughby. It was his first visit to Musketto Cove since he had brought her home four months earlier.

He can do nothing to harm me. Kathryn recited those words to herself like a prayer every time she thought of Willoughby. Her fear, after all, had been groundless—had it not? Nicholas had not been pleased that she had spent that night at Willoughby's plantation, but he had believed her, and not blamed her. The whole business was forgotten.

Yet when Willoughby's ice-blue eyes fell upon her, she felt something colder than the late-autumn breeze. When he quirked one corner of his mouth in a lazy smile, it felt like a threat.

She scooped up Jemmy from the ground. "Bess, watch the children down at your house while Nan, Daisy and I prepare supper. We must ready ourselves for a few extra guests, it seems."

Bess took Jemmy gladly and rounded up Kathryn's older children along with her own, leading them towards her little house. Kathryn turned to Nancy. "What do we need to do to make supper feed three more men?"

"Kill and dress another chicken, if we can spare it."

"And do it lively, like, for the others are already stewing," Daisy added.

"We can spare a chicken. Nan, you do that, and Daisy, get us some more carrots and parsnips—I will see to the ale and perhaps a bottle of wine, if Nicholas wishes to make this a celebration."

When Nicholas pulled her aside, a few moments later, she was able to tell him that she had already anticipated his need: the visitors would dine with them. "They have returned from an expedition into Trinity Bay to seek out the natives, with this man Tisquantum going as their interpreter," Nicholas explained. "We should all hear their tale."

Back in the house, Nancy and Daisy were already at work. Daisy, as usual, kept up a steady flow of chatter as she peeled and chopped vegetables, while Nancy worked quietly, plucking the freshly killed bird.

"'Twill be odd to have a heathen sit down at our table, and serve him as if he was a Christian," Daisy said.

"Hardly odd to me," Nancy said.

"No—of course—you served the native woman in Virginia. But she was baptized and married to an Englishman."

Nancy shrugged. "Cooking a meal and putting it on the table, or scrubbing out clothes and hanging them to dry—work is much the same anywhere. Little matter if it be an Englishman, a Spaniard, or an Indian you be working for."

"I'd not want to keep house for a Spaniard neither—but at least they do be Christians, even if they are filthy papists," Daisy said. "Heathens is another matter altogether."

Nancy shrugged and went on with her work. Kathryn wondered what strange memories were tucked away beneath Nancy's neat white coif: she had said very little about the pirates who captured her, or the

Powhatan princess she had served, or her voyage to England. Only the bare bones, but none of the meat of the tale.

But if Nancy had little to say about native people, the menfolk, when they gathered for the meal, had plenty. Willoughby held court like a lord, telling how himself, Crowder, Tisquantum, and six others who had since returned to Cupids Cove, had set out into Trinity Bay. They had sailed in the barque *Indeavour* to the place where Governor Guy had met with the natives six years earlier.

"Aye, I remember it well," said Nicholas, and Ned nodded. "Truce Sound, Governor Guy called it, for the peace we hoped to make with them there."

"'Twas not the first time returning there," said Crowder. "Two more expeditions went back to that spot, and cruised along the coast looking for more sign of the natives. I went with Governor Mason two years ago, but we saw no sign of the people of the land."

"But this time was different," Willoughby said. "When we drew near to shore there was clear sign they had been there, and recently, too. Then on the following day, while we were aboard ship, we saw them come down to the shore. We waved a white flag—"

"And we know, from our last encounter with them, that they understand this sign," Crowder added. "But they came armed, with arrows on the string, and let fly at us."

"We had Tisquantum here with us in hopes he could speak their tongue," Willoughby said, gesturing at his companion, who had said nothing yet except to thank the women as they put food on the table. "But they gave us no chance. Had we not been so pressed, 'twould have been funny indeed to hear him shouting out in his own language that we came in peace, all the while they were shooting at us."

"D'ye think they understood?" Ned asked Tisquantum. "Would they know your tongue, or you theirs?"

Their guest paused a moment before answering. "They may not. All the languages of the people are..." he hesitated. "Some words are the same. As a Spaniard and a Portuguese might understand some of each other's words, or an English and a Dutch man, you see? If we met, I might have made myself understood to them."

"'Twas no matter, any rate," Thomas Willoughby said, taking the reins of the conversation again. "While they were firing arrows, we got off two shots with the muskets we had aboard, and they ran like rabbits. They are a suspicious folk."

"But they were not so five years ago," Nicholas pointed out. "That time, they were most willing to meet and trade."

"It surprises me not at all," said John Crowder, "nor should it surprise anyone who has talked to the summer fishermen in Trinity Bay. I have met a few fishermen who have had encounters with the natives. More than once I've heard tales that the natives came down to the shore peacefully enough when a boat approached, only for the fishermen to fire upon them with muskets. 'Tis little wonder they have learned to distrust English men and English ships."

While the men talked and ate, the women went back and forth from table to hearth, refilling cups, clearing away trenchers. When Willoughby said, "I do not think the natives here are as peaceable or friendly as in other places—sure, we have heard how down in Virginia they come and go, and trade with the colonists, and some have even become Christians," Kathryn's eyes flickered to Nancy's, wondering if she would speak up. But Nancy kept pouring wine into Willoughby's cup, her eyes cast down and her lips sealed.

"The Wampanoag trade with English—and with Dutch and French also," said Tisquantum. "So do many others of the people. Trade with Portuguese and Spaniards also, in the lands farther south. But it does not always go well. If these people, these Osa'yan'a, or whatever they are called, mistrust Englishmen, it may be they have learned the lesson."

"But we mean them no harm!" Nicholas insisted, at the same time as Ned said, "I think you learned that lesson yourself, did you not? Surely that is the very reason you are here among us?"

Though Nicholas was the master and Ned but a working man, it was to Ned that Tisquantum turned to answer. "Yes. It is so. The English captains came to my home, to Patuxet, to trade. And our sachems were glad to trade." He paused, reached out to touch the iron pot that the chicken had been stewed in. "We had copper, but no iron. Arrows, but no guns. Who would not have iron pots and muskets, if they could get them?"

The other men nodded, but it was Daisy who spoke, the first woman to join the conversation. "I'm sure I don't know how I'd cook anything without an iron pot."

Tisquantum glanced at her, his face briefly lighting up in a smile. "I promise, you would find a way! But once you trade for things, it is good—easier, sometimes—to have those things. So we thought this trade was good, just as trading with the Narragansett and the Nauset and the other people of the land, was good. We traded with English ships, and Dutch, and French—many times, many years."

"Exactly," Nicholas said. "That is what we hope to do here. Trade is a benefit to everyone."

Tisquantum paused, then said, "When the English captains, John Smith and Thomas Hunt, came to Patuxet, they took twenty Wampanoag men—myself one of them—in their ship. Tricked us to come aboard, and bound us in chains. They took us across the ocean to Spain, to sell us as slaves. I am only free because the Spanish priests took pity. My companions—my brothers and kinsmen, my friends—I did not see again. They might live or die in chains."

His words fell into silence as the men around the table shifted awkwardly on their benches and looked everywhere but at Tisquantum. It was, again, a woman's voice that broke the silence, Nancy this time.

"They did the same to the lady Pocahontas," she said. "The daughter of the Powhatan chief. An English captain tricked her to come aboard his ship, and then he took her captive."

"That was Captain Argall," Ned said. "I served under him. A good master to his sailors, but he dealt unfairly with the native folks, as my wife says."

"Well, now. I'll not say I countenance lying, or deceit," said Nicholas. He met Tisquantum's gaze again. "We want friendly, peaceable relations. That is all."

"All the same," said Willoughby, with a touch of irritation, "we can see now that such relations are unlikely to happen anytime soon. The best we can hope for is that we have no violent clashes with the natives. Which raises again the question—what is this colony *for*? What does it hope to achieve, if there is to be no trade with the people of the land? I swear our London masters have no idea."

And they were off at it again, arguing about London men and Bristol men, about who controlled the colony and to what end. Kathryn rose to clear away the last of the meal, with Daisy and Nancy following her lead, as the talk went on.

"I'll leave the ale jug on the table, for this seems a thirsty conversation," said Nancy. She brought a pot of water warmed over the fire and poured it into the bucket they used to scrub out the cooking pots and trenchers.

"Aye, they are kindling a good deal of heat with their words." Kathryn looked up at her friend. "What you said just then—about the lady Pocahontas that you served. You have spoken so little of what happened down there, and I know you have many tales to tell."

"Ah, you know I am no good for telling tales. Never one to spin a yarn."

Kathryn sighed. "And I have not been the best at drawing those tales out of you. I have been—I do not know. Heavy of spirit, since I had the news from home. Like going about in one of those fogs that rolls in off the ocean."

"No-one could blame you."

I could blame myself, Kathryn thought. The truth was, she still did not rightly know what was wrong with her, why grief had crushed her so completely. But when she thought of Nancy's tales, of sitting by the fire on winter nights hearing her stories, or Ned's, or perhaps Tisquantum's accounts of faraway lands, she felt something coming awake in her, like shafts of sunlight beginning to pierce that fog.

Around the table, the men still debated while the women washed the dishes. Willoughby's voice rang out above the rest; when Kathryn looked back, she saw he was standing now, at the head of the table, as if lecturing the men. Nicholas and the others sat as if they were his pupils, save for Tisquantum, who had moved to a stool a little distance away and sat watching, his dark eyes flickering from the men's debate to the women's work.

"Do you want me to go down to Bess's and fetch the youngsters, Mistress?" Daisy asked.

"Ah, no, I think she will keep them down there tonight," Kathryn said. Indeed, she hoped so, and had asked Bess to have them stay. Better they were out from underfoot while the men talked of colonies and conquest, especially with Willoughby here.

Daisy nodded. "If the savage man is staying here the night," she said, lowering her voice to a whisper, "best the young ones are out of the way." Kathryn watched Tisquantum as Daisy spoke and saw him flinch at the words "savage man," as if Daisy had reached out to slap him.

"What, do you think his people eat little English children?" Nancy said, the scorn in her voice cutting like a whip.

"You can't be too careful, is all I'm saying," Daisy retorted.

The other men, paying no attention to the women's talk, were growing more heated.

"...our own charter, our own colony!" Willoughby was saying. "And our own governor, of course. No slight against Mason, but he is a tool of the London merchants."

"This is no more than we have been saying all summer," Nicholas said. He turned to Crowder. "Next spring, when you and your family move up to Harbour Grace—and Holworthy with his family—that will be the time—"

"Why wait? If we get word to Bristol now, before winter—"

"On what ship? Sure there's ice starting to form in the bay already—there'll be no more ships—"

Willoughby cut across the other men's voices. "If we cannot send word before winter, then as soon as may be in the spring. Before some governor gets appointed for us, some friend of the merchants who knows nothing of this land—"

"Now, you cannot say that of Mason," Nicholas said. He, too, was on his feet now, facing down Willoughby. Willoughby outranked him, of course, as a baronet's son, but Nicholas was a cousin of the first governor, the colony's founder, and one of the men who had been here the longest. "John Mason was a sea captain, he's had experience with seafaring, with piracy—I've nothing against him save that he's London's man—"

"Fine! What we need is our own colony, under our own company, and a governor for it who is *Bristol's* man. Someone of the station in life to serve as a governor, but one who knows this land, knows what we aim to do here."

"One quite like yourself, you mean." That was Ned, speaking up as no other serving-man, even a colonist of long standing like Frank Tipton, would have done.

Willoughby's eyes flicked towards Ned, then around the room. "I would not presume to put myself forward in such a way. But I do know, and you'd do well to remember, Ned Perry, that we are all appointed our proper station in life. My father is a man of such station as to have put more into this colony than any other man in England." Then he broke off and smiled—that roguish grin that had once twisted Kathryn's heart like a wrung-out cloth. "I'd not put myself forward, but there's many who'd do worse than I would, I think." His eyes, roving the room, locked on Kathryn's. "Surely even the ladies would agree—is't not so, Mistress Guy?"

Kathryn felt her husband's eyes, too, upon her. She shrugged, made her voice light. "I am sure I know not, Master Willoughby. I leave such business to my husband, who is the only governor I need obey."

Willoughby laughed. "Well said! What a model wife you have, Master Guy. Now, I suppose if we are to get back to Harbour Grace before 'tis full dark, we should be back on the water."

Nicholas made the expected offer that they could stay the night. Willoughby and Crowder declined, but Tisquantum, who had been talking with Nancy and Ned by the fire, said that if Master and Mistress Guy would welcome him, he would gladly stay a little longer.

"We can make up a bed for you in the storeroom with the menservants," she heard Nancy tell Tisquantum, as Willoughby and Crowder got their cloaks and made ready to leave. Just at that moment the door opened and Bess appeared, holding Alice by the hand.

"Sorry, Mistress," Bess said, weaving her way through the throng of men, "I thought the young ones would all be content to stay at my place—Jemmy fell asleep right after supper, and you know Jonathan, he's always glad to spend the night with Will and Matty—but Alice said she must have mama, and would not settle without you."

Alice let go of Bess's hand and ran for Kathryn's arms. As Kathryn knelt to embrace her, she felt rather than heard Thomas Willoughby come up behind them. "So, this is your little one?"

"My daughter, Alice." Her heart pounded.

Willoughby squatted down beside Kathryn, close to Alice. "And how old are you, little Alice? Ah, three years old?" For Alice had held up three fingers. Willoughby smiled at her, then at Kathryn. "Why, you were not even born when I was here in the New Found Land before. What strange times those were—four or five years ago, when we all came out here. I am sure you remember, Mistress Guy."

Kathryn stood up, Alice in her arms, and Willoughby stood also. "I am very glad to have met you, Alice," he said, then to Kathryn, "Who does she take after, with that golden hair, those blue eyes? I cannot see your husband in her, nor much of you either. Some distant relative, no doubt." He smiled at Kathryn. "We can be good neighbours, Mistress Guy. Even a woman, such as yourself, can have a great influence on her husband. What influence you have I am sure you will use wisely." And then he was gone.

NINE

A Feast is Observed

MUSKETTO COVE, CHRISTMAS 1617

To see a neighbour's feast
Adorn it through; and thereat hear the breast
Of the divine Muse; men in order set;
A wine-page waiting; tables crown'd with meat,...
The cup-boards furnish'd, and the cups still fill'd;
This shows, to my mind, most humanely fair.
—Homer's Odysseys, Book 9, 13–19

"IT IS THE ENGLISH CUSTOM, TO BRING BOUGHS OF TREES into the house?" Tisquantum asked as he and Ned carried armloads of spruce and pine branches inside. The women had declared they wanted some to deck the mantel and windowsills.

Ned shrugged. "'Twasn't done when I was a child in Bristol—not in my house nor in my master's house, any rate. I think some of the wealthy folk, merchants and the like, would put holly or mistletoe about."

Eight men, four women, and five small children were now living on Nicholas Guy's plantation. Ned was reminded of that first Christmas at Cupids Cove, seven years ago, when he and the rest of John Guy's men had all lived in the one big dwelling house and tried to make what cheer they could. A man had hanged himself between Christmas and New Year's, which Ned thought went a long way towards saying how successful they had been in making the season merry. This holiday could not help but be an improvement.

"Holly—it was this plant that Master Slany's servants would put about his house. I was with them at Christmas last year," Tisquantum said. "My people do something the same with some of our thanks-givings, using the plants of each season to make all beautiful for our celebrations."

"And do you celebrate anything at this time of year—in midwinter?"

"After the moon of hunting, it is the moon of storytelling—like you, we stay warm by the fire and tell tales in winter. We have rituals for all the turnings of the year—I think perhaps all people do. But this Christmas is to do with your god, yes?"

"Yes—when the Lord Jesus Christ was born on earth," Ned said. He knew that Tisquantum had been instructed in the basics of the Christian faith, but unlike the Powhatan women that Nancy had known in Virginia, Tisquantum had not been baptized or taken a Christian name. He was curious about what the English believed, but his was the curiosity of a traveller, intrigued by the customs of the strange lands he visited.

"Ah yes, gods. Always being born, always dying, over and over," Tisquantum said, a comment that reminded Ned that the world was much larger and stranger than he had imagined it when he was growing up in Bristol.

Nicholas Guy had, at Ned's suggestion, invited the Wampanoag man to spend the winter on their plantation here at Musketto Cove. Governor Mason's plan to have him act as a translator with the native people had been foiled, for now at least, and Tisquantum's plan to find a ship that would carry him to his own country could not happen until spring.

On the day before Christmas Eve, the hall of the big house, always a busy place, was a hive of activity. Mistress Kathryn, Daisy, and Bess were all chopping and mixing bowls full of ingredients for the pies and puddings that would grace the table on Christmas Day. Nancy was not there; she was at Bess's house with the children. Lately the women had developed a pattern on busy days: one of them would take all five children down to Bess and Frank's little house and care for them there, so they would not be constantly underfoot in the main house.

"Where will we lay these?" Tisquantum asked. He stood behind Daisy, who was working with her back to the door, and she gave a nervous jump as he spoke. Ned had noticed that of all the women, Daisy seemed the most uncomfortable about having a native man living among them, and she rarely spoke directly to Tisquantum. But now she turned, gestured to his armful of boughs, and said, "Leave them on the bench—we will decide where to put them when we deck the hall later today."

Tisquantum did so, then took out a twist of cloth he had carried in his pocket. Inside it lay a few handfuls of hard, red berries. "I found these," he said, showing them to Daisy. "Not to eat, but they will look well if you place them among the branches. To make them bright."

"Ooh, lovely," said Daisy.

Kathryn Guy gave the two men a beaming smile. "Thank you so much—I know 'tis a trivial thing when you are all so busy."

"Truth be told, we are not so busy at the moment," Ned said. "There's more men on the place than there is work to be done, now that the snow is down. Mending nets, cutting firewood, and making furniture are all the chores left for the men to do."

"While the women's work never ends," Kathryn said. "Odd, is't not, how men's work goes by seasons, but except for tending the garden, women's work is much the same all year round. People must eat, clothes must be made and mended, no matter the time of year."

The big room was warm and inviting, the fire crackling in the hearth and the air filled with the scents of food. Ned was in no hurry to go back out into the chilly morning. He was glad when Daisy handed a plate of small, spiced pastries first to him and then, after a brief hesitation, to Tisquantum.

"We are trying to save all the good things for the feast," Kathryn said, "but you were good enough to bring in the boughs, so you have both earned a tart. I made them from the dried figs we got off a Portuguese ship in the autumn."

Ned knew that in their first weeks back in the colony, Nancy had been worried for her friend and former mistress. Kathryn's grief over the news of her family's tragedy had been deep. But lately, Kathryn's spirits seemed to be lifting. Perhaps it was the Yuletide celebration that lightened everyone's mood as the days grew darker. Even Daisy cast a tiny smile at Tisquantum as he reached for a second fig tart.

After leaving the big house, Ned parted ways with Tisquantum, who was going back to help with more wood-cutting out behind the byre. Ned took the path that led further along the shore to where Frank Tipton was chopping wood outside his house. "I'll give you a hand with that," Ned said, "after I step inside and say hello to my wife. I've not seen her since before dawn this morning."

"Ah, and that's a long time when you're newly married." Frank laughed. "Wait till you've been a few years wedded, and you'll find you can go all day without seeing her."

Ned laughed. He did not say the truth, which was that after more than three years apart from Nancy, after thinking she was dead, after all the misunderstanding he had put them both through when they found each other—it seemed nothing short of a miracle that they were together again. Sometimes he thought if he closed his eyes at night, he might open them in the morning to find she was gone. He never said this out loud to Nancy. She would tell him not to give way to foolish fancies.

He pushed open the door and entered a room that was a miniature of the one he had just left—a hearth fire, a table with benches on either side, but everything smaller and more modest than in the Guys' house. Instead of the busy hum of women at work, this room was clamorous with the voices of four small boys, ranging in age from Jemmy who was just a year old, up to Jonathan who was nearly five. In between them in age were Bess and Frank's two boys, Will and Matt. All four were engaged in their seemingly endless pursuit of making wooden block towers, knocking down wooden block towers, and arguing over who had knocked down whose tower.

Beside the hearth sat Nancy, with little Alice by her side; Alice rocked back and forth with a cloth poppet in her arms, singing a tuneless lullaby to it, and Ned thought how much gentler little girls were than little boys. Nancy met his eyes as he came through the door and was about to speak when Alice took her poppet and hurled it into one of the block towers as if firing a catapult at the walls of a besieged city. The boys screamed, Alice sat down looking pleased, and Ned revised his thoughts about the gentleness of little girls.

Nancy raised her hands in mock surrender and rose to meet him, picking her way through the tangle of small bodies on the floor. "I ought to chide them and punish them for fighting, but truly, if I did that I would never stop. Bess and Kathryn are as close to sainthood as the blessed Virgin Mary herself."

"More, perhaps, since Jesus was never naughty," Ned said. He bent down to pick up the child who was squalling the loudest—Bess's younger lad, Matt—and said gravely, "Do you see how people don't like it when you knock down the towers they've made? 'Tis not very good, is it?" To Nancy he added, "It might be easier just to whip the lot of 'em."

"I shall leave that to their parents. When I deliver them back to the house I'll simply announce that everyone needs a good whipping, and that will be that."

They both laughed, and the children, responding to their laughter, settled down and began rebuilding the fallen towers, this time with Alice joining in. "After dinner Bess is coming down to watch them, and I will be free to begin cleaning and dressing the pig for Christmas dinner," Nancy said.

"Butchering a pig will seem like a holiday after this lot," Ned said, pulling her towards him for a quick kiss.

On Christmas morning they all crowded into the main room of the Guys' house while Nicholas Guy read the service from the prayer book. It was his custom to do this with the household every Sunday morning, but there was a special solemnity to this gathering on Christmas morning. Tisquantum, who normally absented himself from Sunday prayers, sat with them now, and Ned saw Daisy glancing at him often, as if she were trying to figure out how this heathen man fit into their

Christian festival. Ned laced his fingers through Nancy's as the words of the service unrolled around them.

After the prayers, the women brought out the roast pork, savoury pies, breads and cakes and tarts. Wine and brandy joined the ale on the table, and soon there were songs—first sacred carols, then merrier tunes of celebration—sung as the eating ended and the drinking began.

Many of the adults, not only the children's parents, had spent hours making small gifts for the little ones. These were now handed around with great excitement. There were more carved wooden horses and soldiers than the children knew what to do with—children, Ned thought, who had never seen either a horse or a soldier in their lives. Tisquantum's gift was perhaps more apt, for he had carved five little wooden boats, one for each child; they all understood boats. "You can sail them on the pond in spring," Nicholas Guy said, but spring was an eternity away, so Kathryn filled a shallow basin with a little water so the tiny fleet could set sail. Bess kept a careful watch to make sure the sailors, in their enthusiasm, did not upset the sea and flood the floor.

The women had somehow found time for more knitting and sewing—another poppet for Alice and cloth dogs and horses for the boys, as well as practical gifts for both children and adults: patchwork quilts and rag rugs made from old clothes, and warm knitted shawls, gloves and caps and scarves for the cold months ahead. Rafe had carved three wooden whistles, and one after another the men picked them up to try and play along with Frank's fiddle tunes—with varying degrees of success.

"I've a gift for you," Ned said to Nancy, "but 'tis not here; I will show you later."

"And I have one for you," she said.

He had made a wooden chest, like a sailor's sea-chest; he had cut and finished and polished the wood till it shone. It would be the first piece of furniture for the new home they would build in the spring. He wondered what she had made for him: some item of clothing, no doubt, though unlike the chest it could hardly be so large and unwieldy that she would not give it to him in company.

The shadows grew long and the day darkened to night. Music and games and storytelling would take up the evening and spill out into the days that followed. Some of the men were playing at dice, while Bess had organized the children and a few willing adults into a game of blind man's buff.

"I was thinking today, 'tis a great improvement over our first Christmas at Cupids Cove," Ned said to Nicholas Guy, and the other man smiled.

"Aye, 'twould be hard to have a bleaker holiday than that one. We have come far, and have much to give thanks for."

"I'd wager your last few Christmases have not been such merry times, Ned," said Kathryn from her seat by the hearth with a sleeping Jemmy in her lap. "Or do sailors spend twelve days dancing the hornpipe and drinking brandy?"

"Hardly." Ned laughed. "Most times there's an extra ration of drink, in truth, but 'tis more like to lead to a brawl than a dance. A shipload of men at sea is a dreary place to spend any holiday."

"You have told us so little of your tale—and you too, Nancy," Kathryn went on. "You have had stranger adventures than anyone here—save for Tisquantum, perhaps—and I think it only fair that we should hear some stories."

Ned looked over at Nancy, then at Tisquantum. He saw the same thought in Nancy's eyes as was in his own head—and though he could not read Tisquantum as well as he could his own wife, he thought the man was likely thinking the same thing. All three of them had lived through things that a storyteller would call "adventures," but that would hardly make for cheerful telling around a holiday hearth. But Kathryn looked from one to another of them eagerly, her eyes bright.

There were many stories Ned and Nancy had not told to anyone but each other, and some, he suspected, that Nancy had not even told him, just as he had not told her every story. He had never told her, for example, about the Lenape woman he had bedded in the village where they had met the Dutch traders. But he could tell the rest of that story, leaving out the sin.

"I'll tell you a tale, then," he began, "of a storm at sea, when I was aboard the *Treasurer* with Captain Argall, how we were driven before the wind till the mainmast cracked clean in two, and we took shelter in a bay with two Dutch traders."

Ned told the assembled group about the Dutchmen they had met in the course of repairing the ship, the translator Juan Rodriguez, a man of many tongues and nations, who had made his home among the Lenape, and the feast in the village that night. It reminded Ned of telling stories to his family when he visited them in Bristol: the children so eager to hear tales of sea battles and bloodshed, and Ned wanting to talk about anything else.

His story of feasting with the Lenape led to the company asking Tisquantum about his own people and their customs, and from there, to Nancy telling about her service with the princess Pocahontas.

"'Twas the most like herself I have seen Kathryn since we came home," Nancy said to Ned much later, as they made their way up to the sleeping chamber.

"Aye, she has ever loved a tale—remember when the players would come to Bristol, and she would round up you and me and a couple of the other 'prentices, and go off to see the play?"

"I've no great love for telling tales, but I'll act the player if that is what it takes for her to—oh!" Nancy broke off as she approached their bed.

Earlier in the day, amid the feasting and celebrating, Ned had slipped away and, with Tisquantum's aid, carried the chest he had made up to their bedside. Nancy gasped when she saw it, and knelt to touch the carving on the lid, their initials entwined together. "How beautiful!" she said.

"I hoped you'd like it—'tis the first thing I've made for our house, but 'twill not be the last. Over the winter I'll make us a bench, and some stools and the like. No use to make the table or the bed until we've a house to put them in, but I can begin with a few things while the snow's down, and—"

She sat down on the sturdy lid of the chest and pulled him down beside her, and stopped his words with a kiss. "In faith, Ned Perry, you're as full of plans as ever you were," she said, "and I can scarce wait to see the house you'll build me, and all that you will put into it. But you ought to rearrange your plans a little. Before you get on to benches and stools, put your tools to work building us a cradle."

TEN

New Life Grows in the Spring

MUSKETTO COVE, MAY 1618

A bright board then she spread,
On which another rev'rend dame set bread.
To which more servants store of victuals serv'd.
                    —*Homer's Odysseys*, Book 15, 178–80

T
HE BABY'S WAIL WOKE NANCY FROM DREAMS. SUNLIGHT
poured across the bed, and she sat upright, wondering how
long she had slept. She had woken before dawn to take Lizzie
from the cradle, nursed her, and fallen back to sleep with the baby
nestled between herself and Ned. Now the sun was up, Ned was gone,
and she could hear the rest of the household below, eating breakfast.

Turn your hand to the task at hand, Nancy thought. She had new
responsibilities now that took precedence over any others. She was not
accustomed to lying in bed while others worked, but there was a hungry
infant with a wide-open mouth next to her, so her task was clear.

Nancy knew there was no time in a woman's life when she was
given as much chance to rest as the weeks after her first child was born.
For every baby after this, even in her confinement she would still have

other children to care for. It was likely that until she was an old woman, these would be the only weeks of Nancy's life that she would have but a single task to do. But resting was against her nature.

"Are you awake?" That was Daisy, coming up to the sleeping chamber with pottage, bread, cheese and small ale.

"Ah, Daisy, you've enough to do without waiting on me as if I were an invalid."

"Nonsense! 'Tis, what, only three weeks since she was born?" Daisy laid the tray down on the bed beside Nancy. "All is well in hand. The men are all off working, the mistress is baking pies, and Bess and I are doing the wash. In the afternoon, if the rain holds off, we will go to the garden to begin clearing the ground for spring planting."

Nancy had known little of gardening or farming in her Bristol girlhood, but she had understood that once a patch of ground was cleared for growing things, it generally stayed clear from one year to the next. Such did not appear to be the case in the New Found Land. When the brush had been cut, the rocks removed from the soil, and vegetables planted, the next spring would find a new crop of rocks in the thin soil, turned up by the winter's ice and snow. Now in mid-May, with most of the snow gone, the women and any children old enough to hold a rock would spend a few days picking over the soil. They would add more stones to the growing pile in the corner of the garden, preparing the ground for planting.

"I'll bind Lizzie up in a sling and take her to the garden when you go—the fresh air will do us both good."

Daisy bent over the bed and traced the curve of Lizzie's cheek with a fingertip. "Ah, she's such a bonny thing. Here, little maid, let me hold you while mama has her own breakfast, now." As the baby's head lolled away from Nancy's breast, Daisy lifted her with ease and paced about the room with a practiced rhythm, putting the child over her shoulder and rubbing her back.

How strange, thought Nancy, that she herself, who had never been particularly drawn to babies, should be a mother, while Daisy was childless. Daisy, Kathryn, and Bess all seemed to have a natural ease with children, while Nancy, so deft to sew a seam or pluck a capon or roll out a pastry, found herself awkward and graceless when she picked up Lizzie. She felt a great rush of love for the child, but sometimes doubted whether she was up to the task of caring for her.

Daisy sighed, looking into Lizzie's little round face. "I am so glad you had a girl—in a few years she will be a playmate for Alice. Too many little boys around this place."

"Perhaps Bess's next one will be a lass also."

"Aye, it might be—or happen she'll have twins, as our mother did. There's that many twins in our family, I'm surprised she's not had a set yet." She sighed again. "Truth be told, I never would have thought I'd be five-and-twenty with no child of my own."

"It still might be. Isaac has not given up hope."

Daisy blushed. "Even if I were to marry again, which I will not, Isaac would not be—" She broke off as the baby gave a hearty burp. "There, that's lovely! I'll take this little maid downstairs with me while you get dressed and go to the privy."

The garden, where Nancy joined the other women a few hours later, was a large cleared space of ground between the house and byre, looking out onto the beach where the men readied the boats for the fishing season. It was a fresh, cool spring day with an east wind blowing in off the water, and the four women quickly set to their task, receiving an indifferent amount of help from Jonathan and Will, who were easily distracted from the job of picking up stones.

"That's four years of rocks," Kathryn said as she and Nancy made their way towards the rock pile. Lizzie was snuggled peaceably against Nancy's chest; she was a good baby who rarely cried except when she was hungry. "Though not so many the first year—we only cleared a small patch when we first came. Planted a few carrots and turnips, that was all. But we have added to it every year."

They walked back from the rock pile to find Tisquantum leaning on the garden fence, talking to Daisy and Bess. "Beans are good, but grow better if you plant them with their sisters—that is what we call them." Tisquantum joined the men in preparing for the summer fishery, but he was interested in everything and sometimes discussed gardening with the women, explaining to them how the Wampanoag women used fish to fertilize the soil.

"Their sisters?" Daisy rocked back on her heels. "And what might a bean's sister be?"

Tisquantum smiled. "Beans grow with askutasquash—a vegetable, you can eat the flesh of it—and maize—what you call a grain. We plant all three together; they help each other to grow."

"Well, I don't know what your cootie squash is, I never heard of the like, and we've not had much luck growing any kind of grain here, though the master thinks we ought to try barley again," Daisy said. The settlers were still relying on grain sent out from England on the company ships, which was ground into flour in the mill at Cupids Cove.

"It may be too cold here," Tisquantum said. "Do you not wonder why the people of this land move about, hunt and fish, but do not settle and make farms?"

"Well, 'tis because they are—" Daisy bit off what she was about to say, looking flustered.

Tisquantum laughed. "Because they are what you call..." He paused for a moment, the laughter leaving his voice as he said the word. "*Savages*? That they live like animals? But Wampanoag are also people of the land, and we farm, we grow crops."

"So do the Powhatan," Nancy said, remembering the neat fields she had walked through in the Powhatan village.

"You see, we know how to farm, and to live in villages, as the English do," Tisquantum said. "The people of this land are not savages, no more than Wampanoag or Powhatan. We farm because the land is good for growing crops. Each people knows best how to use their own land. Some lands are good for growing tobacco, some for growing the three sisters, some for hunting and fishing. The people of each land live in the way that is best for that land."

"Can that be?" Nancy wondered. "That we are trying to grow food in a place that is not fit for it?"

Nancy thought she might have imagined it, but the look Tisquantum gave her seemed almost one of pity. "It is not easy, you know this already. But I think askutasquash would grow here, if you could get it. Among Wampanoag, as with you, growing food is women's work, but

I have learned a little from my mother and sisters. A wise man always listens to women." Tisquantum grinned again, and headed towards the beach.

Bess said something quietly to Daisy, and giggled. "She thinks he is handsome," Bess told Nancy and Kathryn.

"Be quiet! I never said no such thing."

"Well, 'tis no more than truth," said Kathryn. "He is a fine-looking man, of his kind."

"Yes, but his kind is not our kind," Daisy said.

"Nancy said the settlers down in Virginia married with the native women," Bess pointed out.

"Some of the men among the settlers took mistresses from among the Powhatan people," Nancy said, "but Master Rolfe was the only one who took one to wife. And I never heard of it going the other way, an English woman and a native man."

"Exactly," said Daisy. "And you all know I am sworn not to marry again. So even if he were an Englishman, it would not happen."

When the work in the garden was done, Daisy and Bess went back to the big house with the children. Kathryn and Nancy, with Lizzie still dozing in her sling, walked along the rocky beach that separated the ocean from the pond. At the end of that beach, across the little cove from the Guys' house, was the clearing where Ned had framed out the house he and Nancy would move into. He, Tisquantum, and Frank were all working on the walls this afternoon.

"They're making grand progress," Kathryn said. "You must be anxious to move in there."

"I suppose I am—are you so anxious to have me gone?"

"You goose! You know I am not—if I had my way we'd sleep in the same bed like we did when we were girls."

"Our husbands might find that an inconvenience," said Nancy.

Kathryn laughed. It was good to hear her laughter again, Nancy thought. Her spirits had been lighter throughout the winter, and when the first ship from Cupids Cove had gone over to Bristol, Kathryn had gotten Nicholas to write a letter to her father and Lily. Writing to them seemed to have brought her a little peace of mind.

"Well, mayhap they would not wish us to share our beds," Kathryn said now. "But Nicholas knows how glad I am to have you back."

Nancy had grown up believing she would always be a servant in another woman's house. A house on its own little plot of land, while still staying close to Kathryn—it was, truly, more than her wildest dreams. That was the prize the colony offered in return for hardship and hard work—that a simple working man and his wife could have a house and land of their own.

"I do look forward to it, truly," Nancy said. "Only I wonder..." She hesitated. "I wonder if I will be able to manage, when I am alone there with the little one while Ned is out in the boat."

"Manage? Lord ha' mercy, Nan, when have you not been able to manage? From what you've said, you managed your way safely off of a pirate ship, from Bermuda to Virginia, over to England and back again. What is't you fear?"

"I know not—only that I see you and Bess with your babes, and you all seem so easy with them. I wonder if I have the knack for motherhood."

Kathryn put her arms around Nancy, an embrace that drew the sleeping baby in as well. "Have you forgotten how frightened and clumsy I was when Jonathan was born, how I was afraid to pick him up lest I break him? Your hands and head were both steadier than mine, in those days. Mothers grow up along with their children, I think."

"I fear I've left it too late," Nancy said. "You say mothers grow along with their children—but I am grown, and closer to thirty now than twenty. I love her—I do—but perhaps I am too old to learn?"

Kathryn's arms tightened around Nancy, and she laid her head for a moment against her friend's shoulder. "Nan, my dearest Nan—'tis not as if you have to do this all alone. Even when you are here in your own house, I am just across the beach—and Bess and Daisy too. We are all here to help one another."

Nancy's throat tightened, and she dared not speak for fear she might cry. All their lives, Kathryn had said they were "close as sisters." Nancy had loved that closeness, but had schooled herself never to forget the distance between them. Kathryn was no grand lady, no lord's daughter or even a merchant's daughter, but she was mistress nonetheless, and Nancy her servant.

Someday, she thought. There would be a time to tell Kathryn the truth, but not today.

ELEVEN

A New Venture is Begun

CUPIDS COVE AND
HARBOUR GRACE, MAY 1618

(W)ho, having freight
Their ships with spoil enough, weigh anchor straight,
And each man to his house...
　　　　　　—Homer's Odysseys, Book 14, 126–28

EVERY LANDING AT CUPIDS COVE REMINDED NED OF THE first time. The dark, tree-covered hills had been unbroken by any building then; apart from a single wharf for fishing vessels, the shoreline all around the cove had been untouched by human hands. When he had set foot on its shore that day eight years ago, Ned had felt as if he and the rest of Governor John Guy's colonists were like Adams in a new Eden, walking on soil that no Englishman, no Christian—perhaps no man at all—had ever before set foot on.

He had made so many journeys since then, away from Cupids Cove to far stranger ports. But Ned still felt a kinship to the little colonial settlement behind its palisade wall that had been his first home in the New World.

He and Rafe had come down in the shallop today with Nicholas Guy to help their old friends John Crowder and Jem Holworthy move up the shore with their families. The voyage would have been easier in the *Indeavour*, which was a fair-sized barque with more room for passengers and goods. But Governor Mason sent the barque to Renews instead. Master Nicholas said that the governor was disappointed with Crowder and Holworthy for leaving Cupids Cove.

"He thinks we Bristol men do be trying to build a settlement that will rival Cupids Cove—a second English town in the New Found Land."

"He is not mistaken though, is he?" Ned said. Crowder and Holworthy had already cleared their land in Harbour Grace last summer, near Thomas Willoughby's place, and as soon as the winter snows melted the two men had returned to Harbour Grace to begin work on their houses.

"Aye, that is the intention," Master Nicholas said. "But why be petty about it, and deny them use of a ship? There is land enough for all—look at this place."

The short sail from Musketto to Cupids Cove showed that there was enough land in the New Found Land for hundreds, perhaps thousands more English colonists. All along the shore, fishing ships had begun to appear, for this was the month when the summer fleets made their way over from Europe. But they were there only for the few short months of the fishery. When winter came the land would be empty of Englishmen. How could men be petty enough to squabble over who ruled what, when there was room for any who wished to come?

When they tied up the shallop at the Cupids Cove wharf, there was no more time for such reflection; the two families who were leaving had boxes, barrels, and bundles ready to load. Jem Holworthy had himself, his wife and two children; Crowder and his wife had one child as well as Sallie Crowder's sister Hannah, a maiden of seventeen. They would journey to Harbour Grace in two boats: Nicholas Guy's shallop, and one that belonged to Thomas Willoughby, who had sent two men to help with the voyage.

Ned was both hungry and thirsty by the time the boats were loaded; not for the first time he wished Cupids were a town large and settled enough to offer an inn. But John Crowder said, "Come along to Whittington's place—he'll bid us a decent farewell before we set sail."

Their little party walked the well-worn path from the wharf up through the settlement. There were some hard stares from folks who did not look happy to see the Crowders and Holworthys leaving. These people were recent arrivals, London settlers who had come out to Cupids Cove since John Mason had been made governor. There truly was a rift between the London men and the Bristol men, and the sense that the Bristol folk were deserting the colony ran deep.

But George Whittington gave them all a welcome at his table, and his wife set out eel pies and fresh-baked bread. "I will come before long to see your new plantations up in Harbour Grace," Whittington said. "You know that while I plan to stay here in Cupids Cove for now, I am heartily in support of a Bristol colony."

Waiting to see which way the wind blows before he jumps, Ned thought. When they had all come out from Bristol all those years ago, George Whittington had been nothing more than a servant in John Guy's household. But George had a gift for ingratiating himself with the masters, for proving himself useful to those with power and loyal to anyone who could do him good. In the division between the Bristol and London men, Whittington balanced a foot on both sides of the chasm.

Nicholas Guy believed that Whittington had a third string to his bow: he was friendly with the pirate-turned-planter Gilbert Pike in Carbonear, who regularly traded with those on the wrong side of the King's justice. Whether it was the London men in Cupids Cove, the Bristol men in Harbour Grace and Musketto Cove, or pirates at Carbonear, George Whittington was going to make sure he had allies in every harbour.

He'll go far, Ned thought sourly. Whittington would be a friend to any man—but he had once been a cruel enemy to a powerless woman whose only crime was to reject his advances.

Still, he forced himself to be polite to his host as he took another cup of Whittington's ale. The little colony of Englishmen in the New Found Land was too small to make lifelong enemies. You never knew when you might need something more substantial than ale and eel pie, even from a scoundrel.

But if Ned tried not to dwell on the past, George Whittington had no similar scruples. As their party left the house, Whittington walked with them down to the shore, falling back to walk alongside Ned as they reached the wharf. Governor Mason and his wife had come out to bid farewell; though the goodbyes were stiff and formal, still there was a show of civility—for again, it was too small a place for enmity.

"Seems a long time since we first came to this land, does it not, Ned?" Whittington said. "Remember how hard we worked those first months, sleeping under canvas until we got a shelter built before the cold weather came?"

"Aye, 'twas hard work."

"I hear congratulations are due—your wife has borne you a daughter?"

"She has, thank you."

"Well, a son next time perhaps. Is she still as much of a spitfire as ever, your Nan? Some men like a little peace and quiet around the hearth."

Ned fought down his rage; knocking George Whittington out with a blow to the jaw would not sweeten their departure. He schooled himself to say, "Some men have the wit to know a good woman when they have one, and treat her as she deserves." He turned his back to walk away before Whittington could say a word, and lifted Jem Holworthy's small daughter over the edge of the wharf, passing her down to her father in the boat below.

The two shallops sailed up the coast to Harbour Grace; one of Holworthy's children was seasick on the way and heaved up his guts over the side. The large harbour was already busy with ships' crews repairing last summer's stages and shelters in preparation for the fishing season, but the little party of colonists made its way to the north shore of the bay, to a long green slope of land not used by the seasonal fleet. Here was the house Thomas Willoughby and his servants had built the year before, and here Willoughby lived with a half-dozen servants who would fish for him this summer. Willoughby's home, along with Crowder's and Holworthy's houses, would be the centre of the new colony the Bristol merchants intended to start.

To reach Nicholas Guy's plantation in Musketto Cove, it was a short sail around the point of land. There was also a path through the woods linking Musketto and Harbour Grace, allowing men and women to travel between the two plantations on foot. Ned pointed out the trail entrance to Elsie Holworthy. "Even if no-one can spare the time to take you by boat, you can go by that trail in less than an hour and be at our plantation. Mistress Guy is there, and my Nancy, and Bess and Daisy. So if you or Sallie or Hannah want a bit of women's company, you are not so isolated here as it seems."

"This is good to know," said Elsie Holworthy. Like Kathryn, Nancy, Bess and Daisy, Elsie was one of the first shipment of women who had come out from Bristol two years after the men. She had been only a servant girl back in England, but she had married Jem Holworthy, the son of a well-off Bristol merchant, a match that would have been unthinkable back home. "We will be right glad for the company of other women."

Ned was proven right before the day was over: Bess and Daisy, with the two older boys, Will and Jonathan, came through the woods to Willoughby's plantation to greet the newcomers with cakes and preserves. The boys were delighted to find new playmates, and took off with many hoots and hollers, while the women settled in by the hearth of the big house with Elsie and Sallie. Young Hannah Porter, Sallie's sister, was outside chatting with Rafe; the two had spotted each other on the dock at Cupids Cove and had barely taken their eyes off each other since.

"I had thought my wife might come over also to welcome our neighbours," Nicholas Guy said to Bess, as the men enjoyed bread and ale.

"We urged her to come. Nancy offered to look to the house and the younger children for her. But Mistress Kathryn said no, no, she would welcome you all to visit her soon, but she did not want to make the journey today."

"What a pity," said Thomas Willoughby. "Mistress Guy was here on an unexpected visit when I had nothing but two servants and a rude tilt to offer her shelter from a storm—I would like to show her how the place is coming along."

Nicholas Guy stood up abruptly, his ale unfinished and his manner suddenly less affable. There was some old coil of trouble there, Ned knew—both Master and Mistress Guy grew uneasy whenever the name of Thomas Willoughby was spoken.

Ned had asked Nancy once what she thought the trouble was. "Thomas Willoughby is too light in his manner with other men's wives," was all Nancy would say. Ned was not sure if that was all she knew, or whether she was being discreet. The ways of women were a great mystery to him.

Nicholas Guy had gone back to his boat, preparing her for the journey home, but the others remained around the table eating and talking. The conversation turned to piracy. "We've had little enough trouble around here these past couple of summers," Rafe told John Crowder. "Fishing ships and fishing stations have been raided, but they've left us planters alone. 'Tis best to be vigilant, though."

"I believe the threat of piracy is much exaggerated," said Master Willoughby.

"All the same, it might be wise to have some guns mounted here, as they have at Cupids Cove," John Crowder said.

"That is the very sort of decision a governor could make—and get the funds from the company to do it, as well," said Willoughby. "I have sent word to my father in England about our need for our own colony with our own governor. I hope before long we shall have news that that has been granted." He raised his cup, and the men around him did the same. "To our own colony, and our future on these shores!"

In the shallop on the way back to Musketto Cove, Ned told Master Nicholas of Willoughby's toast. Nicholas Guy chuckled. "Aye, there is not much doubt who young Willoughby thinks would be best suited as governor. And I do believe he is mad enough to think he might be given the honour, despite his youth and inexperience."

"Surely, sir, if anyone ought to be governor, it should be you. You are kinsman to John and Philip Guy, and you were the first to settle along this part of the shore."

"I welcome your support, Ned, but that is not how governors are made. They are set up by the merchants who finance the colony, and

they choose men of wealth and high standing—not ordinary colonists."
He smiled as they rounded the point and Musketto Cove opened before
them. "But if Thomas Willoughby thinks that he has the ear of every
Bristol merchant, he may be in for a surprise."

TWELVE

A Fatal Misstep is Made

MUSKETTO COVE, JULY 1618

And, full of tears, we did due exsequies
To our dead friend.
                    —*Homer's Odysseys*, Book 12, 16–17

NANCY WAS CLEANING UP AFTER THE EVENING MEAL. With the long evening light, Bess and Daisy had gone down to the flakes along with the men to cover the fish, for the sky promised rain. At the height of the fishing season, all hands were needed. The men fished all morning, then joined the women in the afternoon to split, gut, and salt the catch, turning the fish on the flakes to dry in the sun and protecting it from the rain. Other chores, save those that were absolutely necessary to keep everyone housed and fed, were neglected.

Now Kathryn came down from the upper chamber of the house, where she had put Alice and Jemmy to sleep together in the big bed. Jonathan was outside with Bess's boys, playing on the beach. Nancy's baby Lizzie, in the cradle by the hearth, whimpered for her evening feeding.

"Go see to her—I can finish this," Kathryn said.

"How on earth do you manage when you have more than one child? I never knew or guessed how nursing an infant takes so much strength. Not to mention I still feel sore in a dozen places. In truth, I sometimes think I'd as lief go back to cooking for the pirates as trying to care for a slew of youngsters while still nursing an infant."

Kathryn laughed. "It cannot be so bad, surely!"

"Well, I do not fear for my life or my virtue, so 'tis better here than aboard ship. But 'tis much harder work than I had thought."

"I never thought to see you daunted by any task."

Nancy looked down at her daughter's half-closed eyes, her little rosebud mouth. "I see now why babes are so pretty to look upon—'tis all that keeps us from abandoning them in the woods, to be taken by the fairies." She settled the baby at the breast and felt the steady pull of Lizzie's suckling as she nursed. "I am only surprised that 'tis so much harder than I had guessed. I will be more solicitous of any nursing mother, now that I have done it myself."

"You will have the chance to put that into practice soon, when Bess has hers. And now that we have more women just a short distance away, belike we will be called upon to help each other in different ways."

"'Tis good to have neighbours," Nancy agreed. "Sallie Crowder seems pleasant enough, and Elsie Holworthy always was a sensible woman."

Kathryn laughed. "That is your highest praise for anyone, to call them sensible."

"As well it should be."

"And young Hannah has made excuses to visit three times already, even at the busiest time of year!" Kathryn added. When the women from Harbour Grace had come to Musketto Cove, Elsie Holworthy and Sallie Crowder had chatted with Kathryn, Nancy, Bess and Daisy, exploring the herb garden and the house, while Hannah had hung about Rafe like a bee around a flower.

"We must visit them, the next time Bess and Daisy want to walk over to Harbour Grace on a Sunday," Nancy said. She had been daunted by the rugged woods trail two months ago, when the other women had first moved to Harbour Grace—a walk that would never have troubled her before having Lizzie. Slowly, her strength was returning and she felt ready to brave the trek through the forest.

"Nay, if 'tis on a Sunday, Nicholas will take us in the boat," Kathryn said. "He has said that Reverend Jarrod will come up from Cupids Cove some Sunday in August to hold a service at Harbour Grace, so we will go over for that."

"And we can have Lizzie baptized then."

The light in the room was growing dim; it was almost sunset. Lizzie was restless after her feeding, and Nancy took her up and walked her about the room. Lizzie was beginning to hold her head up, blink her bright eyes, and take notice of things around her. "I think I will walk down to the beach with her," Nancy said, "and come back with Ned and the others when the work is done."

"Wait for me," Kathryn said, shaking out the cloth she had been using to clean the pots and hanging it on a peg near the hearth.

The evening breeze was picking up; the gathering dark clouds overhead promised that the rain would begin soon, and a quick glance down at the beach showed that the work of covering the fish was done. Everyone was busy putting away fishing gear and tying up the boats. Isaac and Rafe worked at the end of the wharf, securing the lines that kept the shallop tied up.

Surveying this busy scene, Nancy and Kathryn paused at the top of the path that led down to the beach. The rocky sweep of barachois stretched before them, beyond the busy hive of activity around the flakes, and on to the other side of the harbour where Nancy and Ned's little house, half-built, waited until autumn to be completed. The thought of moving filled Nancy with two parts anticipation and one part fear.

Kathryn, too, was thinking of their upcoming move, for she was also gazing across the beach and had just said, "Does Ned think you will—" when a sharp cry went up from the wharf.

Everyone on the beach was running to the water's edge. Rafe stood at the edge of the dock shouting, "Isaac! ISAAC!!" over and over.

"What happened?" Nancy asked Daisy, as she and Kathryn arrived, breathless, on the beach.

"I never saw it myself—but they were out on the edge of the wharf—I think Isaac slipped and fell into the water. Rafe threw out a rope—"

In less than a minute, the scene at the water's edge had transformed into one of panic. Rafe hauled back the rope and cast it again into the water. He pulled it up empty, and threw it again. Nicholas Guy put Jonathan down and raced along the wharf to board the shallop. At the same time, the other men hauled the smaller boat out into the water, Ned and Hal jumping aboard and pulling at the oars as Stephen pushed it out into deeper water.

Again, Rafe pulled back the rope. Again, it came up empty.

Tisquantum ran to join Rafe at the end of the wharf. Another throw of the rope. Nicholas had untied the shallop; Ned and Hal were rowing towards the spot where Isaac had disappeared.

Amid the bustle, Daisy screamed Isaac's name over and over.

Jonathan Guy, so recently safe in his father's arms, began to cry too, sensing the adults' panic. As Kathryn rushed to comfort her son, Nancy went to Daisy.

"He was just—they were—'twas so sudden!" Daisy gasped through her sobs. "Just lost his footing, right over there on the edge of the wharf, and—"

"Don't fret now, see, all the men are there—two boats, and they've thrown ropes from the wharf—someone will save him."

"But he's not come up—I haven't seen his head break the water save for the very first time—he went under and—oh, God. Lord, have mercy—this is all my fault."

Lizzie, tiny as she was, could pick up on the tension in the air just as well as five-year-old Jonathan could; she began to whimper. Nancy cradled her fretful baby with one hand and used the other to rub Daisy's back, all the while stifling the urge to shake the other woman. "Don't be talking so. You know 'tis but an accident. It might happen to any of the men, anytime."

How much time had passed since Isaac had fallen in? Two minutes? Five? No, it could not be so long: time must have slowed.

He was just off the end of their own wharf—unthinkable he should drown there, deep though the water was, with half a dozen rescuers around him. But Daisy was right: Isaac's head had not been seen above the surface. No hand broke through the grey waves to grasp any of the lines that were thrown.

None of the men could swim, as far as she knew. Perhaps some of them, who were country-bred, could have swum in a quiet inland pond, but who would brave these deep swelling sea waters, ice-cold even in the height of summer? And yet even as she thought it, she saw that Tisquantum was climbing down the ladder. He had shed his shoes and coat, and now dived into the water.

Daisy screamed again. "No! He'll be lost too, they will both be lost, and 'tis all my fault."

Nancy had not seen Isaac go under the water, but she saw Tisquantum dive beneath the waves—saw, too, that he had the good sense to take hold of one of the ropes as he went under. "Hush now, Tisquantum is no fool. If he's gone in the water 'tis because he knows he can get safely out again. Mayhap he can save Isaac, after all."

Even as she said the words she felt they were a lie. Time was ticking by. Even if Tisquantum found Isaac, would it be too late?

Kathryn and Jonathan came over; Bess and her boys came too, and the women and children huddled together. She heard Jonathan tell Will, "Isaac falled into the sea."

"Is he drownded?"

"Be quiet, both of you!" Bess said. "We would all be best to say our prayers."

"Oh God!" Daisy cried again. "Merciful Christ, spare poor Isaac, and Tisquantum too even if he is a heathen, draw them safe up out of the water."

It seemed like an age, like a hundred years. The grey water rolling, the men shouting and throwing lines, and no sign of any living man out in that dark, chilly water.

"There is Tisquantum!" Nancy pointed; he was emerging from the water, climbing the ladder back up to the wharf. Alone.

"He'll be froze to death," Daisy said.

"Go to the house and get blankets," Kathryn ordered.

The men clustered, on the dock and in the boats. Tisquantum took an age to climb from the water up to the dock, even with Rafe giving him a hand. From his sodden slowness Nancy understood that the urgency was gone. This was no longer a rescue.

Tisquantum spoke to the other men, then left them talking and came down onto the beach, gratefully accepting the blankets Daisy draped around his shoulders.

"We are going to try to cut him—his body—to cut it free," Tisquantum said. "He was not far down—but his coat was tangled, in the—at the bottom of the wharf."

"In the pilings," Kathryn supplied the word. "Lord, if he could have but gotten the coat off, freed himself."

"I have to go back down, cut him free," Tisquantum said.

Nancy handed the baby to Kathryn. "We should build a fire," she said, gesturing to the three small boys. "Help me gather wood."

By the time the sad recovery was complete, the women had a fire blazing on the beach. Tisquantum went to the house to change and returned to the fire for warmth. The other men had only their cold hands and arms to warm, as they had plunged them into the water to help haul Isaac's body to the surface. Now all gathered near the flickering warmth and light, passing around a bottle of brandy.

Those who had seen the accident told the others how Isaac lost his footing, how he had, perhaps, hit his head on the way down. How he had never had a chance, not truly. They congratulated themselves and thanked Tisquantum for salvaging Isaac's body, as if forgetting that an hour before they had hoped to pull him out him alive.

Only Daisy stood apart from the warmth of the fire, away from the group, away from Isaac's body lying on the rocky beach. Away from Tisquantum, who looked at her, his eyes troubled, though he did not go to her.

THIRTEEN

A Gathering is Held

MUSKETTO COVE, AUGUST 1618

Let's to the river, and repurify
Thy wedding garments.
              —Homer's Odysseys, Book 6, 49–50

THE MINISTER HAD INTENDED TO HOLD A SERVICE AT Harbour Grace, but that was before the drowning. Isaac was buried the day after he died, in a little clearing in the woods, a space that Kathryn could not help thinking would someday be full of all their bones.

They could not leave Isaac unburied, but they could have the minister say a few words over his grave when he came, and for that purpose, the Sunday service should be moved to Musketto Cove. So, Nicholas had sent word to Cupids Cove, and word came back: Reverend Jarrod would come to Musketto Cove on the first Sunday in August. He would hold a service, baptize Ned and Nancy's baby, and consecrate the ground where Isaac would, by then, have lain for a fortnight. The Harbour Grace settlers would come to Musketto Cove for the service and a meal afterwards.

All of which meant that Kathryn could no longer avoid seeing Thomas Willoughby.

She had not forgotten his parting words when he saw her with Alice back in the autumn. *I cannot see your husband in her*, and *We can be good neighbours, Mistress Guy*. Now that the Crowders and Holworthys had settled at Harbour Grace, travel along the woods trail between the two communities was commonplace. Kathryn had not gone to Harbour Grace and was relieved Willoughby had not come to Musketto Cove. But he would come, surely, for the service.

Then she had news that pushed even Thomas Willoughby to the back of her mind. Rafe Whitlock came to Kathryn and Nicholas, shy and hesitant, and said that he and Hannah Porter wished to marry, and would they give their blessing for him to bring a wife into the household? "She be a good worker, and 'twould be no harm to have another woman about the place," he said.

"Ah, I see you are a true romantic," Kathryn teased. Then, seeing the young man's mute confusion, she added, "Of course we would welcome your bride." Her mind already raced to think where they could put a new-wedded couple—if Rafe and Hannah wanted to wait until the fish was in and have an autumn wedding, they could have Ned and Nancy's bed, for by that time Ned would have finished work on the little house and moved his family in there.

But Rafe and Hannah had no wish to wait. "We thought, if the minister were coming next week, we could have the wedding then. I know if we were back in England the banns would have to be read, but here…" He waved his hand vaguely around the house, the outbuildings, the cove. In a place with no church building, no regular minister or Sunday service, the formality of reading the banns seemed to belong to another world, one of cobblestone streets and market stalls and church bells chiming the hours.

"So, we will have a baptism, a wedding, and a funeral—the whole of life, from beginning to end," Kathryn told Daisy and Nancy as they planned the menu. It was far from an ideal time for such a gathering, at the height of the fishing season with everyone busy on the water and on the flakes six days of the week. But the rare opportunity of having a clergyman in the cove meant that the day must be seized. "We can expect a dozen guests or more from Harbour Grace—I've not heard if the minister is bringing anyone from Cupids Cove, but I suppose someone will come with him in the boat, at least, so plan for a few more."

"We'll need to slaughter another pig," Nancy said.

"Yes, that will be best." Nothing more needed to be said about that; if Nancy had declared it, she would make sure all was taken care of, from wielding the butcher's knife to baking the pork pies. Sometimes Kathryn wondered how she had managed to run this large and busy household before Nancy returned. "We will need more ale, of course—I will see to the brewing. And Daisy, we must have cakes—you may use the last of the figs, along with some of the berry preserves."

"Aye, 'twill be a sorrowful wedding cake, to be eaten alongside poor Isaac's funeral meal, but I'll bake it nonetheless," Daisy said mournfully.

"She's shed more tears for Isaac since he died than she ever had kind words for him while he lived," Kathryn observed to Nancy later.

"'Tis all to do with this curse she believes she's under," Nancy said. "I've no great knowledge about curses, even though I was tried as a witch, but if you ask me this curse of Daisy's makes no sense at all. She was afeared to marry Isaac, else he'd be cursed to an early death like Matt and Tom were. But now she thinks she cursed him to die by refusing him. What can you make of that?"

Kathryn shrugged. "No curse to it at all, if you ask me. She feels guilty about Isaac because she refused him, and even more guilty that the man she does fancy is one she can never marry. So she's convinced herself that she brought ill-luck on Isaac. The truth is, an accident like Isaac's could strike any of us down, at any time. I have had stern words with Jonathan about running about on the wharf."

On that first Sunday in August, the Harbour Grace settlers arrived both ways, some in boats and some over the woods trail. A pinnace full of fishermen from an English fishing station in Harbour Grace came as well, to enjoy the rare opportunity of a Sunday service preached by a clergyman. Any fishermen who were truly devout had to endure long months without a minister's services, and when their boat arrived with eight men aboard, Kathryn was glad she and her maids had cooked so much food.

Last of all came a small boat from Cupids Cove with three men aboard. James Hill was in command of the vessel, accompanied by the minister. With them was a third man she had never seen before, of middle years and dressed in far finer clothes than any other man present. His peacock-blue doublet and hose, his jacket with its fine lace trim, and his high-crowned hat, all declared him a man of wealth and importance, recently out from England.

Nicholas drew Kathryn forward with him to greet the minister and his guest, whom he introduced as "Master Hayman." She noticed a look exchanged between the men and guessed that her husband knew something about this Master Hayman and why he was here.

But there was little time to wonder: with greetings and introductions out of the way, the church service began. It had to be held outdoors, of course; the men had planned to rig up a piece of sailcloth between some trees to keep off rain if needed. But there would be no call for a roof on such a lovely summer day, and benches were laid out on the grass.

Will we ever have a church here? Kathryn wondered. Even at Cupids Cove, eight years after the first settlers had arrived, there was no church, although the minister resided there and held services every Sunday in the largest house. At Musketto Cove, Nicholas read the Sunday service to the household, and the babies had been christened on visits to Cupids Cove. Now, looking about at the two dozen people gathered to hear Reverend Jarrod preach, Kathryn thought about the future. It would not be a town, not in the way towns were built back in England, but something was needed to link the plantations at Musketto Cove and Harbour Grace into a community. Surely that, as much as prayer, was the purpose of a church.

After the reading of the Morning Service and a blessedly short sermon—Reverend Jarrod was, thankfully, no Puritan—came the other rites. First was the Churching of Women, so that Nancy could be blessed and cleansed after childbirth, then Lizzie's christening, with Kathryn and Nicholas standing as godparents. That was a long time for everyone to sit still, especially the children, but then everyone walked together up to the spot where Isaac was buried. Daisy sobbed as the minister read the service for burying the dead.

The wedding would be held in the afternoon. Elsie Holworthy and Sallie Crowder pitched in to help Kathryn and her servants with the noon meal; Hannah offered to help as well, but the other women told her to sit and enjoy her dinner—it was, after all, her wedding day. After they had eaten, they put aside the pots and trenchers to wash out later. White meadowsweet and wild roses grew all around, and the women made a coronet of the flowers for Hannah's hair and a bouquet for her to hold. She wore a faded red mockado gown that had been Kathryn's own wedding gown nearly ten years earlier; Kathryn had little opportunity to wear a fine gown on the plantation and had altered it to be used by more than one New Found Land bride in the years since.

No sooner had the marriage service begun and Kathryn settled on the bench beside her husband and children, than Jemmy began to make trouble, whinging and crying to be let down to run about. "Sit *still*," Kathryn whispered, but he was not yet two years old, and he had been sitting still a very long time already.

She took him up in her arms and moved a little away from the gathering, to a spot under the pine trees where she could still see and hear the wedding but could let Jemmy down to play in the grass. She ought not have let him have his own way, she thought—Nicholas would no doubt tell her that she should have given him a good smack to teach him manners. But he was so little, and her children were not used to church services that went on for hours.

"A pretty sight, is't not?" She had not heard anyone come up behind her and was startled by Thomas Willoughby's voice. She had been avoiding him all day, but in tending to her son she had become distracted, and ceased to watch for him. He nodded towards the young couple standing before the minister.

"It is always good to see a man and woman unite in holy matrimony," Kathryn said. "As you should know, being a married man yourself. Are you still determined not to bring your wife out to the colony?"

"Not now, certes. If I were to be—well, we shall see. For now I think she is best off back in England. I will make a voyage home this year or next, to see my heir and put another in her belly. She is no sturdy colonial matron like yourself."

Kathryn scooped up Jemmy, who had wearied of poking a stick in the dirt. He often napped about this time in the afternoon, and perhaps by rocking him in her arms she could get him to sleep. But Willoughby was not done with her.

"'Tis a grand little gathering, your husband's people and mine, is't not? Surely we have all we need here to start our own colony."

"That business of starting colonies is beyond a woman's concern." Then, trying not to sound too churlish, she added, "But it is good to see everyone together."

"I would be happy for us to have many more such gatherings," Willoughby said. "And indeed, for us to have our own colony—if we had the right man to lead it."

"Do we need a leader? We are doing well as we are, surely."

"A colony must have leadership. Holworthy and Crowder think your husband is setting himself up to be governor. He is John Guy's cousin, after all—that might hold some sway with the merchants."

"It may be so." For a moment Kathryn thought of it—*a governor's wife!* Though she doubted it would change much of anything in her day-to-day life about the house and garden, still it would be quite an honour for a stonemason's daughter.

But she came to her senses quickly. If Thomas Willoughby was talking to her about who should be governor of the colony, it was not because he wanted her to dream of the honour it would bring to herself and her husband.

"I suppose you would say that if John Guy's cousin has a claim to the governorship, so does Sir Percival Willoughby's son," she replied. "And even your wife might come out if she could be the governor's wife, not simply a sturdy colonial wench like the rest of us."

He laughed softly. "Oh Kathryn, I have ever liked your spirit! You are wasted in Nicholas Guy's bed. But yes, your thoughts chime well with mine. Now, what do you know about this fellow Hayman? When we are talking of a new company and a new colony, surely his arrival can be no coincidence. I have not heard his name before."

"No more have I. Hush now—pay heed to the wedding."

Jemmy had settled to a drowsy rest in his mother's arms, and Kathryn thought she would be safe to sit back down in time to hear the vows exchanged. Thomas only smiled as she slipped away.

When the service was over, Frank Tipton took out his fiddle and folk began to dance—couples in a set, and single men, far more numerous, cutting sprightly jigs on their own. Along with the bride and groom, Ned and Nancy were dancing, as were John and Sallie Crowder; Bess danced with Hal Henshaw, since her husband was the fiddler. Daisy stayed on the edge of the group, watching the children, but when Frank changed the tune and the dancers again arranged themselves into two lines, Kathryn saw Tisquantum reach for Daisy's hand. "Show me how the English dance!" she heard him say, and after a moment's hesitation, Daisy joined him in the line.

Only Jem and Elsie Holworthy stayed off to the side: they were known to have a Puritan way of thinking, and would likely not approve of dancing at any time—but certainly not on a Sunday.

"To my mind," Nicholas said when Kathryn pointed this out as they moved through the steps of the dance, "everyone's principles must bend a bit, here in the colony. 'Tis rare enough to get a day when we can all rest from our work—especially when the fish is in. It could only be on a Sunday, and so Sunday must serve for all things: morning prayer, christening, marrying, burying, feasting, and even the dance. 'Tis not as if we are idle folk with time on our hands, nor as if Rafe and Hannah wanted to wait until winter, when there would have been leisure for a proper wedding."

"And the minister could not have come in winter," Kathryn pointed out. "Who is that Master Hayman, Nicholas? What is he doing here?"

Nicholas laughed. "All in good time, little wife," he said as they parted company at the bottom of the set and changed partners.

When they lined up for the next dance, Master Hayman stood in front of her, holding out his hand. "Your husband has given me leave to partner you in this set, Mistress Guy. Would you do me the honour? I cannot pretend to much skill at these country dances, but on such a fine day and in good company, I want to take my turn."

"Very well, sir—I will be honoured." Whoever he was, he was clearly a man of some importance, and as his hostess she was bound to show him every welcome. She took his hand and led him out onto the grassy clearing that passed for a dance floor.

As it turned out, Master Hayman was a fine dancer, and he thanked her when the dance was over. "I hope to make your acquaintance better while I am here, Mistress Guy, for your husband tells me that you have a fine appreciation for plays, for poetry, and for tales of all kinds."

"Oh—did he say that indeed? He flatters me. I love a good tale—and we have folks here who have the most amazing stories to tell, of the adventures they have had. When I was back in Bristol I loved to go see players and puppet shows when they came to town. But as for poetry, I have no learning."

"But you have the interest, and that is more than I had hoped to find in this far place," Master Hayman said. "I am something of a poet myself, you see, and a land as fair as this, with such unknown adventure stretching before us all—well, it was surely made to inspire a poet!" He relinquished her hand as he brought her back to Nicholas's side. "We shall talk more of poetry when time allows, Mistress Guy." And putting his hand on Nicholas's arm to draw him aside, Master Hayman was gone, leaving Kathryn no wiser about who he was and what he was doing here.

But her curiosity was soon satisfied. When the dancing was done and the women brought out pitchers of ale for the thirsty guests, Nicholas stood up in front of the assembled party. He beckoned to Master Hayman, and the well-dressed gentleman came to stand beside Nicholas.

"I do believe you have all met Master Hayman throughout the course of this day. Master Hayman, I hope you will agree we have a fine colony here," Nicholas said. "Today you have seen my plantation, and tomorrow I will take you to Harbour Grace, where Master Thomas Willoughby has his plantation. You know his father, Sir Percival, of course."

"Yes, yes of course, I know your father well, young man." Hayman looked at Thomas Willoughby and nodded. "He would be very pleased, very pleased indeed with the work you are doing, I think." He drew a deep breath. "How lovely the air is in this country! So clear, so fresh—surely it has a healing effect on all those who live here. So much more beneficial than the air of England—do you not agree, Master Guy?"

"Indeed, it is a fine land—and today is a great day for all of us in this land!" Nicholas Guy turned back to address the gathering. "You all know that the merchants in Bristol who founded the colony at Cupids Cove have been in disputes these last few years with the London merchants, so much so that the Newfoundland Company has been on the verge of splitting apart entirely. For two years now the idea has been suggested that we Bristol men should form our own colony, to pursue our own interests—Bristol merchants supporting Bristol colonists."

A ragged noise of approval came from the small gathered group; a few of the men cried, "Hear, hear!"

"I am here to tell you all today that the Bristol merchants have heard our wishes on this matter," Nicholas went on. "They have drawn up a new charter. Our plantations here at Harbour Grace and Musketto Cove, with further land yet to be settled as far as Carbonear, are now under the ownership of the Bristol Newfoundland Company. For this new colony, entirely separate from the Cupids Cove colony, the company has chosen a new name. There was thought that it would be called Harbour Grace, as that will be its largest and principal settlement, but since it will include Musketto Cove and the southern part of Carbonear also, the company has chosen a name that represents what this colony is. As of today's news from England, we are all planters of the new colony of Bristol's Hope."

Once again, there were a few cheers, which grew in enthusiasm. Thomas Willoughby looked like a man caught off-guard, though he joined in the cheering. Kathryn was certain he had known nothing of this announcement, despite his father's investment in the colony.

Kathryn kept her eyes on Willoughby as her husband spoke again. "Along with this happy news of our new charter and our new colony," Nicholas said, "it is my great pleasure to introduce to you the man the company has chosen to be our first governor: Master Robert Hayman!"

Now Hayman stepped forward to begin a long and flowery speech. *So*, Kathryn thought, *the company has chosen for governor, not Thomas*

Willoughby and not my husband, but a man none of us has ever heard of, who has never set foot in this land before.

That was how things were done, of course; colonial governorships were prizes, given to men of good standing in England. But looking from her husband's face to Thomas Willoughby's, she knew there was more happening here than met the eye.

Long before Thomas Willoughby had thought of making a move, likely as far back as last summer, Nicholas—and perhaps Holworthy and Crowder too?—must have petitioned the masters back in England, asking them not only for a charter and a colony of their own, but for a governor as well. A governor who had come and presented himself first to Nicholas Guy at Musketto Cove; a governor about whom Thomas Willoughby knew nothing.

There was a subtle game being played here, and Kathryn knew she lacked the knowledge to grasp all the undercurrents of it. But it was a game that her husband was in control of, and the moves he was making left Willoughby at a disadvantage.

And that was as it should be. Anything that strengthened Nicholas's position in the colony was surely good for Kathryn and her household, and she would shed no tears to see Thomas Willoughby put out of joint. Only she saw Willoughby's eyes shift from Governor Hayman, to Nicholas, and then to herself. When he met her gaze across the sun-washed clearing, he held her eyes for a moment, then looked to the tangle of children on the ground, where Alice played with the boys.

When he looked back at Kathryn he did not need to speak a warning, not even a veiled one. The warm August afternoon chilled as if a cloud had passed over the sun.

FOURTEEN

A Guest is Entertained

MUSKETTO COVE, OCTOBER 1618

Poets deserve, past all the human race,
Rev'rend respect and honour...
> —*Homer's Odysseys*, Book 8, 645–46

NANCY USED AN OLD SHAWL AS A SLING TO CARRY Lizzie about while still keeping her hands free to work. The baby rarely cried, but she was wide-eyed and curious about the world around her. Since she was still several months away from being able to walk, carrying her about so she could see what was happening seemed the best solution.

It was not a perfect one: just the day before, Nancy had been wearing the sling with Lizzie in it when she went to the communal oven to take out her own loaves of bread. Lizzie had slipped loose, almost tumbling head-first into the oven before her mother caught her. For Nancy, who prided herself on being a capable housekeeper, it was strange how much the addition of a helpless infant made every task more difficult.

She stood now, shifting her weight from one foot to the other because that motion kept Lizzie happy, looking at the plot of land beside their house that Ned had cleared for a garden. Nothing was planted this year;

they had only moved into the little house a fortnight ago. Next year there would be turnips, cabbage, peas and beans and carrots. She would not trouble with her own garden for herbs and medicines; Kathryn was the expert there and had a flourishing herb garden, which Nancy and Bess were both welcome to make use of. But Nancy could grow enough here to feed herself and Ned and Lizzie.

She had never fancied herself a farmer, but in these last years Nancy had learned to do a great many things she had never imagined herself doing. For a time, in the Bermuda Islands, she had even worn breeches and borrowed Ned's name, to disguise herself, and had done a man's work helping to build the fort there. Then, in Virginia, she had worn her own name and skirts again on John Rolfe's plantation, where women helped with the hard labour of growing tobacco. Nancy had learned to make herself over many times, into whatever person the task at hand called her to be. She could do it again; she *was* doing it.

She was glad their new house was part of the larger plantation of Musketto Cove. If she and Ned had been off on their own land far from the other settlers, she would have felt very much alone when Ned was off fishing for the day. As it was, she had fallen into the pattern of doing her own housework in the morning, then crossing the beach to Kathryn's house to help with the noon meal and afternoon's work there.

She planned to go there in an hour or so, but was surprised to see little Jonathan Guy running across the beach. He relished the important task of delivering messages.

"Aunt Nancy! Mama wants you up at the house—she says Guv'nor is coming to visit."

"The governor!" Nancy had not seen Master Hayman since his arrival back in August; after a couple of days at Musketto Cove he had taken up residence in Thomas Willoughby's house at Harbour Grace. Master Nicholas had gone a few times to Harbour Grace on matters of business, but the governor had not returned to the Guys' plantation.

"Hurry back, and tell her I am coming as quick as I might." Nancy untied Lizzie from the sling and changed her apron, stained from the morning's work, for a clean one. She tied a clean white coif around her hair and changed Lizzie's clouts before making her way to Kathryn's house.

Along the beach she had a view of the little round bowl of their cove, the morning sun dancing on the water. On the flakes, fish from the last few catches lay drying in the sun; more was stacked in the storehouse. She knew now that the flat white pieces of salted codfish were as valuable as heaps of silver coins; they were, thus far, the only thing produced in the colony that had value when sold in the markets of Europe. The Bristol merchants gave the colonists trade goods in exchange for fish at the end of the season. Goods were more useful than money, for there were no shops or markets in this land, no place yet to buy or sell.

Now that she had spent time in other colonies, Nancy had a better understanding of what the merchants and the colonists were trying to accomplish here. Codfish served the same place in the colonial economy as tobacco was beginning to do in Virginia; down there, the English had arrived believing they could find vast stores of gold and silver, but they had found that the native people could not point them to the longed-for gold mines. But the tobacco that the local people had been growing all along was in great demand back in England.

Here in the New Found Land, the wealth of codfish in the water had been known in England for a hundred years; the question was whether it was worth supporting colonies of English folk living here year-round, rather than simply sending the fishing fleet across in the summer and bringing them home every autumn.

Nancy did not know which side was right, in that great debate. All she knew was that she and her husband owned a piece of land with a house on it that was theirs by right—Ned showed her a paper Nicholas Guy had drawn up, granting the land to them, though neither Ned nor Nancy could read it. That land, that house, that paper, was all Nancy needed to know about the colony.

Governor Hayman came overland, accompanied by William Spencer, one of the Harbour Grace fishing servants, and a third man that Nancy had never seen before. Spencer had run ahead to bring word of the governor's arrival, then come back to guide the visitors. When they came, Nancy, Daisy and Hannah were preparing a finer noon meal than was customary. Kathryn had put on her best gown, and Master Nicholas changed out of his working clothes into doublet and hose.

Master Hayman was similarly well attired, in forest-green doublet and gold-coloured hose, but his garments looked worse for wear after the trek along the woods path.

"Look at his cap!" Kathryn whispered behind her hand to Nancy. "Are those feathers in it, or did he walk through a bird's nest along the way?"

"Hush," Nancy said, trying to stifle her own laughter at the sight of the bedraggled governor. Despite the mud on his shoes and hose and the pine needles on his doublet, he carried himself with dignity as he greeted the master and mistress of Musketto Cove, bowing over Kathryn's hand and brushing it with his lips as if she were a lady.

"Mistress Guy, how good to meet you again! I look forward to visiting your fine home and meeting your children and the folk of your household. May I present Captain Dermer, come from England by way of Cupids Cove? He wanted to see our fine new colony here at Bristol's Hope, but he especially wants to meet with our native friend."

Captain Dermer was dressed well, though more simply than the governor. Master Nicholas called Tisquantum over, and the men walked some distance away in private conversation.

After the meal and a stroll about the plantation, Governor Hayman settled on the bench outside the big house—he preferred to sit outside, he said, as it was such a lovely clear, fresh day, even though the bite of autumn was in the wind. "What a fair country this is!" he said as Nancy handed him a cup of wine, pulled from the master's stores for a special occasion.

Unlike many men of his class who ignored servants as if they were part of the furniture, he met Nancy's eye and thanked her as he took the cup. "Goodwife Perry, if I remember aright?"

"Yes, sir," she said, dropping a curtsey.

"You are the brave woman who endured such hardships at the hands of pirates. I would hear more of your travels—mayhap you will tell me some tales by the fireside tonight?"

"I—I am not much of a teller of tales, sir. But I will answer any questions you might have."

Kathryn, who had just come from the house, sat down beside the governor. "Nancy makes a great show of modesty and says she does not like to talk of her adventures, but 'tis true, sir, she has seen more of the world than most of us will do in a lifetime. Why, do you know that in Bermuda she went about disguised as a man, and did a man's work in the colony there, to preserve her own virtue until she could get away from that place?"

"Is that so?" The governor looked up at Nancy with even greater interest. "Why, 'tis like something out of a play."

"That is what put the thought in her head!" Kathryn said. "When we were girls in Bristol I used to drag her off to see the players. I love it here in the New Found Land, but in truth, 'tis one of the things I miss in England—the chance to see players, or strolling musicians, or any such thing. We must rely on those who have had adventures, like Nancy and Ned and Tisquantum, to tell us their tales."

"Indeed, indeed." Hayman nodded. "I remember you spoke before of your fondness for tales of adventure, and I have something with me that perhaps we may all enjoy this evening. I brought a few books out from England, and one of them is a new translation into English of a great Greek poet called Homer. Have you heard of the legends of Troy, and the voyages of Ulysses?"

Nancy, having little interest in Greek poets and seeing that she was no longer needed, went back to the house, where Daisy was clearing up from the noon meal and Hannah was rolling out pastry crust for supper. "The governor and that captain are staying the night and likely a few days more," Hannah said, "so me and Rafe'll be put out of our bed, I 'low, to give them a place."

"I'd like to know what that Captain Dermer is up to," said Daisy, "off in corners talking with Tisquantum. Making a load of promises he don't intend to keep, if you ask me."

"What promises would he be making?" Hannah said.

"I don't doubt he's promising that if Tisquantum goes on his ship as a guide, he'll take him back to his own people, his own country."

Daisy's tone was bleak, and Nancy darted a glance at her. She had seen, over the summer, the growing closeness—what she might almost call flirtation or even courtship, if it had been an Englishman—between Daisy and Tisquantum.

"Is Tisquantum like to agree to such an offer?" Nancy asked.

"'Tis not for me to say what he might or might not do. But I do know he wants to go home—more than...more than anything."

"You can't blame him—surely anyone would want the same."

"Would they?" Daisy shot back, wringing out her dishcloth. "All of us here are an ocean away from home. We are content enough to make a life here—could not Tisquantum do the same?"

"Surely 'tis different for one such as him," Hannah said. "He wants to be among his own kind."

"We all chose to come out here," Nancy said. "Tisquantum never chose to leave his home. We cannot all pick and choose our path in life, but to be taken from your home by force is—hard." She thought of the plantation in Virginia, where she had had good work and been treated well. Thought of her friend Omar, who had saved her life in Bermuda—Omar, who would risk anything to avoid being captured back into slavery. Even the poorest and humblest person would surely prefer to chart their own path, if they could. "You cannot blame Tisquantum for wanting to go home."

"I never said I blamed him." Daisy hung the wet cloths on a hook near the hearth and turned to Hannah. "Is that venison ready for stewing?"

"I'll see to the venison," Nancy offered quickly. The week before, a party of men—led by Tisquantum, who was by far the most experienced hunter—had brought home from the forest two of the big stags that Tisquantum called *ottucke*. The meat from one was to be smoked and dried, while the other was butchered for immediate cooking, with some to be bottled and preserved. It tasted much like English venison, and so they called it, though the animals were larger than any deer the settlers had ever seen.

Over supper, the discussion was lively—and, as Daisy had predicted, Captain Dermer spoke of his desire to lead an expedition on the mainland to the south, with Tisquantum as his guide. "I will return to England for the winter to seek a sponsor—'twould be best if Tisquantum could come with me, the better to persuade English merchants of the value of such a venture."

Nancy caught the glance that passed between Daisy and Tisquantum before he said quietly, "When I have come so far to get to this side of the ocean, I do not think I will like to go back to England."

"If you'll not come, I will do my best to persuade a patron to sponsor the voyage myself," Dermer said, "as long as I have your promise that you will come with me next summer."

"Indeed, to return to Patuxet is my greatest desire," Tisquantum said. "If you have a ship to go there, I will be with you." This time, Nancy saw Daisy's eyes flicker towards Tisquantum, but he did not meet her gaze.

Governor Hayman put down his ale and looked around the table. "As you may know, Master Willoughby has taken six of his men in the shallop and gone to Carbonear to explore Sir Percival's land there, with the thought of developing a new plantation," he said. "I bade him before he left, to put in here on his return journey and take us back to Harbour Grace. Captain Dermer and I plan to spend a few days here at Musketto Cove. That will give me time to better know you good folks, and learn more of your plantation, and hear all your tales." He glanced at Nancy with a smile as he said this, and she hoped once again that he would not put her on the spot and have her make some great drama out of telling her story.

In the end it was not so bad; when they sat around talking later that evening, after the work was done, the governor was eager to know more about her travels as well as Ned's. But with Ned and Kathryn helping to draw out the tale, she did not feel as embarrassed as she might have otherwise.

Nancy, Ned, and a sleeping Lizzie slipped away from the fireside to return to their own house, chilly now after standing empty all day. Ned built up the fire to warm the place a little while they put the baby to bed. They sat quietly by the hearth for a few minutes, letting the warmth soak into their bones, chatting about the day's events.

"Will Tisquantum go away with Captain Dermer, d'you think?" Nancy wondered. "Daisy's afraid of it, but it might be the best thing for her, if he goes."

"If Dermer can find someone to fund a voyage to the land of his people, Tisquantum will go for sure. You may be right about Daisy, but I'd not know about that."

In the morning, when her own chores were done and Ned was working on the roof of their house, making sure all was sealed and tight before the snow came, Nancy went to the big house where she found Kathryn and Governor Hayman seated together at one end of the table. Jonathan was kneeling up on a stool next to his mother. A sheet of paper was spread out on the table before them, and the governor had a pen and an ink-bottle—all things he must have brought over from Harbour Grace. The only writing paper Nancy had ever seen at Musketto Cove was the leather-bound book Master Nicholas had for keeping his accounts.

"Now, here is the letter J, that makes your name, Jonathan," Governor Hayman said as he traced out the J on the page.

"Is that feather from a real bird?" Jonathan asked.

"Is—what?"

Jonathan pointed at Master Hayman's quill, which clearly interested him more than the letter J. "Is that feather from a real bird?"

"Ah. Yes, it certainly is."

"'Tis not a seagull. I know what their feathers are like."

"No, it is not, is it?" Master Hayman turned the pen over in his hands, then held it out for Jonathan to touch. "I believe this is a goose feather."

"What is a goose?"

"A bird that lives in a farmyard, like a chicken or a rooster, but much bigger." He looked up at Kathryn. "You have no geese here in the New Found Land yet?"

"Not here. There are some at Cupids Cove—we traded for one last year for the Christmas feast, and might do so again. I could get some goslings to raise here, but they are more work than hens."

"Did you pull the feather off yourself?" Jonathan asked.

"Oh, no no," said the governor, gallantly trying to keep up with Jonathan's curiosity. "Someone else made this feather into a pen."

"Would it hurt the goose? To have the feather taken off?"

"I think not—have you not seen birds' feathers around? They fall off quite naturally. Carefully now, it still has ink in it and might spill."

"Where does the ink come from? What is it made of?"

Governor Hayman was at a loss. "Well, now—I am not entirely sure what ink is made of. I have been writing with it since I was a boy of your age, but I never thought to ask what it is made of."

"Squids have ink," said Jonathan.

"Squids?"

"Like a fish, but not really a fish. They live in the ocean, and when they get frighted they shoot ink out of their bottoms, papa says. If you had a seagull feather and some ink from a squid, could you make a pen?"

Master Hayman chuckled. "It seems your interest runs more to natural history than to learning your letters, young Master Guy. I do not know if this squid's ink you speak of would be good for writing. I shall have to do more study on the matter, and let you know the next time I come. It is a most interesting question. Now, do you want to see the letter K? That is the first letter in your mother's name, Kathryn."

"No, I want to go play with Will and Matty and Alice. But I might try to make a pen if papa can get me a feather and some ink." He slid down from the table.

While this little scene played out, Nancy had put Lizzie down on the floor where the other children were playing. Today was a chilly, damp, grey day and they would be kept inside; they would need to be cautioned not to be too rough with Lizzie, who was just beginning to sit up. As Jonathan went to join the others, Kathryn said, "Oh, Jonathan, you must stay and learn your letters—'tis very good of Governor Hayman to teach you!"

The governor waved his hand. "He is very young, Mistress Guy. It is only natural his attention should not be held for very long, and he is eager to be with his little playmates."

"I wish he would take it more seriously. I should like for him to be a learned man, like you are."

"He will do well enough for his station in life," Master Hayman said. "You must remember that my father was mayor and member of Parliament, and I was sent away to school at the age of twelve. As a planter's son, your boy's main interests will always be practical ones, but there is no reason he should not learn to read and write tolerably well."

Kathryn sighed. "But to be able to read great poems like the one you read to us last night. Nancy, you ought to have stayed to hear Governor Hayman read from this *Odyssey* he was telling us of! I know you will say you have no head for poetry, but truly, 'tis thrilling!"

Nancy smiled. It was grand to see Kathryn so excited, even if it was over something that could have little benefit in their everyday lives. The governor, too, seemed touched by her enthusiasm, for he said, "Can you read at all yourself, Mistress Guy?"

"Oh, only a little. I learnt from the horn-book when I was a child, but only my A, B, C. I can puzzle out a few words, if I have enough time, but 'tis easier for my husband to read and write letters home for me than to try to do it myself." She sighed. "'Tis as you said about one's station in life: 'twould be enough of a chance for a stonemason's son to learn to read and write well, much less a daughter. I suppose some noble ladies get a proper education, but certainly not a working man's wife or daughter."

"And yet I hear the winters in this place are long and cold, with little outside work to do. What a fine time to read and write," said Governor Hayman. "I have plans of my own. I am working on a translation of a French writer called Rabelais, and I have begun writing some verses of my own, a kind of tribute to the New Found Land and the fine life to be had here. I hope by publishing them, to encourage more settlement."

Nancy glanced at Kathryn; she wanted to roll her eyes at the foolishness of the governor's ideas, but Kathryn was looking at him with great respect. "Surely if winter is a good time to read and to write," Governor Hayman went on, "'twould also be a good time to teach and learn? If you are so eager to learn, Mistress Guy—and if your husband has no objection, of course—I should be glad to help you improve your reading. Perhaps by spring you might indeed read Homer for yourself."

FIFTEEN

A Mysterious Disappearance Occurs

MUSKETTO COVE, OCTOBER 1618

Ho! guests! What are ye? Whence sail ye these seas?
Traffic, or rove ye, and like thieves oppress
Poor strange adventurers...
                              —Homer's *Odysseys*, Book 9, 355–57

"THE MAN...O MUSE...IN...INFORME?" KATHRYN HESI-
tated over the fifth word of the line. She knew *the man*, and
O, and had been able to figure out *Muse* with a bit of thought.
"Inform, yes. The poet calls upon his Muse—you know about the muses,
of course—to tell him the tale of Odysseus, who is also called Ulysses,"
Governor Hayman said. He and Kathryn sat at the table; Jonathan had
reluctantly sat through his ABCs and gone off to play. Now, with the
morning meal cleared away and work on the midday meal not yet begun,
the governor was taking Kathryn through the opening lines of the *Odyssey*.

Kathryn had been a little older than Jonathan—six, she thought—
when she had learned her letters, taught by an elderly man on their
street who had a little school in his house for neighbour children. None
of them, girls or boys, was expected to need much reading and writing.
All their fathers were guildsmen; their mothers often helped with the

family business. It could be useful to know how to write down orders and keep simple accounts. But books had formed no part of her childhood; the old man with the little school had died before she had learned more than a few simple words from the horn-book.

The discovery that Governor Hayman had brought a Bible and some books of poetry to the colony with him, and that he cared to take the time to tutor a planter's wife, had opened up a dizzying and delightful prospect. Governor Hayman and Captain Dermer had now stayed three days at Musketto Cove, and, with Nicholas's bemused permission, the governor had spent a little time each day helping Kathryn with her reading and writing. He also read aloud to the household from Homer every night. Soon he would return to Harbour Grace, but he had made a dazzling offer—to leave the book at Musketto Cove so that Kathryn could continue to practise her reading.

Governor Hayman was in his early forties, and widowed, but there was nothing flirtatious in his manner towards Kathryn, and Nicholas did not seem troubled by it. She was accustomed to her husband's attention, and to the improper advances of Thomas Willoughby. Other than those two, every man she saw in her daily round was her husband's servant, and they all treated her with polite deference—save Ned Perry, whose long acquaintance with her made him less deferential; since he married Nancy, she had come to think of Ned almost as a brother. Men of higher status, such as Governor Mason or Reverend Jarrod down in Cupids Cove, barely seemed to notice her existence when she was in the room. A woman was of little consequence save as a man's wife.

And so the attention she received from Robert Hayman was something utterly unique in her experience: he conversed with her as though he were interested in what she had to say. Not as an equal—quite apart from the fact that she was a woman, he was of a much higher station than she. But the governor spoke to her as one man might speak to another: with a kind of interested dignity that she had not realized she craved. Imagine this—putting a book of poetry in front of a planter's wife, just so that she might take pleasure in looking at it!

She had been shy to ask Nicholas's permission for the reading lessons. "I would not neglect any duties in the household, of course, but I would be better able to help the children, once you start teaching them, if I were more skilled in my own letters," she had argued.

Nicholas had picked up the governor's book, turning it over in his hands. "I would have chosen something more practical for you to learn. Scripture, or the prayer book, or perhaps learning how to keep accounts. But I know you care for poetry."

"As long as you do not think it too frivolous."

He smiled at her. "My little wife! I know our life here offers few of the diversions that bring pleasure to women's lives back home. You cannot go to a market, or visit from house to house with many friends, or even go to church. If learning to read poetry gives you some pleasure, then I do not begrudge it. And belike 'twill keep Master Hayman contented too. There are few enough folks here with any interest in his poetry-writing. If we keep him happy, he will be less likely to go haring off back to England."

"And that is your wish? To keep him here?"

"Aye, he is a sensible enough fellow when he is not talking of poetry." Nicholas smiled. "And he is willing to be guided. You know I did not aim to be governor, for the jealousies and resentments it would cause, but neither did I wish a governor who would come in to rule with an iron fist and lay down decrees to men who have lived here for years. With Hayman in charge, and myself and Holworthy to advise him, I think Bristol's Hope will find success."

Still, when Nicholas came into the house and saw Kathryn reading with Governor Hayman, despite the fact that he had given leave for her to do so, she stood up half-guiltily. She could not help feeling she ought to be busy about something.

"How are my wife's lessons progressing, Governor?" Nicholas asked in a half-jesting tone.

"She shows great promise, indeed. I have long thought that women's minds are as capable as those of men, did we but give them the same opportunity to learn."

"If you could teach her to figure and keep account-books, that would be a most useful skill! I have a good crew of men here, but none of them is learned, and I am in great need of a steward to help manage this plantation. But I think my Kathryn has not the head for numbers, though she is a most capable housewife."

"Indeed, if you were to teach any woman to keep accounts," Kathryn said, "it ought to be Nancy. I have never known anyone better at keeping count and organizing things in a household. She lacks only the skill of writing down the figures."

She glanced out the window, as she spoke, at the brewhouse where Nancy and Hannah had just come out after straining the mash to begin a new batch. Kathryn was certain Nancy had an account in her head of exactly how many kegs of ale were in store, along with how many sacks of flour, how many jars of preserves, what vegetables had been harvested from the garden. When the company ship came to take their fish to market and trade them winter supplies in return, Nancy would likewise know how much molasses, grain and other supplies came off the ship in those barrels. Perhaps it would make sense to teach her to write it all down.

"Who knows, our little circle of scholars may yet expand over the winter," said Governor Hayman. "I expect that today Master Willoughby will return to take me back to Harbour Grace. He has already been away longer than—"

"Mistress! Mistress!" Daisy burst through the door. "Bess sent for you. She's having terrible pains, and reckons the baby's coming early."

"Mercy, yes, this is more than a month before her time. I will come at once," Kathryn said. Her three children were all playing while Nancy's baby slept in the cradle, but Nancy and Hannah could take charge of them now. "Your pardon, Governor, I will have no more time for tales today. Jonathan, can you pass mama's bag from the hook there?"

She and Bess had both expected this new baby to be born in November, but babies did not always keep time by their mothers' calendars. As Bess had borne two healthy sons already, Kathryn had good hopes of success this time. She added a few items to her midwife's bag from her store of fresh and dried herbs.

The first birthing-bed Kathryn had assisted at was Bess's older boy, Will. Since then she had helped with Bess's Matt and Nancy's little Lizzie, and of course she had had two more children of her own. What had once seemed a dark mystery was now familiar ground, and she talked to other women whenever she had the opportunity, about what could go wrong at a birth and what a midwife might do to set it right. Elsie Holworthy, who was expecting her next one in the winter, had already said that she would be easier in her mind if Kathryn could be there for the birth.

Frank was pacing the floor of his house with Matty up in his arms and Will clinging to his leg. "It frightened them, when she cried out," he said as Bess shrieked again.

Behind her, Kathryn heard Daisy telling Frank to take the children up to the big house. Kathryn went straight to the bedchamber where Bess half-sat, half-lay against her pillows. As soon as Kathryn saw her, she knew this was no false pain. The mattress was soaked; Bess's waters had broken.

"Too soon! Too soon!" Bess shouted as Kathryn began to peel back her nightdress.

"Nay, nay, we must have been wrong in the reckoning," she said. Daisy, who had come to her sister's side as well, joined in the refrain. "Aye, 'twas a mistake, you were further along than you thought."

"No, no! I know when I last had my flowers, I cannot be near to my time yet! Too soon! Too soon!"

"Hush now, hush. All will be well." Daisy stroked Bess's hair and face, then took hold of her hands. "Hold my hands tight, now. Mistress Kathryn will do what's needful, and when it hurts, you cry out and hold me tight."

We could use a third pair of hands here, Kathryn thought; they needed someone to brew Bess a soothing medicine for the pain. But Frank was already gone. Daisy's task would be to keep Bess calm, and Kathryn's to birth the babe. She had already had her hand up in Bess's privy parts and knew that the way was fully open. She could tell, by this time, how much of a hands-breadth was needed for an infant to be pushed through. Soon Bess would feel the urge to push, that urge that no woman could deny.

When there was a brief lull between Bess's pains, Kathryn bade Daisy to go boil some water. "She'll need a posset made with mugwort if this goes on much longer. We can't let her suffer with nothing to ease the pains." One sure remedy to ease labour was supposed to be giving the birthing woman a few spoonfuls of another nursing mother's milk. Kathryn had never tried this, but it was another good reason to want Nancy here, since she was still nursing Lizzie and might be able to supply that physic.

"Don't leave me!" Bess screamed, grabbing her sister's hands.

Just at that moment there was a noise from the other room. A man's voice, and a woman's. The door closed again, and Nancy was in the sleeping chamber with them.

"Lord ha' mercy. So the baby is coming, is it?" Nancy glanced briefly at Bess. "I'll boil water. You'll show me from your bag what's needed to brew?" she asked Kathryn.

"Yes. Thank you. I' faith, the posset would be good, but there's something might help even more," Kathryn said, and quickly explained the remedy she had learned from her mother. Nancy's eyes widened a little at the request, but she went out into the other room, and returned not long afterwards with two cups, one filled with the herb-infused ale posset, and one with a little milk.

Bess's pains went on all afternoon and into the evening. She was exhausted with pushing, and despite Kathryn's encouragement to try getting onto a stool or squatting on the bed, nothing helped. Neither the posset nor Nancy's milk did much to speed things along.

At one point during those endless hours she heard Nancy talking to one of the men out in the main room and thought that Frank had come to check on his wife. "No, that was Ned," Nancy told her. "A ship has come into the harbour, so they're all busy about that now."

"That must be Willoughby and his men, come to take the governor and Captain Dermer to Harbour Grace," Kathryn said.

"I thought he said a ship, not a boat. It may be the company ship, come to load the fish in the morning."

"'Twill have to be done without my help, then," Kathryn said. The day in fall that the fish was sent to market and the winter supplies unloaded was always a busy one requiring all hands to help, but right now her talents were needed here.

"Perhaps this will be over by morning."

It was over before morning, in fact, just in the hour before dawn, when Bess finally pushed out of her body the small, still, blue-grey creature. Kathryn had known for hours it was unlikely he would survive, and when she saw him she knew he would never draw breath. But she tried all the same, wrapping him and warming him and rubbing him, pulsing his little chest with her fingers, even trying to blow breath into the cold, still mouth. Bess, exhausted, wept into Daisy's arms, and Kathryn remembered her own first birthing-bed, so many years ago. The little bundle that her mother and the midwife had taken away, and how she herself had cried, first in Nancy's arms and then in her mother's.

"It was a little boy," she said to Bess now. "He is gone to be with God already. Do you want to see him?"

Bess did not answer, but Nancy was there with a bowl of water, and Kathryn realized what she must do. She did not know if it was even right, when the baby was so early, and had never drawn a breath, nor did she know if a woman was allowed to perform that simple act. But she dipped a little of the water onto the still, cold forehead and said, "In the name of the Father, Son, and Holy Ghost, I baptize you..." She hesitated, and looked at Daisy.

"Francis, for his father, I suppose."

"Francis Tipton." She did not know if there were any other words that ought to come after that. "May your soul be safe with Jesus, little Francis," she said. When she looked back at the bed, Bess was reaching out her arms for the bundle, and Kathryn bent down to show her the baby.

When Bess had fallen into an exhausted sleep in Daisy's arms, Kathryn put the stillborn baby in a basket. "I will go and break the news to Frank," Nancy offered, "then go down to our house and nurse Lizzie before I go to help with the work today. You should sleep. I got some rest during the night, but you had none."

"We all should rest."

"But if there is a ship waiting to take the fish and put off our supplies, 'twill not be a day of rest. Daisy'll not leave Bess's side anyway; Hannah will be at your house to feed everyone. I want to keep an eye to the supplies. Being there as 'tis all unloaded will help me to plan for what food we have over the winter."

"What will we do with..." Kathryn gestured towards the basket.

"Bring it up to Frank, I suppose. He will have to bury it."

"Beside Isaac. Is it right? To bury it in a graveyard? I hardly know. And I did not know if 'twas right to baptize it, either, only I thought it would give Bess some peace."

"You did right." Nancy stood up, put on her cloak. "I know not what a minister might say, but if the poor thing had a soul, I'm sure God would have mercy on it."

"I suppose I will have to think about such things if I keep delivering babies."

Nancy smiled. "You will have to keep delivering babies, so long as the rest of us keep having them."

Kathryn looked down into her cup. She had brewed an infusion of lavender, not just for Bess but herself and Nancy and Daisy also, to ease everyone's nerves. She remembered that only a few hours before she had been enchanted by Governor Hayman's loan of a poetry book. She thought of Nicholas's pleasure at how things were unfolding in the colony, his sense that this would be a good winter. All those things were still real, but they seemed distant, as if they were happening on the other side of a pane of glass.

After Nancy left, Kathryn built up the fire and cooked some pottage. Then she left the little house, passing the bustling crew on the dock. Boatloads of fish were being rowed out to the ship while barrels and crates of their winter supplies were rowed in. Nicholas was there with his men to take care of it—and Nancy who, as Kathryn herself had told Nicholas, had a better mind for keeping track of goods than anyone on the place.

Exhausted, Kathryn fell into her bed. When she awoke, it was to afternoon light and the sounds of people moving about in the rest of the house. She had slept in her clothes, removing only her coif and apron, but her kirtle had blood on it and she took the time to change both shift and kirtle before going downstairs.

Frank must by now have buried the baby and gone back to Bess, and Daisy was likely still at their house. Bess must be resting well; if she had taken a turn, someone would have sent for Kathryn.

"Nancy told me the two of you and Daisy put in a hard night," said Ned when he saw her coming down the stairs.

"Not as hard as poor Bess."

"Aye, that's true. Frank took it hard, poor fellow. Oh, and the master said to tell you when you woke that he's gone off to Harbour Grace for the day. He and Rafe have taken the governor back in our boat. Willoughby never came back for them. Captain Dermer went aboard the *Susan Mary*—that's the Bristol company ship—he's back to England for the winter."

"Are you hungry?" Nancy was there now, putting a warm bowl of stew in Kathryn's hands. Kathryn sat at the table, and then her children were all about her, pulling on her skirts, Jemmy and Alice wanting to sit up in her lap.

When Nicholas and Rafe returned in the shallop, Nicholas looked troubled. It was almost nightfall. Over the evening meal he told the household what he had seen when their small boat, following not far behind the company ship, had left Musketto Cove.

"We meant to head south, of course, for Harbour Grace, while the *Susan Mary* was sailing northeast. She already made her stop in Harbour Grace yesterday to pick up their fish, and was heading out of Conception Bay and making for St. John's before the crossing back. But she was just past Carbonear Island when we saw another ship, one I've not laid eyes on before, making directly for her. And that ship fired on the *Susan Mary*."

"What? Was it Spaniards? Pirates?" Ned asked.

Nicholas shook his head. "I know not. I could not see their colours. The shot was likely a warning shot and did not hit the *Susan Mary*, but she fired back and grazed their railing. The other ship retreated. Into Carbonear Harbour."

"Seems the pirates were not well prepared, if pirates they were," Hal Henshaw said. "They fired a warning shot, took a single hit, and retreated. Some captain thinking he might make an easy capture, finding one merchant vessel travelling alone."

Nicholas nodded. "That is what we thought as well. Of course, we made for Harbour Grace then, as planned, the governor much shaken by the sight. And at Harbour Grace, Jem Holworthy told me that they've no idea why Willoughby and his six men have not returned, for they intended only a few days' voyage to Carbonear."

There was a moment's silence around the table, then Ned said, "So Willoughby leaves with six men and goes to his father's land in Carbonear—"

"Where we know the Pikes dwell, who have dealings with all sorts of pirates," Kathryn put in.

"And hard on the heels of that, an unknown pirate ship out of Carbonear fires on an English vessel carrying all our summer's fish—our first catch as our own colony, our first chance to establish ourselves," Nicholas finished.

"Willoughby has only a shallop, though," Ned said. "And you said this was a ship?"

Nicholas nodded. "Thirty tons, at least. But if Willoughby and Pike are tangled up in this business, who knows what ships and captains Pike may have connections with?"

"Perhaps 'tis a coincidence," Rafe said.

"That may be," Nicholas said. "Perhaps Thomas Willoughby is a loyal Englishman who has only found himself delayed by a day or so and will soon be back at Harbour Grace."

"A damned strange coincidence, if it is one," said Ned, and all around the table, the men nodded their heads.

SIXTEEN

Advice is Sought

MUSKETTO COVE, DECEMBER 1618

Only this of me
Is the ambition; that I may but see...
My country-earth; since I have long been left
To labours, and to errors, barr'd from end,
And far from benefit of any friend...
                    —*Homer's Odysseys*, Book 7, 207–12

TWO GRAVES, NOW, IN THE CLEARING BEYOND THE GAR-den. Ned wondered, as he passed the spot, who would be the next to lie there. A grim thought; he would not have said it aloud to anyone except, perhaps, Nancy. In the right mood.

They all thought of him as the cheerful one, the fellow whose good humour would keep other people's spirits aloft when the dark winter days closed in. And he was that fellow, most of the time. Or he had been, once, and was trying to find his way back to that place.

Still he leaned for a moment on the railing of the garden, looking at the two wooden crosses. There were no old people in the colony yet; Governor Hayman was the eldest man in Bristol's Hope, and he was hale and hearty. But babies and young children were as fragile as autumn leaves. Ned thought of Lizzie, and under his breath said a prayer that was nothing more than *please, God.*

He and Nancy had suffered so much, separately, these past few years, that now they were together their little family should surely be spared any hardship. They should both get to live and grow old and die in their bed with their perfect, unharmed children and grandchildren all around them, some day forty or fifty years hence. What a fancy, to think any life could be so charmed.

"You are deep in thoughts, my friend," said a voice behind him.

As he nodded a greeting to Tisquantum, Ned thought that perhaps, after all, there was one other person in the cove that he might voice his darker thoughts to. Save for Nancy, of all the folks at Musketto Cove, this was the person Ned felt most at ease with. Perhaps it was because he and Tisquantum were the only men here who had travelled back and forth across the broad ocean, to many different lands. They two, and Nancy, knew more of the wildness and the wickedness that was out there than the other settlers did.

"It is a dark thought indeed," Ned said, and told Tisquantum what he had been thinking. The other man raised his brows.

"It is not strange. Someone will die. Someday we all will die."

"Ah, I knew you would cheer me up."

They both laughed. "Death comes to all, and we are coming to winter, the bad time for sickness," Tisquantum said. "It is natural to think of it."

"*Memento mori,*" Ned said. He knew no other Latin, but he had picked up the phrase in his travels. "I hope we have no outbreak of sickness here this winter. I think of what befell Mistress Kathryn's family. I went to see them in Bristol, and they were all well. I returned a few months later, and half the family was dead."

"So swift it happens. I think of my family and wonder what has become of them. But now I have some hope that I may go and find out."

"You are sure, then, that Captain Dermer will return?"

"Yes. He wants a new land to explore, and his rich men in England want a colony. I told him of Patuxet, that the ground is fertile around there. He was—disappointed, that I would not come back to England this winter. He says these rich men will open their purses more, if there is a Wampanoag man to tell them of our land."

"But you would not go."

"No. I have worked so hard to get this close to my homeland. He says, too, that if he takes me to England, it is better if I am baptized a Christian, so that he can show that the natives will be..." He hesitated, searching for the word. "Converted."

"And you'll not be baptized?"

"No, this I will never do."

Ned supposed he ought to be shocked, or at least to disapprove. But he and Tisquantum had spoken of this before: he would live alongside Christians, learn their tongue and customs and wear their garments, but he would not undergo the rite that would convert him into one of them, even as the price of a passage home. "Well, every man must follow his own conscience," was all Ned said. "Come home and have supper with us."

As they walked towards Ned and Nancy's house, Tisquantum added, "There is another reason I will not go to England this winter."

"Ah. And would that be to do with Daisy?" Ned ventured.

"Yes. The matter is become..." He searched for an English word.

"Tangled? Complicated?"

Tisquantum thought. "I like your first word. *Tangled*. This is like rope, when it is not put away with care, is it not? It makes knots, and is hard to put straight."

"Yes. 'Tis quite the tangle, we might say about a situation that is difficult to solve."

"May I speak of this—this tangle—with your wife?" Tisquantum asked. "I will value the guiding of a woman, but I do not know if it is proper to ask."

"'Tis proper to ask anything at our place."

As they ate, Tisquantum laid out his problem. He was fond of Daisy; if he found her same qualities in a Wampanoag woman she would be an ideal wife. "I think she would accept me as a husband, also, if I were an Englishman."

"You may be right," Nancy said. "She speaks well of you." Privately, Nancy had told Ned that Daisy was like a foolish young maid in love when she talked of Tisquantum, but she would not, of course, say that to the man himself.

"But I am no Englishman, and she is no Wampanoag. Would Daisy come to Patuxet with me, to live as we live?"

Nancy glanced at Ned, as if weighing how much to say. "'Twould be best to ask her yourself. She may believe that you are prepared to stay with us and live as an Englishman. Have you told her you are set against doing that? For if not, she may be spinning herself a fancy."

"Spinning herself..." Tisquantum repeated the words slowly.

"Dreaming of something that cannot come true," Ned suggested, and Tisquantum nodded.

"I fear this very much. Things have so passed between us that I think among your people, it would be required of me to offer her marriage."

"Would it be different, with your own people?" Ned asked.

Tisquantum hesitated. "A Wampanoag woman would have...how do I put it? Our women are more free than English women are, to tell if they want this man or that one."

"She'd have more say in it, you mean, than an Englishwoman might?" Ned suggested.

"Yes, that is so. Among you English, a woman's father or brother often speaks for her, in the matter of marriage. But Daisy has none."

"She is a widow, twice over," Nancy said. "Things are somewhat different for a widow. I doubt anyone would gainsay Daisy's right to choose her own husband, given what she has suffered."

Again, Tisquantum nodded thoughtfully. Any talk of suffering always moved him deeply, Ned had noticed.

"'Twould be simple enough," Ned said later in the evening when he and Nancy lay in bed together, "if Tisquantum would just stay here. He is well liked and a good worker. If he were content to bide here, he and Daisy might marry, and all would be well."

"But it would not be well for him," Nancy said. "He wants to be among his own people. We were both long away from here, and surely you can understand wanting to return home? I know I can."

"Ah, but I thought 'twas me you wanted to return to," Ned said, gently tracing her lips with a fingertip, smiling at her in the darkness. "Was it Cupids Cove that drew you back, or the thought of getting back to me? There was a time I thought I'd gladly live in any little tilt on any shore along the Atlantic, if only I could find you and have you there with me."

He thought Nancy might laugh. Time and love had softened the edges of those hard years' memories, so sometimes they could almost laugh now, about some of what they had gone through. But she was serious, frowning a little, and he traced the frown, too, with his fingers.

"'Tis true. I knew if we found each other, we could make a home anywhere. I was safe and comfortable in Virginia, but I did not want to settle there. I wanted to be with people I felt were my own. And yet... oh, I cannot explain it; you know how I am with words."

"Try," he urged gently. "I know talking with Tisquantum tonight touched on some memory for you. I could see it as we were talking."

"He makes me think of Matachanna, and of Pocahontas, and the rest of them," she said. "They had this longing for Virginia—Tsenacommacah, as they called it. In England they were...like flowers cut from their stems and put in a jug of water. They might look as if they were flourishing, but they were dying, all of them, cut off from their own place. They feel a—a tie, I suppose, to their land. I do not feel that for Bristol, though I was born there. I am sorry. I told you 'twas hard to put into words."

"Some folk feel a stronger tie to home than others, 'tis true," Ned said, "and perhaps all the native people of these parts are like that. So it might be easy for us, and easy for Daisy, to think that the solution is for Tisquantum to stay here. But you think he would never flourish, cut off from his homeland."

"That is how it seems to me," Nancy said. "In tales of romance, true love overmasters every other thing, but I do not think 'tis always so in the real world."

"As long as true love is always the most important thing to you. That is all I ask," he said, claiming her with a kiss.

In the first months after Lizzie was born, they had taken some time to find their way back to lovemaking, for even after Nancy was healed from birthing, she was so often sore and tired from a day and a night of caring for and nursing the child. And those were the summer days when Ned rose before dawn to work at the fish all day, and often fell into bed exhausted, with bed-sport the last thing on his mind.

But now they had begun to find not just tenderness but pleasure again, and as Ned took his wife in his arms, he found he was looking forward to the long, dark winter nights ahead.

Morning came with the baby's cry waking them before the light did. As Nancy fed Lizzie, Ned built up the hearth fire, then went out to the privy. The morning was crisp and cold, with a light skimming of snow on the ground. Soon winter would be here in earnest. He hoped their little house was ready for it. He had already hammered sailcloth over the window, which made the house gloomier inside, but a good deal warmer. "Someday," he told Nancy as they ate their morning meal, "we'll get ourselves a glass window."

"Oh, and how are we to do that?"

"The same way Master Nicholas and Kathryn got theirs. On a ship from England."

"How would we pay for it?"

"Aye, that's the sticking point, to be sure." As long as Ned fished all summer they would have their share of whatever Nicholas Guy's plantation earned in trade from the Bristol merchants, to supplement what they could raise and grow and harvest and hunt. Luxuries like glass windows—well, there was no easy way to get those. Ned was grateful he'd not married a woman with a taste for fine things, but he wanted to give them to her all the same. "If Kathryn Guy and Elsie Holworthy can have glass windows, Nancy Perry should have them too."

"Aye well, maybe we'll get one as the Holworthys did. By moving into someone else's house and taking it over," Nancy said with a laugh.

The big house at Harbour Grace, a match for the Guys' house at Musketto Cove, had been built by Thomas Willoughby the year before as his own home, but when Governor Hayman had arrived, everyone had agreed he ought to board with Willoughby and his servants in that fine big house. Willoughby's man Higgs had cooked for them, as he had done before the governor arrived. Then, when Willoughby and some of his men—Higgs among them—had unexpectedly disappeared a month ago, the governor was left alone in the big house with two fishing servants.

Jem Holworthy, who had been living with his wife and children in a partly finished house, had announced to all that he and his wife would be honoured to serve the governor, and moved themselves into Willoughby's house. Everyone had begun calling it "the Governor's House"; the Holworthys had made themselves quite at home and everyone concerned seemed happy with the situation.

Ned was on his own roof, repairing a leak, when he saw two men approaching on the trail that connected Musketto Cove to Harbour Grace. It was John Crowder and William Spencer, well bundled up against the cold of the day. Now that Ned and Nancy were on the south side of the cove, theirs was the first place anyone passed by when coming by the woods trail from Harbour Grace. The two men, seeing Ned on the roof, stopped to greet him.

"What brings you through the woods today?" Ned wondered aloud.

"We wanted to talk with Master Guy. But 'twould be good if you came along as well, if you can spare a few minutes. We should gather all the men. Governor Hayman said 'twas best we warn you all," Crowder said.

"Warn us? That sounds like a serious enough matter to get off the roof for," Ned said, moving towards the ladder. What, he wondered, could be worth a warning? Once the fishing fleet had left in the autumn, pirates left as well, and the small harbour at Musketto Cove was already partly filled with ice: there was no danger by sea. Danger by land, perhaps? Had wild beasts, or the elusive native people, launched an attack on the Harbour Grace settlers?

The men of Musketto Cove gathered in the fish store down on the wharf, the room still smelling of the salt cod that had been stored there all summer. Perched on boxes and barrels, they listened as John Crowder told his tale.

"These last weeks—since the fishing was over—things have gone missing. Nothing of great value—some rope, a few knives and axes, some nails. We never knew when or how it happened, for 'twas the sort of stuff you'd not notice till you went looking for it. Then Mistress

Holworthy went to the stores t'other day and found that a whole barrel of flour was gone."

"Swiping tools and the like? That's Indians," Frank said with some confidence. "I've heard tales from the summer fishermen. Anything left behind in a fishing station over winter, cooking pots and tools and the like, is gone when they come back in the spring. The natives come and take it." He glanced, half-apologetically, at Tisquantum, who sat on the edge of the group.

Several of the men agreed that they had heard similar stories, but Nicholas Guy said, "I can well believe that might happen when a fishing station is left unguarded over the winter. But to come into a community where people are living? I am not sure the men of the forest would do that."

"There's more than that," Spencer said. "We've six pigs at Harbour Grace, and this morning when Crowder's missus went out to feed them, there was only five. Someone came by night and stole a pig. We never saw no strange boats anytime, but last night there was ice in the harbour, so for certain we know 'twas not done by anyone who came by sea. Someone came overland, brazen as brass, and stole one of our pigs."

"Still sounds like Indians to me," Frank said. "They'd come by land, and they know the country."

"We have another reason to think it may not be the native folk," Crowder said. "The governor has taken a chill since the weather turned cold, else he'd have come himself today," he added. "but he is of the opinion this was done by Christian men, perhaps even Englishmen."

"There was some fair brazen pirates around this autumn," Rafe said. "There was that attack on the *Susan Mary*, and the tales we heard of fishing stations down by Port de Grave that were raided. But pirates don't stay the winter, nor come by land."

"What if they do, though?" Ned found himself saying aloud. "We thought Thomas Willoughby might have turned pirate. And he may well think he has a right to some of what's at Harbour Grace."

Nicholas Guy nodded. "And if he is at Carbonear and has made common cause with Gilbert Pike, why then, there are trails through the woods that he and his men could take. But you said you had other reasons for thinking 'twas done by Christian men?"

"Aye," said Crowder. "With the smaller thefts, there was no sign of who might have come or gone. But this morning, on the wall of the pigsty, something was carved. Not words, nor a name, but like an engraving of a crown. As if 'twas done with the point of a dagger."

"A crown?" echoed Nicholas Guy.

"'Twas no great work of art—done in haste, of course—but 'twas clear 'twas meant to be a crown. Is that something a native would carve? Or would they leave a message for us at all?"

Now Tisquantum spoke up. "In my lands, the people will take things that English or French or Dutch sailors leave behind, when they are gone. Then it is for anyone to take that needs. But to come in like a thief when men are sleeping in their beds? I do not say that Wampanoag would do that. I do not know the people of this land, but it would seem strange to me."

"And would they even know the symbol of a crown, or what it meant?"

"Come to that, even if 'twas carved by an Englishman, what would it mean? If I saw someone leave behind no word save a sketch of a crown," Nicholas Guy said, "I would think that person was trying to say he was acting in the King's name. But who'd steal a pig in the name of King James?"

The conversation went on, 'round and 'round in circles, and then the Harbour Grace men went home and the men of Musketto Cove had to tell the tale to their womenfolk so it could be discussed again. Everyone had a guess, but there was nothing to be had beyond speculation, other than a suggestion that they better secure their outbuildings at night.

Later that evening, back in their own house, Ned asked Nancy what she thought. Could Thomas Willoughby not only turn to piracy, but attack his own former plantation?

"I'd not put it past him, the scoundrel."

"You do not like him, do you? And yet if I remember aright, 'twas he who came to your defense when you were falsely accused all those years ago."

Nancy finished nursing Lizzie and put her down in her cradle. Only a few weeks ago, Lizzie would have lain on her back in the cradle and settled herself to sleep, but now she pulled herself to sit up and look around. She'd be getting herself up on her two feet and trying to toddle about before long, Ned thought with pride.

"Willoughby had his own reasons for defending me," Nancy said. "He was a conceited coxcomb who thought he was too good to work with his hands, and light in his ways with the women. Like the blackguard George Whittington, but with something added. That cocky way that men who are rich and well-born have, of thinking every woman owes them. The way he carried on with Kathryn, I feared 'twould damage her reputation."

"But she'd have had more sense, surely, than to allow him any liberties," Ned said. He was as fond of Kathryn in his way as Nancy was; when they were all young in Bristol and he was an apprentice in Kathryn's father's house, he had fancied himself in love with the master's daughter. That hopeless romance had faded, but the warmth he felt towards her lingered. He could not imagine that she would ever have been foolish enough to encourage Thomas Willoughby.

Nancy laid the bowls back on their shelf, wiped her hands on her apron, and went to the hearth to throw on another log. The bright shower of sparks made Lizzie look up and cry "Ba!"—her only word so far. "Fire!" Nancy said; she and Ned had fallen into the habit that all parents of small children seemed to do, of repeating simple words in response to the nonsense babblings.

Nancy sat down by the hearth and took up her work basket; she was fashioning a blanket from strips of worn-out clothes.

"I do not know that Kathryn would have confessed it to me, if anything improper had passed between them. She would have been ashamed. Indeed, I'd have been best not to speak of it, even to you." She shot Ned a sharp look that told him he needed to keep quiet.

"Surely now, there should be no secrets between husband and wife," Ned said, stooping to kiss her cheek.

"I've none, I know that much," Nancy said. "And I know not whether Thomas Willoughby has anything to do with these thefts at Harbour Grace, but I'd not be one bit surprised if he does."

SEVENTEEN

A Winter Journey is Begun

MUSKETTO COVE AND HARBOUR GRACE,
JANUARY 1619

Unspeakable in length now are the nights.
Those that affect sleep yet, to sleep have leave,
Those that affect to hear, their hearers give.
—Homer's Odysseys, Book 15, 518–20

T HE NEW YEAR WAS RUNG IN, THE TWELFTH NIGHT feast done, and the harbour at Musketto Cove was frozen solid with a layer of snow on top. Everyone on the Guy plantation had gone over to Harbour Grace for Twelfth Night; that had been a clear, bright day and the snow was packed hard, making it relatively easy to travel through the woods. But snow had fallen every day since then, no single storm but a gentle, relentless veil of snowflakes blown about by the wind, and the little cove was cut off from its neighbours in Harbour Grace. By mid-January even the three houses at Musketto Cove seemed to be three separate islands, and the easy traffic back and forth between them that prevailed in spring, summer and autumn had slowed to a trickle.

At least, with the harbour frozen and the woods choked with snow, there was little danger from outside the community. Since the theft of the pig at Harbour Grace, there had been no further mysterious thefts there, and none at Musketto Cove.

Nancy lit rushlights around her house, trying to coax a little more light from the shadows. The sailcloth over the window kept out the worst of the wind but let in little daylight. It ought to have been gloomy, this dark, enclosed winter life, yet she found a kind of pleasure in it. Life was so busy in the other seasons, a constant round of work. There was little time for herself, Ned, and Lizzie to be together in their own house. Now, as winter settled around them, Nancy pulled her little family and their house around her like a blanket for warmth.

This morning, she was mending worn clothes and letting down hems for Lizzie, while Ned worked at carving a wooden headboard for the little bed he was building—a bed that would be Lizzie's when she outgrew the cradle. Lizzie sat on the floor in front of the fire, attempting to bite the head off a rag doll Nancy had sewn for her out of scraps, trying out her four new teeth. She reached forward to grab at her other toy, a cloth ball, fell on her face when it proved to be just out of reach, and howled in frustration. Then she set about figuring out how to get herself upright again.

As Nancy helped her daughter sit up, the door opened with a rush of cold air and flurries. "Mercy, 'tis nice and warm in here," said Kathryn, bursting into the room. "I do think in this weather, a smaller house is better. You've less space to heat."

"And no upper chamber for the heat to escape into," Nancy agreed. "Come warm yourself by our fire; 'tis bitter cold out there."

But Kathryn had something more serious than the weather on her mind. "One of the servants came over from Harbour Grace. Elsie Holworthy's pains have started. Only faint they were this morning, but of course more than an hour would have passed since he left their plantation, and 'twill take me some time to gather my things. I came to ask..."

She hesitated, her eyes dropping to Lizzie. "I should not ask," Kathryn corrected herself. "You cannot leave Lizzie, and come all the way to Harbour Grace just to assist me. Sallie Crowder is over there, and she will be a good enough help. Or I might take Daisy, I suppose."

"Either of them is capable, but I think Daisy is not eager to help in a birthing chamber again, not so soon after Bess lost her baby," Nancy said. "And if there be any trouble, you'll need an extra woman. Sallie has her own work to do, and Elsie's young ones to look to as well. If we bundle her up well, there is no reason I cannot take Lizzie. Ned could come with us in case we run into difficulty on the trail."

"Yes indeed!" Ned stood up and put down his carving knife with such alacrity that Nancy was struck by the quick, unsettling realization that he was eager to be up and doing, perhaps less contented in their safe little winter nest than she was.

James Marshall, one of the Harbour Grace fishing servants, led the way through the woods. Ned, who had rigged up a carrier to put Lizzie on his back, brought up the rear, with the two women in between. The snow was deep, and they made slow progress.

In his first winter at Musketto Cove, Nicholas Guy had discovered a rare opportunity to practise his trade as a cobbler. Some of the settlers had gone out on the ice at the end of winter to hunt and kill the seals that came in close to shore at that season. The meat was welcome, but the seal pelts were even more useful: a warm, sturdy skin covered with fur. Nicholas crafted winter boots for himself and Kathryn out of the first seal pelt he got; they were warmer and drier than any leather boots sent out from England, and since then he had made a few more pairs after every winter's seal hunt. Every man and woman at Musketto Cove now had a pair of sealskin boots, and today Nancy was grateful for hers.

When they passed underneath a fir tree whose boughs were laden with snow, a branch knocked against Nancy's hat and dislodged its cold, wet burden all over her, snow getting even inside the collar of her cloak. "Ugh, this snow is better to look upon than to wear," she said, shaking off the worst of it.

"To think, you might have stayed in Bermuda, or in Virginia," Kathryn said. "No such winter weather there."

Nancy had thought about this often during the two winters that had passed since her return. "Virginia was well enough, I suppose, but 'twas cruel hot in summer. There are worse fates than being cold."

"True enough. I would love to see that land, though," Kathryn said wistfully.

"When people talk of any of the colonies," said Ned, plodding along behind them, "they only tell of the good things—the sunshine and rich soil in Virginia, abundant fish and the clear air out here. But every climate has its hardships."

"I wonder will Governor Hayman be so enamoured of this land, once he has passed a winter here?" Kathryn said.

"I'd say he will have a good deal more respect for woollen undergarments and fur coats," Nancy said. "He'll not have experienced anything like this, living in a fine town house in England."

Governor Hayman was still working on his poems about the New Found Land. "Such an exquisite country, the air so healthful and good for all ailments, the landscape of such stunning beauty. I know if only I could capture it in verse, and have it published in England, we could inspire a good many more folk to come out here," he had told Kathryn.

"But do we want this place to be settled with the kind of folk who read his poetry?" Nancy had asked when Kathryn told her this. And despite her great respect for Governor Hayman, Kathryn had laughed aloud. A settler's life, they all knew, was much better suited to practical folk than to dreamy poets. The governor might think the New Found Land was idyllic, but only because the people around him laboured hard to make it so.

An hour and a half of walking through the snow led them out of the woods trail to the crest of a little hill looking down on the cleared land of the Harbour Grace plantation. It was laid out very like their own land at Musketto Cove, with one big house and two smaller ones flanking it, though in Harbour Grace the houses were all beside each other on the same side of the shore. A byre and other outbuildings were dotted between the houses.

Governor Hayman lived in the big house with the Holworthy family. Jem Holworthy was a famously quiet and reserved man, but his father was a wealthy Bristol merchant, and it seemed he intended to step into the role of country squire here just as Nicholas Guy had done at Musketto Cove. The Crowders had their own smaller house, while the fishing servants who had stayed over the winter lived in the third house, which Holworthy had originally built for himself.

Sallie Crowder, who had been tending to Mistress Holworthy, was relieved to see them. "Oh, Mistress Guy, she is well and her pains still a ways apart, but all the same 'tis glad I am that you are here! I am no midwife, and happy to have one."

Nancy saw the half-smile that flickered over Kathryn's face. *Likely 'tis the first time anyone has called her a midwife*, Nancy thought. And as Kathryn unpacked her bag of herbs and remedies, laying out little pouches and jars on a table in the Holworthys' sleeping chamber, Nancy suddenly saw her friend in a new light. Neither of them was yet thirty years old, and Kathryn, for all she had borne three children, still looked more like a young maid than a matron, with her still-glossy dark curls and softly rounded cheeks. Yet for a moment Nancy could imagine her years in the future, her hair turned grey and lines on her brow, the wise-woman of Bristol's Hope.

"I'll bring hot water from the hearth," Nancy said aloud, to shake off the strange mood. She was not in the habit of looking at people and imagining what they might become in the future. Kathryn simply *was* a midwife, in a place where there were no older women with more experience.

After the terrible time they had endured in Bess's birthing chamber a few months earlier, Kathryn was relieved that Mistress Holworthy's labour was progressing smoothly. "'Twill be some time yet, but I foresee no trouble," she told Nancy. "Go and sit down to dinner with the rest of them. I will call for you if I need you."

Nancy helped Sallie Crowder lay the midday meal on the table and everyone ate together: the Crowders and their little boy, Jem Holworthy and his two children, the servants, and Governor Hayman. The governor always enjoyed having Ned and Nancy about, quizzing them about their travels. Today he wanted to talk with Nancy about the Powhatan people of Virginia.

"I think it will end badly, now that their chieftain's daughter is dead," he opined. "A marriage alliance like that might be one way of binding two such different peoples together, but I do not think her people will take it well that she never returned from England."

"I should think you are right, sir," said Nancy. "Pocahontas was much beloved by her father."

"I would not be surprised if ere long we hear word of open warfare between the English and the natives down there. It makes me think that perchance it is a good thing you folks have had so little contact with the people of the land here," he added.

"They seemed peaceable enough, did they not, Crowder, that first time we met them?" Ned said.

"Aye, but not so peaceable when our last party of explorers went to find them," the governor reminded him. "Any people might seem peaceable until they perceive a threat to their homes and their livelihood. That is the tale of mankind all over the earth." Then, as if a new thought had occurred to him, he said to Nancy, "I suppose your mistress will be far too busy today to sit around and talk of books? I looked forward to hearing what she thought of the last book I loaned her."

"She and Master Guy have read some of it aloud to us in the evenings, sir, so I would say she is making good progress with it," Nancy said. The new book was by a man called Purchas who had collected tales from explorers all over the world. Nancy herself thought it quite interesting, and there was even a bit in there about the New Found Land. Certainly it was more in keeping with the colonists' interests than that old book of Greek legends he had given Kathryn first. "But I think you are right," Nancy went on, "that there will be little time for her to sit and visit today. Excuse me, I must go and see if she has need of me. Ned, I will take Lizzie. 'Tis time for her feeding."

In the upstairs chamber, Kathryn reported that Mistress Holworthy's pains were coming closer together and she had given her mugwort to help with the pain. "I doubt we'll need any such remedy as you gave us to help with Bess's labour," she added with a smile.

"Aye, well, 'tis not costly to give," Nancy said as she laid down the trencher she had carried in and settled herself to nurse Lizzie. "I brought you some dinner."

Lizzie was not as ready to settle as her mother was, and kept twisting about, looking around her with her bright eyes. "See, she knows she is in a different house than yours or mine," Kathryn said, "and she is taking it all in. What a clever little thing she is!"

"Aye, she'll be trying to walk and talk in no time, Ned thinks, though I 'low he's trying to rush things a bit."

"Jemmy started walking just at one year old," Kathryn said. "What about yours, Elsie?"

"Oh...I think 'twas...around that time. A year or so. He was...early to talk." Elsie Holworthy panted a little between her words, but Kathryn looked pleased; if she could carry on a conversation at all then the brew must have worked to dull her pain a little.

"Think of it," Kathryn said, "our children, and Bess's and Sal's, they'll all grow up alongside one another here. They will be the children of the New World. The first English children to grow up in this land."

"I suppose they will."

"Perhaps Jemmy and Lizzie will fall in love, who knows? Your daughter and my son. Then we should be family in truth, Nan," Kathryn said, reaching over to twirl her finger in one of Lizzie's wispy reddish curls.

Nancy nodded, keeping her eyes on Lizzie and her attention on getting her to suckle. She did not, could not, meet Kathryn's gaze or reply to what she had said.

I have to tell her. The thought pressed in, more urgent than ever. For more than a year Nancy had guarded her secret, unable to guess how Kathryn might react upon learning they were half-sisters. But if they had children of the same age, growing up together—well, she must be told.

Nancy had heard of cousins marrying. She had a vague idea it was something wealthy people did, to keep land in the family, but she was also fairly certain that the church forbade it. For the children of two sisters, even two half-sisters, to marry could well be a sin. She must tell Kathryn about what she had learned in Bristol, if she could find the right moment.

"Dear God in Heaven!" A scream from the bed alerted her that this certainly was not the right moment. Kathryn moved to Mistress Holworthy's side, and as soon as Nancy had finished feeding Lizzie she went downstairs to give her back to Ned, then returned to help Kathryn with the birthing.

When Nancy returned to the main hall, it was early evening. As in the big house at Musketto Cove, everyone sat around the hearth talking, drawing a few last moments of light and warmth from the fire. Jem Holworthy stood up as Nancy entered.

"A fine healthy daughter for you, Master Holworthy," she said. "Go up and see her."

Nancy came and sat on a bench next to Ned. "Where did you put Lizzie down to sleep?"

He gestured to a pile of quilts close to the hearth. "They've made up a bed for the children here for tonight, so I tucked her down among them. You and I will sleep by the fire, and Kathryn as well, for there'll be no going back to Musketto Cove tonight."

"No, we will wait till morning, I suppose."

Ned shook his head. "You've been so busy in the birthing chamber, you've not looked outside, have you?" The governor's house had two glass windows in the hall, currently shuttered against the cold and snow. "Have you not heard the wind?"

"I paid it no mind."

"There's a storm on. A great gale and sheets of snow coming down. We may not get back to Musketto tomorrow morning. We'll have to bide here until this passes."

EIGHTEEN

A Storm Arises

HARBOUR GRACE, JANUARY 1619

Then from the angry North
Cloud-gath'ring Jove a dreadful storm call'd forth...
            —*Homer's Odysseys*, Book 9, 117–18

"AND THIS WORD IS...*MONSTROUS*, IS THAT RIGHT? *Monstrous kindness*," Kathryn read, her finger tracing the lines in the book. "Yes?"

"Indeed, monstrous kindness," said Governor Hayman, who sat beside her looking at the Homer book. "'Tis a figure of speech that poets use, to say things that sound opposite to one another."

"Same as to say, that's some wonderful bad storm out there," offered Ned as he carried an armload of wood to the hearth.

"*Stayed at gate*," Kathryn read on. "*And heard within the Goddess elevate, A voice divine, as at her web she wrought, Subtle, and glorious, and past earthly thought.*" She paused and sighed with pleasure. "What lovely words. Subtle, and glorious, and past earthly thought."

It was their second day snowbound at Harbour Grace. The usually slow pace of winter had dropped to a languorous crawl; time seemed to barely move. The house was as full as Kathryn knew her own place at home must be: the Crowders and the serving-men had stayed in the governor's house, so that everyone could share one hearth while the storm lasted. Apart from preparing food, most tasks were suspended and life had contracted to this single room. Even Elsie and her new baby had been moved from the more comfortable bed in the upper chamber to a mattress set up near the fire. Everyone else slept on benches or on the floor near the hearth, drawing what warmth they could.

With little work left to do in caring for the new mother and baby, Kathryn felt at a loose end. Nancy had joined Sallie Crowder in the practical tasks of feeding and cleaning. The men, deprived of outdoor work, were keeping the older children entertained. When Governor Hayman asked how Kathryn was getting on with her reading, she had leapt at the chance to read some more of Homer with him.

Back at home, she had been making her way through the book of travellers' tales the governor had loaned her, sharing it with Nicholas who had read some bits aloud to the household. It was informative, but the ancient Greek poem translated into English that the governor had loaned her first was still the most beautiful thing she had ever read. Now that she was perforce in the company of both Hayman and Homer, with little else to do until the storm stilled, she prided herself on how the words came more easily to her tongue than they had done just a few months earlier.

"I know this tale," she said, a few lines later. "I heard it when I was a little girl—about the witch Circe, and all the men she turned into pigs."

"Not such a great leap, as some men go," said Nancy from the hearth, where she was putting a fish pie in to bake.

"God save us!" Ned cried. "Where is that biddable and dutiful wife I was promised? Governor, can you pass a law in this colony bidding wives to respect their husbands?"

"Aye, there is need for such an ordinance," said John Crowder, stealing a kiss from Sallie as she passed from hearth to table.

Governor Hayman beamed. He was a man who loved company and seemed genuinely to enjoy the enforced closeness in the house. "When I write my poem about the New Found Land, I must be sure to include some verses extolling the women who come out here. What a spirited and sturdy lot of goodwives!"

"We could stand to have a few more of them here," Will Spencer said, "else I'll have to go back to England and find one."

"Kind of you to praise us, sir," Sallie Crowder said to the governor. "Perhaps you might pass a law decreeing that our husbands should pay us such compliments more often."

"Never mind, I repent of trying to bring the law into it. If the governor were to start making decrees about matters between husbands and wives, we should have no peace at all," Ned said. "We will simply have to put up with the wives we have. The quiet, subservient kind would likely not make the voyage over here, or stay long if they did."

"I wonder if she really was a witch," Kathryn said. "Circe, I mean."

"Well, 'tis a very old legend, of course—" the governor began.

"No, I know it is only a story, but even in stories, a good many women are branded witches unjustly." She stole a glance at Nancy, who always became quiet when there was any talk of witchcraft. Though Kathryn would never allude to that cruel accusation when they were in company, it was often in her thoughts. "We know a spiteful person can throw an accusation of witchcraft at any innocent woman. But this tale of Circe and Ulysses—for all we know, she may have had good reason to turn those men into pigs. Belike they were acting like pigs, and deserved it!"

"Ah, that is the trouble with teaching poetry to women," Governor Hayman said. "They always interpret it amiss and sympathize with the wrong characters."

Everyone laughed, and Kathryn went on reading aloud, with occasional corrections or explanations from her tutor, until a faint wail alerted her that Elsie had to nurse the baby again. Kathryn went to get a poultice for the new mother's breasts, to help her milk come in.

She felt useful when helping Elsie and the baby; she felt transported when reading Homer with the governor. But by the time everyone sat down to eat the evening meal, Kathryn felt caged and fretful. She wondered what was happening back at Musketto Cove; she thought of Jonathan, Alice and Jemmy with a sharp pang. Only a short distance away through the snow, but it felt as vast as the ocean when there was no way to get home or to send a message.

She did her best to hide her distress, finishing her meal and helping to clear away the pots and pans and trenchers. But her hands betrayed her: she was holding the ewer that had been full of ale, washing it out in a pan of melted snow water, when it slipped from her hands to the floor, shattering.

"Oh! I am so sorry!" She knelt to pick up the pieces. "Nan, Sallie, keep the children away, they might hurt themselves on the broken shards. What a clumsy fool I am!"

"Nay, fret not, Mistress Guy. Anyone may have an accident. I am sure we have another ewer to replace it," Governor Hayman said in a soothing tone.

"Aye, of course. And if not, you can go to the market and buy one," Kathryn said with a shrill laugh, her hands trembling as she picked up the pieces. "Ah! I forgot! There is no market, is there, not for a thousand miles of ocean. Oh, God's teeth, I've cut my finger." Without warning, she was crying, and Nancy was there with a clean cloth, wrapping it around Kathryn's hand, deftly gathering up the rest of the pieces.

"Forgive my poor mistress. While I have the good fortune to be here with my husband and child, she is stayed away from hers, and 'tis only natural she is troubled," Nancy said to the governor.

"Of course, of course." Governor Hayman turned to John Crowder. "Are such storms as these common in winters? Have you ever seen a worse one?"

As he steered attention away from Kathryn's outburst, Nancy leaned in close to Kathryn's ear. "What ails you? Is't truly only being apart from the master and the children?"

"I—I know not. I was all well the first night, for we were so busy with the birthing that I slept soundly afterwards. And yesterday, I could bear it. But now we are here for yet another day and night, and I—I feel trapped, Nan." Kathryn kept her voice pitched low. "If only I could go outside, walk about, I am sure I should feel in my right mind again."

"Every one of us would like that, but 'twill not happen till the snow stops."

"Will it stop? Will it ever?" Kathryn went to the window; though it had both glass and shutters she could feel the icy wind blowing through it. "What if it keeps coming down till the whole house is buried? If we cannot get out to get wood for the fire…"

"Then we will chop up the tables and benches. We'll not freeze or starve. We are no fools. Come, Kat, why are you so wrought up? Tell me."

"I would if I could—" She broke off, looking back at the rest of the people gathered in the room. "The first time I came to Harbour Grace," she whispered, the thought suddenly forming in her head, "'twas more than a year ago. Before the Crowders or the Holworthys came, when it was only Thomas Willoughby and his two servants."

"You told me of this. There was a storm then also, was there not?"

"Yes, a summer storm. That is why I stayed the night."

"And?" Nancy leaned her head in close. "What came of it? Did he, or either of his men—"

"No! Not a one of them laid a hand on me. But I felt—as I feel now. Trapped. I hate the feeling that I cannot get away, Nan." She wiped her tears away. "What a wretch I am to say such things to you. You, who have truly been a captive. You must think me foolish, and ungrateful too."

"I could never think you ungrateful. And you may sometimes be foolish, but not now. Still, if the place makes you uneasy, there's nothing to be done but bear it until we can leave."

"True enough." She reached out and gripped Nancy's hands, hard. "Nan, I am so glad you are here with me. Not only here in Harbour Grace. I mean, how glad I am that you came back."

"Aye, well, not so glad as I am, I'm sure."

Overnight, the wind died down, and the snow stopped. Kathryn woke from a fitful night of tossing and turning in blankets by the fire, chilled on the cold floor. Jem Holworthy knelt at the hearth, feeding the last sticks of wood on to build up the flames.

"I think the storm be over," he told her. "'Twill take some digging, but we may get out today, and you and your folks be on the way home."

By the time the morning pottage was ready to eat, the men had got the door open and dug a pathway that looked like a deep chasm between mountains of snow. Now that they could get outside the animals must be watered and fed again, and more firewood cut, more snow brought in to melt.

Midmorning, while the other men were busy splitting and hauling wood, Ned announced that he and John Crowder would begin clearing the woods trail to Musketto Cove.

"'Twill be too hard for you and Nancy to go through the snow as it is—hard even for me, if I have the baby with me," he told Kathryn. "If we go first with shovels and clear the way, we can tell the folks in Musketto Cove that we are all well. Then we will come back for you."

Kathryn and Nancy followed the men out into the deep snow outside the house, filling their lungs with fresh air for the first time in three days. The storm had been a cold one, with little moisture in the air, so the snow was soft and powdery. With all the trees and outbuildings capped in white, the plantation had the look of something in a fairy story. Master Hayman, who had attempted to lend a hand with the shovelling before being thwarted by backache, was delighted.

"The snows of England are surely never as pure, as deep, as white as this!" he declared. "How bracing and wholesome the air is! And how happy the children are!"

The children, bundled up in woollens and furs, ran and tumbled about in the drifts, laughing and squealing, working off the energy they had bottled up after being cooped up in the house. Nancy held Lizzie up to see the scene. "Your first winter snowstorm," Nancy said to her. "Wave goodbye to papa now. He is going to clear the path so we can go home." She waved on Lizzie's behalf as Ned and Crowder began shovelling their path between the trees.

Kathryn felt her spirits lift with the fresh air and the plan to return home. Once everyone was back inside, a good deal of time was spent peeling off wet layers of clothing from the children and wrapping them in warmer clothes. Nancy and Sallie cooked a hearty stew that warmed everyone inside and out. The joyful release of getting outside, moving around, then coming in to warm up had so cheered everyone that it was some time before they noticed the slamming of the shutters and howling of the wind outside.

"Wind is up again, from the northeast this time," Jem Holworthy said. "It has veered 'round, coming off the water."

"I hope there is not more snow coming with it. We have had full enough of that," the governor said.

Holworthy went to the door, opened it a crack. "Aye, 'tis snowing again. Seems that was only a brief break in the storm. 'Tis coming thick and fast."

"Surely this latest bout of snow will not last long," Master Hayman said. "The heavens must be near emptied by now."

"No doubt Perry and Crowder will have got to Musketto safely afore it got too bad, and be sheltering there now," said Jem Holworthy.

Kathryn looked at Nancy, who sat by the hearth gently rocking Lizzie to sleep. Neither of them said anything at all.

NINETEEN

A Winter Journey is Ended

HARBOUR GRACE, JANUARY 1619

And forth we made sail, sad for loss before...
　　　　　—Homer's Odysseys, Book 9, 762

THEY HAD BEEN IN THE WOODS FOR HOURS, COVERING what Ned reckoned was less than half the distance between Harbour Grace and Musketto Cove, before he admitted to himself that they were in trouble. "We cannot press on—too far!" he said as the blinding snow slapped his face.

"Turn back!" John Crowder shouted above the wind, and the two men turned around, back the way they had come.

They had enjoyed clear weather at first, and the task, though huge, seemed possible. There was so much snow it was sometimes hard to tell where the trail was, but they pushed forward, shovelling their way towards Nicholas Guy's plantation.

Then the wind sprang up and the snow began again. It was wetter this time, the wind coming directly off the ocean, mixing the snow with ice pellets that stung as they hit the skin. It fell so fast and blew about so much that they had no hope of being able to see where they were going.

Turning back seemed the sensible choice. The path back was already cleared, and their feet might find it even if their eyes did not. Perhaps they could reach the warm shelter of the governor's house before dusk.

They found themselves walking in the still-deep snow, even though they had cleared a path. Walking into the endless veil of more snow. Walking with wet snow caking their boots, breeches, jackets, hats. Ned's legs ached. His arms, his back, his lungs ached whenever he drew breath.

They took turns going in front, breaking ground. The third or fourth time they switched positions, Ned moved to the back and trudged behind Crowder. Blind in the snow, he stumbled a moment later—stumbled over Crowder, huddled on the ground.

"Get up, man, get up! We'll freeze to death here!"

"I cannot—I can go no further."

Ned felt Crowder's words in the centre of his gut. He, too, could go no further. He had fought sea battles, ridden out fierce ocean storms, but he had never felt as exhausted as he did at this moment. The lofty spirits that had carried him out of Harbour Grace that morning were battered beyond recognition.

He pulled Crowder to his feet, the two men bracing themselves with arms on each other's shoulders, heads together. "We must...go on!" They were close enough to whisper had they been inside, but Ned bawled the words so Crowder could hear above the wind.

"I need...to rest."

"No. Think...of your wife. Your children."

They pushed on. Ned could not even be sure they were still on the path. He took the lead position again, and nearly walked into a tree.

He knew little of surviving outdoors in such harsh conditions, but what he had heard from other men assured him that it was deadly to rest in such biting cold. *But if we keep moving, are we even moving towards the plantation?*

They had carried little with them, believing they would be at Musketto Cove in a few hours. But no man was such a fool as to go into these woods with nothing at all: each of them carried a small bag beneath his outer coat. Ned had flint and steel, and a few pieces of ship's biscuit.

He looked up at the sky beyond the snow-laden tree branches. For what seemed like hours it had been a grey-white screen of cloud firing volleys of snow and ice at them. Now he saw it was no longer grey-white, but grey-blue. The short winter day was ending.

Ned stopped, turned around. "You are...right. We must...stop," he said, panting between words, pulling icy air into his aching lungs. "Make...shelter. Build...a fire. Eat. But not...lie down. Not sleep."

They used their shovels, and their failing strength, to build the snow up into a wall on the north and east sides of where they stood, to provide a little shelter from the wind. That done, they each ate some bread, then collected moss from the trees and broke off some dead branches to try to start a fire. It was hard work to kindle a flame, but the effort kept them moving until finally they had a small fire in a hollow in the snow, half-sheltered from the wind.

They shuffled 'round the little fire in a rhythmless dance, trying to keep themselves from freezing, occasionally bending to warm their hands at the flickering heat. Thinking that singing might keep them moving better and raise their spirits, Ned started with "Be merry my hearts, and call for your quarts"; the rowdy drinking-tune was the only song he could think of. He supposed a hymn might be more suitable. Crowder joined in half-heartedly; after the second verse they abandoned the effort and went back to their silent shuffling.

It was almost trance-like, and as darkness closed in Ned found it harder and harder to remember why he should keep moving. His feet trudged the pattern around the fire as if his mind were not needed at all to keep going.

Was it possible to sleep while moving? He was walking, walking so slowly around the fire, his vision clouded by the ice frosting his eyelashes and by the still-falling, still-blowing snow. He looked over; Crowder was wordlessly doing the same. He looked down; the fire was out. Trying to rekindle it now was pointless. Soon the snow must stop. Morning would come.

Another little jump, then, in his memory; he was still moving, but his feet stumbled over something. Something like a tree, lying in the path their feet had been wearing for hours now. How could there be a tree? Ned tripped, went down in the snow next to the thing. Turned it over.

"No! No!" Ned knew this was wrong though he could not remember why. Crowder looked so comfortable, lying on the ground. Ned wanted to lie down beside him. Cuddle in close like he did with Nancy in bed. He and Crowder could keep each other warm. Just for a few minutes...

Get up, you daft fool. Lie down and you'll die. Thinking of Nancy had summoned her voice; he heard it as clear as the howling wind. If he lay down...like Crowder was lying...he would die. Like Crowder?

I cannot die. Cannot leave Nancy and Lizzie. Ned pulled at Crowder's arm, shouted in his face, tried to drag him to a sitting position. He couldn't budge the man.

Save yourself. Keep moving. That was Nancy's voice again. Ned stood up, began to walk again. He swung his arms, hoping to get his blood flowing again. Each time he came to the spot where Crowder lay, Ned made another effort to stir him. It was like moving a sack of rocks.

The snow had stopped falling. The wind had died down. What did it mean, that snow was no longer being driven into his face by the wind? It was always snowing. It had always been snowing. It would snow forever.

Again, his feet stumbled over Crowder's body. He no longer thought of the thing on the ground as Crowder, only as Crowder's body. The sky was growing lighter. Morning must be close.

Morning was coming. The storm was over. Crowder's body lay on the ground. Ned kept walking.

There was something he should do now. Ned could not remember what it was. Crowder might have known, but Crowder was beyond knowing. On the ground at Ned's feet.

Ned's feet. They ached like knives were through them. He could not walk any longer, but he had to keep moving. He stamped his feet, back and forth, feeling the little jolts of pain. Swung his arms. Tried to force sounds from his lips. They were too numb. There was nothing.

Do not stop. Move...move. Be not like Crowder. Stay up. Keep moving.

A sound. A voice. A human voice. He did not know it, did not know what it said.

"Ned! Ned Perry!"

He knew those words from somewhere long ago, from a time before the storm. He did not know what they meant but he knew they were important.

He had heard Nancy's voice earlier; now he heard other voices. They were not real, could not be real, just as Nancy's voice had not been real.

But he saw as well as heard; saw two men coming through the snow towards him. He wanted to move his lips, to tell them that Crowder was on the ground. He could say nothing. He could not see the men clearly, only shapes against the snow.

They were there now, all around him. Touching, speaking. Offering him something. They forced something between his frozen lips; he choked and gagged on burning liquid.

He could make out, through snow-blinded eyes, that they were pointing at the body on the ground, asking something, trying to do something with it. He wanted to say that it used to be John Crowder, but he couldn't make his mouth work. There was ice in his beard. Maybe when it melted, his mouth would be free.

That was Ned's last conscious thought before he collapsed in a heap in the snow.

HE OPENED HIS EYES TO SOMETHING HE COULD NOT UNDER-stand. There was no sky, no snow, no wind in his face. It was cold and dark, but not bitter cold like in the woods. One side of his face was warm. His eyes, still blurred, adjusted to see walls, a hearth, people.

A woman's face, close to his. Frowning. She looked angry. "Can you hear me, Ned?"

Again, he tried to move his lips. He was aware of pain in other places: his hands, his feet, his ears. "I can...hear you."

"Oh, thank the Lord, you're nearly sensible." *Nancy*, he thought, and memory came back, not in a flood but in a trickle. The woman was Nancy, his wife, and he was in the governor's house at Harbour Grace.

He and...Ned strained to remember. He had not been alone, out in the cold and dark. "What...." He struggled to form the question. "Crowder?"

Another face near his, not Nancy's. A man; dark skin, darker hair. He knew this man, though not a name for him. "We found John Crowder lying in the snow beside you, my friend. I am sorry to say he died sometime in the night."

"Crowder...he lay down. I tried to get him up. Never lie down in the snow."

"That is right," the man said. *Tisquantum*, Ned's memory offered the name. "Never lie down in the snow. Good counsel. But sometimes the body gives up."

Nancy again, this time with a spoon and some hot broth in a bowl. "Here. Drink some of this."

Gradually, his senses returned as he drank the broth and rested. He began to piece together what had happened. He and Crowder had set out for Musketto Cove, been caught in the second storm, tried to survive outdoors all night. When the snow stopped, Tisquantum, Frank, and Rafe had set out from Musketto Cove on the same mission, to clear the trail and reach the other plantation. They found Ned and brought him back to Harbour Grace with Crowder's body.

Sallie Crowder was hysterical. She fired questions at Ned like gunshot. Why did he let John lie down? Why couldn't he keep John alive? Nancy steered her away from Ned, and then Kathryn took Sallie and her son down to the Crowders' own house.

"I do feel it," Ned told Nancy. "Guilty. I tried so hard. We both did all we could to stay alive."

"There's no rhyme or reason in why one person is taken and another spared. Sallie will know that when she is in her right mind. No-one blames you for not saving John."

I do, he thought, but tucked that thought inside. "I would have been dead in the snow beside him, if it had been another hour before the men came to find us."

"Spencer and Marshall headed out also, from here, once the snow stopped. They would have found you, only Frank and the others started earlier. How are you feeling?"

"My feet are all wrong. It makes no sense, but—'tis like I cannot feel them, and yet they still hurt."

"You are right, that does make no sense," Nancy said, but Governor Hayman said, "That is frostbite. I have heard tell of men suffering with it in northern climates. Few Englishmen ever venture far enough north to be troubled by it, but it is known to explorers in the far northern oceans."

"Is there a cure for it?"

"I...er, we ought to consult with Mistress Guy. She is the most skilled healer among us, though perhaps a ship's surgeon, if we had one..."

"God's teeth, a surgeon! Do you mean I am going to have my feet cut off?"

"Be still, now, and stop your foolishness," Nancy said. "No-one has said anything about cutting off your feet."

Of all the people in the room, now that Sallie Crowder and her little boy had been removed, Governor Hayman seemed the most distressed. He paced about, shaking his head and wringing his hands. "Such a tragic outcome, that one man might freeze to death and another nearly so, half an hour's walk from the house! While we were all safe and warm inside, and supposed them to be safe at Musketto. How cruel the winter winds can be."

"'Tis a harsh land, sir," Nancy said. "We have done well here, but we never forget what kind of country it is."

Ned reached out for her hand. He felt Nancy's fingers tighten on his.

"Indeed, sir," he said. "No-one should take this place lightly."

A Remedy is Proposed

MUSKETTO COVE, MARCH 1619

Men's own impieties in their instant act
Sustain their plagues, which are with stay but rackt.
                    —*Homer's Odysseys*, Book 22, 532–33

"LORD HAVE MERCY! I KNOW 'TIS UNCHARITABLE AND I be a shrewish wife, but I had to get out of that house," Nancy said as she carried her baby and a basket of sewing into Kathryn's house. "Only for an hour or so, let me have some peace to sit and work by your fire."

"Aye, if you can call this peace." Kathryn laughed. She was sewing also, while Hannah prepared the noon meal. Kathryn's three children played on the floor before the hearth, breaking out into frequent loud exclamations for Kathryn to look at what they were doing, or making, or destroying. Nicholas Guy was repairing shoes at a smaller table in the corner of the room, the tap of his cobbler's hammer punctuating everything.

"Is anyone moaning and complaining about how they cannot walk about properly, six weeks after almost freezing to death? No? Then 'tis peaceful enough for me." Nancy sat down, put Lizzie down near the older children, and took out her mending.

"'Tis very hard on poor Ned, hard for any man to know he cannot work, and hard to stay quiet and recover," said Nicholas Guy.

"Oh, I know it, indeed I do," Nancy said. "I told you I was only being shrewish. But I need a change, or we will fall to quarrelling."

"Then sit down, and we will talk of other things," Kathryn said. She promised herself she would go that evening and have a look at Ned's feet; his frostbitten toes were not healing as she had hoped they would after that deadly night in the woods, and none of her salves or remedies seemed to be helping. Nancy, who was anything but a shrewish wife and had taken good care of Ned, deserved her few moments of comparative peace.

"Daisy must be at Bess and Frank's place, is she?" Nancy asked.

"So she told me." Kathryn glanced at Nancy, and saw that her friend understood the look. Sometimes when Daisy said she was going to her sister's house, Kathryn suspected she was stealing a few moments alone with Tisquantum. The pair were never more than friendly and courteous in company; anything more tender between them was carried out entirely in secret, and secrecy was hard to come by in Musketto Cove, especially in winter when everyone was living out of each other's pockets.

Kathryn wondered if she should say something to Daisy, command her to put a stop to whatever relations she had with Tisquantum, but it was hard to censure something that was kept so quiet. Perhaps only a woman who had once carried on a secret affair herself would recognize the signs. At any rate, the ice would soon be out of the harbour and Captain Dermer would return to carry Tisquantum off to his own land. There would be an end to the problem, except for poor Daisy's broken heart.

Nicholas, meanwhile, had left his cobbler's bench and come to sit beside the women. "I had hoped you had come for another lesson, Nancy. Have you been studying your figures with as much devotion as my wife studies poetry? I am more in need of a bookkeeper than ever."

"If you give me the slate, I will show you what I can work out," Nancy said, with an eagerness that surprised Kathryn. She had been speaking in jest, months ago, when she suggested Nicholas could teach

Nancy to do her sums. But Nicholas had taken the suggestion to heart, and begun teaching Nancy to add and subtract on a slate, a skill she already had in her head from years of keeping track of household stores and provisions.

They passed the afternoon that way, Nicholas quizzing Nancy on her sums and discussing with her whether the plantation could yet support a cow and calf, while Kathryn watched the children and did her sewing. When Nancy and Lizzie returned to their own house, Kathryn went with them.

Ned sat by the hearth, mending a broken chair. Kathryn, opening her bag of remedies, asked him if he had been up and walking about yet today.

"Hobbling around a bit like an old man—nothing useful."

"Well, you can be useful sitting down if you'll take this one off my hands while I go out to fetch more wood," Nancy said, depositing Lizzie on his lap as Ned laid aside his work. Kathryn knelt at his feet, pulling off the thick woollen stockings that covered the bandages, then removing the bandages themselves.

Ned had, for the most part, recovered from the ordeal that had killed John Crowder, but he had two frostbitten toes on one foot and three on the other, and they were not healing well. She had seen frostbite only once before: Rafe's ears when he lost his cap during last winter's seal hunt. But with time and care Rafe had recovered, and apart from the tip of one ear looking oddly white, they had returned to normal. She had hoped for the same of Ned's toes, but they were not healing, and as she undid the bandages, the sickly smell she had dreaded rose to her nostrils.

"'Tis not good, is it, Doctor?" he asked, and she saw in his eyes and heard in his voice how hard he was working to keep a cheerful face in front of her.

"No, Ned, 'tis not good. I have a salve here I will put on them, but 'twill be of little benefit, I fear." She looked up, reluctantly meeting his eyes. "They are not healing; the flesh is beginning to die. You know what that means."

"Aye. Lose the toes or let it keep going and lose the feet—or perhaps the legs—altogether."

"We cannot let that happen. A ship's surgeon would be of more use here than a cunning-woman. I would like to be able to talk to anyone who had more experience of this malady."

"You are as skilful as any man in treating illness and injury, Kathryn. I will trust you to do whatever is needful with my poor feet." She noticed he had dropped the "Mistress" in front of her name. Both he and Nancy usually addressed her formally, at least when others were around, but the friendship among the three of them was old and deep and tested by much hardship. In this moment she knew Ned was not addressing the lady of the manor, nor even the colony's healer, but the old friend whom he trusted.

Nancy came back in with an armload of firewood. "Nancy my love, my toes will have to go," Ned said to her, striving for a light tone. "God's bones, what a choice for a man to have to make—lose a few toes now, or risk losing the whole foot later!"

"I think 'tis not a choice you will have to make, Ned," Kathryn said, as gently as she could. "I've heard tell in some cases the toes come off of their own accord, and I think this one on your right foot is near to doing so. But if they do not, then yes, someone will have to play surgeon and take them off. I hope it does not come to that, but I see no hope of saving these others."

"Think of that," Ned said, "dead toes falling away like dead leaves off a tree in autumn. 'Tis quite a picture, is't not? Better to have all that's dying cut away, I suppose." His voice was grim.

"If 'twill prevent the infection spreading, it must be done," Nancy said.

"What do you think, Lizzie—shall your papa have his toes snipped off, snip-snip?" Ned laughed, but the laughter barely masked his anger and fear.

"Papa!" echoed Lizzie, which distracted all the adults for a moment.

"La! Would you hark to her? She's not said that before, has she?" Kathryn wondered.

"She's not said either papa, or mama, or anything you could call a word," said Ned. "She knows 'tis papa who needs consolation now, I suppose."

"I will come again tomorrow, first thing in the morning, and we shall see what is to be done," Kathryn said, trying for a calm confidence in her voice that was much at odds with the knot in the pit of her stomach. She had sewn up wounds and brought babies into the world and pulled rotten teeth, but she had not thought life would lead her to a place where she had to consider how to remove a man's toes.

TWENTY-ONE

A Journey is Suggested

MUSKETTO COVE AND HARBOUR GRACE,
MAY 1619

She her way went, and I did mine dispose
Up to my ship, weigh'd anchor, and away.
                              —*Homer's Odysseys*, Book 12, 220–21

"EASY NOW, NED—I WILL GO FIRST," NICHOLAS GUY SAID
as the two men turned the small fishing boat over on the beach.
A thoughtful gesture, but an unnecessary one; Ned was fully
capable of lifting and turning a boat. The solicitous kindness drove him
nearly mad, but he kept a still tongue, knowing it was kindly intended.

Six weeks had passed since he had lost his toes, three falling off
of their own accord and two cut off by Kathryn. Twelve weeks since
the night in the snow that had made it all necessary. Learning to walk
properly had taken a bit of trouble, and for the first few weeks, he
hobbled about with a stick like an old man. He had given up using the
stick now, and walked with only a slight limp, though he occasionally
stumbled or lost his balance.

He was tired to the bone: tired of pain, tired of how slow he was to
get his strength back, tired of being careful about his footing when he'd

always been swift and nimble. Tired of feeling a step behind the other men. Now that the colony was waking from winter and everyone was preparing for the fishing season, he found he could keep up well with most tasks. He was tired of his kind neighbours waiting for him, making allowances. Looking at him as if he were less than the other men.

Ned Perry did not think he was a proud man. He had been born to a humble station in life. Moving to the colony, and the adventures that had happened to him since, had given him unexpected opportunities to better his station, and he was grateful for that. When he had come home two years ago from his wanderings, wedded to the woman he loved, he had been convinced that he had everything he would ever need to make him contented in life.

He had not reckoned on an injury leaving him crippled, even in a small way. He knew the risks in a colonist's life, knew that so many worse things could happen to a man than losing a few toes to frostbite. He reminded himself every day that John Crowder had died in that snowstorm. Isaac had died falling off the wharf. Back in Cupids Cove, when they first came out all those years ago, a man had cut his leg with an axe while chopping wood. The wound had turned septic, as Ned's toes had, and then it had killed him. An injury or illness that did not kill a man might still leave him permanently lamed. Against those ever-present possibilities, what had happened to Ned was a trivial thing.

So why did it eat at him so? Why did he bristle and have to bite back an angry retort when anyone asked if he needed help? He did not always bite it back in time; sometimes he snapped at the other men, or even at Nancy. Then cursed himself for being cross. 'Twas no shame to lose his balance and need to steady himself. And yet shame was what he felt—shame, and anger.

For no good reason, he had been thinking more and more lately of the darkest time in his life, those two years when he had sailed the southern seas with Captain Elfrith and the men of the *White Lion*, when he had believed Nancy drowned in a shipwreck. When he had seen things that shocked him, and done things he despised. Then he had found Nancy again, and while things had not been set right immediately—for he was too lost in his own guilt and anger to reach out to her—they had found their way back together, and all was well.

It still is well, Ned reminded himself as his hands went through the familiar motions of scraping down the hull of the boat. *All is well. I got frostbite and lost a few of my toes; 'tis hardly some great tragedy. Stop making so much of it.*

As he worked, his eyes scanned the horizon, looking at the small stretch of ocean that was visible beyond their cove. At this time of year, the waters that had been empty all winter were coming to life with ships again. They had already seen fishing vessels heading down the coast and knew from their neighbours at Harbour Grace that some of the summer fleet had begun work in that harbour. What had not come yet, and what they were all waiting for, was a ship sent out by the Newfoundland Company of Bristol, the ship that would bring trade goods in return for the salt fish they had shipped out in the fall.

Since Ned and Nicholas had been working on the boats this morning, they had seen three ships pass the mouth of the cove, too far away to tell what colours they were flying. "The governor said he would send someone over with a message when the first company ship comes in," Nicholas said. "I wonder if that may be it?"

Sure enough, less than an hour later Will Spencer arrived, running down the path from the woods to the beach with his news. "Two ships into our plantation!" he announced. "The *Bountiful* and *Godspeed*, both out of Bristol. The *Godspeed* has our trade goods and supplies, and the *Bountiful* is Captain Dermer come back again. He wants to meet with you, sir, along with the governor and Tisquantum," he added to Nicholas.

"Well, he will get to meet with us, and anyone else he likes, for I doubt anyone will want to miss the first ships of the season. The womenfolk will come and all, so they can pick and choose from the cloth, the foodstuffs, and all the rest. We'll rig up the shallop to go this afternoon, Ned. All those who cannot come by the shallop will go by the woods trail. You and Nancy will come with the mistress and myself."

When the boat from Musketto Cove got to Harbour Grace the two ships were anchored a little offshore, with their boats tied up to the wharf. Most of the trade goods had already been unloaded and brought ashore, with Governor Hayman overseeing the business.

"Ah, at last, Master Guy and his Musketto folk are here, and we may begin," the governor said. "We have waited, for I wanted to be sure that the division of goods is fair, based on the fish landed at both plantations last year. I have it all here in my ledger—and I see you have brought your own account-books as well, so we can be sure all is done aright."

It was a long and somewhat tedious business, and Ned well knew that Nancy would make sure their household got what was coming to them. He'd often thought it was a risky thing that neither he nor his wife could read or write, and so were dependent upon others to tell them if their share was fair. He was a trifle amazed when Nicholas Guy had begun teaching Nancy her sums, for she took to it as naturally as if she had been taught from childhood. He hoped their children could learn to read and know their numbers; he did not want them to grow up thinking that the folks in the big house were the only ones who could deal with the merchants.

When the men had claimed the fishing gear and the women began dividing up the bolts of cloth and barrels of grain, molasses and the other staples amongst the families, Ned drifted away from that centre of activity. He found Captain Dermer sitting on the stagehead with Tisquantum, Will Spencer, and Hal Henshaw.

"I've a charter, a ship, and a crew," Dermer was saying. "My orders are to take the fishermen that are already aboard the *Bountiful* as far as Monhegan to fish for the summer, and to go on with a small crew from there, to explore and seek out good land for a new English settlement. I've two men already who will go with me on that voyage of exploration, but I mean to hire the rest of my crew over here, from men who know the New World and will be well suited to help with this venture."

"Are you planting a settlement, or only seeking out a site for one?" asked Hal. "I might go along if 'tis a voyage of exploration, but after this summer I mean to go back to England. I'm not cut out to be a colonist all my life."

Dermer laughed. "I have heard tell that spending a winter in a colony often leads a man to that conclusion! I have need of a crew only for the summer. Anyone who signs on with me will return here to the New Found Land when the voyage is done. I am not tasked with founding a new colony. There are those who wish to come out and do so; my orders are to explore the coast and find a place suitable for settlement."

"Who are these folks who want to settle? Bristol folk?" Ned wondered.

"Nay, I know them not. I've heard there are Puritans and Dissenters who broke with the Church of England, who want their own colony where they can make the rules to suit themselves," Dermer said. "And to grow rich, of course, for what else does any man want from a colony, when all's said and done?"

"Not many of us growing rich 'round here," Ned said. "Indeed, we were lucky to survive the winter. Not all of us did."

Dermer nodded. "I heard about Crowder. 'Twas a grave loss." He looked at Tisquantum. "Our friend here has agreed to come along as our guide. We will explore the territory of his people and see if there is a place there where an English settlement could be planted. There, his people can set up a profitable trade with the English."

"If it brings me to my home and my people, I am glad to be your guide," Tisquantum said.

"You would stay there, then?" Ned asked him.

"You know this has always been my plan," Tisquantum said. They both looked to the beach where the women were gathered, comparing lengths of cloth and talking amongst themselves. Daisy stood a little apart from all the wives; there was something melancholy about the sight of her.

But Tisquantum's and Daisy's troubles were far from the forefront of Ned's mind. "Have you need of a ship's carpenter?" he heard himself asking Thomas Dermer.

"I have need of all sorts. If you have been a ship's carpenter, that may be of use, but I'll take any good seaman who has experience in the New World. I mean to make the voyage in the ship's boat—she's a five-ton shallop—after we leave the *Bountiful* at Monhegan, so I'll want a crew of eight or ten men at most."

At day's end the Musketto Cove men loaded the Guys' boat with their supplies. Some of those who had sailed with them earlier in the day were returning by the woods trail, although Nicholas Guy offered to make a second trip back to pick up anyone who would prefer to sail rather than walk. He darted a glance at Ned as he made the offer.

"We are fine to go back by the trail, are we not, Nancy?" Ned said. "Lizzie can ride on my back."

Nancy did not ask if Ned could manage the woods path; she helped secure Lizzie onto his back and then joined him on the trail. They quickly fell behind the others. Ned's feet were, indeed, not used to this rugged path, and he walked more slowly than the rest of the travellers. But Nancy only asked did he want her to take a turn carrying Lizzie, and nodded when he said no.

"You enjoyed today, did you not?" he said. "It reminded me of a market day."

"Aye, I thought the same. The closest we ever get, here, to a market or a fair."

"Do you miss it? Towns, markets and fairs?" He thought of walking through Bristol streets with Nancy by his side, past stalls selling meat and vegetables and fabrics and tools and a hundred other things. Buying a hot pie from a pie-man and eating it as they walked along, hand in hand, looking at the abundance of things to buy.

"Betimes I do," she said. "But then I think that if I were back in England, shopping at the market, we'd go home to rented rooms in someone else's house. Everyone gives up some things to gain other things in this life."

"True enough. You have the spirit of a colonial woman, in truth. 'Tis not every woman can adjust to this kind of life."

"Don't put it all on the women, longing for the comforts of home! There's a good many men want to turn around as soon as they see there's no alehouse on the corner, no guild to meet and drink with at the end of a working day."

Ned laughed, and they walked in silence for a few more minutes. He had to tell her, sometime, about his conversation with Dermer, and yet he was strangely reluctant to speak of it. He thought of how angry she would be, if he went ahead and made such a plan without talking to her, though of course it was a husband's right to do so.

"Does this trouble you?" Nancy said. It took him a moment to understand that what she was asking had nothing to do with the thoughts in his head. She was looking at the woods around them, the branches above them. They had come into a broad space in the path, almost a clearing, and through the spring buds on the birch trees above them he saw a sky beginning to deepen towards twilight. "Every time I come over this trail I wonder if 'twas about here, or here, that you and Crowder spent the night."

"Oh. In truth, I could not tell you. It all looks so different now." Save for the day in January when the other men had pulled him back from Harbour Grace on a sled, this was his first time on the woods path since his ordeal. "I cannot tell you how different it was then. We could barely see, hardly knew where we were. The snow made it like—like a dream. A nightmare. I would not know that spot where Crowder died if I were to stumble on the very place again."

Nancy put her hand in his. He knew by the weight slumped against his back that Lizzie had fallen asleep. "'Tis wicked of me," Nancy said, "but whenever I see Sallie I thank God that it was John who was taken and not you. I could have been in her place."

Ned drew a deep breath. "Do you think we would be safer, if we never set foot away from Musketto Cove again?"

"Ah. So, you are thinking of going on this voyage with Dermer and Tisquantum?"

"I should have known you would be a step ahead of me."

"Daisy is distrait that Tisquantum means to go back to his own people. And I heard that Dermer is recruiting men for his voyage."

"'Twould only be for the summer. I thought that if you continued working onshore with the other women, Master Nicholas would make sure we got a share of the summer's fishery, and I could earn extra coin by sailing with Dermer. A glass window for the house, perhaps? I've no fancies about finding gold in New England and becoming wealthy, but 'tis a small way for us to get ahead, if I take the occasional voyage."

"A glass window would be lovely." She looked up at him, a challenge in her face. "But a little coin in your pocket and glass windows is not your only reason for wanting to go."

They walked in silence for a few minutes. His feet were indeed aching now. He could feel the missing toes as if they were still throbbing. "'Tis not that I want to leave you and Lizzie. But there is something I do miss about it, the life at sea."

"What a twist of events for the lad who was so seasick on his first voyage he swore he'd never go to sea again."

"True enough. Life takes some odd turns." His thoughts took odd twists and turns, too, ones he could not quite put into words. "I cannot tell you for certain why I want to go, only that I will return, and that 'twill be good for us all if I go."

"You have nothing to prove to me, Ned. Nor to other men."

"Ah, I know that." *But to myself*, he thought. This longing, the pull of the sea and the world beyond, had been in him ever since their return to the New Found Land. He had thought it was something he could ignore, a call he would resist. Now, he was tempted by the idea that if he were at sea again, he would not feel half-crippled. He silently thanked Nancy for not asking whether his broken feet would hold firm on the deck of a ship, whether he could climb into the rigging if needed.

"You must do what you think is needful," she said. "As you say, 'tis a good opportunity to earn coin you could not earn here. And a growing family, after all, may need the odd coin here and there."

He glanced at her again, at the self-satisfied smile she wore. "So you have news for me, also?"

"I was not sure of it until a day or so ago. But, yes. Another babe, God willing."

"When?"

"Before winter, I think. November?"

"I would be back by then. Unless you would rather I did not go at all, if you are..."

She gave him a playful push on the arm—lightly, so as not to throw off his balance. "A woman expecting a child needs no special care. Go off on your voyage, for I know you long to be back at sea. Go earn me that window-glass, and then come home to me."

TWENTY-TWO

An Expedition is Launched

CUPIDS COVE, MAY 1619

This said, he choos'd out twenty men, that bore
Best reckoning with him, and to ship and shore
All hasted, reach'd the ship, launch'd, raise'd the mast...
　　　　　—Homer's Odysseys, Book 4, 1054–56

NED HAD NOT VISITED CUPIDS COVE SINCE LAST SUMmer, when he had helped the Crowders and the Holworthys move to Harbour Grace. He welcomed the chance to visit with some old friends. Will Spencer, who had come from Harbour Grace to join the voyage, did the same with the men he knew at Cupids Cove, while Dermer and Tisquantum met with Governor Mason to discuss their voyage south.

"'Twas a hard winter here," George Lane said in reply to Ned's query. "We had another bout of the scurvy and lost two folks—Henry Hill, and Sam Butler's missus. And Edward Hallett's wife birthed a child, there about Christmas, but neither her nor the babe lived. None of the women here now is skilled as a midwife. Mistress Butler used to do what she could, before she took sick. We've sore need of a wise-woman."

"Mistress Guy is the midwife for the women at our place and in Harbour Grace, and I am sure she would come to Cupids Cove if someone sent a boat for her," Ned said. "We lost one babe and one man over the winter. Bess and Frank Tipton's baby was stillborn, and poor John Crowder froze to death when himself and myself was caught out in a storm."

"Aye, that's a terrible thing," Lane agreed. The Cupids Cove settlers had already had the news of Crowder's death, but Lane listened to Ned tell it again, nodding at the grim details.

"So, you've got a taste for adventure after all your travels?" Lane asked Ned later, walking along the stone-covered beach by the wharf. "Or is married life sending you off to sea again? I know there's times, with Jennet and all the youngsters, I half think I might go to sea myself, just to get a bit of peace and quiet."

Ned laughed. "Nay, I've no complaints about married life. If anything, 'tis for Nancy and the children that I want to go. We've one fine little maid now, and another on the way. I want the chance to earn some money of my own. If you've a mind to go, Dermer is looking for more men for his crew."

Lane shook his head. "Jennet would kill me. 'Tis another summer of fishing and making fish for me, I 'low. I'd hoped by now this place might have grown to some size of town where I could follow another trade besides fishing."

Ned knew that George Lane's father was a baker, operating the same kind of little shop that Ned's brother had married into back in Bristol. The youngest of four boys, George had grown up with no hope of inheriting the family business and thought he would have a better chance in the colonies.

"The day may come when you can turn your hand to bread and pastries again," he said, but Lane sighed.

"Truth is, we all came over here thinking we'd build something like an English village. Not a place the size of Bristol or London, of course, but where there's a butcher, a baker, a candlestick maker, and the like."

"Did you ever truly know a candlestick maker? Sure even back in England I doubt there'd be enough work to keep a candlestick maker busy all the time."

"Likely not." Lane laughed. "How many candlesticks does a man need? I've an uncle who was a chandler, though—that's a good trade. But still, after ten years in this place, every man has to work at fishing, and in the meantime has to be his own carpenter and boatbuilder and farmer."

"While his wife must be the butcher, the baker, and the chandler," Ned agreed

"Myself and Jennet were talking of building on our own piece of land down the shore a ways," Lane said. "There's a few folks here who have done that, just as you lot are doing up by Harbour Grace. If we must fish and farm, a small grant of land would suit us well."

"'Tis not a bad life. There's a good deal to be said for being your own master."

"Aye, there's truth in that," Lane said. He pointed at a stretch of shore some distance from the settlement. It was filled with the pines, silver birch, spruce and fir trees that covered nearly every piece of uncleared land on the island. "There is the spot we were thinking of."

"'Tis a fine spot. But have you thought of moving up to Bristol's Hope with us? We need more planters there if the colony is to thrive, and we Bristol men ought to stick together."

"I will give it thought," Lane said. "Mayhap I'll go up to Harbour Grace and talk to your governor there about what it might take to get a piece of land for my own house, byre and stage. What more does a man need, after all?"

What more does a man need? Ned tucked that question away in the back of his mind. If he answered that, would he have some kind of an answer to why he was sailing south with Dermer instead of getting ready to head out to the fishing grounds for another summer?

After a meal in the governor's house that night, Dermer told his crew that two Cupids Cove men were going to sail aboard the *Bountiful* with him: James Hill and Dickon Sadler. They would join Dermer, Ned, Spencer, Tisquantum, and two men who had come out from England with the express purpose of going on the voyage of exploration—the navigator and mapmaker Samuel Hollett, and a seasoned sailor named John Harvey who had explored the same part of the coast years earlier with Captain John Smith. These eight would sail on the *Bountiful*, intending to leave her when they reached the fishing grounds, and then set off in a shallop to explore the land of Tisquantum's people.

Having heard Dermer announce this, Ned was surprised the following morning when the men gathered at the Cupids Cove wharf to see not only Hill and Sadler, but a third man coming with bags and bundles. He was even more surprised to see that the other man was George Whittington.

Ned said nothing to Whittington, and had no opportunity to speak to Dermer until they had all rowed out to the *Bountiful*, boarded her, and brought the shallop aboard. When they were sailing out through Conception Bay, Ned went to the captain's cabin and asked to speak with Dermer.

"Sir, I wish I had known you had engaged Whittington."

"Why is that, Perry? 'Twas only last night he spoke to me of joining us, and I think he will be a fine addition to our party. I want an even number of men for the boat crew. Tisquantum aims to leave us when we reach his homeland, and if we set off with nine, that leaves eight after he is gone. Governor Mason tells me this Whittington is a clever fellow, looking to make his fortune. He is one of Guy's original colonists, like yourself, is he not?"

"He is, sir. And 'tis not as if you have to consult with the crew about the men you take on—I know that. 'Tis only that I do not trust Whittington. There is bad blood between us, I admit, but the fault is more on his side than on mine."

"Is this going to cause trouble, Perry? I cannot have fighting among my crew."

Ned paused. They were at sea. The only thing he could ask was to be put off in St. John's station and find passage back to Cupids—and lose his opportunity for a summer earning good money. He straightened his shoulders. "Nay, sir. At least, if there is trouble, I'll not be the one to start it."

"That's as good as any man can promise," said Dermer. "I will take your warning to heart and keep an eye to him. You are dismissed."

The *Bountiful* sailed around Cape St. Francis, then on for a brief stop in St. John's before continuing south. They had fair winds and clear skies all along the stretch of open sea to the south of the New Found Land. Ned remembered sailing these waters with Captain Argall six years before, when they had gone to Port Royal to attack and burn the French settlement.

For the first time in years, Ned wondered about those Frenchmen. Had they gone back to France, or rebuilt Port Royal, or found a new colony? He supposed one of the masters could tell him—Governor Mason or Governor Hayman or even Captain Dermer. Englishmen who were concerned with planting colonies kept close track of what rival nations were doing in the same line of business. Ned had never thought to ask.

He had believed at the time that it was a cruel thing to do even to enemies, burning the homes other men had worked hard to build. But the longer he had stayed at sea, the more inured Ned had become to cruelty, so that he had hardly thought of Port Royal for years. At least he had taken no lives there.

He told the story to Tisquantum as the two stood their turn on watch that night. "'Twas a terrible thing we did," Ned said.

"It is the kind of thing men do in war," Tisquantum said with a shrug. Above the ship, seagulls wheeled and cried out.

"Your people, also?"

"All men everywhere attack their enemies. My people are not—what would you call it? Angels in your paradise. We have wars."

"You had no guns, though, until we brought them."

"That is true. But your own people had not guns in the time of your ancestors, yet still you had many wars."

Ned turned Tisquantum's words over in his head as he listened to the splash and boom of the ship's bow rising and falling with the waves. "So our people are not so different from yours, then?" he asked.

"That may be so. You have the guns—that is a difference." He looked sideways at Ned with a trace of a smile. "Only now, after so many years of trading with you, we are beginning to have them also."

Tisquantum was different, Ned thought, since this journey had begun. He would have expected his friend to be in a lighter mood, happy at the prospect of returning to his home or his people. But whether it was the parting from Daisy, or that returning home made him relive the circumstances of his leaving, Tisquantum kept to himself far more than he had done in Musketto Cove.

The ship passed a small island that the French called Cap de Sable, then tacked westward across another stretch of open sea. To their north lay the French Bay—the bay *Fundo*, as Portuguese sailors called it because of its depth. To the south, the long stretch of coastline running down to Virginia and beyond.

On a brisk, sunny morning nearly a fortnight into the voyage, they came to the island of Monhegan. It looked like the harbours around the New Found Land at this time of year, with many ships like their own moored off the island, and smaller fishing boats out at sea. Here they would leave the *Bountiful* and most of her crew to fish, while Dermer and his group of explorers took the shallop along the coast.

They all went ashore; the shallop crew brought their belongings from the *Bountiful* and stowed them aboard the small boat. Everything needed to be packed as neat and as watertight as possible, for there was little extra space and no cabin or shelter to provide protection from the sea and the elements. Food stores and gear—including the notebooks, pen and ink that Samuel Hollett had brought for recording their discoveries and mapping the coastline they explored—were stowed fore and aft and beneath the seats.

Ned had spent a good bit of time aboard boats this size, for Dermer's shallop was much like the boats that were used for fishing and travelling short distances around the New Found Land coast, though a little larger than some of them. But he had never made a voyage of any length aboard one. In the early years at Cupids Cove, when Ned had gone with Governor Guy aboard the *Indeavour* in search of the natives, a second, smaller crew had gone along in a pinnace, but Ned had been aboard the *Indeavour*, and been glad for that berth. He had been a poor sailor in those days, not accustomed to the sea, and had pitied the men on the smaller boat, who were even more at the mercy of the waves.

The *Bountiful*'s men ate on the beach that night, visiting with some of the other fishing crews, and slept one last night on the 'tween deck of the ship. In the morning they finished loading the boat, adding casks of fresh water to the items already stored. The shallop had two sails, but neither was raised for the short journey from Monhegan to the mainland; instead, the men rowed. Ned was paired with Tisquantum, and wondered, as they pulled together at the oars, whom he would row with once Tisquantum had returned to his own people.

They made landfall about midday at a spot Tisquantum indicated. After they ate a simple meal of ship's biscuit and dried salted pork, Tisquantum said, "There is a village near to here. These people are not Wampanoag, but my people have trade with them. It is strange that nobody has come yet; they would be watching the shore for boats. I will go alone and tell them I am here."

"No," said Dermer sharply. "I should come with you, and a few others."

There was a pause. "I am not under your command, Captain," Tisquantum said at last.

Dermer shifted his weight from one foot to another. "That's as may be, and I will not force you. But we planned this voyage together. I ask you to bring us with you, to find the natives."

Tisquantum looked for a moment as if he would defy Dermer, but said only, "Very well. Come with me, if you will."

Dermer chose Whittington and Hill to stay and guard the shallop and gear, while the remaining men, led by Tisquantum, set off along a well-marked trail into the woods. They had walked about half an hour when they came to a clearing that reminded Ned of the Lenape village he had visited so many years ago with Argall's crew. The houses were built in a similar style to those Lenape dwellings, wood-framed domes with reed mats draped over them for roof and walls. The place had an eerie, deserted air. There was no busy hum of activity as one would expect on a summer morning. Canoes were pulled up on the grass by a river; empty circles of cook-fires showed not even a wisp of smoke.

Dermer made as if to call out, but Tisquantum stopped him with a hand on his arm. He went ahead of the Englishmen, walking past the dwellings, calling out in his own tongue, and after a moment a boy who looked to be nine or ten years of age came out of one house. He was thin, his clothing ragged; he looked ill-cared-for.

Tisquantum spoke to the boy for some time, then turned back to Dermer. "There has been a sickness in this village. A plague. The boy, his mother, and his grandfather, and two children of another family, are the only ones left alive."

"God's teeth! And how many folk were in the village before?" Dermer wondered.

Tisquantum looked about at the clearing. "This is a place where eight or ten families would have their summer dwelling. Fifty, seventy people, perhaps."

"Christ, what misery. What should we do for the poor savages? Leave them food? Take them to some other village?"

"I will speak to the boy's grandfather—their sachem," Tisquantum said. "Their tongue is not mine, but I know enough to be understood." Turning away from Dermer, he followed the boy into the dwelling.

When Tisquantum emerged some time later, an older man came with him. Tisquantum translated as he spoke to Dermer. "Go away and leave us alone, Englishman. We have nothing to offer in trade. Sickness has taken all from us."

"Tell him we want nothing from him," Dermer said. "We would help, if we can, though we have little food to share."

Tisquantum did not bother translating this. "They have food all around," he said to Dermer. "It is not a famine. What they do not have are men to hunt, women to farm and gather food. There is nothing you can offer that would help."

He spoke again to the elder at some length, then turned back to Dermer. "There is another village a day's walk from here. They are waiting for the woman and the youngest child to recover enough to travel, then they go to this village. They want no help from Englishmen."

"Were Englishmen here before? Or other Christians?" Dermer wondered. "Did we spread this disease to them?"

Tisquantum raised his hands as if to ask *Who knows?* "All the peoples along this shore have traded—some with English, some with French, some with Dutch. There were not such plagues before the trading began. I remember sickness when I was a boy, but no great plague that would wipe out a whole village."

The English party returned, sobered, to the beach. "Let us not linger here," Dermer decided. "I would visit the site of Popham's colony, where we may spend the night, and mayhap we will find natives there to see how they fare. Then tomorrow, we sail on for your land," he added to Tisquantum, "and hope to find better tidings."

"May it be so," Tisquantum said.

The place that Dermer called "Popham's colony," which Tisquantum called Sagadahoc, was at the mouth of a river. It was cleared for settlement, though the forest had begun to take the land back. The buildings that still stood were not the dwellings of the local people, but English-style wooden houses, abandoned and fallen into disrepair.

"Ten—no, twelve—years ago," Captain Dermer said as they went ashore, "a company of Englishmen tried to plant a colony here, the same year as the settlers went to Virginia. It lasted barely over a year, and the settlers went back to England."

"I hardly blame them," said Whittington. "It does not seem this coast is a good place for settlement. The air here must surely be unwholesome."

"They had no sickness while the colonists were here," Dermer said, "only money troubles. Their patron back in England died, and the investors withdrew their funds."

"The air here is clean, the land is sweet and good," Tisquantum said. "Plagues come in every land from time to time. You have it so in England also."

"Aye, we have all lived through plague," Dermer agreed. "But back in England we tell folks that the New World has more healthful airs, that they will escape the plagues of London by coming out here."

The mood of the whole party was bleak, and spending that night on the shores of an abandoned settlement did nothing to lift their spirits. Tisquantum went off by himself into the forest, and this time Dermer did not attempt to stop him or send a party of men with him. Tisquantum returned before dusk to report that he had found another abandoned settlement.

"Could it be plague there as well?" John Harvey wondered aloud when Tisquantum reported this.

"It may be," Tisquantum said. "But I saw no sick, no signs of recent dead. It may be only that they have moved on, abandoned that place." He looked at Captain Dermer. "We leave here tomorrow. I will guide you on to Patuxet as I said I will do. But I do not know what we will find there."

TWENTY-THREE

A Grim Discovery is Made

PATUXET, MAY, 1619

But, if thy soul knew what a sum of woes,
For thee to cast up, thy stern Fates impose,
Ere to thy country earth thy hopes attain,
Undoubtedly thy choice would here remain...
— Homer's *Odysseys*, Book 5, 270–73

"NOW THIS—THIS IS GOD'S COUNTRY!"

Ned looked up from the oars—it was a calm, windless day—to see the view that so impressed Captain Dermer. They were entering a great bay where the land reached out into the water like a giant fishhook, with sandy beaches giving way to gentle green land. It did indeed look welcoming.

"This is Patuxet," said Tisquantum.

"Captain Smith called it Plymouth, after the city in England," Captain Dermer observed as they hauled the pinnace up on a beach.

There was nobody on shore; all was silence but for birdsong in the trees. Domed houses, such as they had seen in other native settlements, stood well back from the shore. But again, there were no signs of life or activity.

"This is wrong," Tisquantum said as they hauled the shallop ashore. "There should be men out fishing, women working in the fields."

"Perhaps they have moved on to some other campsite?" Dermer suggested.

Tisquantum shot him a look that might have been contempt. "This is not some hunting camp. This is Patuxet land, where we live spring and summer since—since the beginning." He pointed at the dwellings in the distance. "When we leave for the winter, the mats that cover these wetus go with us to the winter camp. You would see only the frames here, if my people ever left Patuxet in summer. But we would not." He took a further step up the beach towards the empty fields. "We did not."

They all knew, of course. Since the first plague-ravaged town they had visited, the same thought had likely been in all their minds. Certainly, Ned thought, it must have been in Tisquantum's mind.

When they came to the dwellings, Tisquantum looked inside a few. "There are tools, clothing, all manner of things left behind. I think it is last year, at least, since anyone lived here. If—" He broke off, looking around at the empty houses. "There is a place I must go." He indicated another path that led into the woods. "Alone. You go back to the boat."

"There's a good deal more to see here," Dermer said. "If we were to go off on that broad trail there—"

"No. Go back."

Ned could almost see the struggle in Captain Dermer, to assert his authority as ship's captain and as an Englishman. But since they had first made landfall on the shore near Monhegan, Tisquantum had changed his manner towards Dermer; they were in Tisquantum's territory now. After a moment, Dermer led the sailors back down the path to the beach, while Tisquantum went alone into the woods.

It was late afternoon. Whittington and Dermer caught a few trout in a brook, while Ned built a fire and Hollett walked about the empty settlement, making notes and sketches. They ate the fish for supper with ship's biscuit and spread out their bedding on the shore to sleep. Tisquantum did not return.

In the morning, the sun spilled its radiance over a landscape that looked, if possible, lovelier than it had the day before. In the morning light the green of the grass and trees, the richness of the soil, the sparkling water of the brook that ran down to the sea, all looked inviting. A place to build a home, Ned thought, just waiting for settlers to come across the sea.

Dermer announced they would no longer abide by Tisquantum's order to remain on the shore, but would explore some of the other forest trails. The men set off in pairs, walking down well-cleared trails. "The natives have been settled here for a long time, and a good many of them," Ned observed to Dickon Sadler as they made their way down a path wide enough for the two of them to walk side by side.

George Whittington made the grimmest discovery, and did it with his usual lack of grace. "Little doubt what happened here," he said when the crew met in a clearing where several paths converged. "There's a load of fresh-digged graves over there. Then there's bodies on the ground, wasted away but not buried. I suppose the last ones left alive put the rest in the ground and then went to the graveyard to lay down and die."

"God's teeth," said Dermer. "No more than what we expected, but still, 'tis grim to see."

"It might be worth our while digging around there," Whittington said. "I've heard tell some of these natives believe in burying a man's most valuable goods with him, so who knows what we might find?"

"No!" Dermer said sharply. Ned wondered if he thought it was sacrilege to disturb graves, even though they were not Christian. But Dermer said, "These folk died of a plague. Stay well away from the bodies that are above ground and do not disturb the graves. They may—"

"Hush!" said Ned, cutting the captain off and gesturing. From a different path that led deeper into the forest, Tisquantum approached.

Tisquantum said nothing to his shipmates, but spoke to Dermer. "There is a Wampanoag village a day's journey inland. I did not go all the way, but travelled far enough to see signs there are men still alive there. I will go to them. You will leave this place."

"Indeed we will not," said Dermer. "We came here to bring you to your own people, to treat and trade with them and learn about this place. Take us to this other village with you."

"They will not be glad to see you."

"I will chance it."

After some further discussion, Sadler and Hill were sent back to the beach to guard the boat, while the rest of the crew set off into the woods, Tisquantum in the lead. The sun was full overhead, the day promising to be a hot one. Even the trees shading the path did not shield them from its heat as the morning wore on.

It was the longest Ned had walked in some time. His damaged feet ached within an hour, and hurt worse as the miles of uneven forest path went on. He had imagined he would talk to Tisquantum, wondered what he might say about the devastating discovery of the abandoned settlement at Patuxet. But the moment did not arise. Tisquantum led the column of men, and when they stopped briefly for water or rest, he spoke only to Dermer.

"Does Dermer know he may be leading us into a trap?" George Whittington said to Ned late in the afternoon, after they had stopped for a brief meal of ship's biscuit and dried meat, and continued on the path again.

"I do not think Tisquantum would lead us to our deaths."

"Would he not? What reason has he to protect Englishmen? The man is stolen from his home, kept captive for years, and now comes back to find all his family dead. Why would he not want his revenge?"

"'Tis not as if Englishmen killed his people!" Master Hollett said. "It was plague."

"Tisquantum is not a man to want revenge," Ned said.

"How do you know what kind of man he is?" Whittington shot back. "Even a Christian would want revenge in such a case. How much more would a savage?"

"I know Tisquantum. I count him a friend."

"Then I count you a fool—not that there is anything new in that," Whittington said, and spat on the ground. "There can be no true friendship between Englishman and Indian, Christian and heathen. You delude yourself."

"Do you call me a fool?" Ned said, lunging at Whittington. He had spent the weeks of this voyage choking back his old anger at

Whittington, telling himself that if he, Ned, had grown wiser with the years, it was possible the other man could have changed as well. That he might not be the same man who had tormented and falsely accused Nancy all those years ago. Now that anger rose again, as Whittington taunted him for trusting Tisquantum.

Dermer turned back. "Peace! No brawling. We must stand together."

Will Spencer laid hold of Ned's arm, pulled him away from Whittington. Whittington muttered, "You will be sorry if you lay hands on me, Perry," and turned away, both men falling back into line. Spencer walked between them. Ned pushed his anger at Whittington back down to the deep place where it always lay. There were bigger concerns to deal with today.

An hour later, Wampanoag scouts from the inland village met their party, and the Englishmen hung back while Tisquantum talked with them. Then they fell into line and began walking again, led by Tisquantum and three other Wampanoag men.

The settlement, when they arrived, looked as if it, too, had been plague-stricken: there were people there, but far fewer than the number of dwellings and fields might suggest had once lived there. People gathered around Tisquantum, some clearly recognizing him, surprised to see him alive. They cast suspicious glances at his English companions.

But no-one offered violence, though Tisquantum insisted the English lay aside their muskets and pistols. Once disarmed they were given food. Tisquantum told them that the sachem of this village was going to send a message to a larger Wampanoag settlement, where a greater chief lived, who would come or send men to parlay with Captain Dermer.

It was much later that evening, while the Englishmen were being shown a place to sleep in one of the many empty dwellings, that Ned saw Tisquantum standing alone. He hesitated a moment, then approached him.

"'Twas a terrible thing, what we found at Patuxet," Ned said. "But these are...Some of your people are alive here?"

It was a foolish thing to say. Was Tisquantum supposed to rejoice about that? But he only said, "These here are not men of Patuxet, they are Pocasset. But both are Wampanoag." Seeing that Ned did not understand, he added, "It is as if you said, I am a Bristol man, this other fellow is a London man, but we are both English."

"Ah. I see." Ned tried to imagine returning to Bristol, finding everyone he had ever known dead. "I am terrible sorry that it had to end like this."

Tisquantum inclined his head briefly. "I like to think that if those English had not taken me prisoner, I could have saved my people. But most like I would have died with them." He drew a deep breath. "That would have been for the best."

"No. Surely not. 'Tis a blessing you were spared."

"Every man wishes to live and die among his own people. Now I cannot." He looked at Ned, for the first time seeming to soften a little. "You must tell Daisy. I told her I would leave her only because I must be with my own people."

"She will want to know why, if your own people are all gone, you cannot come back to her."

"That could never be. I cannot live among the English again."

"You hate us," Ned said.

"Do you blame me?" Tisquantum turned away from Ned. "Tell Daisy I wish her well. Or perhaps tell her nothing. You will know best." He glanced back and added, "You are not the worst Englishman I have known, Ned Perry." For a moment the crooked half-smile Ned was used to seeing on his face flickered, then it was gone. "But you are not different from the rest of them."

He watched Tisquantum walk away, rejoin the other Wampanoag men, and vanish into the darkening night.

TWENTY-FOUR

A Warning is Sent

MUSKETTO COVE, JUNE 1619

It was the hateful man that his conceit
Before suspected, who had done that ill...
— *Homer's Odysseys*, Book 22, 199–200

F OR ONCE, THE HOUSE WAS NOT FREEZING COLD WHEN Nancy woke in the morning. The slow, reluctant New Found Land summer was coming at last, and the sun was beginning to give warmth as well as light. She built up the fire in the hearth and had pottage cooking and bread dough rising before Lizzie woke and called out, "Mama!"

Lizzie was toddling about now, getting into everything with the curiosity common to a child who had passed her first birthday. She had outgrown the cradle, which stood by the hearth waiting for the new baby who would be born "when papa will be home," as Nancy often said to Lizzie—and sometimes to herself.

She and Lizzie spent much of their daytime hours in the Guys' house, Nancy helping the other women with their work as the children played together. But there was a pleasure she could not quite explain in crossing the rocky beach at the end of the day, entering her own little house, and closing the door behind her.

Sometimes she thought of the only other place she had lived in her life that had been hers alone: the cook's cabin on the ill-named *Happy Adventure*. There, she had shut the door and prayed for safety and escape. She used to drop the bar across that cabin door, shutting out not the unknown dangers of the forest, but the well-known dangers of evil men.

She was safe in Musketto Cove, as she had not been aboard that pirate ship. Even with Ned away, she had the encircling arms of the whole plantation. Yet with all that, there was a pleasure in barring her own door at night.

After they had eaten the morning meal, she carried Lizzie on her hip and the pot with her loaves of bread in her other arm, across the beach to the oven where Daisy was just putting her own bread on to bake. "Now, stay by me," Nancy said as she put Lizzie down on the grass.

"I used up the last flour in the barrel," Daisy said. "Good thing the master's off to the mill today."

At the wharf, Master Guy and Stephen were loading sacks of grain aboard the boat; they were going to Cupids Cove for the day. Nancy had already discussed with Master Nicholas whether their grain stores, once made into flour in the mill at Cupids Cove, would be enough to keep them supplied with bread until the sack ships came again at the end of the fishing season. She enjoyed this work for the master, liked learning the mysterious skill of writing down figures and calculating sums, liked to keep record of their stores and supplies, the credit earned for their fish and the value of trade goods. "We will have plenty of flour when they come back this evening," she said now.

"Aye," said Daisy wistfully, watching as the shallop pulled away from the dock. After a moment she said, "When do you expect Ned back from this voyage with Captain Dermer?"

"Ned thought they might return by August or early September. They will want to make good use of all the fine weather to explore the coast, but be back in port before the autumn storms come."

"But Tisquantum will stay there."

"'Tis most like he will. Captain Dermer needs Tisquantum as a guide, but Tisquantum wants only to go back to his own people." She darted a glance at Daisy, who stood with her hands in her apron pockets looking out to sea. "You'd know more than any of us, I 'low, about what Tisquantum's plans are."

"I know he wants to go home—but why? He was here with us, with good Christian folk, learning our ways, speaking our tongue. Why would he go back to live wild in the woods?"

"I suppose he misses his family, his friends. And he may very well like the way they live. 'Tis what he grew up accustomed to, after all."

"I do not know why he could not have been contented here with us."

Lizzie, playing in the grass, let out a little whimper and put her arms up to her mother. Nancy scooped her up. How easy it was to comfort a tiny child, and how hard to comfort Daisy! Daisy's heart had already been broken so many times, and Nancy had no soothing words to offer.

In spite of, or perhaps because of, Nancy's silence, Daisy went on. "I never told no-one this—not even Bess, for I didn't want her to think ill of me—but before Tisquantum went away, I told him that if he wanted it, we could. Well. We could lie together, like man and wife."

That was a surprise. Not that a couple would come together in that way—plenty of folks did, before they could get themselves in front of a preacher. Nancy and Ned had done so themselves, and in this remote land, where ministers were scarce, such pairings would likely be more common even than back in England. But in such a case promises would be made, even if not before a minister. No woman who was virtuous, or simply prudent, would lie down with a man who would not promise to stay by her and look after any child that might be conceived.

"Did you think...that he would stay, if he got you with child?"

Daisy looked as if she were fighting back sobs. "I hoped so. But he said—he said among his folks, 'twould be dishonourable to do such a thing and then leave me, and he thought 'twas the same among the English."

"He was right to say so. Where would you be now, if you were carrying his child?"

"I would have it, at least!" Daisy said with sudden fierceness. "I married Matthew, and he died with no child to remember him by. And then I married Tom, and 'twas the same. I thought at least—" She wiped at her face with the edge of her apron, and Nancy turned away so as not to see her tears. "He told me—he said he would not stay here, but I could go with him, and that his people would welcome me. To live among the natives, can you imagine?"

Nancy said nothing. It would be strange indeed for Daisy, living among a different people, whose language and customs were so remote. After her time in Pocahontas's household, her friendship with Matachanna, Nancy did not see the native people quite the same way as the other settlers did, yet even she could not imagine living in the Powhatan village as one of their people, the way Pocahontas and her kinswomen had lived among the English settlers. This was not something she could find words to explain to Daisy, and even if she could, what good would it do?

Daisy sighed heavily. "There's a deal of work to do today, I hardly know why I be standing here gossiping." She marched ahead of Nancy, back to the Guys' house.

There was, indeed, a deal of work to do today, with the master and Stephen gone off to Cupids Cove and the rest of the men out fishing. Young Hannah, six months pregnant, watched the little ones while the other women weeded between the newly planted rows of crops. In the afternoon, the women moved to working on the flakes, splitting and salting and turning the cod.

It was later, after the evening meal but before dark had fallen, that the shallop returned from Cupids Cove and the men went to the dock to help unload barrels of flour. Nancy and Daisy put out the pork pie, bread, and cheese they had laid aside for Master Nicholas and Stephen. But they did not come alone; Governor Hayman was with them. He, too, had been at Cupids Cove today, and come back to Musketto Cove with tidings for the folk there.

"'Twas most fortunate I found Master Guy in Cupids Cove today," the governor began, "for I had gone there to bring Governor Mason troubling news that touches on both our colonies, Cupids Cove and

Bristol's Hope alike. We have had word of a pirate attack on a fishing station between here and Cupids Cove, at Port de Grave. A dozen men were taken captive, along with the fish they had already caught and made so far—not much, for 'tis early in the season. We think their chief aim was to take men rather than goods, though they did make off with some of the stores as well."

"Turks? Or do we think 'tis Englishmen again?" Frank asked.

"There was no-one left of that vessel's crew to tell us what the men who attacked them were like," Governor Hayman said. "The captain and two of the ship's officers were slain, and the rest taken. But just yesterday—which would have been a few days after this attack occurred, judging by what we could learn from other fishing crews—we had something quite disturbing come to our own settlement."

"More thievery?" That was Kathryn, listening wide-eyed to the governor's tale. There had been no more thefts since the pig had been stolen from Harbour Grace late in the autumn, but the thought of piracy had been much on everyone's mind.

"They did not steal anything this time, but delivered a warning," Governor Hayman said, taking out a piece of paper from his inner pocket.

"A warning?" Rafe repeated, incredulous. "How, tied to a bird's leg?"

"'Tis the same as the thefts back in the autumn," said Governor Hayman. "The message was found in the morning, at my very doorstep, so it must have been delivered by night—but there was no sign of any unfamiliar boat putting into shore. Once again, 'twas someone who came overland, through one of the woods trails."

"And what does it say?" Kathryn asked.

The governor opened the paper and read aloud.

"Governor of Bristol's Hope, greeting and fair warning. We hope that the colonists at Harbour Grace and Musketto Cove will have more good sense than those at Cupids Cove. You shall see that by settling this shore you are come into our territory, and you must not try to abide by the King's law, or call upon his Majesty to save you. If you prove yourselves our friends and show it by tribute, we will not trouble you further—"

"Tribute!" That was Frank again. "We'll not pay tribute to no pirates, will we, masters?"

"We do not intend to," Nicholas Guy said. "But let the governor read the rest."

The governor went on. There was a list of everything the pirates wanted in tribute. So many pigs, and so many chickens, barrels of flour and sugar. Nancy tallied their stores in her head as he read out the list; they could never survive the rest of the fishing season if they gave so much of their goods away to pirates.

There was a time given, as well. "On Midsummer's Day," it said, "we will come to Harbour Grace and receive your tribute, if you wish to live in peace."

Governor Hayman read the conclusion of the letter. "If ye be not our friends, and show your friendship by tribute, we will not stop at your livestock, fish, and goods. Who knows but that we may come for your sons and even your fair-haired daughters? Beware to the mothers of Bristol's Hope, be sure your husbands are wise and not rash!" Governor Hayman looked up. "'Tis signed, The Prince and the Duke of Carbonear."

Kathryn, who along with Bess had gasped at the line about the mothers of Bristol's Hope, cried out now, and Nancy looked over at her. Kathryn's hand was pressed to her mouth. She had Alice up in her lap and was clinging to the child as if a pirate might come even now and rip the little girl from her.

Amid the chorus of voices that broke out as the governor finished, Rafe said, "The prince and the duke? What is that folly about?"

"'Tis often in the manner of pirates to give themselves grand names and titles, whether they own them by birth or not," Governor Hayman said. "But we have our suspicions as to the identity of these two."

"Gilbert Pike of Carbonear—of course we have suspected him for some time," said Nicholas Guy. "And he may well be—"

"Calling himself the prince," said Kathryn. "For we all know his wife puts on airs of being an Irish princess."

"My thought exactly," Nicholas Guy said.

"And it takes little wisdom to guess who might style himself duke, if he has turned to piracy," Governor Hayman said. "We wondered what had become of Thomas Willoughby. His father is but a baronet back in

England, certainly nothing like a duke! But here in this wild land, men may give themselves titles they could never carry in the old country."

The room became a babble of men's voices then, talking about how to respond to the pirates' demands, about preparing defenses. Nancy thought of the great mounted guns at Cupids Cove—would they need one here, in their quiet harbour?

She excused herself, with Lizzie half-asleep in her arms. Nancy knew better than anyone, even Master Nicholas, what stores and supplies they had; she could discuss with him what could be spared, but it seemed that none of the men was even considering paying the tribute. It was time to go back to her house and bar the door, and try to banish all thoughts of pirates.

Yet she was barely there half an hour, Lizzie abed while Nancy prepared for the next morning, when someone tried the door and, finding it latched, knocked softly. Not the heavy fist of an intruder, but the light touch of a friend.

She let Kathryn in, and built up the fire again. It was evident her mistress had come to settle in for a talk. They pulled stools up to the hearth, and Nancy took up her knitting, which she could do even in the half-light. Kathryn had brought no work with her; her hands knotted in her lap.

"Have you come to tell me why this letter from the pirates troubled you so?" Nancy said, when Kathryn showed no signs of beginning the conversation. "For I saw you when he read it out. You feel more fear than the rest of us do."

"'Tis true—oh, to my shame! I was a fool, Nancy, and I have kept this secret so long, but now I fear 'twill destroy me, and destroy us all."

"Well, tell me the tale first, and after that we can unravel how to keep it from destroying you." Nancy had her suspicions; she had had them for a long time, but she did not know the whole of the story, and perhaps Kathryn was now going to unfold it.

"I had best—I need to tell it from the start," Kathryn said. "That summer six years ago, when we were both at Cupids Cove. You remember?"

"I am not like to forget being accused of witchcraft and put on trial before the masters of the colony, no."

"Of course. And you remember—you remember that when they did try you, Thomas Willoughby spoke in your defense?"

Nancy was silent a minute. "I do recall it. It surprised me, for he had never taken the slightest notice of me, but I knew he had a quarrel with Governor Guy and Master Crout. I thought 'twas only a matter of him trying to assert his own authority, nothing to do with me or my case."

"I suppose there was something of that to it," Kathryn admitted. "But I doubt he would have spoken out, if not for..." Her voice trailed off.

Nancy tried to think of a way to say it, to make it easier for Kathryn. "You...struck a bargain with him?"

The fire crackled in the silence. Kathryn nodded. "I take no pride in what I did."

Nancy poured a mug of ale for each of them. "You did this for me? To win his support?"

"Yes! I swear I'd never have been unfaithful to Nicholas if not for that. But you must know, I—I desired it. Desired him—Thomas."

"So, you made a sacrifice, but 'twas no hardship to make it." Kathryn looked up then, looking for that judgment in Nancy's eyes, and Nancy smiled at her. So many years had gone by, after all.

"Yes, well, there was passion between us. I'll say that much and no more."

"That's well enough, I don't need chapter and verse of the tale."

"It would have been over and done, if Thomas had not returned here. But even before he came back..."

Nancy saw it all then, the pieces fitting together. "Oh. Alice? Of course."

"I do not know for certain. But she was born at the end of that winter, in March, just a year after Jonathan."

"So, the time is right. And she looks not like you or any of your family, nor like your husband or the boys."

Then the rest of the tale came out, the part Nancy had already heard, of how Kathryn had been lost in the woods, how Willoughby had found her and taken her to his house at Harbour Grace. The parts she had not heard: how he had asked Kathryn to leave her husband, stay with him and be his mistress. How he had held it over her, that he could tell Nicholas the truth and ruin her. How he had seen Alice at Musketto Cove.

"You heard what that letter said, about fair-haired daughters? If Thomas truly is one of these pirates, then that is not simply some poetic flair. That is a message, intended for me." Kathryn pulled her shawl tighter about her shoulders. "We've only three daughters among us, between here and Harbour Grace—Lizzie, Meg Holworthy, and Alice. And only Alice is fair-haired."

Nancy sat silent for a few moments, turning it over in her mind. "I fear you may be right," she said at last.

"Oh, Nan! I thought—I half-hoped if I told you the whole tale, you would tell me I was being foolish, making up some grand story in my head, as you know I am wont to do. But if you truly think there is something to it, what can I do? What can I tell my husband and Governor Hayman to convince them to pay the tribute? They'll not listen to me, but perhaps you could talk to Nicholas. You know all about our supplies and what we have in store. You are the one woman whose counsel he might heed."

"But he would want to know why I would counsel paying tribute to pirates. We could not afford it." Nancy paused, thinking back to those months she tried hard to forget, sailing under Captain Sly and then Captain Fitzpatrick. "Even if we could, 'twould be folly to give in to such men. There are seaports that exist only to support the trade of piracy. It seems the Pikes and Willoughby mean to turn Carbonear into such a port, to make it a base to prey on fishing ships and merchant vessels."

"It seems so."

"I know little enough of great men and their business and politics, but I do not believe any good can come of having truck with pirates, and making this New Found Land a den of thieves. 'Tis only sensible that the Governor and your husband would take a stand against such, and fight back if need be."

"Fight back! Nan, if they try to resist at all, Willoughby will use what he knows against me. My husband will cast me aside, and perhaps Alice, too. What will I do then? Not go to be Willoughby's doxy, that's for certain!"

"Of course not. If it came to that, you could live here with me and Ned, or go back to your father in Bristol, who would be glad to see you again. You are not without a friend in the world, after all." *I'd not see my own sister cast out*, Nancy almost said. But there was no time tonight for that story.

"But I do not want to be cast off!" Kathryn said, her voice breaking into a sob. "It happens I am quite fond of my husband, not to mention my home, and my sons. For even if Alice were cast aside with me, Nicholas would never let me see the boys again." Now the tears were coming hard and fast. "You are right, we cannot bend the knee to the so-called prince and duke. But I cannot risk Willoughby's revenge, either!"

Nancy laid down her knitting and came to kneel beside Kathryn. She took Kathryn's hands in hers and rubbed them briskly. "Hush, hush now, Kat. Do not cry."

"I must, Nan! I know my troubles are as nothing compared to what you have been through, but this is serious indeed—"

"No, I mean hush, or you'll wake—ah, there she is." A child's wail drifted from the sleeping chamber at the back of the house, and Nancy stood up. "I must go to her, try to put her back to sleep before she wakes up in earnest. But look—we will find a way past this. I promise you that. I know not how just now, but surely you and I together are more than a match for Thomas Willoughby."

TWENTY-FIVE

An Enemy is Given Aid

MUSKETTO COVE AND
CARBONEAR, JUNE 1619

And leave revenge of vile words to the Gods...
—Homer's Odysseys, Book 22, 367

KATHRYN SLEPT BETTER THAT NIGHT THAN SHE HAD
expected. Nancy's assurance that together they were a match
for Willoughby made no practical difference to her situation,
yet it comforted her. But her dread returned the next morning when
Hannah came in from feeding the chickens and said, "There's a boat
just tied up to the dock. Fellow in it says he's from Carbonear."

The name laid a cold hand upon her heart. *Carbonear.* This must
have something to do with the Pikes, with Willoughby, with the letter.

But the stringy young fellow with the strong Irish accent who came
to the door a moment later hailed her with relief. "Mistress Guy! Be
you the midwife?"

"Yes," she said, claiming the title without thinking.

"I serve Master and Mistress Pike at Carbonear. The mistress, she's
in a bad way in childbed. She's never had no midwife before, but the
master says she be like to die if I don't get someone."

Mistress Pike in a bad way. "Wait for me—I must pack a bag. I will be ready to return with you in half an hour," Kathryn said, moving towards her still-room as she spoke.

Sheila Pike had certainly colluded with the pirate attack on the Guys' first plantation, and might even now be in league with Thomas Willoughby to threaten Harbour Grace and Musketto Cove. But as Kathryn packed a bag with everything needful for a difficult delivery, she could not think about the grudges she held against Sheila Pike. She would not refuse to help at a birthing-bed.

"You ought not to go alone," Nicholas said. "I should come with you."

"You were gone all day yesterday; you should be here today. If anyone is to come with me, it should be one of the women, to help with the birthing." Nancy had been a good, steady helper at Bess's and Elsie's childbeds, but she could not ask Nancy to come to Carbonear for an unknown length of time; either leaving Lizzie behind or bringing her would be difficult.

In the end, Kathryn took Daisy, and told her husband he did not need to go himself, nor to spare one of the men who should be out fishing today. "Whatever the Pikes are, they surely would not call me for help and then threaten or hurt me," she assured him, with more confidence than she felt.

There was no sign of Thomas Willoughby, nor of Gilbert Pike or any other man, when they got to the Pike plantation on the north side of Carbonear harbour. The Pikes' menfolk were all out fishing. The house was a woman's domain: one maid trying to care for the children, another running to the door shouting, "Thank God you've come, mistress!" And Shelia Pike, in her sleeping chamber, screaming as if she were being attacked.

Later, when there was time to think, Kathryn reflected that this was by far the most difficult birth she had ever attended. The loss of Bess's babe last winter had been a terrible blow, and she felt, as she had then, that she was unlikely to be able to save the baby. But she had never seen a mother bleed so much, cling with such a faint thread to life.

The child came out, finally—a boy, still and grey. He was not breathing, and she could not make him cry. Kathryn wrapped him in a blanket and told one of the maids to put the little body in a basket by the hearth while she worked to save the mother's life.

In the end, she thought, her herbs and potions, and the little skill she had, did not make much difference. Sheila Pike seemed to cling to life through her own fierce determination, more than anything Kathryn had done. As the late-afternoon shadows lengthened, Kathryn thought the worst was over, and that the woman would live. Daisy brought in the cordial she had brewed from the Kathryn's herbs. Sheila Pike could only manage a few swallows before she closed her eyes, but it looked as if she were sleeping naturally rather than slipping into unconsciousness. She had not asked about the infant.

"Will she live?" one of the Pikes' serving girls asked when Kathryn told her to stay by her mistress.

"I have hopes she will. She is through the worst of it now, but the next few days will be uncertain."

"Will you stay here in case she has need of you?"

Kathryn wanted very much to be back at Musketto Cove, but she looked at the sun dipping towards the horizon and sighed. "We will stay tonight. If she is well enough in the morning, we will have one of your men take us home."

Gilbert Pike made his first appearance in the house as Kathryn was finishing her meal. "How fares my wife?" he said, without greeting or preamble.

Kathryn's last meeting with this man had not been a pleasant one. Three years ago, her husband had almost had to haul her away from the Pikes' wharf as she accused Gilbert Pike of planning the attack on the Guys' plantation. They had not met since.

Briefly, she told him of Sheila's condition and the chances that she would make a successful recovery. He nodded. "'Tis a shame the child did not live. I'll see you're paid for your trouble. I will settle with your husband."

He turned to leave the house, but Kathryn followed him out. "Master Pike, a word, if I may?"

He eyed her warily. No doubt he still thought of her as a spitfire and a disobedient wife, and she had been unable to save his infant son.

"There is one thing my husband would like in payment for my saving your wife's life," Kathryn said. "If you are in league with Thomas Willoughby and know where he is to be found, we would appreciate you telling us."

Pike spat on the ground. "I was thinking more in the line of a few chickens as payment."

"Fowl are always welcome, but information is worth more. We know you are working with him against us, and yet you send to us for help when your wife is in childbed. 'Tis bold of you to think that we would be willing to help. But as you see, I came at once."

"Birthing and dying is women's matters. Business and trade is men's matters. You've tried to meddle in men's matters before, and I told your husband he needs to control you better."

She stifled the flare of rage in her chest and kept her tone as even as she could. "Men's matters, was it, when pirates attacked our home, when one of my maidservants was wounded and another taken captive? How is it a men's matter, if women are the ones who suffer?"

Pike turned his head to spit before looking back at her. "That's no business of mine, one way or t'other."

"So, you will tell me nothing of Willoughby? Not even where he may be found?"

"He is not here on my plantation, I'll tell you that much."

"But he is not dead, or gone back to England? You have seen him?"

"You've earned no help from me. All I've got out of this business is a dead brat and a wife who might or might not live to bear me more. You'll be doing well to get a brace of birds out of this day's work."

She turned back up the path towards the house, fists clenched. Nothing could be gained by getting angry at this man.

Sheila Pike's children were playing in the grass, watched over by one of the maids who was also feeding the hens. Two of the menservants were turning fish on the flakes down by the water. The life of a plantation went on, regardless if a baby was born or died, if a mother survived or succumbed.

Kathryn did not like Sheila Pike, had never liked her since their first meeting and since then had accumulated many reasons for her dislike.

Even after spending hours trying to help her survive, she still could not feel any warmth or fondness for the so-called princess. But she felt a kinship with her, all the same, as she looked at the work going on all around and thought how none of it would be possible but for women. If Sheila Pike had died in childbed, her husband would likely have taken one of the maids to warm his bed; the women were both essential and expendable.

"Mistress!" Daisy threw open the door, clutching a blanket. Kathryn opened her mouth to ask what she had there, but then she saw.

"I looked—into the basket, I was adding wood to the fire, and—I saw it. Saw it move—the hand." She thrust the blanket-wrapped bundle, the baby that was supposed to be dead, into Kathryn's arms. He was still little and pale, but the grey-blue tinge had gone from his skin. His eyelids fluttered.

"He might yet survive," Kathryn said. "We will put him back by the fire for now, for surely 'twas the warmth that brought him around. And when Princess Sheila wakes, we will give the child to her to nurse. There is colewort in my bag; boil some in ale and I will give it to her when she wakes, to bring in her milk."

It was a miracle, but such a fragile one. Later, Kathryn took the baby and laid him on his mother's chest.

"I thought...he was..."

"We all thought so. But he is alive. Look you, you have a miraculous baby who has come back from the door of death. Feed him; 'twill do you both good."

It did, indeed, seem to do them both good, and Gilbert Pike returned to the house to find his wife nursing the son he thought dead. Kathryn thought of asking him, *What do you owe me now?* but said nothing.

In the end, it was Sheila Pike who paid the debt, not her husband. She slept a little more that night, woke with better colour in her cheeks, and was able to take some ale and pottage for breakfast. The babe slept cuddled in beside her; he too had a better colour.

As Kathryn was bidding farewell to Mistress Pike with some final instructions, the Irishwoman gripped Kathryn's arm. "I owe you great thanks, Mistress Guy."

"I did my duty. I am glad the outcome was so happy."

"You might have left me to die, and my son as well."

"I would not do that," Kathryn assured her. "If I can save life, I will."

"I am—sorry, for things that have passed between us."

"There is no changing the past." Kathryn paused. "But the present and future—that is another matter. If you can do something to help us now, it would be all the payment I require for my services."

"What matter?"

"I mean the prince and the duke. I mean these demands your husband and his allies have made to my husband and Governor Hayman, their demand that we pay them tribute. Most of all, I mean Thomas Willoughby. If you know where he can be found, I would be most grateful for that information."

"I cannot...I cannot tell you that."

"Cannot or will not?"

Sheila Pike was silent, looking down at her son in her arms. He was still so tiny, so frail. When she looked up at Kathryn again, her expression was wary. "Will you come back?" she said. "If I need you again, or if the babe does?"

"I do not know how much I can do, beyond the remedies I am leaving with your women. If you need me..."

"You will come, if I give you the information you seek."

Kathryn willed herself to keep still. The thought of trading care for information would not have entered her mind, but Sheila Pike was a woman who judged other people by her own measure, and enjoyed having power over them.

She wished she had brought Nancy, instead of Daisy, with her. She remembered one of Nancy's tales about her time on the pirate ship, how she had told those men that she had once been accused of being a witch, but also told them it was true, she did have a witch's powers to curse those who harmed her. *I am no witch*, Kathryn thought, though she knew in some people's minds the lines between midwife, wise-woman, and witch were very faint. *Sometimes it may not hurt to let people think you are more powerful, and more cruel, than you truly are.*

"Willoughby has a house here, in Carbonear," Sheila Pike blurted. "At the far end of the harbour, near the mouth of the river. It cannot be seen from the shore; it is well back in the woods. He has a ship, but 'tis not always there. He has men working for him. That is all I know, I swear." She hesitated, then added, "And yes, my husband and I have made common cause with him, but—I will put a stop to that, if I can."

Kathryn held her breath. This was more than she had hoped for. The Irishwoman went on. "It is Willoughby, not my husband, who wants to threaten Bristol's Hope. We never wanted English settlers on this shore, but now that you are here, we have no quarrel. I will try—try to make sure our business does not touch upon yours, that Bristol's Hope is left unharmed. Will that content you?"

"There is only so much that we women can do to affect the decisions of men, Mistress Pike. If you vow to me that you will do your best, that is enough for me."

It was not, of course. But it would be enough for now.

TWENTY-SIX

An Attack is Averted

MUSKETTO COVE AND HARBOUR GRACE,
JUNE 1619

There, close upon the sea, sweet meadows spring;
That yet of fresh streams want no watering...
—*Homer's Odysseys*, Book 9, 203–4

O N THE VOYAGE HOME, IN A SHALLOP ROWED BY ONE of Pike's men, Kathryn said nothing about her conversation with Sheila Pike. Daisy had no need to know about it. When she got home, Kathryn planned to tell Nicholas of the promise she had managed to wring from Sheila. She would not tell him what Mistress Pike had said about Willoughby having a place in the woods at the end of Carbonear Harbour; she could not risk a confrontation between Nicholas and Willoughby.

Daisy was lost in her own thoughts. "'Tis a hard thing, bearing a child, is't not?" she said as they rounded the point past Carbonear Island.

"Aye, it can be. Few women have as hard a time as Mistress Pike, but she and the babe both survived, which is more than many can say."

Daisy was silent again for a few moments. "Perhaps 'tis not so bad, to be spared all that."

"It might happen to you yet, Daisy."

Daisy shook her head firmly. "No. I was right before. After what happened to poor Matt and Tom, I'll not marry again." The morning light slanted on her pinched little face. Daisy was no great beauty, but she looked sweet and almost young in the soft sunshine. "Even poor Isaac. I never cared for him, and told him I'd not marry him, but he died anyway, just because he fancied me. And Tisquantum—"

"He cared for you, and you for him. But he did not die."

"For all I know, he could be dead. He's gone off to sea. Who knows what may happen? If he lives, likely 'tis because he never stayed here with me." She drew a deep breath. "I did the right thing, for him and for myself."

Who can ever know when we've done the right thing? Kathryn wondered. She told her husband what had passed between herself and the Pikes, leaving out the information about Willoughby's whereabouts. With Nancy she discussed the whole matter thoroughly. And then all she could do was let time pass for a fortnight, until it was Midsummer's Eve.

Nicholas said he would spend the night at Harbour Grace. "'Tis best I be there first thing in the morning, and you as well, if you would come with me. Governor Hayman, Holworthy and I have talked it over, and we believe that is where these pirates will approach, since 'twas there the message was sent."

"Unless they do not come at all," Kathryn said.

"That is our hope," Nicholas said. "If your skills as a healer have won us a reprieve, the whole colony will be grateful to you. But we cannot rely on it. Pike may not honour his wife's promise, and even if he does, he may not be able to sway Willoughby."

There had been no time to put in any sort of defenses, though Nicholas had already spoken to the governor about getting a big gun for Harbour Grace, similar to the ones at Cupids Cove. In case there should be any attack on Musketto Cove, he had told Frank, Rafe, Stephen and Hal to take their muskets out in the fishing boats with them today, and to stay near the mouth of the cove.

Kathryn asked Nancy if she minded being left at Musketto Cove while Kathryn and Nicholas went to Harbour Grace on the morrow.

"Nicholas seems very sure they will not land here, but I hate to think of you being here if—" She broke off, unable to put it into words. Surely the horror of that attack six years ago could not come a second time? "Come to Harbour Grace with us tonight. Or I could stay here with you."

"Nay, be not so foolish," Nancy said, with a lightness of tone that Kathryn suspected was more than half a pretence. "If they are more like to land at Harbour Grace than here, why would I want to run there? 'Tis right for you to go, and for me to stay."

Kathryn was still uneasy. But her place, she thought, was at her husband's side, so she went with him and left Nancy behind.

At Harbour Grace everyone was going about their evening chores with an air of tension, waiting to see what the morning would bring. They dined with Governor Hayman and the Holworthy family, and talked about the news at both plantations in an attempt to avoid talking about the prince and the duke.

"And what of your own house, Jem? Are you working at that still?" Nicholas asked.

"Nay, we have laid aside plans to finish that house ourselves, and turned it over to young Marshall here," Jem Holworthy said, nodding towards James Marshall. "He's having a wife sent out from England, by special order."

The young servant ducked his head as his cheeks coloured. "The maid is a cousin of my stepmother. We knew each other a little when we were younger, before I came out. I sent word, and it seems she is willing to give life in the colony a try. She will come out on the company ship at the end of the fishing season, and we will be wed."

"And glad we will be to have another young couple to begin a family here. I have invited the Holworthys to make our arrangement permanent, that they will remain here, in the governor's house," Governor Hayman said, pouring himself another cup of ale and passing the jug on down the table. "It is as much their home as mine—more, perhaps. 'Twill be good to have someone in the place over winter, too, so that it falls not into disrepair."

"Ah, then you mean to go back to England, and not stay a second winter here?" Kathryn asked him.

"Yes, I have business in England that I must attend to. There is little work to do here once the fishing season is over. Nothing you brave colonists cannot manage for yourselves. I will, of course, return on the first vessel in spring."

"Of course." Kathryn hid a smile. As the first snows fell last winter, Governor Hayman had waxed poetic about how clean and lovely the blanket of snow was, how fresh and healthful the air, how clear the skies. But after the long, cold months of winter, after snowstorms and supplies running low and John Crowder freezing to death in the woods, he had apparently decided his new territory was best governed in the summer months.

She and the governor read aloud from Homer that night, and the governor commended her on the few lines of script she had produced. For the first time, she had written something of her own rather than copying lines from the book she was reading. "Why, this is quite good. You have a good turn of phrase, as well as your hand being clear and easy to read," he said. "If you had been born to a higher station in life and been educated earlier, why, you might be one of our lady poets. Another Countess of Pembroke, perhaps. You might be the first poetess of the New World."

"Ah, you flatter me! I could never be a poet. But if I could get hold of paper, I have thought I might keep a kind of journal—an account in plain words, of what it is like to be a planter's wife here in the colony. Has such a thing been done before?"

"Scarcely by anyone, and certainly not by a woman, but I believe you have the skill. I myself will arrange for paper. If you keep an account over the winter, I will be most interested to read it next summer."

That night, in a spare bed in the governor's house, she told Nicholas of the conversation. "Would you have any objection to me trying to write? A simple account of this place, perhaps to note down some of the plants and remedies I have discovered here, and a record of what our days are like? Such a record would be useful to share with other women who are thinking of coming out to the colonies."

"You are so busy already with the house and children, the garden and the animals, I scarce can see when you would find time to write.

But if anyone can set herself up as a diarist, it would be my little wife. To think, she scarce could read a letter when first we married, and now fancies she can write a book!"

"I could work on it in winter, when there is not so much outside work to do."

"The main thing now is to ensure that we continue to have a safe colony here, before we trouble to write down any accounts of it," Nicholas said. "And whether we are to have that, we will see on the morrow."

In the morning, the fishing boats from the Harbour Grace plantation did not put out to sea. The governor ordered all the men to stay ashore. The boats from the summer fishing stations were out on the water, but no large vessel rounded the point or sailed into Harbour Grace. By midmorning the governor gave the order for everyone to resume their usual tasks.

The midday meal came and went, the afternoon lengthened, and at last Governor Hayman said, "It looks as if the prince and the duke, whoever they are, have decided to let us bide, and not demand tribute."

"Then we owe thanks to my good wife, and to God for sparing the life of Master Pike's wife and child, so that his heart was softened towards us," Nicholas said.

Back at Musketto Cove, their family and neighbours had also passed an uneventful day, with no sign of pirates. Nancy had taken advantage of the weather to put herself, Daisy and Hannah to work washing out all the bed linens, which now draped over bushes all about the property. "So, we will have no sheets to sleep in tonight, but all will be fresh tomorrow," Nancy announced to Kathryn.

As she greeted her children, sweeping Jemmy up in her lap and cuddling Alice and Jonathan close, Kathryn allowed a wave of relief to wash over her. Perhaps the good work she had done at the Pikes' plantation had been enough. Perhaps Gilbert Pike had been able to prevail upon Thomas Willoughby, that the little colony at Bristol's Hope was to be left in peace. She pushed aside the troubling question of where Willoughby was and what his aims were, and decided to simply enjoy the relief.

It was durable, that sense of relief. One day passed into another as June warmed into July. She worked, and watched her children grow, and when Hannah's baby came in August, Kathryn helped with the quick and uncomplicated birth. Nancy was starting to show a belly now, and Bess confided that she thought she might be expecting again too. The women of Musketto Cove were as fruitful as the sea and the land around them; it was a summer of warm days, soft rains, plentiful fish, and good crops in the garden.

There were still rumours of pirate activity about, but the attacks they heard of were on foreign vessels, never on English fishing stations or on English settlers. Kathryn had not yet received the promised gift of paper and ink from Governor Hayman—that would come with the ships in the autumn—and was too busy for writing now anyway, but all summer long she tucked away bits and pieces of information, incidents, and ideas that might form part of the journal she would write in winter.

She was no poet like Master Hayman, but she would write, as he did, that the New Found Land was a good place, and though a settler's life was hard, it was rewarding. She would write about the fish drying on the flake, the turnips and carrots growing in the thin, rocky soil, the berries that ripened on bushes in the fall, and the joy of watching her children tumble about and play and grow strong on land that was their father's, and would be theirs in time. When she had time, and paper and pen, she would write that this was a good land, and that she lived here without fear.

In August, the second letter came, this time to her door.

TWENTY-SEVEN

Safe Harbour is Reached

VIRGINIA, AUGUST 1619

And this port
Were we arriv'd at, by the sweet resort
Of some God guiding us...
                    —*Homer's Odysseys*, Book 9, 217–19

THE SEA WAS CALM AT LAST. FOR DAYS THE WIND HAD driven Dermer's shallop before it, tossing the boat about so they could not even safely make landfall. Ned had brief flashes of memory from his voyage years ago from Cupids on the *Indeavour* with Governor Guy; how the barque had been accompanied by a pinnace, and that smaller boat dashed on the rocks on the homeward journey. He often feared this shallop would suffer the same fate—when he had time to think about fear.

Most of the time, there was no room for thought at all. Only action: bailing out the boat, trying to save their supplies or tossing them overboard to lighten the load, constantly trying to adjust the boat's heading to keep the stern to the wind. All the while being slapped in the face by sheets of rain, so cold and wet and miserable that you wondered if it was even worth surviving.

On the second day, some planks in the boat's hull had worked loose, and water came flooding in. The men had worked quickly to stuff the gap with the blankets and coats, prayers and curses mingling as they did so. That temporary solution slowed the rush of water, but could not stop it completely.

Ned had weathered out storms at sea—bad ones—in larger ships, but nothing could have prepared him for facing a storm in an open shallop. They were all experienced sailors, but every man aboard puked up his guts, and that was far from the worst of it. With no chance to go ashore or even piss or shit over the side of the boat, men soiled themselves and sat in their own filthy, sodden breeches. They licked rainwater to slake their thirst and crammed what they could of the soggy ship's biscuit into their mouths, only to throw up when the boat began to pitch in the heavy seas.

It had been two days, or perhaps three. Day and night, light and dark lost their meaning, and nobody was sure how long the storm had gone on. All this time the wind had blown them south, with the coast still visible on their starboard side but impossible to reach. Now, with the sea calm at last, they rowed to a small, empty cove where they could go ashore, rest, and take stock.

"God be praised, we did not lose a man in all that turmoil," Dermer said. "And we are further along our way to Virginia than we would have been in calmer seas." But nobody felt thankful; they were hungry, thirsty, and exhausted.

Ned's first thought was of sleep, even before food. He drank some fresh water from a nearby stream and then stretched out on the beach, waiting for the ground to stop rocking beneath him. It was late summer in a hot country, and though the heat might feel oppressive before long, being dry and warm was a luxury now.

When he awoke, he joined the other men in foraging for something to eat. Nothing was left of their food stores, but they were able to refill their casks of fresh water, and Dermer had set a few men to gathering oysters in the shallow water, while others picked plums from the trees nearby. With their need for rest and food at least partly satisfied, most of the men also took the opportunity to bathe in the warm water and clean their clothes as best they could.

"God's truth, I don't know if I can get back into that boat," James Hill said as they hung their breeches to dry over some bushes. "I'd walk overland back to Cupids Cove if I could."

Will Spencer nodded. "We should have gone back on the *Bountiful* at Monhegan."

After the encounter with the Wampanoag in Tisquantum's homeland, the crew of the shallop, without Tisquantum but with the addition of two Frenchmen who had been shipwrecked sometime earlier and stayed with the Wampanoag ever since, retraced their voyage back to Monhegan. The Frenchmen were transferred to the *Bountiful*, whose captain would soon return to England with his cargo of cod. But Dermer intended to take the shallop south again, making for Virginia and exploring the coast along the way.

Ned had not been happy with that plan. He and the other New Found Land men were eager to get home once that sobering voyage to Patuxet was over. But the *Bountiful* was going straight back to England. They were welcome to go with it, Captain Dermer told them, and find their own way back to Cupids Cove from there. But if they wanted to complete their service to him and earn their promised pay, they would have to continue on to Virginia, where merchants would honour his credit and allow him to pay his men. There they might find a ship bound for the New Found Land.

So they had turned south again with their small crew—Captain Dermer, Samuel Hollett, John Harvey, James Hill, Will Spencer, Dickon Sadler, George Whittington, and Ned. Weeks passed. They had had more encounters with the natives—at least one of which might have turned violent, had it not been for the timely intervention of a native man who, like Tisquantum, had spent some time as a captive in England and learned the language.

Between the hardships these captives had suffered, and the plague that had ravaged the native settlements, the local people offered little of the open-handed welcome Captain Dermer had hoped to find. Most of them wanted nothing to do with the English. Ned was not surprised. Tisquantum's parting words still lingered in his brain weeks later: *You are not the worst Englishman I have known. But you are not different from the rest of them.*

Once the storm blew up, there was no more time to think of home, nor of whether they were welcomed by the people of the land. The events of those weeks felt like a dream ending in a nightmare.

Ned wrung out his shirt, laid it alongside his breeches. "I had that thought also," he confessed to Spencer. "That we ought to have gone on the *Bountiful* when we had the chance. But then we would be across the ocean in England, looking for a passage home, and might have had worse storms befall us. We cannot be far from Virginia now."

Indeed, they were not. After taking time to repair the damage to the shallop as best they could, Dermer's crew put to sea again. Another day's sailing brought them to a port where the masts of ships rose up to welcome them, the first place since Monhegan where they had seen that welcome site.

"This is the cape they call Point Comfort," Captain Dermer said, "the boundary of the Virginia colony. We'll find good welcome here. Mayhap we'll not even have to go on up the river to James Fort. You Cupids Cove men will likely find a ship here that will take you back home."

"And you will find someone to honour your credit so that we'll go home with coin in our pockets?" Ned asked.

Dermer laughed, "Aye, Perry, you'll get your pay as promised." As though it were a light matter, for a working man to give up his whole summer and then insist on payment for it.

When they went ashore and began to walk along the docks, Ned's attention was diverted by two of the ships at anchor, for he knew them both well. One was the *Treasurer*, which he had sailed on under Captain Argall, and the other the *White Lion*, the ship he had served on under Captain Elfrith's command. Both, then, were still plying the seas down here in Virginia.

Most of the folk on shore were sailors, but there were landsmen there too—some of the Virginia colonists, Ned guessed. Point Comfort did not seem to have many dwellings, but from the dress of the more prosperous-looking men he could guess that the colony's merchants came here to do business with the ships in port. There was the usual busy bustle of boxes and barrels being loaded on and off ships, and amid the noise and hurry he was not wholly surprised to hear a familiar voice call out: "Is that you, Ned Perry?"

"Are you known in these parts?" George Whittington asked, with a hint of surprise.

"I sailed on both those vessels," Ned said, nodding towards the *White Lion* and *Treasurer*, "and a few of my old shipmates are likely still aboard." He hurried ahead of the rest of Dermer's men towards the burly fellow leaning over the rail of the *Treasurer*, waving a greeting. And once he went aboard to greet Red Peter, it was no surprise to see Francis Withycombe climb down from the rigging to say hello as well.

It was not the first time he had encountered these inseparable old friends in an unfamiliar place. Three years earlier, a chance encounter with these two men had led to Ned's second voyage on the *Treasurer* and his reunion with Nancy. "Still aboard this same old ship, are you, then?" he asked.

Francis jumped lightly onto the dock. "Aye, we shipped out with another captain for a while there, for they made Captain Argall governor of Virginia, and the *Treasurer* was back in England. But you know how ships and captains move about. Your old master, Captain Elfrith, has command of the *Treasurer* now, and the *Lion*, that he used to captain, is under a Dutch master called Jope. We saw action alongside of them a few weeks ago—fought and boarded a Portuguese vessel, and took prizes."

"Gold?"

"Slaves," said Red Peter, nodding towards the dock. There, from the vantage point of the *Treasurer*'s deck, Ned saw what he had not seen before: behind the men doing business ashore was a fenced enclosure where two dozen Africans, both men and women, were penned.

"We've about the same number in our holds," Red Peter went on, "and when we came into port yesterday and found the *Lion* had already traded their captives for stores of food, we thought we'd have the same good fortune. But things are not going so smoothly for Captain Elfrith."

"No?" Ned was not surprised Elfrith was in some trouble. His old captain had ever been one to sail close to the edge of the law. But he was distracted by the chained Africans on shore. "These folk were bought as labourers here in Virginia? I thought there was no slave trade in the English colonies."

When Ned had sailed with Elfrith years ago, they had captured African slaves from a sugar plantation in the Indies. The slaves had to be sold in a Spanish port, for Elfrith had said there was no coin to be made selling them in Virginia or Bermuda. The English colonists were not accustomed to slave markets.

"Folks here are beginning to think differently of the trade, now they see how much work it is to grow tobacco. It needs more hands than the settlers have to spare," said Francis, whose brother was a Virginia planter. "The natives have the knack of it—they grew it before we did, after all—but they have no will to work for English planters, and cannot be forced. Captain Elfrith says the Virginia settlers may call the Negroes indentured servants if they don't like to call 'em slaves—he gets paid either way, so it makes no difference to him."

Ned stared at the penned captives. He wondered for a moment why they stayed inside the fence, then realized they were all shackled at the ankles, the chains binding them to each other and to the posts at the corners of the pen. A small group of men huddled together, perhaps working at the locks to try to free themselves, but there was nowhere for them to flee to even if they could break their chains. A woman near the fence called out to passersby, but they either ignored her, or pointed and stared.

He remembered the Africans he had helped to capture. They were already enslaved—had been for years, perhaps all their lives—yet they had fought fiercely to avoid being taken aboard Elfrith's ship, into some new and perhaps worse captivity. These men and women here on the Virginia shore had been taken from their homeland across the ocean, then transferred from one ship to another, to be sold on a foreign shore. Were their spirits crushed by all they had endured, or would they, too, fight for their freedom if given a chance?

Ned supposed he was one of those Englishmen who still found something distasteful about the trade. But perhaps Francis was right. The day was coming when slave markets might be a common sight in English colonies, and he would have to accustom himself to it.

He turned away and pulled his attention back to his friends, who invited him to share a drink as they told him the news of the last few years. "Peter's been made bo'sun now, you can see how it's gone to his head, swelled him up with pride," Francis teased.

"Gone to my head and turned it grey, more like," Red Peter said.

Francis and Ned were of an age, but Red Peter was a few years older than they were, likely in his late thirties now. It was true, Ned thought, that by the look of his once-fiery hair they would soon have to call him Grey Peter. His smile was as warm as ever; becoming a ship's officer had not made him more formal.

"And what of you, Ned?" Francis asked after they had told him their own stories. "When you left Captain Argall's service in London you were going off to join your Nancy. Yet here you are at sea again. Did she turf you out on your arse?"

"I well deserved it, but nay, she did not." It was Ned's turn to tell tales. He told them how he and Nancy were married, with one child and another on the way, that they owned their own house and plot of land. He told them the other side of it too: the hardships of life in the northeastern colony, the bitter cold of the winters, losing toes to frostbite and seeing a friend freeze to death beside him. The long, hard hours out in the fishing boat, then salting and turning the fish on the flakes. Even as he spoke he thought it was no worse, in its way, than the work that folk in Virginia put in on the tobacco plantations, or the killing heat of their summers and swampy air.

"I'd best not complain, for truth is I love it there," he finished, "and I know I am Fortune's favourite, to have landed in such a good place with a good woman. I'd not be gone from home now, only I am trying to earn some extra coin to better our lot."

As he spoke, he wondered if that was wholly true. Apart from the money, and despite all the hardships of this journey, he could no longer deny that something about the sea, and the wider world it led to, had drawn him back. Would it continue to do so, the pull of home and away ever tugging at him like the ebbing and flowing tides?

He knew better than to ask Francis and Peter if either of them had taken a wife or had thoughts of settling down ashore. Neither of them had interest in a life on land, and Ned knew, though he did not fully understand it, that neither of them wanted a woman either—not for a lifetime, or even for a night. The only steady companionship either of them wanted was each other's.

Dermer's men dined aboard the *Treasurer* that night, welcomed by Daniel Elfrith, who was also glad to see Ned. "Never had a ship's carpenter as reliable since. Are you sure you'll not come back to the sea, Perry?" the captain asked.

"Nay, he's a wife and a tidy little plantation awaiting him up in the New Found Land," Red Peter said.

"That barren place? 'Tis so far north, man—not fit to live in!" Elfrith protested. "If you'll not come back to sea, come back to Virginia—or to Bermuda. Like as not I'll head there next, for the masters here are making trouble for me. Little matter of my letter of marque no longer being valid. I managed to sell a handful of the slaves I took, but the rest will go to Bermuda."

"Begging your pardon, Captain, but for all you say of the harshness of the New Found Land, you could do worse than to set your sights there—at least for this cargo," George Whittington said. "Fishing and making fish is hard work, and the Africans might be well suited for it. 'Twould be worth seeing, at least, if the governors in Cupids Cove and Harbour Grace might buy some off you."

"Nay, Whittington," Captain Dermer said, "Captain Elfrith and I already spoke of this. I told him, I doubt there will ever be much market for African bond-servants in the New Found Land. Their breeding is ill-suited to the climate, and the fishery, though 'tis hard and back-breaking work for those who do it, hardly requires the sheer volume of labourers that tobacco and sugar do."

"That may be, but surely we ought to think of—"

Dermer waved off Whittington with a gesture. "I daresay the odd English settler may have a private Negro servant or two in the New Found Land in time, but there's no money to be made in importing them in large numbers."

"And 'tis too far to go for a gamble," Elfrith said. "I know I will have better luck in Bermuda. As for you fellows who want a passage home, there's a ship called the *Fair Isle* in port here. You might speak to her captain. I hear he's bound north for the New Found Land."

The next morning, Ned said goodbye to Francis and Red Peter. "I'd say we'll not meet again in this life, but I thought the same when I bid ye farewell in London two years ago, and here we are again."

"Aye, the great thing of life on the sea is you never know where you may end up," said Francis. "Someday we may even sail into your little cove in the New Found Land, and you and Nancy and your half-dozen children will have to give us supper at your table."

"I'd like nothing better." Ned laughed. It had lifted his spirits to see these old friends, he thought, as he stood on the dock watching the *Treasurer* lift anchor and sail away from Point Comfort bound for Bermuda.

Ned remembered how Elfrith had once brought a much-needed cargo of grain to sell in that colony, not knowing or caring that it contained a swarm of black rats that plagued the island for years afterwards. Daniel Elfrith knew it was a privateer's business to capture and sell whatever cargo would make him a profit, and he wasted no worry on what might happen once that cargo was ashore. No doubt he thought of his human cargo in much the same way as his rat-infested grain.

Meanwhile, Captain Dermer was having better fortune with the Virginia merchants than Elfrith had. His patron's credit was good enough that he was able to give the New Found Land men each a small purse of coins before they set sail for home aboard the *Fair Isle*. If seeing Francis and Peter had cheered Ned, having a pocketful of money did even more so.

TWENTY-EIGHT

The Innocent are Slaughtered

MUSKETTO COVE, AUGUST 1619

An eagle rose, and in her seres did truss
A goose, all-white, and huge, a household one...
                    —*Homer's Odysseys*, Book 15, 206–7

A T THE END OF AUGUST, THE WEATHER TURNED CHILLY, recalling the fog and northerly breezes of June. Nancy wrapped a cloak around herself and a shawl around Lizzie before they left the little house in the morning.

Already, the fishing boats were out on the water. Nancy pointed out at them as she carried Lizzie across the beach. "Look, someday papa's ship will come into the cove there. It might be today."

"Papa?"

Would Lizzie even remember Ned when he came back? He had been gone three months, an eternity to a child whose entire life encompassed only fifteen months. "Down!" said Lizzie, and Nancy put her on the ground, to toddle along the beach.

The older children were running about outside the Guys' house, despite the cold wind, the bigger boys waving sticks in the air. "Lizzie!" cried Alice, who had recently decided that she was Lizzie's guardian and best friend. She came over, enveloped Lizzie in a hug, and then with some effort picked up the child and carried her to where they were playing.

Jonathan Guy ran towards them as well, but he was interested in Nancy, not in the baby. "Auntie Nan, do you know what papa said? When I am seven years old?"

Nancy squatted down to the boy's level. "No, what did papa say?"

"When I am seven, I can be breeched, and we will have a celebration. I will wear breeches like papa and all the men do!"

"And I will too!" shouted Will Tipton.

"Not until you are seven! I will be breeched first, because I am oldest, and because my papa is the master!"

"Well, it will be six months yet—half a year—before you are seven, and then your papa and mama will decide what to do about breeching," Nancy said. "But you know, when you are a big boy rather than a little one, you will have to work hard, just as the grown folks do."

"I can work hard!" Jonathan insisted, and Will echoed, "Me too!"

Nancy remembered this ceremony of putting on breeches for the first time, that ritual of growing up, from long ago in Bristol when Kathryn's little brother had gone through it—young John, now dead. How quickly time turned, she thought. The little boys at Musketto Cove ran about in the same homespun petticoats that Alice and Lizzie wore, but that would soon change.

Kathryn came out of the house, a basket over her arm. "Ooh, the wind is in off the water," she said, coming down the steps to join Nancy. "It will rain before the day is over, I've no doubt. Boys, be careful with those sticks now, we'll not have anyone hurt today."

"Rain is not so bad. We've had such a hot, dry spell, it will be good for the gardens."

"If only 'tis not cold enough for a frost." Kathryn was on her way to the henhouse to feed the chickens, and Nancy fell into step beside her.

"Surely we'll not have it that cold—not yet." Nancy did not like to think of autumn coming; she wanted Ned safely home before the chilly weather closed in.

They were almost at the henhouse when Nancy realized that something was wrong. The sounds of the morning were the same as always—the chatter of the children at play, the crash of waves on the rocks, the cries of seagulls, the snorting of the pigs in their sty. But this close to the henhouse there should also be the frantic clucking and squawking of hens waking to a new day, ready to be let out into the yard. They were silent, even the cock, who had not crowed since Nancy had come across the beach to the Guys' property.

She felt a sudden, sick pang of apprehension as Kathryn opened the door to the henhouse.

It smelled bad. Of course, it was a henhouse, and would smell of chickens and their dung. But it should not smell of the heavy, metallic tang of blood. Nor should it be so darkly, deeply silent.

Sixteen hens, and one proud cock. Some on their roosts, and some on the floor of the henhouse—every one of them dead. Not with their necks wrung, as one killed a chicken for the pot, but with their throats cut. A slaughter.

The two women stood frozen in the doorway, trying to take in the fantastical scene before them. Blood, feathers, and the still bodies of chickens that had been alive the evening before.

"God in heaven," Kathryn said, her voice shaken. "What—who could have done this?"

Nobody here, Nancy knew at once, though she did not say it aloud. There was not a person in Musketto Cove who could or would do such a thing. "Could—might a wild animal have got in? A fox, perhaps?"

It was the sensible guess, though how a fox might get into a barred henhouse with a sturdy door, built to keep out just such predators, Nancy did not try to imagine. The bodies did not look torn apart, as an animal might do to its prey: when she knelt to look at the chickens on the ground, their necks looked as if they had been cut by a knife. All the same, she said, "Perhaps the door blew open, and a fox got in."

"I heard something—late in the night," Kathryn said. "Some clucking and squawking. I did think some creature was on the place, perhaps prowling around outside. But then they were quiet again, and I thought whatever had scared them was gone."

Any thought that this was a natural disaster was dispelled when they turned back to the door. On the door of the henhouse—not on the outside, where they would have seen it first, but on the inside, to show that an intruder had been here—a piece of paper was stuck to a nail.

Kathryn took the paper, and Nancy followed her outside, away from the scene of carnage. Already Nancy's mind was working, wondering what could be salvaged from this slaughter. Would chickens killed in such a manner be fit for the pot? But Kathryn had eyes only for the paper she held in her hands. After a moment she stopped walking.

"'Tis addressed to my husband," she said. "*Master Nicholas Guy.*"

"Who would do such a thing, and then leave a letter? There was no strange boat in the cove last night, was there?"

"Remember the letter that came to Governor Hayman in the spring, and the thefts from Harbour Grace last autumn?" Kathryn said. "All done during the night, by someone who came unseen through the forest." Her voice trembled.

"What does it say?"

Kathryn began to read aloud. "*O Jerusalem! How often I would have gather'd you under my wings lyke a hen gathering her chicks but lo you would not!*"

"That is Scripture, is't not?"

"I believe it is. Hens and chicks." Kathryn drew a deep, shuddering breath, then went on. "*Poor hens! But lyke to Jerusalem in our Lords day you folk of Musketto have hard Hartes, that will not yield to gentle...*" She hesitated over the next word, shaping it with her mouth before she read on. "I think it says *supplication—will not yield to gentle supplication. So I must take a Firmer Hand. Like Mother Hen will doe all she may to Protect her Chikins, so any Mother will Protect her childe, even the blue-eyed Girl Childe that looks not like the Others. Your good wife I know is a good Mother to all her Children, and knowes best what is her duty towards her Lorde and Master. I ask only what I have askd before, that I bee Free to carrie out my Trade, and that No-one shall Interfere. Leeve me bee—or you will loose more Chikins than these.*"

"It sounds...in truth, it sounds like the ravings of a madman," said Nancy.

"Does it?" Kathryn turned the paper over in her hands.

Nancy said nothing. She thought of the other message from the pirates, the one that also made mention of a fair-haired girl child. "This one is not signed by anyone styling himself a prince or a duke," she said.

"No, it does not need to be. Look at the bottom. The same little sketch—like a crown. It was on the other letter too, and carved into the wall of the pigsty at Harbour Grace."

"Stealing a pig—now that, I can understand," Nancy said. "I could have understood someone stealing some of our chickens, even. But killing them like this? And leaving such a strange message?"

"Oh Nan. What if Nicholas had found it first? Would he have understood? Thomas came by night to do this deed, and left this letter for my husband—but the message is meant for me. He wanted to remind me that he still has the power to ruin me by revealing that he is Alice's father—"

"Yes, I understood that bit."

"If Nicholas had read this, surely he would know, surely he would suspect—"

Nancy took the paper from Kathryn's hand and studied it, though the marks on the page meant little to her. Likely Thomas thought Kathryn would not have been able to read it either, for he could not have known of her lessons with Master Hayman. After a moment, Nancy folded the paper and handed it back.

"'Tis no matter to say, what if Nicholas had read it," she told Kathryn, with more firmness than she felt. "He did not. By great good fortune, it fell into your hands first."

"But what am I to do with it? He says that we should not interfere with his business, but we have interfered already, if the Pikes have truly broken ties with Thomas. What more does he want, except to ruin me?"

"You told me that he asked you—twice—to leave your husband, and come be his mistress. Do you think he might be mad enough to believe you would truly do such a thing?"

Kathryn put the paper in the pocket of her kirtle. "I thought him many things—handsome, once upon a time. Reckless, certes he was that. Dangerous, even. But I never thought him mad." She did not look at Nancy, but down over the little slope of grass to where the children played, Alice's golden head bright against the rest. "What if Nicholas had gone to the henhouse this morning? What if Nicholas had noticed how quiet it was, and gone to see what the matter was?"

Then Daisy came out of the house, and Nancy could see the effort with which Kathryn pulled herself together, arranged her face. "Daisy, 'tis terrible news, and all my fault, I am sure, for I was last to the henhouse last night." Her eyes met Nancy's for a second, and Nancy knew what Kathryn would say next. "I must not have latched the door properly. I believe it blew open in the night, and a fox must have gotten in. It is a terrible loss, Daisy. All our chickens are dead!"

By the time the little bodies had been collected, and what could be salvaged had been saved to eat, everyone had heard the story. Nancy and Kathryn took care of disposing of the bloody evidence themselves, so that no-one else need examine the scene and notice that it did not look like the work of an animal, nor that none of the bodies had been carried off for the fox's dinner. Kathryn played her part as well as any player on a stage: she was shocked and horrified at the loss, but gave no hint of a human hand at work.

"Is't not best your husband knows, at least?" Nancy asked her when they were alone. "And the governor, perhaps? If Willoughby is making threats against us, surely they need to know."

"How can I tell them? *What* can I tell them, that will not lay bare my shame? Nicholas must never see the letter, for I cannot explain what is behind it."

"Then what will you do?"

"What will I do? I will—with your help—have all these poor birds buried before Nicholas comes in for his dinner, while Daisy makes chicken broth. And then—not today, but next week, when I know Nicholas means to go down to Cupids Cove for night or two—I will go to see Thomas Willoughby."

"You are mad! What good can come of that?"

Kathryn looked up from the letter. She had been staring at it all this time, and when she met Nancy's eyes she looked strange, faraway. *Like someone fairy-led*, Nancy thought. "What good? None, perhaps. But you must see, Nan, there is no other way out of it. I cannot tell my husband the truth about this, nor can we ignore it. Either way, Nicholas will find out that I was unfaithful, and cast me aside."

"And what will happen if you go to Willoughby? He will take advantage of you—or worse, he may hurt you. No good can come of it, Kat."

Kathryn crumpled the letter in her fist; Nancy took that fist in her own hands.

"I must try, Nan. I must make him see reason. He does—he did—care for me, some little bit. I can use that, whatever fondness he feels for me."

"No. That will never work with a man like him." Nancy knew that much. If a man like Thomas Willoughby found a woman beautiful and desirable, that would not dispose him to be kind towards her. Desire would not make him gentle.

"Mama!" The inevitable cry came from the clutch of children near the doorstep of the house, and Kathryn stood up. "We'll talk no more of this. My mind's made up," she said.

They did not talk more of it—not during the day, when they were busy about their work. But in the evening, Kathryn walked across the beach with Nancy as she took Lizzie home. "I hope you have changed your mind," Nancy said.

"Not a bit. I have been thinking of it all day, and I see no other way about it. I will tell everyone I am going berry-picking, or some such thing. I know the path to Carbonear. It leads all the way around the harbour to the Pikes' plantation, and that is a good half-day's journey, but I need not go so far. Willoughby's place is at the mouth of the river, so Sheila Pike told me. I can get there in two hours."

"You have planned your excuse and the path you will take, but you do not know what you will do when you get there."

"I told you—plead with him. Make him see sense."

"It will not work."

"Perhaps not!" Kathryn's voice was so sharp it sounded as if she were about to cry. She walked ahead of Nancy, so quickly that she turned her ankle on one of the round beach stones, and then she did cry out. When she looked back at Nancy there were tears in her eyes. "Perhaps it will do no good, but I must try! What else can I do?""

"Is your ankle hurt?"

"No, 'tis nothing." She stumbled on across the beach, limping a little. Nancy hiked Lizzie further up on her hip and hurried to catch up with Kathryn.

"Very well. I know I cannot change your mind, once you have made it up. But there is one thing I do insist upon—you'll not go alone."

"I will—I must. He will never trust me if I bring anyone with me."

"Say what you will, Kat, 'tis not safe for you to go alone to that man's house, supposing you even find him. And if your tale is to be that you are going berry-picking, 'twill make sense if we go together. No-one will credit it if you go off alone. Daisy can watch Lizzie, along with your young ones. If you are determined to do this mad thing, I will go with you."

"No. You cannot. I will not put you into danger."

"So, you admit there is danger."

"Of course there is!" Kathryn turned to face her, and Nancy saw she was truly crying now. "There is danger, but I must face it alone."

"No. You must face it with me." Doubt edged at Nancy's mind: was Kathryn really going to confront Thomas Willoughby? Or was she going to offer herself to him, as she had done before? A sacrifice, or a willing gift?

They were off the beach now, nearing the steps of Nancy's little house. She made the decision on impulse. For two years she had told herself, *Not now, the time is not right*. But it was the last thing she had to offer: the truth.

"Come into the house with me, while I put Lizzie to bed," she said. "Have a cup of ale by my fire, and I will tell you why I must come with you to Thomas Willoughby's house."

TWENTY-NINE

A Secret is Revealed

MUSKETTO COVE, AUGUST 1619

This eas'd her heart, and dried her humorous eyes,
When having wash'd, and weeds of sacrifice
Pure, and unstain'd with her distrustful tears,
Put on, with all her women-ministers...
　　　　　　　—Homer's Odysseys, Book 4, 1020–23

KATHRYN KNELT IN FRONT OF THE HEARTH IN NANCY'S house, building up the fire as Nancy put Lizzie to bed. She had sat by Nancy's fire so many evenings, but tonight felt like an eerie echo of the night a few months earlier when she had finally told Nancy the truth about her affair with Thomas Willoughby. How frightening, yet how freeing, it had felt to confess!

Now it was Nancy who had something to tell her, some secret that Nancy thought would convince Kathryn to bring her along when she went to confront Willoughby.

It would not work; Kathryn had already made up her mind to that. If she went alone, she could convince Willoughby she was coming to him willingly. If she brought a servant, he would never believe that.

She still had no clear plan of what she would do when she confronted Willoughby, but she knew she could not bring Nancy with her—and that was leaving aside the fact that Nancy was six months' gone with child, and would be walking over a rough woods trail towards an unknown destination. Kathryn knew she must do this alone.

Nancy came back into the main room. "Ah, thank you for seeing to the fire. Do you want something to drink?" She moved to the table, took two cups and a pitcher, just as she had done on that other night.

"It matters not what you want to tell me. I will listen, out of love for you, but 'twill not make a difference. I am going alone."

Nancy sat down across from her. In the firelight, it was hard to read the expression on Nancy's face. "That's as may be. But 'tis something I have had to tell you for a long time. It has nothing to do with you and Thomas Willoughby, but when I have told you, you will see why I am determined you cannot go alone." Nancy's hands were busy smoothing down her apron: it was strange to see her without sewing or knitting to occupy her.

"Very well then. Tell me."

Nancy was silent for a moment, as if gathering her thoughts. Finally she said, "There is two ways to tell it—a bare fact, and a story, I suppose. No need to ask which you'd prefer."

"The story, always."

"I will try my hand at it." Another pause. "Your mother and father were married, what, a year, before you were born?"

Whatever Kathryn had expected, it was not this—a tale that would take her back home to Bristol, to before she was even born. "I believe so, yes. About a year, or a little less."

"And when they married and moved into their house, your father hired Tibby as their maid."

"Yes." Kathryn knew it was a small point of pride for artisans and craftsmen like her father to be able to employ a servant so that their hard-working housewives would have some help. It was a little luxury that set them a step above mere labourers. Tibby—Aunt Tibby, she had grown up calling her—had been a fixture in the family for Kathryn's whole life.

"Very well. This is the difficult part," Nancy said. "I learned of it when I went back to Bristol two years ago. It seems that when your mother was carrying you, your father—well. He did as many men do, I suppose. He was not faithful. He—he strayed from his marriage vows."

"What?...Oh." Kathryn had been about to ask *with whom*, but Nancy, bad as she claimed to be at storytelling, had already given her the answer. The whole story unfolded before her like a piece of fabric laid out for cutting.

"I never told you, because I'd not have you think the worse of your father. He is a good man, even though he made that mistake. And he was good to Tibby, too—did not put her out in the street as some men would have done."

"Do you think—did my mother know?"

"Tibby told me that when you were a babe, when she could no longer hide her own belly, she said she had to go home to her sick mother. She came back to work for your parents after I was born. She left me in care of her sister and husband for a few years, until they both sickened and died."

"So that much was true." The story they had both been told as children was that Nancy's parents had died of plague, and the Gales had generously allowed her aunt Tibby to raise her in their household.

"Aye, it was," Nancy said. "And your mother died believing that was the truth of it—so Tibby thinks, anyway. She said there was never a hint of anything in your mother's manner that would suggest she knew the truth."

"So, all this time—more than two years—you have known. That we are half-sisters."

Nancy looked down at her hands, then back up at Kathryn. "Yes. If it had been only that—that we are sisters—I would have told you long ago."

If Kathryn had wanted something else to fill her mind instead of the coming meeting with Willoughby, she had it now, with a vengeance. How could her father have been so callous—to have another woman under his wife's roof? And to keep the woman there, and her bastard child? And what of Tibby? Did she go with him willingly, which would make her a trollop? Or unwillingly, which would make Kathryn's father something even worse? There was no way to hear this story that did not make her think ill of someone she loved.

"Why tell me now?"

"Because you always treated me as a sister, even when you thought I was only a servant. I knew when I was taken captive that you would do anything to bring me home if it was in your power, just as much as Ned would. And that was even without knowing there was a blood tie between us."

"True enough."

"And I would have done the same for you, in any danger, in any trouble you faced. All the more so, now that I know we are sisters. If you will not hear it from your friend, Kat, then hear it from your sister: if you are hell-bent on going to confront Willoughby, you must do what you think best. But I will go with you. I have the right by blood, as well as by friendship, to demand that."

FIVE DAYS AFTER THE SLAUGHTER AT THE HENHOUSE, KATHRYN told Daisy that she and Nancy were going off berry-picking, and not to worry if they were away until suppertime. Nicholas had taken the shallop to Cupids Cove to consult with Governor Mason about some matter of business. With the children in Daisy's care, the two women set off through the woods path that led north from Musketto Cove, hugging the coastline towards Carbonear.

"Are you sure this is not too much for you?" Kathryn asked. Nancy would never admit weakness, but surely she must find this rough trek tiring.

"Sure, I walked to Harbour Grace with Daisy only last week, though that trail is better cleared than this one." Through a break in the trees, they could see the ocean; they were quite near the coast now. Nancy scanned the ground ahead of them. "I believe the path goes this way," she said, pointing. They were a good distance from Musketto Cove now, beyond the paths where they usually travelled for berry-picking or wood-cutting or other ventures into the forest.

"You have been this way before," Kathryn said. "I had forgotten."

"I had almost forgotten, myself," Nancy confessed. "It was only once, and long ago—and coming the other way, of course."

Kathryn had been at Mistress Pike's house in Carbonear on that fateful day six years ago when Musketto Cove was attacked by pirates. But Nancy and Ned had gone home the day before, over this same wooded trail, and spent the night together in the woods. It was on that long walk that they had finally pledged their love and promised to marry—only to be torn apart when Nancy was taken captive.

"How strange," Kathryn said, "to think all that happened so long ago. How different everything would have been, if the pirates had not come then."

"Would it all have been so different?" Nancy wondered aloud. "Or all the same, only a few years sooner? You and Nicholas would have gone on building the house at Musketto; Ned and I would have married then. Daisy would be married to Tom, I suppose, for he would still be alive. But for the rest of us, it seems we have ended up in the same places where we began."

"Yes, I suppose so," Kathryn said. She hiked up her skirts to scramble over a fallen tree trunk, then turned back to help Nancy over. "I suppose so, only—so much happened, in those years. I wonder would we be the same, if—if all those things had not happened?"

"Hard to say." Kathryn knew Nancy did not think about things the same way she did. In Nan's orderly mind, things happened, and you did what you must do to survive them. Nancy never saw any sense in stewing over what might have been. No amount of unpicking or unravelling could change the pattern, once it was knit.

But Kathryn could not stop herself thinking that way. If she had never slept with Thomas Willoughby, then he would have no hold over her. But then, she might not have Alice—if Alice were truly his daughter. Perhaps, without Thomas's support back in Cupids Cove, the masters' decision might have swung the other way, and Nancy been condemned and hanged as a witch. Kathryn had committed a sin, but could she wish a sin undone, when it had brought good as well as ill in its wake?

Now the path had widened, and the trees were more sparse. They could walk side by side, and the sea below them was clearly visible, the sun sparkling on waves. "Thank you," Kathryn said, "for telling me the truth about—about my father. About us. 'Twas no easy tale to hear, but I am glad I know it now."

"I am sorry to have kept it from you so long."

"If this were a tale, my father would be a wealthy man—a king, perhaps—and after all these years we would learn that the little servant girl raised to serve the princes was really a princess herself, and heir to half his kingdom."

Nancy laughed, and despite the dire uncertainty she was walking towards, Kathryn's spirits lifted at the sound. "I've no wish to be heir to half a kingdom, or even to half a stonemason's shop."

"All that is Lily's now, at any rate. I have no inheritance to share with you. And in truth, I know not what to make of this tale, or what to think of my father, and what he did."

"Do not think too harshly of him," Nancy said again. "He loves you, whatever else is true."

"And whatever happens, 'tis most like I will never see him again," Kathryn said. Then she reached for Nancy's hand. "Come, then. We've a ways to go yet."

THIRTY

A Traveller Turns Homeward

AT SEA, AUGUST/SEPTEMBER 1619

Glad he stood with sight
Of his lov'd soil, and kiss'd it with delight...
— *Homer's Odysseys*, Book 13, 529–30

THE CAPTAIN OF THE *FAIR ISLE* MADE NO BONES ABOUT the fact that his business was piracy. Men like Samuel Argall and Daniel Elfrith might mince words about the difference between legal privateering and piracy, might trouble about whether they had valid letters of marque or not. But the sailors on the *Fair Isle* were outlaws, plain and simple, and did not trouble to hide the fact.

"'Tis as honest a trade as any," their ship's carpenter, MacLeish, said to Ned. He was a short, sinewy Scotsman who had been at sea since he was thirteen, and was happy to while away the hours aboard ship chatting to another man who knew his craft.

"Honest?" Ned echoed.

"Very well then, if you mislike the word *honest*, say *decent*. The merchants, the privateers, His Majesty's Navy—all of 'em are scoundrels. I'd as soon sail with men who are truthful about being scoundrels."

Ned laughed. "Aye, that may be. 'Tis glad I am of a ship that will take me home, so I'll not argue with you. My only quarrel is with pirates who attack defenseless folk, especially women and children."

"We've never done that," said the Scotsman. "And we've not taken slaves, neither, for we've two blackamoors among the crew and captain says 'twould cause unrest. Taking a merchant ship loaded down with cod coming back from the New Found Land, now—we'll do that, but we don't trade in human cargo."

Ned could have argued with him about decency. The fishermen aboard those vessels, or the settlers ashore, depended on that cod for their livelihood. But it would be easy for the other man to argue that the merchants who owned the ships and controlled the trade were the greater rogues. And Ned was not in an arguing mood. The winds were fair, the seas quiet, and every day's voyage north brought him closer to home and to Nancy.

When they came within sight of the southern coast of the New Found Land, Ned and the men from Cupids Cove asked Captain Bellamy what port he planned to put into.

"I am not stopping at St. John's, nor will I go all the way to Cupids Cove, for we do not trade with the folk there," the captain told them. "But we have business at Carbonear—that is close enough for you, I imagine."

"Ah, you trade with Master Pike?" George Whittington asked. "I have had some dealings with the Pikes myself—good, sound folk."

Ned kept the coins Dermer had given him close to his person at all times, especially when he slept. Beyond that, he did not bother much about whether the *Fair Isle*'s trade was in legal or illegal goods. But George Whittington had had several private conferences with Captain Bellamy, and Ned wondered what they were discussing.

"Like as not he's trying to get a cut of the business," James Hill said as he, Ned, and the other New Found Land men stood at the rail, watching the rocky coast slip past. "He's a sharp one, is Whittington, always with an eye to profit."

"I heard he was talking to the captain about African servants—trying to convince him to bring some to sell here," Will Spencer said.

MacLeish, who was also nearby, shook his head. "There's no market for slaves in the north," he said, as Captain Dermer had said back in Virginia.

"'Tis a dirty trade, anyhow. I'm as glad to steer clear of it. Treating men and women like cattle," said Hill.

He lowered his voice a little as he spoke, for both the African sailors were working not far away on the deck. Neither of them had had much to do with the passengers during the voyage, but now one of them spoke up. The crew called him Jack, or sometimes Black Jack; he was a slight man who looked tough and wiry and climbed the rigging like a boy, though he was Ned's age or older. "It is common enough in some places," he said now. "Those slaves who were taken to Virginia—they are all from the land the Portuguese call Angola. My father and grandfather called it Ndongo, and there is a great trade in slaves from there to the colonies in the Indies."

"Aye," said Spencer, "and I've heard tell that the Africans there round up their fellow men and sell them to the slavers. Before white men ever came there, your people used to capture each other as slaves, trading back and forth in times of war."

Jack eyed Spencer with a steady gaze. "So you think, then, it is the natural way, for men of our complexion to be in bondage?"

"Ah—no, I never said—"

"But then, if rich men in Africa owned slaves, perhaps we are the natural slave owners, no?" His quick smile did not cover the knife-sharpness of his tone.

"It is not the same," said the other African. He was a bigger, burlier fellow whose name Ned still did not know, so much did the man keep to himself. "You cannot know the life that awaits those poor wretches aboard the slave ships. It is not a life where you might serve another man in his house, have some dignity, win your freedom in time. They are slaves for life, far from home—and not only for their own lives. The children are born into bondage. It is forever, with no hope of freedom." He had been looking at the Englishmen; now he turned his gaze to his fellow African. "You do not know, Jack—you have lived free all your life. Be thankful for it." To Ned and the others he added, "I was born a slave, in Santo Domingo. I am free now, and I will not crew aboard any ship that trades in slaves."

"Nice to be so high-minded you can afford to turn down work," said MacLeish.

"There are worse things than being poor," the black man said.

Later, the same man sought Ned out by the ship's rail. "Your name is Ned Perry? From Cupids Cove colony?"

"I am Ned Perry, yes, and when I first came out from England I settled at Cupids Cove."

"Ah. Then I should tell you that I have known you before. Your name, at least."

"You have? I am sure I'd remember if I met you."

The man laughed, looking down into the churning grey waters below. "I knew a woman who tried to disguise herself as a boy, and called herself Ned Perry. She was not good at fooling people, but she was very brave. Did she find you?"

Ned felt as if the other man had grabbed him by the throat. Meeting Francis and Peter and Elfrith again had been chance enough, but this was like meeting a character out of a tale or legend. "You are—you must be Omar."

The man laughed. "I have gone by that name, and others, yes. And if you know my name, then you must have found Nancy."

"I did. She is my wife now. I am going home to her."

"Ah. It is good to hear a story that has a happy ending."

"What can I tell her of you? If you are alive and free, then I suppose your story has had a happy ending also."

"You may say so. Although I suppose no man's story has an ending as long as he lives."

"If the ship is long enough in Carbonear, would you come home with me and visit us? We are a short sail from there, and I know Nancy would be glad to see you again."

"I do not know our captain's plans when we reach the New Found Land. But I am glad to know she is well."

"I wish you had made yourself known to me sooner." How strange, Ned thought, that he had been near three weeks on this ship, and all this time in the crew had been the man who had done far more than he himself had done to save Nancy—though truly, she had never needed saving.

"I waited, once I heard your name," said Omar. "I wanted to see what manner of man you are."

What a thing to tell Nancy, when they sat by their fireside and he told the tale of his travels! He looked forward to telling her those tales, showing her his earnings, talking over with her what they could buy. Looked forward to seeing her belly rounded with the new babe—praying to God all was still well—and counting off the days and weeks till the child was born.

For as long as he could remember, even when they were apart, Nancy was the only one he could imagine sharing his thoughts with. He longed to be with her again. And he vowed once more that he would not leave her to go to sea again—but he thought of Omar saying that no man's story was ended as long as he lived.

Omar returned to his duties, and the other men drifted away. Ned stood alone at the rail, watching as the ship tacked southwest, around the point of Cape St. Francis. Almost home, now.

"You are lost in thought, Perry," said George Whittington, coming to stand beside him at the rail.

"Aye, that I am," Ned said. Another reason to be glad they were almost home: he would soon be out of Whittington's company.

"'Tis most interesting, is't not, that these fellows have an established trade in Carbonear, so close to the new settlement at Harbour Grace?"

Ned shrugged. "Master Guy and Governor Hayman know well that there are pirates in Carbonear. I am sure you know it too."

"It seems short-sighted, to me, that both Governor Mason and your own Governor Hayman look so sternly on men who are but trying to make a living."

"I cannot speak for the governors, but do you not think Nicholas Guy has a right to be chary of dealing with pirates? They burned his plantation and attacked his servants."

"Aye, but that was years ago. Time moves on." Whittington laughed and slapped Ned on the back. "And we must move on as well, Perry—no need hanging on to old grudges, is there?"

If I timed it right, I could push him over the rail into the sea, and no-one would be the wiser. Instead he said, "Fare thee well, Whittington," and went below decks.

There he found James Hill, packing his few belongings into a well-worn bag. "What will you do when they put us ashore in Carbonear?" he asked Ned. "Myself, Dickon and Will was just talking about how we'd get home from there."

"I can walk from Carbonear if I have to. I have done it before," Ned said. "Will, you can come with me back to Musketto, and on from there to Harbour Grace."

"Aye, if you're along to show the way. I've not been this far north of Harbour Grace before," Will Spencer said.

"As for Dickon and me, we'll hope to find a boat at Carbonear that's going down to Cupids Cove and can take us home," Hill said, "and I suppose Whittington, as well."

"Whittington can bloody swim to Cupids Cove for all I care," Ned said, "but if you fellows cannot find a boat to take you, walk to Musketto Cove with me and Will. Someone there, or at Harbour Grace, will take you home."

He was surprised, when the *Fair Isle* entered Carbonear's deep bay, that they sailed right past Gilbert Pike's plantation. He had assumed all this time that if a pirate ship had dealings in Carbonear, it would be with the Pikes. Carbonear was a busy harbour at this time of year; the fishery was in its final weeks, and numerous ships were moored, with small boats out fishing and men making fish ashore. The *Fair Isle* passed all of these, making straight for a single dock that sat alone at the far end of the harbour with no sign of houses or buildings nearby.

"Whose place is this, then?" Ned asked MacLeish.

"Damned if I know. Some English nobleman that's come out here and set himself up as a trader. He's got a ship of his own, and does a lively trade, and he don't ask questions about how the goods were got."

"An English nobleman? Sure that must be where Thomas Willoughby is hiding himself. His father owns land here, and there's no other nobleman around."

George Whittington laughed. "Had you not guessed as much? Willoughby is going to make himself a very rich man here, and anyone clever will do business with him."

It all made a kind of sense, Ned thought—Willoughby setting himself up as a New World trader doing business with pirates, and Whittington ingratiating himself into that company of rogues. Whittington had risen in the colony by attaching himself to powerful men and doing their bidding, by playing all sides of the game to see where the most profit was to be made.

Now they were all about to dock at Thomas Willoughby's wharf, it seemed, and find out what his business was. *But at least*, Ned thought, looking at the tree-lined hills that rose up from the water, *I know my way home from here.*

THIRTY-ONE

A Debt is Paid

CARBONEAR, SEPTEMBER 1619

But all these wrongs revenge shall end to thee...
　　　　　—Homer's Odysseys, Book 11, 151

KATHRYN AND NANCY SAW WILLOUGHBY'S PROPERTY as they approached the brook that widened into a pond on the south side of Carbonear harbour. Almost invisible from the water save for a single wharf, it was impossible to miss when approaching by land. It did not look like their own plantation, or those at Harbour Grace or Cupids Cove, or the Pikes' plantation further along the Carbonear shore. There was no cleared land by the water for fish flakes and stages, no storehouses, no fleet of little boats. This was not the home of someone who meant to make his fortune from fishing. Nor was there any farmland, or outbuildings for livestock. There was a wharf with a single pinnace moored there, and a little off shore, in deeper water, another ship approaching. A path wound through the woods from that wharf to a clearing about half a mile inland. And on that clearing, Thomas Willoughby had built no byres, no garden, none of the simple structures Kathryn had come to expect to see in the New Found Land settlements. He had built himself...

"A mansion," she said aloud. "The bloody great fool's tried to build himself a gentleman's manor house, or something like it."

Though it was built, like all the settlers' houses, from the rough-hewn wood of the New Found Land forest rather than from English stone, the house yearned to be a manor house. Most houses in the colony were similar to a labourer's cottage in England: one large room containing the hearth and everything a family needed to live, with a sleeping area that might be walled off from that room or might simply be part of it. Nancy and Ned lived in such a house, as did Bess and Frank, and the Crowders at Harbour Grace.

Kathryn had a larger house, befitting her husband's status in the colony. The Guys' house, like the governor's house at Harbour Grace and the Pikes' house in Carbonear, was built in a similar pattern to the first dwellings at Cupids Cove. The main hall took up the most of first floor, with a storeroom at the end of it, while a second story with sleeping chambers was built upstairs. Kathryn and her husband and servants even had the luxury of having the sleeping chambers divided, for privacy. She had never imagined that anyone, here in the colony, would attempt to build any house grander than that.

The house Thomas Willoughby had built was both longer and taller than her own. It had two full storeys, with a peaked roof high enough to contain a storage space above the second floor. Built into the front of the roof was a little gabled turret and in front of that, a small walkway such as Kathryn had never seen on any house, even back in England—it looked like some foreign style. But she could see the point of it at once: it would allow someone standing there to see above the treetops and out to the ocean beyond, like the crow's nest on a ship. Willoughby's house was well-hidden from the shore, but from this eyrie he could watch ships coming and going throughout Carbonear harbour.

She counted six glass windows from where she stood; this was a house built to be imposing, to tell its neighbours that a man of wealth and position lived there. All the more incongruous, then, to see it standing alone in a clearing in the woods at the end of Carbonear harbour, with no neighbours to impress.

"What does he fancy himself—king of his own private realm?" Nancy said aloud. "What does a man need with a house like that in this country?"

"I mean to find out," Kathryn said. The two women climbed down to the river and picked their way across on wet, slippery stones, careful of their footing lest they slip into the fast-flowing water. Then Kathryn led the way along the path towards the great house.

When they emerged from the woods into the clearing, the silence was eerie in a way that reminded her of the henhouse full of slaughtered fowl. The pig stolen from Harbour Grace, if it was taken here, must have been killed for the table at once. She could see now that there was one small outbuilding—a storage or work shed of some kind, no doubt—but no pigsty or henhouse or byre. Kathryn was used to the constant noise of plantation life: animals, children, men and women at work. But she saw no workmen going about their business, and certainly there were no women, children, or animals on the place.

"There was a ship approaching," Nancy said. "Perhaps Willoughby and his servants are down at the wharf."

"Most likely," Kathryn agreed. From here, the dock was hidden beyond the trees. "Still, I am going to the house, to see if he can be found."

"Very well," Nancy said, following her.

"No. I am going alone."

"What? I have told you—"

"You asked to come with me, and I agreed. You are here. But I must speak to Willoughby alone. He must believe there is a chance—even a small chance—that I am coming to him as he asked me to."

"'Tis not safe, Kat, I cannot let—"

"If you love me at all, Nan, help me by keeping watch. Stay hidden among the trees. You can see if anyone is coming, and if I need your help, I swear on my life that I will call to you."

Nancy did not promise to obey. But after a moment she nodded slowly, and stepped back into the shadow of the trees as Kathryn crossed the open ground between the forest and the house alone.

Kathryn climbed the three steps to the door. It was painted red—he had must have had paint brought out from England. He had also fitted it out with a great brass door knocker. She knocked three times, wondering if he had tricked out one of his servants in footman's livery, to complete the illusion.

But no servant dressed in fine doublet and hose came to the door—not even a fisherman in homespun tunic and breeches. *He is not here*, she thought after knocking a second time. Would he be at the wharf waiting for the ship that was arriving? Or was he gone altogether?

She stepped away from the door and looked around, wondering what to do next. She glanced back towards the trees where Nancy was waiting.

"D'you know, this is the first time since I had that door hung that anyone has knocked at it?" The voice came, disconcertingly, from above her.

He stood on the small walkway in the roof, leaning against the rail that surrounded it, gazing down at her. "At last, I have a neighbour visiting. Pardon my rudeness. My men are all down at the shore, for a trade ship is arriving. Do let yourself in."

She opened the red door and stepped inside. Thomas Willoughby's attempt at grandeur had not yet reached the interior of the house: his great hall looked very much like the main floor of her own house, with a hearth, a table, and benches. There were no wall hangings or cushions about; this house had no evidence of a woman's touch, but the daylight streaming in through so many windows made it bright and welcoming.

She was still standing there, looking about, when Willoughby came down from the chamber above. "Mistress Guy," he said, crossing the floor quickly and taking her hand. "What an unexpected pleasure."

"On the contrary, you must have expected me to come. After all, you visited my home first."

He did not let go of her hand, but brought it to his lips. When she tried to draw it back, he tightened his grasp.

"Ah yes. I am sorry about the chickens. I did not want to deliver a message in such crude terms, but your husband and his pet governor seem to be quite determined to ruin my business."

"My husband never saw the letter. I found it first, so your attempt to ruin me failed."

"You read it yourself? But that is better than I could have hoped. You never cease to delight me, Kathryn, with every new thing I learn of you. So beautiful, and also learned!"

"Whatever this business of yours is, it cannot have been harmed too badly, for 'tis clear you are thriving here."

"Oh, I am glad you approve of my house. A great deal of time and expense to build it, of course, but if I am going to make my fortune in this land, I need a place worthy of my name. Come, let me show it to you."

She followed him around the hall. "It is so grand, I thought you must have brought your wife out from England," she said. "Surely no single man needs such a place for himself and his servants?"

He laughed, pausing at a set of shelves that flanked the fireplace, and took down a silver tankard to show her. "A pretty thing, is't not? With the family coat of arms. I made a brief trip back to England, and brought a few things out with me to make my sojourn here more comfortable. Elizabeth was—not one of the things I brought back. I am happy to report that I was there long enough to get her with child again. Another son, it is to be hoped."

"So, it is quite a bachelor existence, then?"

"For the moment, yes. I have six men working for me. I brought a serving girl with me from England, thinking she could cook and provide a few other comforts, but she did not last long, poor thing. Not every woman flourishes in this climate as you have done. One of my men is a passable cook—Higgs, you might remember him."

He paused at the foot of a flight of stairs that led to the second storey. "Come up and see. I have made it as comfortable as I can here. I think you will approve."

She followed him up the stairs, wondering if this was a bad idea, a terrible idea. "You are not fishing or farming—how do you mean to make this fortune?"

He laughed as he led her upstairs. The main room up there was lined off with beds in two tiers for his servants. A door at the end of that room led to a separate chamber. Thomas opened it and stood aside, gesturing for her to come in, but she stayed in the larger chamber, loath to put a door between herself and the stairs.

"I think you know a good bit about how I make my fortune," he said. "Now your husband has turned Master Pike against me, which makes my business more difficult. Oh, Pike still has dealings with pirates, no fear of that, but only with those who prey on French or Spanish ships. He has said he will have no part in attacks on English vessels, English fishing stations, or, most particularly, English plantations and settlements. Quite a change of heart for the brave Pirate Pike and Princess Sheila."

"He was the king, and you were the duke?"

Willoughby laughed. "A small impertinence, to grant ourselves such titles. But now that our partnership is sundered, the Duke of Carbonear answers to no prince. I still have some allies."

"And these allies—is it one of their ships putting into your dock now?"

"Indeed. I was up in my lookout watching. I can see the water from there, though my house cannot be easily spied from the deck of a ship—a nice trick, is't not? Then I spied you instead, a much prettier catch. But you seem so shy, dear Kathryn. Do you not want to come into my bedchamber, as you once welcomed me into yours?"

"That was a long time ago."

"Yes...so long one might almost forget. If you did not have a pretty little reminder running about at your heels every day."

She drew a deep breath, wished that they were standing out in the open instead of inside his house. "You threaten to reveal my sin to my husband—to claim that my daughter is yours as well. What will that gain you? What good can it do?"

"Why, none at all." His face brightened with the wry smile she once found so intoxicating. "Your husband might well challenge me, and that would end with one of us dead. But you would come out of it worst of all—your reputation sullied, your position lost. None of us wants that, do we?"

"Then what *do* you want?" she almost cried. "I do not have the influence with my husband that you seem to think! I could not sway either him or the governor to turn a blind eye if you are attacking English ships and planters."

"So, you have come instead, to offer yourself to me, in hopes I will abandon my quarrel?" His smile was different this time, slow and brooding. "You are right—it is quite a bachelor existence here, and this place still has want of a woman's touch. A great many Englishmen, you know, have a legal wife at home England and another out in the colonies. Most often 'tis a native woman or a slave, but both are hard to find in these parts. At any rate, I prefer my sweet English rose." He reached out, caressed her cheek, and she took a step closer to him. The door of the bedchamber stood open, inviting her in.

"So...if I were to come to you—"

"You have already come to me."

"If I were to stay with you, would you leave off attacking our planta-tion? Leave my husband, my children, our people in peace?"

"Of course. I would still send men to attack the odd English vessel, but I promise to leave the humble planters alone. Your people may split and gut and salt fish to their hearts' content, year after year, until they die."

"And my children?"

"Unfortunately, those you would leave behind. But you would in any case, you know—that is the law. They are your husband's children. I suppose we might make an exception for little Alice—that is her name, is it not?—but it would be hard to spirit her away without your husband learning of it. He must not know that you are here with me."

Of course. This mad plan of his could hardly go forward if he were known to have abducted or seduced the wife of another planter. Nicholas's honour would not stand for that. As she tried to frame a response, Thomas's face softened. Gone was the wry, sardonic smile; he drew her closer to him, closer to the open door.

"So I would simply...disappear from my home, my family?" she asked.

"Sadly, people disappear all the time. They will think you lost in the woods, perhaps. You must have given some excuse for leaving today. In time, your people will believe that an accident befell you. Attacked by the wild men of the woods, perhaps, or more simply, fallen over a cliff into the sea. They will mourn, but you will be safe here with me."

He did not know, of course, that Nancy had come with her, that any such "accident" would require Nancy's complicity. Was that why Nancy had insisted on coming, so that Kathryn would not be tempted to give in to Willoughby? Her mind spun like a child's top, but she said only, "You have given this a good deal of thought."

"I hope you truly have come to me with a good heart and a true intention, my Kathryn," he said softly. "Do not think me cruel. I have been kind to you before, and will be again." He brought his lips towards hers. She began to pull away, but then moved towards him, allowing him to kiss, to claim her. He put an arm around her waist, drew her close. Her heart beat so hard she thought he must be able to hear it.

When he ended the kiss, he kept his arm around her. She tried to steady her ragged breath. "You make a persuasive argument, Master Willoughby."

"I hope you do not forget the pleasure we once enjoyed together."

She smiled, aimed for a light and flirtatious tone. "Oh, indeed, I remember. You offer me a return to that pleasure, plus all the grandeur of your lovely home. And all the wealth you can earn from your trade?"

"All that and more, in time. It may be a solitary life, but it will be a comfortable one—even luxurious. I can bring out women servants from England. You will not be a housemaid, but will have women to help you, and every finery you may desire."

Women servants. She thought of that tossed-aside line about the young woman he had brought out as a maid—*but she did not last long, poor thing.* What tale of horrors did that handful of words hold?

"It is tempting," she said, still striving for the manner of a silly flirt-gill, the young bride she had been when she knew him first. "But I am lady of a fine plantation already at Musketto Cove. You must show me your lands, if you would convince me it is worth making the trade." She laughed. "Before I will go into your bedchamber, take me up to the place where you were when I came to the door. Show all your lands from up there."

He laughed, too, and his laughter lifted a little of the fear she felt. "What a minx you still are. You have come here, choosing me over your husband, and yet you still want me to woo you with promises of land and ships and wealth? Very well, I will show you. I am proud of what I have built here. Mind your skirts, now—this one is a ladder, not a proper set of stairs like the other."

He led her away from the gaping door of the bedchamber, beyond which she could now see a well-appointed bed with rich velvet hangings. In the middle of the larger chamber, a ladder led up into the roof.

She climbed the ladder behind him, and came out into a small, square gable room with a door where the window should be. Outside that door was the walkway where she had first seen him standing. She followed him out there. He put his arm around her waist again, holding her close as he pointed towards the sea.

"There, you see. The ship has dropped anchor, and though we cannot see it for the trees, my men are now rowing out to her, to unload cargo and bring her men ashore for refreshment. They will be landed within the half-hour, and I shall go down to greet Captain Bellamy. He does business in the Indies, and is bringing me some fine goods for trade before going to my business partners in England. I have not the same access to the Irish trade since Gilbert Pike has sundered his connection with me, but in time...in time, I will have markets that rival his. I have, thus far, only one ship of my own—a little barque currently sailing down to Renews. But I have arrangements with the captains of several vessels, and I will have more, in time."

"You truly are building something here. I can see it."

"Next year I will hire men to clear more land. One must grow a little food, and keep a few animals, but I do not aspire to be a planter."

She looked up at him. "Was this always your intention, when you came back here?"

The smile left his face. "I can hardly tell what my intentions were. I was sent to this damned country like a boy sent for a whipping, when I was nineteen years old, because of some trifling matter of gambling debts that my father said brought shame on our family. Forced out here to live and work like a peasant."

"I know. 'Twas hard for you."

He went on, paying no heed to her attempt at sympathy. "When my penance was done, I thought I could go back home and live in my proper station. But England is no country for a younger son. Even if I kept my record clean, I could not gain the stature that my brothers had. So I tried—I truly did. Came out here again with my father's name and

blessing and credit, and tried to begin my own plantation at Harbour
Grace. But then—"

She had made a mistake; she had worked so carefully to bring him
to flirtation, then to pride, but she had gone wrong by asking him about
the past, and now he had turned to anger. Any thought she had of
finding a soft spot, of making a space in which she could appeal to his
kindness—that was quickly slipping away. She cast about for what to
say next.

"But you have done so well now! This beautiful house—"

"Because I was forced to it! I'd have turned the house at Harbour
Grace into such a fitting home, had I been allowed. I thought that with
a charter for the new colony, my father's name and credit would earn
me the post of governor. And then the—the company, those fools, had
to bring out a prattling poet instead, and put him in as governor—a
puppet for your husband. And I, a baronet's son, was supposed to have
no more standing in the colony than Nicholas Guy or Jem Holworthy
or any of these low-born planters! D'you think I'd stand for that?"

His eyes were glittering now, and his arm about her waist was tight
enough to hurt. He was a strong man. Almost any man was stronger
than any woman, especially when he was angry.

"No, no, of course. I understand. You—you deserved to be governor.
You deserve—"

"I deserve my rights," Thomas Willoughby said, "and if I cannot have
them, I will take what I can get. I will take what wealth my ships can
gather from other merchants, and I will take the service of the men in
my pay, and I will take *you*, my little minx. I hope you did come here
meaning to stay, Kathryn, for you must not think I'll ever let you go."

He pulled her closer still, covering her mouth with another hard,
bruising kiss. *If I cried out now, Nancy would hear me*, Kathryn thought.
Perhaps she can even see us, up here. But Nancy would be running into a
trap, as Kathryn herself had done.

"I will come to you," she said when the kiss ended, and they were
breathless in each other's arms. "Do not doubt me. But I must go home
to—to see to things. To make sure my children are—are cared for. I
will return—"

"You little fool. Do you think I would let you go back to your husband now, and prattle all to him?"

His two fingers on her jaw, drawing her face up to his, were just hard enough to hurt. Another kiss. She remembered, as distant as the ships out on the bay, the pleasure she had once known in his arms, the way he had awakened her body to desire and delight.

Desire and fear felt so much alike. She had been frightened ever since she bade Nancy to wait in the trees. Into the house, up the stairs, up the ladder—every step had made her more afraid.

But if desire and fear felt alike, so did fear and anger. She thought of her slaughtered chickens; small victims, but victims nonetheless, whose deaths would mean a little bit more hunger and hardship for her people, her beloved Musketto Cove. One more thing taken from her, by a man who believed it was his right to take. He would take and take and take, Thomas Willoughby and men like him. No woman would ever be permitted to say no.

She did not last long, poor thing—some little unnamed servant girl, likely from his father's estate or from the Bristol docks. Used by Willoughby and his men in a dozen ways, now lying beneath this ground in an unmarked grave.

She thought of Nancy, captive on a pirate ship, of the righteous Puritan pirate who had defended Nancy's virtue until he wanted it for himself. She remembered Nancy telling how that man had begged for forgiveness before he died of a battle-wound, and how Nancy had refused to give it, let him to go to God with the sin of rape on his conscience.

When the kiss ended, Kathryn saw the triumph in Thomas's eyes; he was smiling again now. "See?" he said. "It will not be so bad, will it, being here with me? Your husband has never been able to compare, has he?"

One more image flashed into her head: her father. Not the dear, kindly father she remembered, but a young husband swiving both his wife and his maid, betraying the trust of both the women who had raised her. She placed her hands on Thomas Willoughby's chest and smiled up at him.

"You are right," she said. "Those few nights I spent with you—I have spent six years dreaming of them. Not a single moment with my husband has been as sweet as those nights you were in my bed. It is worth everything—any shame, any hardship—to be here with you again."

He moved the hand that was holding her waist, brought it up to her cheek so that he cradled her face, ever so gently, in both his hands. "My sweet Kathryn," he said.

She put all of it, every ounce of the fear and anger, even the memory of that long-gone desire, into her hands. She put in her anger on behalf of the slaughtered hens, the dead servant girl, her own mother and Tibby, Nancy, and finally, herself—anger for every woman ill-used by men like Willoughby. Her fury was the only power she had.

Even as she shoved him with all her strength, she thought, *I am a fool.* He would grab hold of the railing, find his footing, and then—what? *He will throw me off instead.* But no—he would not give her such an easy death.

It was only a moment, a flash of thought. He reached for her as he fell backwards over the railing, grabbing for her arm, but she jumped back, too quick for him. She watched, hands covering her mouth, as Thomas Willoughby fell backwards, collapsing like a rag doll, over the roof of his proud new house, turning over as his body hit the roof's edge, landing face-down, two full storeys beneath her on the ground.

She stood frozen, staring down.

Willoughby's men, his servants, were not far away, down at the shore unloading the ship. They would come back and find their master— dead? Was he dead?—on the ground, and Kathryn would be trapped in this house, accused of murder.

Accused. Justly. She had murdered him, had she not?

She must run, leave this place, get away. But they might pursue her through the woods. Surely Willoughby's men would not think their master had simply fallen from the roof to his death?

Still unable to move, Kathryn saw the sight she had feared—someone running from the woods towards Willoughby's still form. Too late, now, for her to escape.

Then she realized the running figure was not coming from the trail that led to the shore, but from the forest to the south, the trail she and Nancy had travelled along.

Nancy.

It was Nancy running from the shelter of the trees, running towards Willoughby's body. Her skirts were hitched up in one hand, and with the other she gestured urgently to Kathryn: *Come down out of there!*

Kathryn turned back into the house, down the ladder, then faster down the stairs, out through the red door. Onto the ground outside, where Nancy now knelt next to Willoughby's body.

"Is he—"

"Dead, near as I can tell," Nancy said.

"Oh, Lord, what have I done?"

Nancy shot her a quick glance. "What you had to do. Protected yourself. And rid the world of a nasty piece of work in the bargain."

"But I—Nan, I could hang for this."

Nan looked up, her hand still on Willoughby's head as if to make certain he would not open his eyes. "You could—but you will not. Now, you take his feet, I will take his arms."

"What?"

"You heard me. If we are found here with his body, I will swear to my death that I saw him attack you up there on the roof, and that in the struggle you pushed him over the railing. 'Tis little more than truth, after all. But 'twould be better by far to have no questions asked at all, and for us to be far from here when the body is found."

"What do you mean to—"

"Take hold of his legs, and help me lift him." Nancy stood up and got her hands under Willoughby's armpits. "Try to lift, not drag him, so we'll not leave as much of a trail. Keep him turned face-downwards, like he is. And *make haste*! I can hear voices on the trail to the wharf."

Willoughby was not a very large man, but he was a solid burden for two women, one six months pregnant and the other shaking in her shoes. Kathryn could hear them too, now—the men coming up from the shore. It seemed impossible that she and Nancy would get the body into the cover of the trees before they were seen.

Almost as impossible as believing that a few moments ago, that this had been the living man who was trying to seduce her away from her husband and home. Threatening her, if she did not bend to his will.

They were almost to the edge of the forest now, the boundary of Willoughby's cleared land. She could hear the men's voices on the other trail more clearly now; they were coming closer. She tripped on a tree root, her ankle turned, and she dropped Willoughby's legs.

"Hurry!" Nancy hissed. "We cannot tarry. Pick him up again!"

Kathryn gripped Willoughby's ankles, hoisted his weight again. "I doubt I can carry him much farther."

"There's not much farther to go." Nancy, staggering forward with her end of the body, glanced back over her shoulder. "Don't fret yourself, Kat. I have a plan."

THIRTY-TWO

A Journey is Concluded

CARBONEAR, SEPTEMBER 1619

Fell from the very roof, full pitching on
The dearest joint his head was plac'd upon,
Which, quite dissolv'd, let loose his soul to hell.
—*Homer's Odysseys*, Book 10, 693–95

As THEY APPROACHED THE DOCK, NED SAW SOME SIGNS that the place was occupied. Above the treeline was something that looked like a tower or a turret, presumably on the roof of a tall house. A path led through the forest from the wharf where a pinnace was tied up. There was some running back and forth, the men on the wharf vanishing into the trees, reappearing on the shore, talking amongst themselves.

When they drew into shallower water, the *Fair Isle* dropped anchor and began to put down its boat. At the same time, two men from the wharf climbed into the pinnace and began to row towards the *Fair Isle*.

Captain Bellamy and his quartermaster went aboard the boat, along with several barrels of goods, and rowed in to meet the pinnace. Aboard the *Fair Isle*, the sailors lowered the sails, while Ned and the other New Found Land men stood with their small bundles of belongings on deck, waiting for a boat to take them ashore.

Across the small stretch of water, he heard the conversation as the two boats drew abreast of each other. "Is Sir Thomas on the wharf?" Captain Bellamy asked. Ned was fair certain that Thomas Willoughby had no right to style himself "Sir Thomas," but this far from England, who was to gainsay?

"Ah, that's the trouble, Captain, the master's not here," said one of the men in the boat. "We was all down here making ready for your arrival, and the master was up at the house keeping watch. When he'd not come down by the time you dropped anchor, I sent Smith there up to fetch him. But he's not at the house, Captain."

"What do you mean, not at the house?" Captain Bellamy roared. "Where the bloody hell else would he be? Not as if he's gone round to the tavern now, is it?"

So, they were going to Thomas Willoughby's house, but the man himself had disappeared. A pretty pickle, Ned thought, but as long as it landed him ashore, he did not care overmuch. There was more talk between Captain Bellamy and Willoughby's men, and then the two boats began making the journey back and forth from ship to dock, bringing the cargo ashore. Ned, James Hill, and Will Spencer rowed to the wharf along with two heavy crates.

By the time they were all ashore and the goods unloaded, Willoughby still had not appeared, and his men were uneasy. Ned recognized a few of them, for they had been at Harbour Grace with Willoughby two years ago, and must have fled to Carbonear with him. The fellow who had first spoken with Captain Bellamy, a stocky man of about forty who was something of a leader among his fellows, was William Barry; Ned had a nodding acquaintance with him from the times they had met at Harbour Grace.

Barry said, "'Tis most unlike him indeed, Captain, and as you say there is no place for him to go without a boat. We looked all around the house and grounds and even called for him in the woods. I know not what to tell you."

A little silence fell. Captain Bellamy apparently did not know what to say either.

"Most unfortunate, and I am sure Sir Thomas will reappear in time, but in the meantime, we can surely still bring our trade goods into his house, can we not?" George Whittington's voice boomed. "We can take our cargo in while we await his arrival, and your cook can prepare a meal for us."

"Yes sir, we will, sir," said Barry, and turned to another man nearby. "You heard Master Whittington. Go on up to the house and begin preparing dinner for the crew. The rest of you, begin taking this lot up to the house."

Master Whittington? Ned thought. Even stranger than calling Willoughby "Sir Thomas" was that these fellows apparently knew George Whittington of Cupids as "Master." The men onshore looked relieved to have someone take charge—a few of them nodded greetings at Whittington, whom they clearly had dealt with before. Even Captain Bellamy seemed to accept Whittington's authority.

"Quite the place he's built for himself, ain't it?" James Hill said to Ned as they each carried a sack of flour up to Willoughby's house.

"Quite the place, indeed. No wonder he goes about calling himself Sir Thomas," Ned agreed, looking at the two-storey house that was much grander than any other house yet built in the New Found Land. Willoughby must be setting himself up not just as a planter who happened to trade with pirates, like Gilbert Pike, but as some kind of a merchant prince, the first nobleman of the island.

That being the case, it was hard to understand why he was not there to greet his guests. Some of the men carried out a brief search in the woods, but found no trace of their master. In the meantime, Willoughby's cook, Higgs, put on a meal of roast pork for the hungry sailors and their passengers that felt like a feast to men who had spent so long at sea.

"All very well, but sooner or later we'll have to be paid or take the goods away again," Captain Bellamy said as the men passed around Willoughby's brandy after dinner.

"There be no need for that, surely, Captain," said George Whittington. He turned to the fellow who appeared to have some command over the others. "Barry, you have the key to Sir Thomas's strongbox, do you not? Wherever he has gone, he would not want to lose out on good trade. As I have done business with him before, I would gladly give you the authority to pay the good captain, in your master's absence."

Yes now, I suppose you will, Ned thought. George Whittington was making himself very comfortable there in Thomas Willoughby's big chair.

"We should strike out for home soon," Ned said aloud to Will Spencer, who nodded agreement. To Hill and Sadler he added, "Will you come with us, or stay here and see if you can find a ship to take you back to Cupids Cove?"

At that moment two of Willoughby's servants, running as if bears were chasing them, burst into the house. "We've found him! We found the master!" one cried. From their manner it was evident that they had not found him hale and hearty.

Thomas Willoughby had been found face-down in the river that bordered his property. It seemed likely he had stumbled on the wet rocks while crossing the stream, perhaps striking his head and losing consciousness so that even though the water was not very deep, he'd drowned in it.

The river was not far from the house, but neither was it on the way between the house and the wharf. None of the men could explain why Willoughby had been crossing the river. Since Barry and the other servants had seen their master only an hour or two before, the accident could not have happened long ago. But it was far too late for Willoughby by the time he was found.

A second group of servants went out to retrieve the body. "What do we do with him?" one asked, and William Barry looked to George Whittington for an answer.

"You must dig him a grave. Does any man here know the words of the Burial for the Dead? Yes, you?" He nodded at the *Fair Isle*'s quartermaster, who had likely had to say those words over men who died aboard ship. "Very well, then if you do not mind lingering until poor Willoughby has been put beneath the soil, would you be good enough to recite what must be said over him? Then your ship will be free to depart." He turned back to Barry. "Have you had cause to bury anyone here yet? Is there a spot?"

"Yes, sir," said Barry, "down by the pine grove, where we laid poor little Annie—the serving maid who died last winter."

"Excellent. I mean, 'tis a sad duty, but good that you have a place set aside already. Go see that it is done." He turned back to Captain Bellamy. "I will write a note to be delivered to Sir Percival about his son's sad death. You may carry it back to Bristol, and see that it gets sent to the Willoughby estate."

"Didn't know you could write," Ned said quietly to Whittington, when the gravediggers had gone about their business and Whittington had taken a piece of paper and a pen from Willoughby's desk.

"I have taught myself these last few years—enough to get by. Very useful for keeping figures and account-books, you know, which will come in handy now when I get a chance to look at Willoughby's ledgers." George smiled up at Ned, a sunny smile that was so nearly innocent Ned wondered if there were any way George could possibly have killed Willoughby himself, even while he was still aboard the *Fair Isle* out in the bay. Whittington certainly seemed to be stepping neatly into the dead man's shoes.

"Oh, and of course Hill, or Sadler—one of you," Whittington said to the two Cupids Cove men, "I will want you to bring a message to my wife. Tell her that I will be here seeing to matters of business for a while, but that I will either come myself, or send a boat, for her and the children to join me here." He looked around with pleasure at the broad expanse of Thomas Willoughby's house.

"You mean to stay? To make this your home?" Hill said.

"What, do you think I should leave my friend Willoughby's house and business to be run by poor Barry and these other servants? They are grateful to see someone take charge. And I'll note that none of them is shedding any tears over their master's death. I am sure he was a hard man to work for." He folded the letter, then, after a moment, took out sealing wax. "I had better be sure they take off his signet ring before they put him in the ground."

"Will we stay, see him put in the ground, and the prayers said over him?" Will Spencer asked as he and Ned walked back outside.

"Not I." Ned picked up his bag and slung it over his shoulder. "I've no cause to mourn Thomas Willoughby, and no desire to stay here currying favour with George Whittington. If you ask me, Carbonear has replaced one scoundrel with another—but 'tis no business of mine. Come, boys," he called to Hill and Sadler. "If you want to come with us as far as Musketto Cove, we will take to the trail now, and be there in time for supper with my good wife."

Epilogue

MUSKETTO COVE, JUNE 1620

"ANOTHER DAY OF CAPLIN WEATHER, LOOKS LIKE," NED SAID, coming in from the privy. Chilly air followed him into the house. The month of June had been wet, cold, and foggy, but the little fish that rolled up on the beaches during that dreary weather had come in good numbers and were supposed to be an omen of a good season for cod. Today the fishermen of Musketto Cove would put their boats out and discover whether that omen proved true.

Nancy laid a bowl of pottage and the last of yesterday's bread, along with a chunk of cheese, in front of her husband as he sat down. She captured Lizzie, who was careening about the room, and sat her on the bench to eat, then sat down herself to nurse little Henry.

When Ned had gone out on the water and Nancy had cleared away the meal, she banked the hearth fire and took the two children across the beach to Kathryn's house. The sun was already burning through the fog; today might be a clear day after all. Another good omen, she thought, if the first day of the fishing season also felt like the first of summer.

Today the women were planting turnips. The children played while their mothers worked, except for the two big boys, Jonathan and Will.

Despite Jonathan's protests that he was the elder, both boys had been breeched together in the spring; they were now expected to take their part in clearing the ground and digging holes for the seed. At midday the men came in with the morning's catch, as plentiful as they could have hoped for the first day fishing.

Later in the afternoon, the Holworthys' shallop sailed into the cove. By that time, the sky was clear and sunny, and the day had warmed enough that the women had put aside shawls and stopped trying to keep the children bundled up. Governor Hayman was aboard, having recently come over from England for the summer.

Everyone crowded into the big house for supper; Nancy and Daisy convinced Kathryn to sit at table and play hostess while they served the meal. The governor had much news to bring from England and the wider world. Nancy paid little heed to most of it, more concerned with keeping an eye on her children while making sure every dish got safely from hearth to table.

But she noticed when Governor Hayman said, "There are plans made for another English colony to the south in the autumn. I have heard there are two ships full of English Puritans leaving Holland for the New World."

"Puritans?" Master Holworthy echoed with some interest. "Are they that crowd of separatists in Leiden? I have heard of them."

"Yes, those are the ones—a goodly crew of them, so I hear, setting off for someplace in Virginia. To the north of James Fort, I believe." The governor glanced at Ned. "It may well be the same lands you explored with Captain Dermer last year."

"Not Patuxet, or anywhere in Wampanoag country, I trust," Ned said. "I know not if Captain Dermer ever went back or sent word to England, but surely anyone planning a voyage to those lands should know that Tisquantum's people will not be friendly to settlers."

"Tisquantum lived friendly enough with us for nigh on two years," Nicholas Guy said. "I know not why he would be hostile to Englishmen now."

"Ah well, I believe they are bound further south from there, and had not even got as far as England, much less set off across the ocean, when

I left the country," Governor Hayman said. "But are you quite sure, Perry, that Tisquantum's folk would be unfriendly to settlers?"

Ned had an answer for that. Nancy, distracted by Henry who began just then to cry, did not hear what it was, but she felt the swell of pride she always felt when she saw Ned talking to the masters of the colony as if he was their equal. He knew his place, but he also knew that he had seen more of the world than most of them, and they listened when he spoke.

As Nancy settled by the hearth with the baby, the men's talk turned to colonial ventures closer to home. A nobleman named Calvert had gotten a grant for the land down around Renews, where two efforts had been made to start an English settlement already. He was talking of sending out colonists next year. From there they talked of John Guy's first attempt at Renews, thwarted by the pirate Easton, and then it was only natural for the governor to ask if there had been any trouble with pirates since he was last in the country.

The mysterious death of Thomas Willoughby had been a subject for much conversation last autumn. Now George Whittington had moved his family into Willoughby's house, and it was an open secret that he, like Gilbert Pike, carried on a lively trade with pirates. However, none of those lawless captains had troubled the settlers, either in Bristol's Hope or Cupids Cove.

"As long as Pike and Whittington do not trouble us, 'tis no business of ours," Jem Holworthy opined. "They've no wish to cause mischief for us planters, as Willoughby did, so what trade they do at Carbonear does not concern us."

"Perhaps not," said Nicholas Guy, "yet I hardly think Sir Percival Willoughby will be happy to know how his property is being used. Whittington makes out as if he is Sir Percival's agent, having stepped into his dead son's shoes, but I know there has been no such agreement. I have written to Sir Percival to let him know of the goings-on at Carbonear. Things may change once I receive his answer."

The two women remaining at the table, Elsie Holworthy and Kathryn, excused themselves from the talk of politics and piracy. Kathryn came to sit on the bench by Nancy. "All's well?" Nancy asked softly.

It was a kind of cipher between them. Whenever the topic of Thomas Willoughby's death came up in conversation, the two women would seek each other out, and Nancy would ask Kathryn if all was well. It was the closest they ever came to speaking of that day.

Kathryn sat now with her hand on the mound of her belly where her new babe was growing. Jemmy toddled over and reached up his arms to sit on his mother's lap, and just afterwards Lizzie did the same, so both Nancy and Kathryn made room on their laps for their sleepy children.

"It is well, truly," Kathryn said softly, under the noise of the men's talk. "I will always know it was a sin, but in faith—I cannot imagine how much worse things might be, had he not died that day."

Nancy also kept her voice low. "Perhaps a time will come when he is altogether forgotten, and you will never have to hear his name again."

"It would be a blessed day, indeed." Kathryn looked down, stroking her little boy's soft curly hair. "I am at peace," she said, though something in her eyes belied the words. *That fool plagued her in life and haunts her in death*, Nancy thought. Nothing she could say would entirely banish Willoughby's ghost.

Kathryn drew a deep breath, as if she, too, needed to quiet that uneasy spirit. With the hand that was not caressing Jemmy's hair, she reached for something on the bench beside her and showed it to Nancy. "See what Governor Hayman has brought me."

"Another book of tales for you to read on winter nights?"

"No—perhaps better." She passed over the book, and Nancy, opening it, saw that the pages were blank. "'Tis for the journal I hoped to keep. I can begin this winter, when the fishing is over, to start keeping record of my herbals and remedies, and an account of our lives here." Kathryn looked at Nancy again. "Am I a fool, to think I could pen such a thing?"

"Not a bit of it. If anyone can write it, 'twould be you, Kat."

Soon after, the party began to break up. The governor and the Holworthys wanted to sail to Harbour Grace before dark; Bess and Frank collected their children and returned to their own house, and Ned and Nancy said their farewells to everyone.

They walked across the beach in the slanting golden light of early evening, a tired Lizzie riding on Ned's shoulders, Henry snuggled in a shawl against Nancy's chest. With his free hand, Ned reached to hold Nancy's hand as they watched the Holworthys' shallop catch the evening breeze and sail out of Musketto Cove.

Nancy's mind drifted back to the dinner-table conversation, to Ned's keen interest in the new colonies and in the fate of Tisquantum and his people. "Do you wish you were out there?" she said.

"What, out in a boat? Sure, I was fishing all morning."

"You know what I mean." Not the daily routine of the fishing boat, or the occasional voyages over to Harbour Grace or Cupids Cove; her fear was that those did not slake Ned's desire for the sea.

"Ah, love, I told you. After all I went through last summer with Dermer, I am more than content to stay and fish in Musketto Cove this year."

And next year? And every year after? She did not frame the questions aloud; it was not her way, to be a nagging wife. But he heard the words she did not speak.

"I'll not lie to you—there is something about it that draws me. When I hear the governor and the masters talking as they did tonight, about things that are going on in the wide world..."

"You want to be out there again."

"Perhaps. I know not, in truth." He squeezed her hand more tightly. "You and I both have that in common, after all. We have seen more of the world than just Bristol and the New Found Land."

"True enough. But those journeys left me with no desire to wander further. If I never set foot off this island, never on the deck of a ship again, I will be glad of it."

He smiled. "When you first came out to Cupids Cove, I told you— d'you remember?—that was the difference between men and women. That men want to explore, while women want to stay home and tend the hearth. I am not sure anymore if that's the whole truth, but it might be the difference between you and me."

She felt a little touch of fear across her heart: he would go away again, and every time he went, she would live with the fear that a shipwreck or a pirate attack would keep him from ever coming home. She thought of the pirate attack that had taken her away and killed Tom Taylor on this very beach; she thought of Isaac falling to his death off this wharf. No place was truly safe: who knew that better than she did?

"I know well that you may go to sea again someday," she said as they reached the steps of their own little house. "And I am sure our fortunes will be all the better for it, if you do."

Ned lifted Lizzie off his shoulders. "Can you walk into the house? No, too sleepy? Come on then—one step, two—here we are." He swung the child across the threshold, then turned back as Nancy came inside, and closed the door behind them all, dropping the bar across to lock out the world. "The one thing you can be sure of," he said to Nancy, "is that I will always, always come home to you."

Outside, the sun had begun to set behind the trees to the west. But their only window—their new glass window—faced east, out on the cove and the sea beyond, where the last light of day was still shining on the leagues of water that stretched between them and England.

Nancy turned from the window back to Ned. "You will if you know what's good for you," she said, and tilted her head to meet his kiss.

Afterword

MANY OF THE CHOICES I HAVE MADE IN WRITING THIS TRIL-
ogy have already been addressed in the afterwords of the two earlier
books, *A Roll of the Bones* and *Such Miracles and Mischiefs*. In bringing
this series to an end, I will mention here a few topics not fully covered
in those earlier volumes.

Cupids Cove and Bristol's Hope

Cupids (also known as Cupids Cove, Cupers Cove, and various other
spellings) was the original English colony on the island of Newfoundland,
founded by John Guy in 1610. I feel I owe something of an apology to
the people of Cupids who have been so supportive and encouraging of
this project; I named this series *The Cupids Trilogy*, but only the first
volume is set mainly in Cupids Cove. In this third book my focus is on
the second English colony, founded a few years later after divisions
between London and Bristol investors led the Bristol men to form a
new colony.

The second colony, called Bristol's Hope, was established in 1617.
Although the main settlement was at Harbour Grace, the Bristol merchants' grant extended north to the south side of Carbonear, where it
adjoined land held by Sir Percival Willoughby, and included the tiny

place in between called either Musketto, Muskets, or Mosquito Cove, where I have chosen to situate the Guy family.

Confusingly, Musketto Cove, also sometimes called just Mosquito, was renamed Bristol's Hope in 1904 and is known by that name today. However, "Bristol's Hope" originally referred to the larger colony, not to that one small cove. In practice, the Bristol's Hope colony was often referred to not by that official name, but by the name of its largest settlement: Harbour Grace.

Less is known about Bristol's Hope and how it operated as a colony, than is known about the early years of Cupids Cove. As always in researching this series, I have relied heavily on the expert knowledge of archeologist and historian William Gilbert, whose archeological work at Cupids and detailed knowledge of the period are unsurpassed.

Nicholas Guy

While many of my main characters are fictional, Nicholas Guy was a real person. We know he was one of the earliest colonists at Cupids, and his last name suggests he might have been a relative of the colony's founder, John Guy. We know that Nicholas Guy's wife, unnamed in the records relating to Cupids, gave birth to a male child there in March of 1613. (As a parenthetical note, in this trilogy I have followed modern dating conventions, starting the new year on January 1, as I thought dating events as the seventeenth-century colonists would have done, with the new year beginning in March, might be confusing to a modern reader.)

We also know that Nicholas Guy remained in Newfoundland but left Cupids; by 1631 he was acting as Sir Percival Willoughby's agent at Carbonear (a development lightly hinted at in the Epilogue of this novel).

The original Governor John Guy and his brother Philip most likely both returned to England within a few years of the founding of Cupids Cove, though some evidence suggests they may have made later visits to Newfoundland. Nicholas Guy and his wife remained in Newfoundland, and their family became long-standing planters and landowners in Conception Bay.

Census records for Newfoundland show that in 1675 both a John Guy Sr. and John Guy Jr. were living in Carbonear, and a Lewis Guy was living in Harbour Grace. The 1677 census also lists a Nicholas Guy living in Carbonear; and a list of planters, compiled in 1708, recorded a Nicholas Guy fishing out of Bay Roberts that year. It is quite likely these men were the descendants of the original Nicholas Guy.

Robert Hayman

When the new colony at Bristol's Hope was formed, Robert Hayman was appointed its first, and only known, governor. Hayman was a scholar and a poet, and the author of the first book written in Newfoundland, his *Quodlibets*. Some of these short poems deal with life in Newfoundland and were likely meant as recruiting material to encourage more English people to settle here. Hayman spent his last summer in Newfoundland in 1628, and died in 1629 while on a voyage of exploration in Guyana.

Readers of this series may recall that the chapter headings of *A Roll of the Bones* were quotes from Hayman's *Quodlibets*, and an excerpt from that poem is reproduced as the epigraph to this book.

The chapter headings in this book are taken from Chapman's translation of the *Odyssey*, first translated into English in 1616. We do not know that Robert Hayman owned a copy of this book or that he brought it to Newfoundland with him, but it would have been a likely volume for a man in his position to have owned.

Homer's *Odyssey* is the story of a man returning home from a great adventure, and this novel, for me, largely addresses the question of homecoming: What do we do *after* we've had our great adventure, and what does "coming home" mean? Before reading Chapman's 1616 translation I read Emily Wilson's lively and engaging 2018 translation, and it was in her commentary that I encountered an idea that has stayed with me: in the course of Odysseus's search for his own home, his acts of violence ensure that many other characters never make it home safely.

The same is true of our colonizing English ancestors—their quest to build a home in the New World dispossessed the people whose homes were already there. For all these reasons, I was drawn to the *Odyssey* as a text to be read within the story itself, and used for the chapter headings.

The idea of Governor Hayman teaching a planter's wife to read and write is entirely my own invention. Women settlers were often illiterate and, even if they were literate, were unlikely to have access to the free time and materials needed to write. For those reasons (and because of the vagaries of time and document preservation) no document such as Kathryn Guy's intended journal exists from any woman settler in Newfoundland in those early centuries. If such a journal did exist, it would be a priceless treasure indeed.

Pirates

In setting this third volume of the trilogy in a small cove between Harbour Grace and Carbonear, I am stepping into an area of Newfoundland history where pirates loom large. While the amount of time Peter Easton spent in Newfoundland is often exaggerated, and the adventures of Gilbert Pike and Sheila Na'geira rest on oral storytelling rather than on documented evidence, it is undeniable that piracy posed a genuine threat to shipping, settlement, and the migratory fishery during these years. It is also true, as I have tried to portray throughout this series, that the line between "piracy" and legal "privateering" was often blurred. Many ship's captains, as well as the merchants and shipowners with whom they did business, moved back and forth frequently over that line.

There is no evidence that Gilbert Pike (who, with his Irish wife Sheila, likely did not exist—at least, not in the form legend has given them) and Thomas Willoughby (who did exist) ever tried to set up Carbonear as a pirate headquarters. But given the prevalence of piracy in this region and time period, the storyline seemed like a reasonable leap of imagination.

The delivery of a shipment of captured Africans to Virginia by Daniel Elfrith and another captain in August 1619 is a well-documented event which is often seen as the beginning of the slave trade in the English colonies in North America. I have had to fictionalize the timelines a little bit to allow Ned to be present for this event—in reality,

Thomas Dermer's crew likely arrived in Virginia a month or so later than the slave traders.

George Whittington

I gave this character the name of one of John Guy's original 1610 colonists, who occasionally turns up in documents related to the colony. When I first introduced him in *A Roll of the Bones* as a servant of John Guy, my keen-eyed history expert William Gilbert pointed out that the real George Whittington must have been of a higher status in society, since he is referred to in some documents as "Master Whittington." I have chosen to portray my fictional George Whittington as a character of low social position who rises in status in the colony due to conniving, manipulation, and shameless currying favour with those in power. Nothing more is known about the real George Whittington, and if any of his descendants are living in Newfoundland today, I apologize for making him a villain.

Thomas Willoughby

Thomas Willoughby, who appears first in *A Roll of the Bones* and briefly in *Such Miracles and Mischiefs*, is another character with real historical roots. The son of Sir Percival Willoughby, an investor in the Newfoundland Company, Thomas was sent out to Cupids as a young man in 1612 under the supervision of his father's agent, Henry Crout. The implication seems to be that being sent to the colony was punishment for an unspecified misdemeanour by the young Willoughby. Crout's journals suggest that Thomas Willoughby did not adapt well to a colonist's life. He returned to England in 1613, but by 1616 was back in Newfoundland and apparently back in his father's good graces, attempting, without great success, to further the family's business interests.

A petulant and resentful young man of good family exiled to Cupids was a character I could not resist including in *A Roll of the Bones*. Picking up his story in this novel, I have once again indulged in some fictionalizing of history, adjusting the date of his return to Newfoundland from

1616 to 1617. I have also changed his location: his letters indicate that he built a house and attempted to establish a plantation on his father's land at Carbonear. I have taken the liberty of having him settle first at Harbour Grace, only later moving to Carbonear to pursue piracy (something the historical record does not associate him with).

The most intriguing part of Thomas Willoughby's story is that, after another brief mention in the family records, he disappears completely from the historical record after 1621, suggesting either a further disgrace leading to a permanent split with his family, or an untimely and unrecorded death. I chose to have him meet his death in Newfoundland in 1619.

The fate I have imagined for him is entirely my own invention, but it did give me a lot of satisfaction.

Tisquantum

Throughout this series, one of my goals has been to explore the experience of early English colonists in the light of the impact their arrival had on the Indigenous population. Despite several attempts by the colonists to establish a fur trade with the Beothuk, only a few encounters with them are recorded between 1610 and 1620. Of these, John Guy's meeting at Truce Sound (Bull Arm) in 1612 is the best known. Henry Crout encountered a group of Beothuk at the bottom of Trinity Bay in 1613, and around 1619, a Captain Whittington met and traded with some Beothuk in the same area.

According to a 1639 account by David Kirke, a year after the 1619 encounter the Beothuk returned to the same spot to meet with English settlers but instead encountered a group of migratory fishermen who fired upon them; this incident fueled mistrust and suspicion and led to a breakdown in friendly relations. I have alluded to an encounter of this nature in Chapter 8 of this novel, setting it a few years earlier.

Another key piece of English–Indigenous relations in Newfoundland falls neatly within the time period of this book: in 1617 to 1618, a Wampanoag man named Tisquantum (sometimes called Squanto) spent an unspecified amount of time at Cupids. The settlers most likely wanted to use him as an interpreter in their attempt to establish trade with the Beothuk; Tisquantum, who had been kidnapped from Patuxet several years earlier and lived in Spain and in England, probably just wanted to get home.

In Newfoundland he met Thomas Dermer and joined the voyage of exploration that brought him home to what is today Massachusetts in the summer of 1619—to the devastating discovery that his people had been largely wiped out by an epidemic. He later acted as a translator between the Wampanoag and the *Mayflower* settlers who landed at Patuxet in 1620 and renamed it Plymouth.

Tisquantum's time in Newfoundland is mentioned only briefly in a couple of sources; I have taken some liberties in having him spend his time at Musketto Cove rather than Cupids, and having him stay in Newfoundland longer than he probably did, giving my characters and the reader time to know him better.

In researching Tisquantum and his culture I was helped by David J. Silverman's book about the Wampanoag, *This Land is Their Land*; Neal Salisbury's article "Treacherous Waters: Tisquantum, the Red Atlantic, and the Beginnings of Plymouth Colony"; and a lecture by Andrew Lipman, author of the upcoming book *The Death and Life of Squanto*. While both Lipman and Silverman are non-Indigenous scholars and their versions of history differ in some respects from Wampanoag oral tradition, they have researched English documents relating to Tisquantum's people far more thoroughly than had been done previously. Listening to interviews with Darius Coombs of the Mashpee-Wampanoag nation and Loren Spears of the Niantic-Narragansett nation (on the American history podcast *Ben Franklin's World*) also helped develop my image of Tisquantum and his people.

The English settlers were interested in contacting the people who were indigenous to this island and establishing trade with them, but they did not know them by the name Beothuk, and would not hear this name until much later. In this novel, I have theorized that Tisquantum might have known of the existence of the Beothuk through the trading networks that reached far enough north to include the Mi'kmaq, and that he might have heard a Mi'kmaq term, Osa'yan'a, for the people we now know as Beothuk. But this is, of course, speculation: Tisquantum was asked to act as a translator between the English and the Beothuk, but we cannot know how much he would have known about the Indigenous people of Newfoundland, and there is no record that he ever had the opportunity to carry out that role.

As in the first two books of the series, I have tried to portray the attitudes of settlers towards Indigenous people in ways that are accurate to the times, which include using language and stereotypes that we rightly consider offensive today. In particular, the word "savage" has a painful history and is not one I would condone using outside this context, but I felt that leaving it out would gloss over the way my settler ancestors viewed the Indigenous population. I do not want to absolve these ancestors of blame for their treatment of the people of this land.

As with my previous book, my thinking about Indigenous–settler relations, and specifically about Tisquantum, was greatly helped by my conversations with Indigenous Sociocultural Consultant Leahdawn Helena, and her thoughtful critiques of the manuscript.

Grappling with our own history is always complicated. I was first drawn into this story by the way women's experiences were erased from the recorded history of early English settlement on the island of Newfoundland; this series is largely an attempt to use imagination to fill in the gaps of history. But in celebrating the courage and perseverance of those women colonists, I found I could not disregard the larger project of which they were a part: the even greater erasure of other cultures, of Indigenous histories.

Both things can be true: that these English women were strong and courageous, *and* that they helped to perpetrate one of history's great crimes—the theft of their "New World" from the Indigenous population. The tension between these two truths has stayed with me throughout this writing.

Acknowledgements

As always, I am grateful to my circle of family, friends, and fellow writers for their support throughout the process of writing this book.

To my first readers and critics, including Michelle Butler Hallett, Christine Hennebury, Jennifer Morgan, and Lori Savory: I am forever grateful for your insights. To my editor Kate Kennedy, cover designer extraordinaire Rhonda Molloy, and the rest of the Breakwater Books team: this would have been impossible without you. Eternal gratitude to Rebecca Rose who was willing to commit to publishing an entire trilogy before reading a word of it—an almost unheard-of vote of confidence from a publisher.

In the notes above I have mentioned the contributions of William Gilbert and Leahdawn Helena, both of whose expertise was essential to my understanding of the history behind this project. I am also grateful to author Derek Yetman for answering many questions about ships and providing helpful clarification and insights, as well as to Dr. Beverley (Bly) Straube, Dr. Sonja Boon, and Dr. Neil Kennedy, for providing further historical background and insight. In the case of these people and others who have answered various questions about this project, I am grateful for their input and take full responsibility for any errors, anachronisms, and blunders that have made their way into the text.

I am deeply grateful for the support of the Newfoundland and Labrador Arts Council and specifically for the Professional Project Grants I received in 2021 and 2022.

Thanks also to the leaders and participants in the "Go and Write" September 2021 Kingsbrae writing retreat, for the inspiration and setting that allowed me to figure out how to start this novel.

Thanks to my dad, Don Morgan, for endless encouragement and a careful reading; to my husband, Jason Cole, for always supporting my writing career and making life easier than it has any right to be. Love forever and always to Chris Cole and Emma Cole as you continue on your own voyages of discovery; home is the place you can always return to.

Trudy J. Morgan-Cole is a writer and teacher in St. John's, Newfoundland. Her historical novels include *By the Rivers of Brooklyn*, *Most Anything You Please*, as well as *A Roll of the Bones* and *Such Miracles and Mischiefs*, the first two volumes of the Cupids Trilogy. She is fascinated by the forgotten or ignored stories of women in history and loves to create fiction out of the gaps history leaves behind. Trudy is the mother of two young adults and lives in Rabbittown, in the heart of St. John's, with her husband, Jason, and the world's most beautiful rescue dog.